WITHDRAWN
REDWOOD
LIBRARY
NEWPORT
R.I.

Egypt's Road to Jerusalem

Boutros Boutros-Ghali

❖ ❖ ❖

Egypt's Road to Jerusalem

A Diplomat's Story of the Struggle for Peace in the Middle East

Random House New York

Published in the United States by Random House, Inc., New York, and
simultaneously in Canada by Random House of Canada Limited, Toronto.

All of the photos without credits are from the author's personal collection.

Library of Congress Cataloging-in-Publication Data

Boutros-Ghali, Boutros
Egypt's road to Jerusalem : the memoirs of a diplomat / Boutros Boutros-Ghali.—1st ed.
p. cm.
Includes index.
ISBN 0679-45245-1
1. Boutros-Ghali, Boutros, 1922– 2. Diplomats—Egypt—Biography.
DT107.828.B68A3 1997
327.62'0092—dc21
[B] 96-39810

Random House website address: http://www.randomhouse.com/

Printed in the United States of America on acid-free paper

24689753

First Edition

To the memory of my grandfather
Boutros Ghali Pasha,
whose devotion to Egypt inspired me
to follow the road without turning back

❖ ❖ ❖

Acknowledgments

My original diary of more than a thousand manuscript pages in Arabic from which this book was drawn has been deposited with the Hoover Institution at Stanford University, where, after ten years, anyone may examine it.

I wish to thank Hoover Institution Director John Raisian and Deputy Director Charles Palm for their invaluable assistance, Africa and Middle East Collection Deputy Curator Edward Jajko and Library Specialist Amal Dalati for their skillful translation, and editor Romayne Ponleithner for her outstanding contribution.

Contents

❖ ❖ ❖

Introduction

With a regularity that is virtually involuntary, I have recorded the events of my life daily ever since boyhood. Remarkably, when my pleasant life as a university professor was suddenly transformed into that of a minister of state, with all the evening meetings and social functions that accompanied official life, I continued the practice of noting and reflecting upon the day's events. I came to realize that this was a means by which I could sort out, order, and begin to comprehend what had befallen me and thereby prepare myself for the next day to come. This process was itself therefore a necessary form of relaxation.

This book is drawn directly from these daily records and describes events from late 1977 to late 1981, the seminal years of negotiations to achieve Palestinian rights and peace in the Middle East.

Anyone who endeavors to write of the past recognizes that fundamental decisions of style, structure, and even philosophy must be made. Important events rarely take place as in a coherent, sequential story; they occur in moments scattered across time, and their significance is not grasped until well after the fact. On the other hand, when all the various aspects of an issue are brought together, far greater coherence emerges than ever existed in reality. Thoughts and actions that took place in a random and sporadic fashion emerge in a coherent and continually flowing chronology. Thus reality as it happened in fact is incomprehensible; as it is usually recounted it is inevitably distorted. The author must find a balance somewhere.

Historians, years after the fact, survey what each participant did and pass judgment on an event in its complex entirety. The record I have set down in this book tells a story that is at once more limited yet more honest. Life as it is actually lived must be conducted on partial information. I have tried to preserve that reality in these pages. This volume therefore does not convey the whole story, but it undeniably conveys what it was like to be an Egyptian diplomat at the time, and to have to act on what I knew when I knew it.

To be true to this recognition this book is drawn from the record that I made contemporaneously with the events described. The story told here does not, therefore, go beyond what I knew or felt at the time. When these pages reveal that I was wrong about a fact at the time, I have allowed that error or unawareness to remain in the text. I have followed this rule even when it concerns events or ideas about which I now, informed by hindsight, know that my decision or emotion then was entirely unwarranted or unfounded. For the information and greater interest of the reader I have, however, added comments about the fate of certain personalities and projects in the years that have followed the 1977–1981 time frame of this text; the reader should have no difficulty in recognizing where these afterthoughts and comments appear in the book.

My intention in this work is to present this record as a journal of Egyptian diplomacy, as the story of an Egyptian diplomat, and as a portrayal of an Egyptian initiative that began a process of immense importance to international peace and security.

—Boutros Boutros-Ghali

Egypt's Road to Jerusalem

Chapter One

❖ ❖ ❖

The Road to Jerusalem

Selection by Sadat

Tuesday, October 25, 1977, began like any ordinary day of my academic life. Early in the morning I went to the offices of the Faculty of Economics and Political Science of Cairo University, which I had helped found in 1960. I was proud of the college and proud to work there.

A bit later I went to the Al-Ahram building on Galaa Street, to my office in the Center for Strategic and Political Studies, which I directed. I was editing the January 1978 issue of the quarterly *Al-siyasah al-dawliyah* (International Politics), which was already behind the printer's schedule.

That afternoon, I visited an exhibit of paintings by an American woman artist at the American Library in Garden City. My nephew had strongly insisted that I do so. The artist was the wife of the professor who was overseeing his doctoral thesis in economics at the Massachusetts Institute of Technology. Afterward, I went to Cairo International Airport to meet my wife, who was returning from Italy.

As I entered the airport building the journalist Hidayat Abd al-Nabi saw me from afar and ran toward me in excitement. "The Presidency of the republic has been looking for you everywhere. Where have you been? A thousand congratulations, Doctor, on the ministry!"

As soon as my wife, Leia, arrived and saw my expression, she asked what had happened to me. I replied that I was threatened by a calamity that could turn her life and mine upside down.

On the way back to our house in Gizah, I told my wife that I would decline the appointment to the ministry. I felt no hesitation in the matter. I had arranged my life very satisfactorily. I could do serious academic work. I could travel frequently to gatherings of professional international societies in pleasant places. I was a member of the political bureau of the Arab Socialist Union, the one party of the Egyptian political system, with branches all over the country. Stability, respectability, and variety were all in balance in my affairs. I decided to go immediately to the Presidency of the Council of Ministers to put an end to the subject and explain my refusal to the prime minister.

I entered the building in Qasr al-Dubarah, which had been the palace of Princess Chevekiar, the first wife of King Fuad and the elegant arranger of festivities for King Farouk. The princess had been a dear friend of my mother, who was a faithful royalist. In my youth I had happily attended parties at the palace in honor of King Farouk. Photographers and journalists surrounded me, offering congratulations and asking me questions that I was unable to answer.

It was eleven o'clock at night when Prime Minister Mamduh Salim received me. We had not met before. A tall and imposing man, Mamduh Salim had a reputation for honesty, self-control, and careful and infrequent speech—a rare combination in the Arab world. Above all, he was a security man, a policeman.

Mamduh Salim spoke: "The president of the republic has decided to appoint you to the new cabinet which he has asked me to form."

My true feelings came out as I told him of the many obstacles to this appointment. "How can I take such an official position?" I said. "All Socialist laws are applied against me, from the first Land Reform Law of 1952 to the third Land Reform Law."

Mumdah Salim replied, "We are aware of that."

My wife's fortune, I said, had been sequestered; a government trustee paid her a limited allowance each month. Members of our family had experienced similar treatment. We were not, therefore, in high standing politically in the eyes of those who had made the revolution.

Mamduh Salim responded, "We are aware of that."

The Egyptian Revolution of 1952 had imposed socialism. My family's properties, which had been extensive, meant that we were considered "feudal." Nationalization, which was a form of confiscation, had been imposed upon all of us. I had lost 90 percent of what I had inherited from my father. I had lost my political rights at first, but was later exempted because I was a professor at Cairo University. A respect for intellectual achievement still existed, and I was considered a potential asset to the regime. As a result of the exemption I had stayed in Egypt, but my two brothers were compelled to leave the country to have any hope of successful careers.

It was nearly midnight. I was oblivious to the fact that Mamduh Salim had been at work for twelve hours. "Your laws have made me an enemy of the people," I said to Mamduh Salim. "It is not in the interest of Egypt to offer me this appointment."

"We are aware of that," he said.

I persisted. "I am a member of the Committee of Experts of the International Labor Organization, which is equivalent to an international court. It is responsible for evaluating the extent to which the various nations honor international labor conventions. I am also a member of the Commission of International Jurists, which monitors the practices of nations in the field of human rights. Taking a ministerial position would mean having to resign from these international bodies, because it would not be right for me to judge and be judged at the same time. Although I am personally proud to be a member of these organizations, what is important is that Egypt be represented in these organizations and that the membership of our country not be lost. And that is not all," I continued. I then explained at length the extent of my concern for my academic work.

Mamduh Salim listened with patience despite the lateness of the hour. "You may retain those positions along with your new position," he said.

Suddenly I realized that I did not know what ministerial position had been offered to me. So I asked, with some embarrassment, "What is the ministry that you are thinking of assigning me?"

Mamduh Salim started and asked, "Don't you know?"

I explained that everyone had only said, "Congratulations, you have been appointed a minister." Mamduh Salim laughed and said, "You have been appointed a minister of state. You will work with me here in the Presidency of the Council of Ministers."

I did not know what that meant. "In general, you will assist me in preparing the meetings of the Council of Ministers. During the next few days we can discuss the other duties that will be assigned to you," he explained.

I felt the noose tightening. The president of the cabinet, through his generosity and responsiveness to every obstacle I raised, was closing off any way out. I declined once again. I said that I wished to convey to President Sadat the extent of my gratitude and appreciation for the great honor and the generous gesture, but that I could serve Egypt far better outside than inside the cabinet.

The patience of Mamduh Salim was running out, but he said with his usual calm, "Dr. Boutros, you are fussing, but the hour is late. The president of the republic has issued his decree already."

I found myself interrupting: "Can't you talk to the president and explain the special circumstances that force me to decline? Can't you explain to him that I am completely ready to serve the nation and the government and the party without the need of a ministerial position?"

Mamduh Salim replied, "Doctor, the hour is late. You must prepare yourself mentally to take the new position. The republican decree on the composition of the ministry, and your membership in it, has been broadcast on the radio and television and will appear in tomorrow morning's newspapers. You have no choice."

He broke off the conversation. "I want to see you early tomorrow morning in Abdin Palace, where you will take the constitutional oath. You have pursued thirty years of academic life and have lived with theories, far from reality," he said. "The time has come for you to enter the practical sphere and to pursue a public life serving Egypt. For many generations your family has had a rich tradition of service to the country. Now you have to assume your share of that national service."

In fact, my grandfather had been prime minister and minister of foreign affairs when Egypt was part of the Ottoman Empire. My uncle had been minister of foreign affairs in the time between the two world wars. Another uncle had held a similar position from 1914 to 1922 during the British protectorate. Cousins of mine had been ministers and members of Parliament and in the diplomatic service. But all this was before the Egyptian Revolution, when such positions were predominantly held by members of the "two hundred families."

My father had always pressured me to enter the field of diplomacy. When I came back from taking my doctorate in Paris, he scorned my determination to be a scholar and teacher. Then the Revolution changed the social scene, and families such as mine were dissuaded from having such ambitions.

Why had President Sadat chosen me? I did not know. I had met him at the start of the Revolution. He had been one of the members of the innermost group of the Council of the Revolution. We had been on a platform together for a program marking United Nations Day in October 1954. "I know nothing about the UN," Sadat had said to me. He read the questions we were expected to discuss and threw them aside, saying that he did not intend to be examined like a schoolboy. But when the program began, he answered the questions knowledgeably and in depth. He was highly intelligent, but he often tried to conceal his cunning and his superior mind. He read extensively despite a reputation for never having time to read. Over the years I had published in daily papers and specialized journals many articles on major issues in Egyptian foreign policy. I had had little contact with President Sadat, but I knew that he had read my articles. Could it be, I thought, that the president has selected me for this position in preparation for naming me minister of state for foreign affairs? My father's prodding and my own awareness of my family's long tradition had mentally prepared me for this, despite the different path my career had taken.

I returned home furious with myself. My fury increased when I found friends waiting for me and asking whether I had submitted to the attractions of power. I replied that I had tried to decline but had been unsuccessful. "That is what they all say" was their reply.

I was upset at being condemned to give up intellectual and international life, research, studies and conferences, my students and colleagues, all for a position whose purpose I did not know.

I learned from the newspapers that the new cabinet would include about thirty ministers with specific portfolios and three ministers of state without portfolio, myself and two others.

On Wednesday, October 26, 1977, I went to Abdin Palace to take the oath of office. Abdin had been the royal palace of King Fuad and King Farouk. Its huge rooms shone with gold decoration. I found myself shaking hands with numerous people I did not know. I took refuge with my two new colleagues, Dr. Na'im Abu Talib, professor in the College of Engineering of Alexandria University, and Dr. Ali al-Salmi, associate professor in the Faculty of Commerce of Cairo University.

Dr. al-Salmi said that he was to be responsible for restructuring the organization of the Egyptian administration. Dr. Na'im said that he was responsible for handling the technical side of various problems. One thing was clear: our jurisdiction as ministers without portfolio was unclear.

I found among the members of the cabinet a number of other friends and colleagues: Hamed al-Sayih, a brilliant economist; Ibrahim Badran, Egypt's most famous surgeon; and Abd al-Mun'im al-Sawi, the influential reporter and publicist. They helped me overcome the feeling of isolation that I had felt as I entered the great hall.

Small cards were distributed on which was printed the constitutional oath we were to take: "I swear by Almighty God that I will faithfully protect the republican order; that I will respect the constitution and laws; that I will look after the people's interests to the fullest extent; and that I will preserve the independence of the homeland and the security of its territories."

I was agitated and worried that I would find myself unable to recite the oath without mistakes, so I read the text over and over. When I looked around, I found my new ministerial colleagues also immersed in studying that simple text.

A small problem seemed to be of the utmost importance: Should I wear my glasses while taking the oath or take them off? As I pondered this dilemma I found myself standing in front of the president of the republic with my glasses on. To the right of President Sadat was Vice President Hosni Mubarak; to his left was Mamduh Salim, president of the Council of Ministers. I took off my glasses, slowly pronounced the oath, and returned to my place.

Suddenly an air of gaiety prevailed and my fellow ministers began to congratulate one another with evident relief. We gathered on the steps of the great staircase for the traditional photograph. New colleagues were making strategic and studied maneuvers to occupy a prominent position in the picture. Because of my inattention, I found myself in a humble spot in the last row, next to His Excellency Sheikh Muhammed Mitwalli Sha'rawi, a fiery preacher and commentator on the Koran. We shared a cordial relationship. He later became one of the most popular figures in Egypt, who might be called a Billy Graham of Islam.

When I returned home, I found many bouquets of flowers and hundreds of congratulatory telegrams. The telephone rang incessantly. In Egypt, from pharaonic times to the present, the tradition is one of al-Hakem, the ruler. One is the ruler or one is nothing. Therefore, the highest position to which one can aspire is in the service of the ruler. To be a minister in the cabinet, as I had become, was to possess far greater prestige than an artist, scholar, or man of wealth. In the developing countries there are only two kinds of real power: political power and religious power.

The next day I went to the Council of Ministers, expecting to begin my first day's work as a minister of state. There was no office for me. But I was welcomed and assured that within less than a week a suitable office would be prepared with an adjoining office for a secretary. Telephones and equipment would be installed, I was told. I returned home, more angry than ever at my inability to escape this ministerial position.

On the following morning I paid an official visit to the patriarch, often called the pope of the Coptic Christian church, His Holiness, Anba Shenouda. His new Coptic cathedral was built just behind the Boutrossiya, a church built as a memorial to, and named for, my grandfather Boutros Ghali the prime minister. It was the burial place for my family, and my father's tomb was there. The compound in which the cathedral is set is the "Vatican" of the Coptic faith, but it is of modest scale and condition. The Coptic Church had once been a great landholder in Egypt and extremely rich. After the Revolution, its holdings were limited by the various agrarian reform laws. In Egypt, which is overwhelmingly Muslim in population, the tradition has been for a Copt to be among the Council of Ministers to look after and, if need be, defend Coptic interests affected by the government.

The pope, in a very nuanced and roundabout way, asked if I would be taking that responsibility, for the previous Coptic minister had recently left the Council. I felt that the pope was not reassured by my assumption of this role, for although I came from a noted Coptic family active in Church affairs, I myself had not been active in the Church. I said that my responsibilities still had not been defined. Sensing Pope Shenouda's concern, I promised to go to the president of the cabinet to convey the views of the patriarch.

The first meeting of the new Council of Ministers convened on Sunday, October 30, 1977. It pleased me that a familial air prevailed. I followed the discussion with interest but was content to listen. I had in mind the academic custom that a new member does not speak at his first meeting.

The next days were taken up with visiting my colleagues to inquire about my duties. One official directed me to the room assigned to me, whispering that I was too late to choose the best office for myself. The other minister of state, Dr. Na'im Abu Talib, he said, had been there early that morning and taken the biggest and nicest of the offices. I tried to convince him that I was concerned about my job, not about the kind of office I would have. He did not take me seriously.

By the end of the day it was clear to me that a minister of state was a minister without a ministry and must struggle to find work for himself. At the request of Mamduh Salim, president of the cabinet, I drew up, with some hesitation, my suggestions for the responsibilities I should take up.

1. Continued work to deepen the understanding of Socialist democracy.
2. Contacts with foreign political parties and organizations.
3. Egyptian-Sudanese relations.

4. Contacts with international nongovernmental organizations (NGO).
5. Contacts with international learned societies.
6. Foreign information.

In fact, I was already responsible for a number of these activities in my role as a member of the political bureau of the Arab Socialist Union. In his efforts to encourage closer contacts with the West, Sadat had no objection to using personalities who were perceived as pro-Western, even though they belonged to the ancien régime.

I was stunned when, on November 2, 1977, the text of my memo was published in the newspapers exactly as I had written it, with no alteration except for the omission of the point dealing with foreign information. The newspaper also reported that one of my colleagues would be in charge of monitoring the implementation of the state five-year plan. My other colleague would be in charge of defining the basic problems that lessened administrative efficiency. My fears were confirmed. We three ministers of state had no defined tasks. There was nothing to justify our appointments to these positions.

My first concern was to go every morning to check on the preparation of my office. The undersecretary for procurement would greet me each day with:

"*Alf Mabrouk* [A thousand congratulations]; the paint has been applied."

"*Alf Mabrouk;* the draperies have been hung."

"*Alf Mabrouk;* the telephone has been installed."

"*Alf Mabrouk* . . ."

On the evening of Wednesday, November 9, I went to the People's Assembly chamber and sat with my colleagues to await the arrival of President Sadat, who was expected to make a speech of major importance. The chairman of the Palestine Liberation Organization, Yasir Arafat, was seated at the front of the chamber as an honored guest. He was making *salaam* to everyone, putting his palms together and raising his hands above his head.

In the course of his speech, President Sadat declared, "I am ready to travel to the ends of the earth if this will in any way protect an Egyptian boy, soldier, or officer from being killed or wounded. I say that I am ready for sure to go to the ends of this earth. I am ready to go to their country, even to the Knesset itself and talk with them."

Chairman Arafat was the first to burst into applause at these words. Neither Arafat nor my colleagues nor I understood the implications of what the president had said. Most of us took his words simply as indicating his readiness to exert the utmost effort to achieve peace.

As soon as the speech was over I joined a number of the ministers and the members of the People's Assembly in debating what the president had said. The feeling began to spread that what had been taken for mere rhetoric really meant that President Sadat might in fact intend to go to Israel. I did not agree. I felt that the president had scored a propaganda coup but that talk about his intention to go to Israel had no basis in fact.

I later learned that Sadat, before giving his speech, had revealed to his closest aides that he was thinking of declaring his intention to go to Jerusalem as a way of breaking the diplomatic deadlock. His aides had argued vigorously against this idea, and Sadat's prepared text contained no reference to Jerusalem. He had given them the impression that he accepted their point of view. But when he began his speech, Sadat suddenly departed from his text and extemporized, stating his willingness to go to the Knesset. His aides were astonished—and horrified.

I stayed up most of that night reading once again the doctoral dissertation prepared by Mrs. Nazli Mu'awwad. Despite my new governmental position, I was still the dissertation supervisor for several students, a responsibility that could not be abandoned without harm to a young scholar's progress. In the morning I returned to the university campus to attend her dissertation defense. I realized how deep was my relationship to the university and academic work and how much it would cost me emotionally to be separated from it because of my new ministerial position, where my duties seemed to have no purpose but to keep me busy.

On Wednesday, November 16, 1977, my new office was finally ready for occupancy. I received a telephone call asking me to see the prime minister. In a mysterious and rather pompous way, Mamduh Salim told me to go at once to Qasr al-Urubah, the residence of the vice president, Hosni Mubarak, in Misr al-Gadidah, a suburb north-east of the city. A former commander of the air force, Mubarak was a war hero. He had led the first air strike that enabled the Egyptian army to cross the Suez Canal and break the Bar-Lev Line in 1973. Mubarak had chaired a commission of scholars and generals chosen to write a history of the Egyptian Revolution. The books were never written; the project fell into disarray, like most government commissions. As a member of the commission, I was amazed nevertheless by his patient attempt to make a collection of individuals, each trying to make his own views prevail, into a productive and coherent whole.

At Qasr al-Urubah I entered a salon to the right of the entrance. In a few minutes Mubarak entered, smiling and pleasant. "President Sadat admires your intellectual and political writing," Mubarak said, "and knows of your contacts in international circles. He has therefore decided to assign you an important and secret duty. He requests that you prepare an outline for the speech that the president will give next Sunday—in Israel! A speech that the president of Egypt will give before the Israeli Knesset!" It was a double surprise for me. For the first time I realized that President Sadat actually intended to go to Israel.

A few days before, when I had been trying to find and arrange my ministerial office, a Jewish American representing the Peace Now movement came to ask me if I could manage for Sadat to send a message of congratulations to a Peace Now conference that would be held in Jerusalem under the chairmanship of Pierre Mendès-France, the former premier of France. "You must be mad," I said. "Sadat would never agree to such a thing." Nonetheless I telexed the presidency about the request. Three hours later I received a telegram from Sadat: "I agree. Prepare the text of the message." I did so, but the question was how to convey such a message to an enemy country with which we had no communications. Then I saw that we could pass it through the French, or through the Romanians, or through our own ambassador in Cyprus. I chose the third way with the agreement of the president. Despite this signal from Sadat, I had not realized what he had in mind. The telegram was seen by the Israelis as the first bird of spring. I later discovered that someone had removed it from the archives, apparently because of its historical value.

But now I was to be at the heart of this historic event, charged with preparing the speech! Mubarak made clear to me that the president's peace gesture would not mean relinquishing any rights concerning either the Palestinian issue or Arab territories occupied by Israel since 1967. The speech must clearly reflect this.

I took down notes on a small piece of paper. Many questions passed through my mind. I preferred simply to listen. The vice president said that the outline should be prepared in English. I said that because English was my third language, after Arabic and French, I would like to ask the assistance of a colleague to assure that my English was accurate. The vice president agreed but reiterated the need for secrecy.

French had been the international language of the Egyptian elite since Napoleon invaded our country at the end of the eighteenth century. The Egyptian commitment to French language and culture was reinforced by the British imperial presence in Egypt as a means of protesting that presence. Egypt was playing France against England as it would later, in the cold war, play the United States against the USSR. At the moment, however, I had to function in English, and I needed help.

I returned home and sat at my desk to arrange my thoughts. This speech was unprecedented in history. How can a president of one country address the parliament of another country while a state of war prevails between them? What would he say about the past? And what would he say about the future? How could I make it clear that his trip to Jerusalem was not an act of surrender or weakness but of strength and conviction?

I searched my library for legal and philosophical publications on peace. I read speeches made by leaders during World War II. I looked at the preparatory documents of the San Francisco conference that gave rise to the United Nations. I studied the preamble of the United Nations Charter, which treats the issue of war and peace, and the basic charter of UNESCO, which includes paragraphs on the sources and causes of war. I located in my library the important decisions relating to the Palestine issue. I also consulted the shelf of books written by Zionist and Israeli leaders like Herzl, Weizmann, Ben-Gurion, Dayan, and Begin. I had collected them for use in constructing arguments to attack Israel; now I would try to draw something positive from their pages.

I sat before the blank page with stacks of references piled on my desk, pen in hand, and a thousand and one ideas crowding my head. Then I realized that there were no precedents in the references, so I put them aside and mentally adjusted myself to confront a unique situation.

I thought for hours—until someone reminded me of the cabinet meeting at 6:00 P.M. I took my place among the ministers but was unable to follow the discussions. My mind was completely occupied by the task of the speech. I took out of my pocket the slip of paper on which I had taken down Vice President Mubarak's instructions and read them for the tenth time.

Nine o'clock came and the cabinet was still in session. I went to the prime minister and whispered in his ear that I must excuse myself and return home to continue work on executing the task I had been assigned. Mamduh Salim looked surprised. "You should not have attended this meeting," he said. "You should devote all your time to your new mission."

I returned home to the blank page on my desk. I wrote three pages, but was not pleased by what I read. I was exhausted and decided to postpone writing until the morning.

I woke up early and hurried to my study. In the quiet and peace of the morning my pen began to move across the paper. I wrote ten pages. Then I began rewriting entire paragraphs, omitting and adding and rearranging the thoughts.

In the afternoon I called my friend and colleague Dr. Magdi Wahba, a professor of English literature at the Faculty of Letters at Cairo University. Magdi came from an old and respected tradition. His grandfather had been prime minister and his father a minister. They were one of the "two hundred families." We had been children, students, and colleagues together. As a scholar and member of the Arab Academy, he was deeply admired for his comparative studies of English, French, and Arabic literature. I told Magdi that I was in desperate need of his help and hoped he would set aside all his time for me the following day and come to my house.

On Friday, November 18, 1977, Magdi came at ten and brought with him a typewriter. We worked together until four in the afternoon, when the phone rang. It was Mubarak's office informing me that the text of the speech was needed immediately. I apologized, as I had not yet finished writing it. I promised that the speech would be ready at seven o'clock.

Before half an hour passed, another telephone call came. It was Mubarak again. I started apologizing for the delay but he interrupted. "I am not calling you about the speech. There is another important issue. A presidential decree has been passed assigning you the post of minister of state for foreign affairs and acting foreign minister. As such, you are to join the delegation accompanying the president on his trip to Israel tomorrow, Saturday." I said that I was prepared to serve the country in any capacity requested of me. "Take it easy," Mubarak said.

But the surprise of my new appointment as head of the Foreign Ministry and Egyptian diplomacy did not make it easy for me to finish the speech. At exactly seven the doorbell rang. A representative from presidential headquarters came in and I turned the speech over to him after rereading it again and again. I then sat down to worry about my duties as a member of the delegation accompanying the chief executive on a mission that exceeded in delicacy, difficulty, and importance any other in memory.

It was widely known that Ismail Fahmi and Muhammad Riyad, who had been, respectively, foreign minister and minister of state for foreign affairs, had resigned rather than having to accompany President Sadat to Jerusalem. They were opposed in principle to the president's initiative, and appeared to fear repercussions. The fear in the air was palpable. My telephone again was ringing incessantly. "Don't go. The airplane will never reach Jerusalem. You will be assassinated like your grandfather," friends warned me. Others hoped that I would accept this historic mission. The Arab press was vicious. No Muslim, they wrote, would agree to accompany Sadat, so he chose the Christian Boutros-Ghali, who has a Jewish wife. The telephone calls, most of which were made to my wife, urged her to try to change my mind. Leia said she would support my decision, whatever it was. None of this affected me. My acceptance of this mission had been instantaneous. I felt it was my patriotic duty, but I was also attracted by the extraordinary challenge.

On Saturday morning, November 19, 1977, Ambassador Saad Hamzah, head of protocol, telephoned to congratulate me and inform me that decisions by me were required. He requested that I go to the ministry. I had hoped to devote the few remaining hours before the plane took off to thinking and reading. I had gathered the writings of Moshe Dayan, Israel's foreign minister, with the intention of rereading parts of them. But I was so nervous that I could neither concentrate nor even remember what I had read already.

But at Saad Hamzah's insistence, I hurried to the Foreign Ministry's old building on Midan al-Tahrir. It had once been the palace of an Egyptian pasha. The protocol chief led me inside. "Here is the office of the foreign minister on your left," he said, "and here is the office of the minister of state for foreign affairs to your right. You can choose between the two offices because you are both acting foreign minister and minister of state for foreign affairs." The former was higher in prestige than the latter. The foreign minister dealt with the overall administration of foreign policy; the minister of state for foreign affairs dealt with specific problems and undertook special assignments as requested by the president. Both were members of the cabinet and, almost by definition, were destined to be competitors. I didn't hesitate at all and entered to the right, to the office of the minister of state. I knew only a few people in the Foreign Ministry, although more than 50 percent of its personnel had been my students in political science at Cairo University. And I knew very little about the Foreign Ministry's methods of operation.

After a few hours in my new office I went to the airport and boarded the president's aircraft, which, a few minutes later, landed at Ismailia, where President Sadat came on board. He was quiet and at ease, as though this were a normal trip. He chatted with his friend Osman Ahmed Osman, the construction-company millionaire; they were telling jokes and laughing pleasantly. I suspected that Sadat's calm was a deliberate pose. How could anyone not be filled with emotion at the outset of this unbelievable journey?

In less than an hour the lights of Tel Aviv suddenly appeared through the airplane window as we began to descend at Ben-Gurion Airport. I had not realized the distance was so short! The doors opened. Lights shone on the steps of the Egyptian aircraft that had landed at the Israeli airport. I felt I was looking at a page of history being written with letters of fire. Israel seemed as strange to me as a land in outer space. For decades it had been the enemy, the cancer in the body of the Arab world, which we had to do all in our power to destroy.

I noticed again the calm that enveloped President Sadat. His features gave no indication that the moment was in any way unusual or caused him any excitement or nervousness.

Sadat stood bathed in the glare of what seemed like a thousand floodlights. His presence seemed like a biblical vision. The blinding light made it impossible to see the crowds surrounding the aircraft and its space on the tarmac, but I could hear the intense, excited murmur of many voices and the incessant clicking of cameras as if made by a cloud of unseen insects.

The official reception ceremonies were over quickly. In a car speeding toward Jerusalem, on my left sat Moshe Dayan, foreign minister of Israel. His chief of cabinet, Elie Rubinstein, a fluent Arabic speaker wearing a yarmulke, sat beside the driver. Circumstances did not make for easy conversation. I began to speak about archaeology because I knew that Dayan was fascinated by it. I said that my first wife had interested me in archaeology. At the University of Paris she had been doing her doctoral dissertation on depictions of Helen of Troy on red and black pottery at the same time that I was working on a doctoral dissertation on international law. Together we had closely followed the course of the dig on the island of Thasos in the Aegean Sea, not far from the city of Kavalla, a location I knew as the birthplace of Mehmet Ali, pasha of Egypt in the early nineteenth century and founder of the Egyptian royal family. But, I said to Dayan, that marriage ended after a few years, and with it ended my interest in archaeology. Dayan laughed and said that his interest in ruins continued after he separated from his first wife.

As the car climbed the hill to Jerusalem, crowds lined the road, waving Egyptian and Israeli flags. Mothers held up their infants to see our motorcade. I told Dayan about my emotional, personal, patriotic, and historical ties to the Palestinian issue. I pointed out to him that while he knew the issue from a practical standpoint, I had long experience with it in the academic world. I had devoted the academic year 1954–55 at Columbia University in New York to the Palestine problem. And I taught and lectured about Arab problems for almost three decades all across the Arab world, from Morocco on the Atlantic to Kuwait and Abu Dhabi on the Gulf.

It was clear to me from the conversation that Dayan cared little for Egypt's role in the Palestinian issue. To him it was a matter only of Palestinians in the West Bank and Gaza and the Palestine Liberation Organization. He seemed indifferent to the profound Pan-Arab and Islamic dimension of the issue. When we see a Palestinian brother living under the weight of occupation and thrown in jail, I said to Dayan, we all feel like Palestinians whose rights have been violated; we feel the anguish and bitterness of having lost a homeland. The entire Arab world is a single whole. Arabs still feel the loss of "Andalus" (Spain). The loss of Palestine was a colonialist imposition upon the Arab world by the great outside powers.

Dayan was impervious to my words. He said he wanted me to convey a message to President Sadat. If Sadat's speech to the Knesset included any reference to the Palestine Liberation Organization, "this will not facilitate the new atmosphere of reconciliation that we want to promote." Should such a reference be made, he said, Menachem Begin would be obliged to attack the PLO. I did not tell Dayan that the speech I had drafted included a reference to the Palestine Liberation Organization.

We reached Jerusalem. We could scarcely believe what we saw—an Egyptian flag flying on an Israeli car making its way with difficulty through huge crowds shouting welcome to President Sadat. Egyptian flags were everywhere. I had never seen such a manifestation of popular emotion!

The King David Hotel was packed with security men and world media correspondents. Arnaud de Borchgrave of *Newsweek* approached me, furious that the *Time* correspondent, Wilton Wynn, had been permitted to fly with President Sadat to Jerusalem. He demanded that I get approval for him to be on the return flight. I proposed this, but the president flatly rejected the idea. He was not on speaking terms with de Borchgrave; I never learned why. I repeatedly tried to promote a rapprochement between the two, but Sadat would not relent. Even today, when de Borchgrave and I meet in New York, we speak of Sadat's enmity toward him as a mystery.

Moshe Dayan escorted me to my bedroom door on the top floor of the King David. The first thing I did on finding myself alone in the room was go to the window and gaze at the lights of Jerusalem. I wondered why this city, which symbolized peace, had always been a place of bloody confrontation. I saw the immense amount of Israeli construction and feared, with a shudder there in the night, that the Arab world would never be able to recover Jerusalem. I saw myself as a small boy, watching my mother, Sophie, preparing her kit for her pilgrimage from Cairo to Jerusalem, as important a journey for a Copt as is the hajj for a Muslim. I felt the excitement of my family as my mother boarded the train for Jaffa in Palestine, where from the station she would go up to the Holy City. And I recalled her return and how she felt blessed by the pilgrimage she had made.

I stared for a long time at Arab Jerusalem and felt the awe of the moment. But I also felt fear because of the bold step we had just taken. It was extremely important, but it was also a dangerous step on a long and unknown road. I was entering the most important chapter of my life. How could I make the most of it? How could I summon the energy? These thoughts passed through my mind as I looked from the window of the King David Hotel at Jerusalem—Jerusalem—Arab Jerusalem—occupied Jerusalem—stolen Jerusalem.

We woke at dawn. We went to Al-Aqsa mosque, where the president and his entourage said prayers. I was standing near them while those praying were bowing and kneeling, glorifying Almighty God. I cannot describe the emotion that overcame me on this occasion and in this holy place. I was about to cry. To overcome it, I made myself think about my shoes outside the mosque; what if I could not find them in the heap there? I also could not help thinking about King Abdullah bin Hussein of Jordan, who had been assassinated by a Palestinian in 1951 as he was entering Al-Aqsa to pray. He was accused of collaborating with Israel. President Sadat was risking the same fate. Israeli security personnel were everywhere, peering into every corner of the mosque and Haram al-Sharif; it was clear that they too were thinking of King Abdullah. We left the mosque and entered the open area amid a demonstration by protesting Palestinians.

We then went to the Church of the Resurrection, where Amba Basiliyus, the Egyptian Coptic archbishop of Jerusalem and the Near East, greeted President Sadat warmly. The Egyptian Coptic shrine in Jerusalem, Deir es Sultan, was occupied by the Ethiopian Copts; Israel would not return it to the Egyptian Copts because Israel wanted Ethiopia's cooperation to permit the emigration of the Falasha, the Jews of Ethiopia. The archbishop delivered a fiery speech strongly attacking the Israeli occupation and its practices. His face was red, his hands trembled with emotion, and his white beard waved as he spoke in a booming voice, as though he were rousing a vast throng by his oratory. President Sadat listened to the archbishop impassively.

From the church, we went to Yad Vashem, the memorial to the Jewish victims of Nazi persecution. I had visited Auschwitz and felt keenly the tragedy of the Holocaust. At Yad Vashem, President Sadat's face revealed nothing. He refused to put on the yarmulke that was offered to us to cover our heads in the memorial, and I, imitating him, also declined the offer of a yarmulke.

We then returned to the King David Hotel. President Sadat, Dr. Mustafa Khalil, and I were joined for lunch by three Israelis: Prime Minister Begin, Deputy Prime Minister Yigal Yadin, and Foreign Minister Moshe Dayan. During lunch, Begin suggested the opening of a direct hot line between Cairo and Tel Aviv to continue the dialogue and to provide a quick and secure means of communication. President Sadat listened silently.

Begin had noticed that sometimes Sadat called me Boutros and at other times he called me Peter. Begin took me aside and asked me, "Why the two names?" I replied that Sadat called me Peter—Boutros is the Arabization of the name of the apostle Peter—when he was feeling cordial toward me. When Sadat was not so happy with my behavior he called me Boutros. Begin was fascinated by this and began to adapt the practice with a code of his own. Begin knew that the Latin name Petrus meant stone or rock. So when Begin was annoyed by my resistance to his diplomacy, he called me Peter; when he felt that I was a good boy, he called me Boutros. Sadat soon realized that Begin had turned Sadat's own meanings of the two names upside down and enjoyed playing with Begin about it as a kind of continual joke.

Dayan spoke of the necessity of agreeing on a framework and schedule for negotiation in the coming period. President Sadat replied with visible coldness, "We have to concentrate on the heart of the issue, not on technicalities and formalities. What is important is the issue of content, not details and framework." It was obvious from the start that the president was not comfortable with Dayan and his sullen, prickly personality.

Before Sadat came to Jerusalem, his opinion was that Dayan was "reasonable" and that Ezer Weizman, then Israeli minister of defense, was a "warmonger." Weizman, despite an injury to his leg, had been in the receiving party and had jauntily saluted Sadat with his cane; Sadat liked his style. But he regarded as very bad form Dayan's insistence on pressing me for a separate Egypt-Israeli peace while we were riding in the car to Jerusalem.

Dr. Mustafa Khalil interrupted the conversation, and so did Yigal Yadin, the deputy prime minister. We all worked at lightening the atmosphere by bringing up nonconfrontational issues. It was clear throughout lunch that everyone was anticipating the speech that President Sadat would make that afternoon in the Knesset.

At the Knesset, Speaker of the Assembly Yitzhak Shamir gave a short introduction welcoming the Egyptian president. Then President Sadat began his historic speech. Until that moment I had imagined that he was going to give the speech that I had outlined. But the wonderful speech he gave was completely different. He spoke in Arabic; I had prepared a speech in English. Not a single word, phrase, or idea of mine did he speak. I learned that I had been one of three who had been asked to write his speech. The speech Sadat delivered disappointed his audience, but that was no consolation to me.

When President Sadat finished, Prime Minister Begin rose and gave a harsh, impromptu speech. It was clear that he was unable to rise to the historic occasion. Sadat had spoken in a lecturing tone; Begin spoke in a hectoring tone. Each seemed to be posturing to impress his own side rather than to communicate with the other.

After the session was over, we returned to the King David Hotel to attend a dinner party for fifteen Egyptians and fifteen Israelis. President Sadat was seated between Menachem Begin and Moshe Dayan. I was seated next to Dayan. The atmosphere was tense, and although the heating was turned on in the hall of the big hotel, I felt a strong chill in the air. The Israelis were clearly disappointed with President Sadat's speech and the Egyptians were shocked by Begin's response.

It was now evident how wide a gap separated the Egyptian and Israeli positions. The hope of bringing down psychological and political barriers through this visit was fading. For a moment, the

Egyptian delegation had felt that President Sadat's visit, like magic, would solve everything. Osman Ahmed Osman, hardly a diplomat, volubly complained about Begin at the official dinner.

The personality of Ezer Weizman stood out during the dinner. Weizman, who had been in a car accident, had left his hospital bed to attend the dinner. He did his utmost to lighten the atmosphere with his stories, reminiscences, and jokes. I joined him in trying to ease the mood with small talk. Mustafa Kamil, an official who would later create a new Egyptian political party with Sadat's encouragement, also tried to enliven the occasion. The rest of the Egyptian delegation were silent.

When dinner was over, Dr. Mustafa Khalil suggested to Weizman that we meet with him, and I suggested to Yigal Yadin that he join us. We did not ask Dayan to join this meeting, although he had accompanied me in the car and had sat beside me at dinner, where we had talked at length. Dayan impressed me as a complicated, introverted personality with whom I found it hard to exchange opinions. The situation was entirely different with Weizman and Yadin. The personality of leaders and the chemistry between them affect the course of negotiations and great events. The Marxist belief that history proceeds with scientific ineluctability fails most notably in its disregard of this important reality.

In Dr. Mustafa Khalil's hotel room, Yadin, Weizman, Khalil, and I sat at a round table with a bottle of whisky and talked deep into the night. So a Scottish whisky served as the first "hot line" for communication between Egypt and Israel. This session was the opening of Egypt-Israel negotiations. Weizman began the conversation, reminiscing about the Cairo he had known when he was a pilot in the Royal Air Force during World War II. The Cairo of the forties was not the Cairo of the seventies, I replied. The Cairo Weizman had known was a chic European city, I said; today it is a crowded Asian metropolis.

I described the effect of the population explosion on economic and social conditions in Egypt. Egypt needed peace, I said, so that it could confront its urgent economic and social issues. I wanted to convince the two Israeli ministers of the seriousness and sincerity of the Egyptian quest for peace. I wanted them to understand that President Sadat's initiative was not a tactic we were using to regain our land in order to prepare for the next war. I wanted to assure them that Egypt truly sought to establish peace, security, justice, and stability throughout the region, for all countries and peoples. I recognized how deep were the doubts of the Israeli officials, doubts that were ingrained in the Jewish personality by the tragedies and persecution that the Jewish people have known throughout history.

The conversation in the room in the King David Hotel turned to military matters. Yadin and Weizman were soldiers. I was bored by the technical talk of the generals, but Dr. Mustafa Khalil amazed me with his knowledge of military issues. Suddenly he turned to Weizman, asking, "Does Israel have the atom bomb?" The Israeli defense minister did not answer. He rose from his place with his empty glass and walked very slowly to a nearby table to fill it with Scotch and began to drink. Then he spoke on a different subject, as if he hadn't heard the question.

Our four-way meeting ended about two o'clock in the morning. I felt that negotiations had already begun. We had overcome the first obstacle, the lack of trust between two Egyptian officials meeting two Israeli officials for the first time.

The next day Mustafa Khalil, with Sadat's permission, arranged a meeting for the president with Weizman. The two were instantly compatible, and a kind of affection developed between them. Weizman's lighthearted and enthusiastic nature made us feel that he was closer to the Egyptian personality than either the academic Yadin or the cold and introverted Dayan. But I knew that we should not ignore the influential Dayan.

I again rode in Moshe Dayan's car as we headed for the airport to begin the trip home. I sought to convince Dayan that Egyptian diplomacy was aiming at a comprehensive peace and that we were not thinking at all of a strictly bilateral solution between Egypt and Israel.

Dayan responded with derision: "How will you be able to negotiate in the name of the Palestinians, the Syrians, and the Jordanians if they reject the principle of negotiation?" I replied that Egypt's task was to convince the Arab sides of the necessity of negotiation and that negotiation could lead to positive results. If Israel, in fact, wanted to live in security and peace, it could participate in that process by adopting positions that would demonstrate that negotiations could succeed.

Egyptian diplomacy could also work, I said, toward a framework that would help the Arab states decide to negotiate with Israel. Do not forget, I said, that Egypt has an Arab dimension imposed by history, geography, and national ties founded on culture and a shared language and religion.

Dayan was not convinced, so I brought up a new idea that had just occurred to me. It should be possible, I said, to complete Israeli withdrawal from Gaza before the rest of the occupied Palestinian territories. Egypt had a special responsibility toward the Gaza Strip, having administered it from 1949 to 1967. If Egypt were to regain the administration of Gaza, it could assist the Palestinians there in developing an independent state that could be the nucleus of the larger state desired by the Palestinians. I explained that such a move would inspire trust in the sincerity of Israel's intentions and embolden the Arab sides to undertake negotiations with Israel. Dayan rejected the idea, saying that the Gaza Strip did not have sufficient economic and financial resources to exist as an independent state, which was proved by the fact that forty thousand Gazans were working inside Israel. We spoke also about Jerusalem, and once again I glimpsed the vast gulf that separated our two positions.

Whatever I felt about Dayan's personality, his conversation was frank, decisive, and clear. Dayan's style was in marked contrast to Weizman's, which tried to overcome obstacles through personal warmth and dynamic optimism. Weizman and I agreed on a telephone contact in Paris through which Egypt and Israel could pass messages without going through a third government. This was the only agreement we reached in Jerusalem.

At Ben-Gurion Airport, the farewell ceremonies were completed swiftly, and I found myself in the airplane sitting with President Sadat. He asked me to call together all the ambassadors accredited to Cairo to explain to them the purposes of his trip and the political objective of the venture he had begun.

As the plane gained altitude and was about to leave Israeli airspace, we saw F-4 Phantom fighter jets of the Israeli air force on both wings of Sadat's aircraft. "Yesterday they were fighting with us," the president said, "and today they are sending us off."

A huge crowd awaited our return; it seemed as though the entire population of Cairo had turned out. With peace, they cried, all the problems of Egypt will be solved.

Mustafa Khalil looked at me. He was a realist. "Do you believe they will give Jerusalem back to us?" he asked. "All that construction! I fear that Jerusalem is lost to the Arabs!"

"Even if true," I said, "we must believe the contrary. Otherwise all is lost." I suggested that a formula similar to that adopted for the Vatican and the Christian holy places in Rome could be the compromise. "At the end of the road beyond Jerusalem we will find Jerusalem," I said.

Disillusion in Ismailia

Tuesday, November 22, 1977, was a packed and hectic day. I was told to go to the television building to be interviewed on the peace initiative by French television. This was to be my first television appearance in my capacity as Egyptian foreign minister. Later I was interviewed by a beautiful French journalist, Josette Alia, whom I had known for many years as an editor for the French weekly *Nouvel Observateur.*

I spoke about the psychological shock to Israeli public opinion of President Sadat's peace initiative. Egypt could not have presented a stronger indication of its true and sincere desire for peace than Sadat's visit to Jerusalem. The journalist was interested in my relations with Moshe Dayan. I said that I had tried to explain to Dayan the meaning of Arab solidarity and the depth of feeling of a shared destiny that strongly united the peoples of the Arab nations. I had tried to convince Dayan that differences among Arabs, however long they lasted and however deep and numerous they might seem, would ultimately be settled amicably within the Arab family. Thus, I said to the French correspondent, I had tried to make it clear to Dayan that peace in the region had to be comprehensive or there would be no peace.

I had long been convinced of the need to provide foreign governments and the world press with more information about Egypt's foreign policies. Now, after President Sadat's astonishing journey, our foreign policy had to be clear to both friend and enemy. I would have to expend great time and effort in this informational work.

The following day I began my briefings for the diplomatic corps with the African ambassadors, because Africans were the largest group of ambassadors in Cairo, representing fifty nations, and because I wanted to emphasize Egypt's African connection. I felt that most Egyptian diplomats did not give sufficient importance to our relations with African countries. They were Europophiles and regarded Africa as peripheral. Assignment to Africa, they felt, was not to be compared with assignment to glamorous European capitals.

I explained to the African ambassadors—saying everything twice, once in French and once in English—that President Sadat's visit to Jerusalem was an unprecedented attempt to break the deadlock and achieve progress in regaining the Palestinian people's rights.

The Africans were concerned about Israel and South Africa. Did working with Israel mean Egypt was going to work with South Africa? I stated emphatically that it did not. I reiterated Egypt's opposition to South Africa's hateful practices of racial discrimination.

In the afternoon the Arab ambassadors arrived. I was apprehensive, fearing that this meeting would be strained. But it was friendly and the discussion was calm and useful.

The next day, Thursday, November 24, I met with ambassadors from Asia. The ambassador of Thailand read to the group a letter from the king of his country praising President Sadat for his courageous initiative and declaring Thailand's support for the visit to Jerusalem.

In the evening I met first with Western European ambassadors and then with those from Eastern Europe. The evening began with a protest by the Albanian ambassador, who had been invited to attend my briefing as part of the Eastern European group. He refused, saying that Albania would not have its name associated with the Eastern European Socialist bloc in any way, as they were not "real" communists. This created considerable confusion among the officials organizing these meetings until someone suggested to the Albanian that he join the group of Western European states. The ambassador agreed at once to sit with the capitalist nations and participated in the meeting comfortably. After the meeting was over, he whispered to me that he preferred a thousand times over to participate with those who opposed Marxism and Leninism frankly and openly rather than with those who betrayed those principles and conspired against them.

Then came another surprise from President Sadat. He announced in the People's Assembly that he was calling for an informal meeting in Cairo to prepare for a return to the Geneva Conference. He wanted to invite Israel, the United States, the Soviet Union, Syria, Jordan, and the Palestine Liberation Organization to Cairo. On the basis of this meeting, Sadat would try to set the structure and pace of negotiations by reconvening the major international conference at Geneva involving all the parties and aimed at a comprehensive solution.

The Geneva Conference on the Middle East had been convened on December 21, 1973, under the auspices of the United Nations secretary-general, with the United States and the Soviet Union as cochairmen, and with the foreign ministers of Egypt, Jordan, and Israel in attendance. The Syrian seat remained unoccupied. The letter of invitation to the conference stated that its purpose was to start the negotiations called for in Security Council Resolution 338 of October 22, 1973, "aimed at establishing a just and durable peace in the Middle East." The conference then recessed and did not meet again in plenary session. Though dormant, it continued as a symbol of the need for a comprehensive solution.

President Sadat was not opposed to the U.S.-USSR-chaired Geneva Conference, but he realized that it would be very difficult to resume negotiations. When Sadat asked me to organize an informal conference in preparation for Geneva, was he in fact camouflaging his determination to negotiate bilaterally with Israel and forget about the Arabs? Surely he was tempted to do so. After all, Egypt had agreed to a bilateral armistice with Israel in negotiations on Rhodes in 1948. Egypt and Syria had made a bilateral agreement with Israel after the 1973 War. Sadat was very aware of these precedents, but I felt that he had not yet made up his mind.

As soon as the meeting of the People's Assembly ended, the president summoned me to his private salon in the assembly building and asked me to begin preparing for the conference immediately. He said it would be held on December 3—in eight days! The president said that the invitations must go out immediately. I suggested that Lebanon be included, and he agreed. He also agreed to extend an invitation to the United Nations. For me, the involvement of the United Nations was imperative. The United Nations had accepted Israel as a legitimate member state. And UN Security Council Resolution 242 was the basis of the Arab-Israeli peace process.

The president asked, "What is wrong with you, Boutros? Why are you afraid?" I replied that holding an international conference, especially under these delicate political circumstances, could not be done within a few short days. Sadat would not hear of this: "What are you afraid of, Boutros? The conference must and will be held on December third. You have to manage. You can have everything ready in time."

I sat up for long hours in the night thinking about the thousands of problems I would have to solve to prepare for the conference. I was a beginner. What would be the level of representation? Where would the sessions be held? What would be on the agenda? In whose name would invitations be extended? How would Israel be informed of the invitation in the absence of diplomatic relations between us? December was the peak of the tourist season in Egypt. How would we find rooms for the delegations in hotels packed with tourists? Would we find the necessary translators, stenographers, and secretaries? How would we handle hundreds of representatives of the world media? And the security problems . . . all in eight days?

I convened a working group at the Foreign Ministry. I talked with Sadat by phone several times. We agreed that the conference would be held at the technical level rather than the ministerial level. Opinions differed about location. Some wanted the Socialist Union building on Corniche al-Nil so the delegations could be housed at the adjacent Hilton Hotel. Others favored the headquarters of the Union government in Misr al-Gadidah. I suggested Mena House.

This old hotel at the foot of the Pyramids had been the scene of important meetings during World War II, among them the meeting that brought together Chiang Kai-shek, Winston Churchill, and Franklin Delano Roosevelt, and that confirmed China as one of the Big Four allies and Taiwan, a Japanese colony, as an integral part of China.

Another consideration influenced me. I knew that ancient Hebrew history and culture were essential to Israel's self-image. Holding such a meeting as this beside the Pyramids would emphasize the unparalleled richness of the Egyptian past that could not be ignored by the Israelis. I remembered a phrase that Arnold Toynbee had written: "It is as if the pyramids are saying, 'We were here before the arrival of the prophet Abraham,'" an attitude I wanted to convey to the Israelis at the Mena House. But such historical considerations were far from the thinking of the security people, who objected strongly to the choice of the Mena House. They explained the dangers to me at length and in detail, pointing out the five entrances to the hotel and gardens. But I stuck to my opinion and decided to hold the conference at the Mena House.

After long discussions with the working group about the agenda for the conference, I realized that some officials of the Foreign Ministry possessed documents of the utmost importance, documents they were concealing from me. I was enraged. I could sense that these officials regarded me as an outsider who might not remain long in the ministry and that they felt entitled to keep me in the dark.

I then faced the problem of choosing the Egyptian delegation. I reviewed the names of several Egyptian diplomats and hesitated. In the end I decided on Dr. Esmat Abdel Meguid, Egypt's permanent representative to the United Nations in New York. I had known Esmat since the forties, when he was studying for his doctorate in Paris. I fully trusted his deftness and ability to manage the conference. I called Sadat, and he agreed to my choice with indifference.

I met with Dr. Osama al-Baz, an éminence grise of Sadat. I had appointed him to the board of the Center for Strategic and Political Studies, which I had opened at Al-Ahram a few years earlier. I had wanted him as my adviser on the Jerusalem trip but found that he was already a member of the delegation. Small, slight, with a raspy voice and a superb intelligence, he had studied at Harvard and became in Egypt the consummate political survivor and all-purpose savant. Osama drafted the invitation to the Cairo conference in English and in Arabic. This took the form of a letter addressed from me to the foreign ministers of the countries invited and to the secretary-general of the United Nations.

The letters were prepared, and in the afternoon I summoned the American ambassador, Hermann Eilts, a professional of immense self-confidence leavened by good humor, and gave him the letter directed to Secretary of State Cyrus Vance. It invited the United States to send a delegation to an informal meeting to be held in Cairo on December 3, 1977, in order to prepare for the Geneva Conference.

Then it was Soviet Ambassador Vladimir Poliakov's turn; I gave him a similar letter. Poliakov had a split personality. When speaking in his personal capacity, he would use Arabic and be amiable; when speaking officially, he would use Russian and be pompous. His interpreter was with him at all times. I explained to Poliakov—through his interpreter—the importance of the Soviet Union's accepting the invitation. The Soviet Union, I said, is the cochairman of the Geneva Conference. Egypt regards a Soviet presence in the Middle East as necessary to maintain a balance between the two superpowers and to reinforce our commitment to nonalignment, the cornerstone of Egyptian foreign policy.

Then I met with Dr. Ahmad Sidqi al-Dajani, a member of the Palestine Liberation Organization's supreme executive committee, and delivered to him the invitation extended to the organization to take part in the Cairo preparatory conference. Ahmad Sidqi al-Dajani was not a stranger. We knew each other from the Institute of Arab Studies affiliated with the Arab League. He was a prolific scholar and I had felt the depth of his learning as well as his clear thinking, which he expressed in husky tones, slowly articulating his words in a highly sophisticated Arabic.

This invitation took the form of a letter written in Arabic dated November 26, 1977, addressed from me to Mr. Yasir Arafat:

> Mr. Yasir Arafat
> Chairman of the Palestine Liberation Organization
>
> Warm greetings:
>
> I would like to advise you of the Egypt Arab Republic's initiative to hold an unofficial meeting in Cairo in which all sides of the conflict in the Middle East, the President of the Geneva Conference and the Secretary-General of the United Nations will take part with the purpose of preparing for continuing and completing the work of the Conference in order to reach a complete solution to the conflict in the Middle East and achieve just and lasting peace in the region.
>
> Accordingly, I invite you to assign your representative to take part in this unofficial meeting to be held in Cairo starting 3 December 1977.
>
> Respectfully yours,
>
> Dr. Boutros-Ghali
> Acting Foreign Minister
> Arab Republic of Egypt

I spoke to Sidqi al-Dajani at length about the purpose of the meeting. The participation of the PLO would be of maximum importance. The presence of the Palestinian delegation at the negotiating table with the Israeli delegation would serve as unprofessed mutual recognition. I pointed out the necessity of not wasting this opportunity and of taking advantage of the momentum from President Sadat's visit to Jerusalem.

I discussed with him more than one solution through which the problem of PLO representation—because of Israel's refusal to deal with PLO members—might be overcome. For example, I said, the PLO might charge an Arab personality, or one of the important officials of the Arab League, with representing the PLO in the workings of the conference. I was also prepared to adopt the formula that had been used at Dumbarton Oaks, where, because the Soviets refused to sit with the Republic of China, two tables were set up, one with the USSR, one with China. The other parties then could move from one table to another as needed.

What was of paramount concern to me, I said, was that the Palestine Liberation Organization be represented in the meeting and that the Palestinian flag fly next to the other flags at the conference site. He listened and promised to convey the arguments and opinions that I had put forth. The Arab press outside Egypt was soon complaining that no invitation to the PLO had ever been issued by Egypt. Since then I have often used this letter to prove to Palestinians that they had missed an opportunity to talk directly with Israel. Sixteen years later, when I sat in the White House grounds listening to Rabin and Arafat speak of their agreement, I felt with satisfaction that I had been right. But in retrospect I also had to admit that the sixteen intervening years meant that the talks we were proposing at Mena House were well before their time.

I likewise presented a letter of invitation to Ambassador Ahmad al-As'ad, chief of the office of Syrian relations in Cairo—the name given to the chief of the diplomatic missions of Syria and Libya after the establishment of the United Arab Republic, a confederation of Egypt, Syria, and Libya. The Jordanian and Lebanese ambassadors also were given invitations.

I instructed Ambassador Esmat Abdel Meguid in New York to invite the secretary-general of the United Nations. I also charged him with extending an invitation to Israel via its permanent delegate to the world organization. There was, of course, no official or unofficial relationship between the Egyptian delegation and the Israeli delegation, and the time had not yet come to establish direct contact between the two. For this reason, Esmat and I agreed on a plan by which the Dutch ambassador to the United Nations invited both Abdel Meguid and Ambassador Chaim Hertzog, the delegate of Israel, to his mission at the same time. At this meeting, "in passing," Esmat submitted the letter of invitation.

On Monday, November 28, 1977, the Turkish chargé d'affaires came to discuss arrangements for the visit of his foreign minister, who was to arrive in Cairo on November 30. I had inherited this visit from a former foreign minister who had invited his Turkish counterpart. I found it embarrassing, considering the shortness of time, to ask for a postponement or cancellation of the visit.

The motivation of every chargé d'affaires is to be promoted to ambassador, and this Turkish diplomat was greatly excited as he prepared for the visit of his foreign minister, perhaps with such a promotion in mind. He presented me with an outline of a joint communiqué about discussions that had not yet taken place. I could not face this excessive zeal and turned him over to the undersecretary of the department dealing with Western Europe.

I had inherited another visit as well—from the foreign minister of Chile. I felt there was no choice but to postpone this visit because of the swiftly approaching Mena House conference. When I conveyed this news to the Chilean ambassador, he seemed to lose his senses completely. His face darkened. He began to utter unintelligible phrases, first in English, then in Spanish. I tried to calm him down and got him a glass of water. When he was able to speak clearly again, he said that his diplomatic future depended upon the minister's visit. Indeed, his life depended on it, he said, because postponement would be considered a personal disaster and a failure of his mission, and that, therefore, he would not hesitate to commit suicide!

I retreated in the face of this threat and abandoned the idea of postponing the visit. But the ambassador would not rest easy until I had called in Ambassador Saad Hamzah, our director of protocol, and, in the Chilean's presence, ordered that the visit go forward without alteration or postponement.

Then the tide turned.

Ambassador al-Hindawi of Jordan came to see me and officially conveyed to me his government's regret that it could not participate in the Cairo conference.

That afternoon Ambassador Poliakov requested an urgent meeting. He arrived with a letter from his government: Moscow declined to attend the Cairo meeting. I rebuked the ambassador and made my disappointment clear to him. Poliakov tried to excuse his government's decision by saying that Moscow considered the Cairo conference illegal. Egypt, he said, did not have the right to extend invitations to such a conference. That was the prerogative, he claimed, of the United States and the Soviet Union, the two states that had cochaired the Geneva Conference in 1973 and remained nominally in that role.

I discounted this as a ploy to rationalize a political position. Yes, the United States and the Soviet Union were cochairmen, but it was the United Nations secretary-general who issued invitations to Geneva. Sadat insisted on this procedure, even though both the Soviets and the Israelis disliked giving the UN such a prominent role. The conference Egypt was proposing would be unofficial, I argued, and simply a way to lay the ground for reinvigorating the moribund Geneva Conference and to contribute to its ultimate success. This negative posture on the part of Moscow, I said, could cost it the opportunity to participate in this new and unprecedented peace effort.

Then it was the turn of the Lebanese chargé d'affaires, Zaydan Zaydan. His government declined the invitation to the Cairo conference, claiming that it had not been invited to participate in the original Geneva Conference in 1973. I explained to Zaydan Zaydan that the Cairo conference would be an unofficial gathering. Nothing prevented Lebanon from participating if his government was interested in a peace settlement in the Middle East. And Lebanon, I said, had a vital and pressing interest in peace for the region. I found myself repeating the same arguments over and over to all those who came to decline to attend the conference.

When the foreign minister of Turkey, Ihsan Sabri, arrived, I found to my relief that he was a man of pleasing personality, broad culture, and keen intellect, fluent in both French and English. Despite his advanced age, he was light of movement, quick of wit, and good company. Most important, he supported the Egyptian peace initiative. Turkey was strong and independent enough to stand against an international tide that had begun to run against the conference.

On Friday, December 2, 1977, I had a new experience: my first press conference. There was a huge crowd of representatives of the international press and radio and television stations. I had long ago become accustomed to facing crowds in lecture halls, but harsh lenses and lights were something quite different. I felt that the eyes of the world were upon me and my every word would be scrutinized.

Scores of questions came in Arabic, French, and English; I answered each in the language of the questioner. Everyone concentrated on the Soviet Union's refusal to take part in the Cairo preparatory conference. I repeated what I had told Poliakov previously: that the Cairo conference was unofficial and that there was, therefore, no obligation to adhere to the rules and procedures of the Geneva Conference. I left the press conference drenched with perspiration despite the cool weather but satisfied with myself. I had been able to control the situation and answer all the questions with clarity and without losing my poise or my temper.

While the Cairo conference was under this fundamental assault, bureaucrats in the Egyptian government, including some ministers whose responsibilities had no connection whatever with the subject, were trying to insinuate themselves into every detail of it. As denunciations mounted from without, disorganization mounted from within.

On December 3, I met again with the American ambassador, Hermann Eilts, to discuss arrangements for the Cairo conference. Despite the Soviets and Jordanians, we were still planning to go forward. As Eilts got up to leave my office, he said to me, "When you arrived at this important position, you enjoyed an international reputation and much respect in intellectual and academic circles. Boutros, you have credibility. This credibility is something of a challenge to you now that you have a political responsibility. Simply put, the challenge is whether you will be able to maintain this credibility and that respect."

I made no comment, but after the ambassador left I thought long about what he had said. My academic and intellectual background gave me a double responsibility. And the minister should not abandon the scholar!

Shortly after the Turkish foreign minister left Egypt, the Chilean foreign minister arrived at Cairo International Airport. He presented me with the Order of Merit of Chile, first class. When a dear friend with known leftist tendencies stopped by later, he was angered by the Chilean decoration. How could I accept a medal awarded by the reactionary Pinochet government that had eliminated Salvador Allende and his Socialist experiment, and that bore responsibility for massacres and the ending of freedom in Chile! In fact, the decoration—my first medal ever—should have been presented to my predecessor, the one who had extended the invitation to the Chilean minister. I received it merely by chance and had done absolutely nothing to warrant the recognition. I said nothing of this to my friend; I offered only what I intended to be a diplomatic smile, a smile that I would come to use frequently in the future.

On the afternoon of December 6, I held my second press conference. Its purpose was to explain Egypt's decision to break diplomatic relations with Algeria, Syria, Libya, and South Yemen. Without consulting anyone, President Sadat had decided to cut our relations with all those who opposed his initiative. I was left with the job of convincing the journalists that breaking diplomatic relations would not mean that all consular, commercial, and economic relations would stop and that people-to-people relations would not be interrupted.

But their questions revolved around the Cairo preparatory conference. Because of the wave of international opposition, we were compelled to lower the level of the conference and to postpone it. I confirmed that the conference was now planned for December 3 at the Mena House. The parties that had accepted were the United States, the United Nations, Israel, and Egypt. I stressed the hope that other Arab parties would understand the importance of the conference and would agree to join at the last minute.

One journalist asked me whether President Sadat's approach to Israel would lead the Arab League to move from Cairo to another Arab capital. I replied by referring to the charter of the Arab League signed on March 22, 1945, in which, in Article 10, Cairo is declared to be the site of the general headquarters. Therefore, I said, it would not be legal to move the headquarters without amending the charter under prescribed procedures in accordance with Article 19, which requires a two-thirds majority. My dry and technical reply was in marked contrast to the virulence of the Arab press. Sadat, they hissed, was a traitor to the Arab cause; I was the traitor's apprentice.

The next day, Prime Minister Mamduh Salim called to tell me he had decided to close the consulates of the Soviet Union in Port Said, Aswan, and Alexandria, as well as the consulates of Poland and Czechoslovakia. He requested that I inform those governments of the decision so that they could comply with it without delay.

I began to question the wisdom of this decision and its political consequences. Mamduh Salim interrupted: "The decision has been made; these are the instructions of the president." President Sadat, he said, was determined to counterattack harshly all those who condemned his initiative. This was a pretext, I believed. Sadat despised the Soviets and their satellites and wanted them out of Egypt.

On Saturday, December 10, I went in the early morning to the Nile Hilton Hotel to accompany Cyrus Vance, secretary of state of the United States, to Al-Qanatir al-Khayriyah to meet with the president. We rode in an armored car. Hermann Eilts was with us, and as we rode along he briefed Vance on the extent of Arab opposition to Sadat, especially among communists and Islamic fundamentalists.

At Al-Qanatir al-Khayriyah was a villa amid a garden built near the oldest barrage on the Nile, north of the city. President Sadat met first alone with Secretary Vance; then we were invited to join them. On the Egyptian side were Hosni Mubarak, Mamduh Salim, Lieutenant General Abd al-Ghani al-Gamasi, Hasan Kamil, the grand chamberlain, and myself. On the American side were Hermann Eilts, Roy Atherton, Harold Saunders, and Philip Habib. It appeared to me that this session was nothing but a diplomatic show, a "photo opportunity." Vance confirmed his government's support for Sadat's initiative and its participation in the Cairo conference. Sadat said that he would insist on the importance of the American role in the peace efforts in the Middle East and in any efforts to find a solution. The real issues were being discussed tête-à-tête. Vance informed his colleagues later what had been said behind closed doors. Whenever we asked Sadat, he would say he could not remember. Only later did I learn that the Americans regarded the meeting as important because Sadat convinced them that he was ready to move ahead on his own.

On Sunday, December 11, I met with the committees on Arab affairs and foreign affairs and defense in the People's Assembly. The meeting was headed by Dr. Gamal al-Utayfi, the chairman, a lawyer and politically ambitious party activist. We had gone through a difficult time during the Nasser regime and later strengthened our ties during twenty years' association in Al-Ahram, which was not only a newspaper but also a major center for studies and publishing on public affairs.

Speaking in the Assembly was a new experience for me. I decided to speak extemporaneously, thinking that this would permit a freer flow of ideas and arguments. And there was perhaps another consideration: mistakes of grammar might be forgiven more easily in an extemporaneous speech than in a formal written text.

I described President Sadat's initiative to the members and informed them of my meetings during the past week with the chiefs of the diplomatic missions stationed in Cairo. I then explained the goals of the Cairo preparatory conference. I referred to the conference that the Arab rejectionist front had just decided to hold to oppose Sadat. The rejectionist front was made up of those Arab states that rigidly followed the "three noes" of the 1967 Khartoum conference: no recognition, no negotiation, no peace with Israel. This gathering would have no political effect, I said, because continuing rejection could not be a substitute for a studied strategic policy. I ended my remarks by announcing the decision of Egypt to close the consulates and cultural centers of several communist-bloc countries. I noted that they were conducting improper activities that raised concerns for Egyptian national security.

Albert Barsum Salamah, a former cabinet member and a lawyer from Alexandria, asked about our contacts with nonrejectionist Arab states—would they participate in the Cairo conference? I said we were undertaking extensive communications. We had not yet received a response from Syria or the Palestine Liberation Organization or other Arab parties. We continued to hope that they would participate.

Mumtaz Nassar, an Assembly leader with a quick legal mind, asked me if Egypt continued to recognize the Palestine Liberation Organization as the sole legitimate representative of the Palestinian people. Choosing my words with the greatest care, I replied that the first invitation to attend the Cairo preparatory conference had been to Mr. Yasir Arafat. I confirmed Egypt's recognition of the PLO as the legitimate representative of the Palestinian people. Taking precautions for the future, I avoided using the expression "sole representative." If President Sadat's initiative went forward, Egypt might at some point have to negotiate on behalf of the Palestinians with the approval of non-PLO Palestinians.

How different was an academic lecture—which must treat all aspects of an issue with frankness and detail—from these parliamentary and political discussions in which the speaker is forced to adhere to the official government position and to expound one side of an issue and ignore all others.

While we continued to plan for a Cairo conference that could lead the parties back to Geneva and comprehensive negotiations, the preparations for the conference led us to put the date off from December 3 to December 14. The Cairo preparatory conference met from the fourteenth to the seventeenth of December at the Mena House, close by the Pyramids. Only four parties participated: Egypt, Israel, the United States, and the United Nations. It was a meeting of "experts," not ministers, so I did not attend.

Egypt, which had led the movement to unify the Arab world, was now spurned by its Arab brethren. It was Nahas Pasha, prime minister of Egypt, who presided over the conference in 1944 that drew up the Protocol of Alexandria, the first draft of the Arab League charter signed in Cairo on March 22, 1945. Cairo became the headquarters of the Arab League. More than 50 percent of the population under the League was Egyptian. The largest contributor of funds was Egypt. The secretary-general was always an Egyptian. Egypt was the originator of the pact of collective defense and economic cooperation of June 17, 1950, which was modeled on the NATO pact. It was Egypt that promoted the first Arab summit, under the chairmanship of King Farouk. And it was Egypt that successfully countered the Baghdad Pact concocted by the United States and Great Britain in the cold war. Egyptian leadership in the Arab world now seemed at an end as the Arab world turned against Sadat. Had Sadat realized this would happen when he went to Jerusalem?

On Saturday, December 24, 1977, President Sadat asked me to meet him in Ismailia, at the halfway point of the Suez Canal, where he was to meet with Prime Minister Begin, who was coming to

Egypt in return for Sadat's visit to Israel. I went to Almaza airport, where I found a helicopter waiting. It took off carrying Dr. Mustafa Khalil, the secretary-general of the party, and al-Nabawi Isma'il, the minister of the interior, who deals with security, and me. We flew over the site of the Farouk summit, which had taken place at Inchass, a small palace on the road to Ismailia. All the surrounding land had once belonged to my family; when the Khedive expressed interest in the area, my grandfather had sold the land to him. The helicopter landed in Ismailia and cars took us to the beautiful villa that served as a rest house not far from the airport. There we found Prime Minister Mamduh Salim and sat with him to await the arrival of the president.

Mamduh Salim asked me about the appointment of a new Egyptian ambassador to Yugoslavia. The former ambassador, Mourad Ghaleb, a former foreign minister and a physician of powerful personality, had resigned in protest over Sadat's new policy. I said that I had been in contact with Gamal Mansour, our ambassador to Syria, who had just returned to Cairo because of the breaking off of diplomatic relations between Egypt and Syria. As a young army officer at Cairo University, he had been my student at the end of the 1940s and later became a general in the army. I had agreed with him that, with Sadat's approval, he should travel to Belgrade without delay. Mamduh Salim asked, "Would it not have been better to wait for the opinion of the foreign minister?"

At first I could not understand what Salim meant. Then I realized with a shock what the prime minister was trying to convey to me in a roundabout way. I was upset by this news, and even more so by the way I was being informed. Why had I not been told sooner and in a frank and direct way? After a few minutes of silence I asked Mamduh Salim about the identity of the new foreign minister. He whispered a name, which I heard to be Hasan Kamil. I imagined that the head chamberlain had been appointed to the post of foreign minister. I recalled the efforts Hasan Kamil had made during the past weeks to focus attention on his ceremonial efforts at the Mena House conference. But President Sadat came into the room before I could confirm the identity of the new minister.

We sat around a long table. The gathering included Vice President Mubarak; Speaker of the Assembly Sayyid Mari; Prime Minister Mamduh Salim; Mustafa Khalil, secretary-general of the party; Minister of War General Abd al-Ghani al-Gamasi; Hasan al-Tuhami, special adviser to the president; and Minister of the Interior al-Nabawi Isma'il. The president spoke about the importance of his meeting with Begin and then asked me to report to those present about preparations for the Cairo conference. I did this and then read an outline of a joint declaration to be issued after the president's meeting with Begin. Afterward, General Gamasi gave a quick review of his discussions with Weizman. When Gamasi concluded, President Sadat commented, "Ezer Weizman is the only Israeli personality I can deal with." Then the president looked at me, saying, "Boutros, you will participate as of today in all the National Security Council meetings." I wondered if this was another way of telling me that I was not to be foreign minister. The foreign minister would of course attend National Security Council meetings as part of his job.

When the meeting was over I asked Mamduh Salim who the new foreign minister was. The prime minister smiled with mock astonishment, "Do you not know Muhammad Ibrahim Kamil, Egypt's ambassador in Bonn? He is a pleasant personality. No doubt you will get along with him and you will both work together in a brotherly spirit and fruitful cooperation." This was entirely understandable, as Sadat and Muhammad Ibrahim Kamil had been friends of long standing; they had been imprisoned together for political activities before the Revolution. Sadat probably had intended all along to name Muhammad Ibrahim Kamil. I was not downcast by this. I knew that Sadat considered my role as minister of state for foreign affairs to be functionally equivalent to foreign minister and the duties I was being assigned proved that Sadat had great confidence in me. It was now clear that when I had selected the office of minister of state for foreign affairs rather than the next-door office of foreign minister, I had unwittingly predicted my future.

I returned to Cairo and to my home, where I found a friend who criticized me severely. "How can you agree to work under the direction of Muhammad Ibrahim Kamil?" he asked. But I was *not* working under Muhammad Ibrahim Kamil, and I knew that my friend was only trying to provoke me. "How can you accept such a disgrace? How can you remain quiet after such dishonor? Muhammad Kamil is less than you in age, stature, and learning; he is a second-class diplomat. Do not forget that you were the one who went to Jerusalem with Sadat and carried the burden of that risk, from both a personal and political standpoint."

I smiled quietly and explained to my friend that life had prepared me for this. Professors and assistant professors who worked under me and whom I promoted had become dean or taken other leading posts in the university. Thus my students became my superiors. I accepted this situation, I said, and did not find in it anything to compromise my dignity or to imply an insult to my person. The issue is not age or knowledge or experience. Political appointees will always impose leadership on those in public service.

In the afternoon back in Cairo I participated in the cabinet meeting. The prime minister declared that the next day's Ismailia conference between President Sadat and Prime Minister Begin would result in agreement on the most important foundations of a peace treaty. I had to comment on this as a point of intellectual and politically honesty, and asked for the floor. Peace negotiations take a long time, I said. The effort to achieve peace will be long and hard and could continue for months and even years. I gave as an example the peace talks to end the Korean and Vietnam wars. These talks were based on principles and served the interests of the parties; the Ismailian talks would undermine the principle of Arab unity and sacrifice the interests of the Palestinians.

What I said did not appeal to Prime Minister Mamduh Salim. I could see the displeasure in his face. There was, he declared, a big difference between the Ismailia talks and the Korean and Vietnamese talks. I was about to ask for the floor again when I felt someone nudge me and whisper that there was no need to upset the prime minister. I turned around to find it was al-Nabawi Isma'il providing this brotherly advice. I said nothing and the meeting ended.

In the car on the way home I reviewed what had happened. I had tried to give the ministerial council a lesson in international relations and negotiations as though I were back in the lecture hall. But I had been learning about the chemistry of life in the high circles of government.

From then on events seemed to rush at me nonstop.

A snapshot at Ismailia: the second meeting with Menachem Begin, Moshe Dayan, Ezer Weizman, and General Avraham (Abrasha)

Tamir. Begin's stony personality was apparent in every word he uttered and every movement he made. This man, who was a statesman and diplomat, was bellicose and struck me as a danger to peace and the peace process. On the other hand, Weizman, who was a great military man, charmed us with his lighthearted style, and his presence eased the atmosphere. Dayan was unpredictable. One moment he would be arrogant and bitter; the next he would propose creative solutions and move the process forward.

A second snapshot: my first meeting with the new foreign minister, Muhammad Ibrahim Kamil. I found from the start that getting along with him would not be difficult. He had a pleasant and easygoing personality and spoke honestly and clearly in words that revealed a big heart. I had repeatedly been warned that relations between the foreign minister and the minister of state for foreign affairs traditionally had been bad. I heard stories of friendship turning into animosity, of foreign ministers who isolated ministers of state, and of ministers of state intriguing to get rid of foreign ministers. But my meeting with Muhammad Ibrahim Kamil made me feel that we could work together in honesty and loyalty to our country.

A third snapshot: the luncheon party held at the pretty villa in Ismailia. The wife of Israel's former foreign minister, Abba Eban, sat beside me. She was born in Ismailia and grew up there. When she learned that Begin would meet there with Sadat, she had asked to accompany the Israeli delegation, and Begin had agreed. Mrs. Abba Eban asked me questions all through lunch. Questions political and unpolitical, personal and impersonal. Most of these questions were far from diplomatic. What is the truth about relations between Sadat and Mubarak?—even as they sat at the same table with us! What is the role of the prime minister in the negotiations with Israel?—even as the prime minister sat nearby! Why was I not appointed foreign minister? Why does not Sadat eat the same food his guests eat? Is special food prepared for him? Does he not have lunch? Is he fasting? I told the Israeli lady that I was still in the A-B-C stages of diplomacy and so could not answer her specific questions. I could, however, speak about all aspects of the Palestinian issue and explain its historical, legal, and political aspects from an academic standpoint. She laughed and said her husband was also an academic and his conversations also were in this vein, no matter what the topic.

Another snapshot: President Sadat mentioned that today was his fifty-ninth birthday. Strangely, no one had known this. The news created a joyful atmosphere; al-Gamasi congratulated him, and Begin stood up and gave a speech praising Sadat's manners, character, and achievements. But Begin exaggerated his praise to the point where he seemed to be sneering and mocking us. However, Begin ended his talk on a different tone. Jewish tradition, he said, calls for wishing a friend on his birthday that he live one hundred and twenty years. "I know this may be difficult to believe, but I wish, from the bottom of my heart, for Anwar al-Sadat to live one hundred and twenty years and beyond." President Sadat smiled broadly and thanked Begin, and an atmosphere of happiness prevailed among us.

Intensive talks took place at Ismailia for two days, which began with a closed session between Sadat and Begin. I spent my time in conversation first with Weizman in one room and then with Dayan in another. My aim was to balance my relations with what appeared to me to be two opposite Israeli poles. I soon learned that there was deep solidarity between them.

After half an hour, Begin and Sadat emerged to join us. The Israeli prime minister looked happy and relaxed; this worried me and I wondered what could be the source of his pleasure. Soon I learned that Begin had received Sadat's approval to form two committees, one military and another political, at the bilateral level. The first would involve the defense ministers of both countries, and the other would include the Egyptian and Israeli foreign ministers and be held in Jerusalem.

As soon as the Foreign Ministry "gang," as the Israelis called us, found out about this agreement, we tried to alter the two committees so as to make them comprehensive rather than bilateral sessions in which Egypt would be in an inferior position, inasmuch as Israel still held Egyptian territory. We sought to conform the talks to the planned Cairo conference, which so far had been accepted by the United States and the United Nations in addition to Israel and Egypt. I feared that Israel wanted bilateral talks in order to make a separate peace with Egypt. This would prevent us from advancing Palestinian rights and at the same time would split the whole Arab camp.

We succeeded in changing the political committee to a quadrilateral body to include the United Nations and the United States, but the military committee remained bilateral. We got agreement that both committees would report to the Cairo preparatory conference and that those next invited to Mena House would be at the ministerial, not expert, level. Thus we were able to link the two committees to the Cairo preparatory conference as a way to keep the process under the Geneva Conference approach, which was comprehensive rather than bilateral. But all our efforts would be undermined repeatedly because the Arabs rejected Sadat's initiative and because the Israelis kept pushing for a separate peace with Egypt that would exclude the Palestinians. Thus a bizarre, objective alliance emerged between the Arab rejectionists and the Israeli hard-liners.

Then Begin spoke for hours and hours—or so it seemed—explaining his project to achieve Palestinian "self-rule." To me, his vision involved a kind of amputated Palestinian entity, one that would create the perception of self-rule but leave practical control in Israeli hands. As he spoke, he repeated this argument time and time again. He declared that the settlements that Israel had built in Sinai, between Al-Arish and Rafah, and on the road from Eilat down to Sharm al-Sheikh, must remain and must continue under Israeli administration.

President Sadat answered forcefully, saying that Israeli forces should withdraw from all lands occupied in June 1967 and enable the Palestinian people to exercise their right to self-determination.

The next day we entered into extended discussions about the joint declaration, and Sadat agreed in principle on the outline presented by the Israeli side. But the Foreign Ministry gang objected. There was no need for a joint declaration because nothing had been achieved.

To conclude the Ismailia summit, Sadat and Begin did, however, hold a joint press conference in a large tent erected behind the villa where they had met. A huge crowd of journalists from different parts of the world was there. The president read a declaration that clarified the differing positions of both sides. An Egyptian journalist directed a question to Prime Minister Begin in Hebrew. Begin seemed delighted by this and congratulated the questioner on his command of the Israeli language.

When the press conference was over, I could see relief on the faces of Sadat and Begin. They seemed pleased despite the failure of the meeting to achieve real progress and the revelation of the immense gap between the two states.

On the helicopter carrying us from Ismailia to Almaza airport, it seemed to me that without a doubt the Ismailia meeting had failed. It had an impromptu quality to it and the negotiations had been disorganized. We had prepared studies, memoranda, outlines, and research, but they were neither read nor used. Dayan himself revealed his discomfort and said to me that the Ismailia meeting had failed and that nothing could be achieved in the future if the work continued in this unplanned style. Our Foreign Ministry gang for its part had tried to convince Sadat that as no joint declaration had been achieved with the Israeli side, the agreement regarding the formation of the two committees could not be implemented. Sadat rejected that, saying, "I gave my word to Menachem Begin and cannot go back on it." We tried to convince him that the negotiations needed greater planning, but he refused to discuss it.

I was overcome by a feeling of failure and depression. The Ismailia meeting made clear to me several sides of Anwar Sadat's personality. I wrote down in my notebooks the main points as I saw them.

First, Sadat had no patience with details. He chose to leave decisions about them to his assistants, which allowed him to overturn or bypass them at the last minute.

Second, Sadat's one goal, it was clear to me, was to regain Egyptian land—the return of the Sinai to the motherland. All other issues were secondary and could wait until the first priority was achieved.

Third, Sadat's apparent indifference to the Palestinian issue reflected his conviction that the Egyptian and Palestinian issues could not be dealt with at the same time, and that trying to do both at once would weaken our ability to achieve either of them. In other words, Sadat had concluded that Egypt could not undertake a major effort to gain the legitimate rights of the Palestinian people as long as Egyptian territory lay under Israeli occupation. By contrast, I was convinced that no treaty of peace could endure unless it included measures for Palestinian rights, the minimum being the right of self-determination.

Fourth, Sadat did not adhere to the Geneva Conference. It was clear that the Mena House conference in his mind was not a preparation for a return to Geneva but a preliminary to direct negotiation far from the comprehensive, all-parties structure of the Geneva Conference.

And fifth, Sadat negotiated, maneuvered, and argued not only with the Israeli side, but also with his own Egyptian officials—and perhaps even more so. He seemed to want both to encourage yet contain our disagreements with him. Sadat wanted to show Begin that he was faced with internal resistance as well as with opposition from the larger Arab world.

The Ismailia meeting had given me a chance to study and analyze Israeli thought and behavior. I could see that Israel's goal was to make a separate peace with Egypt and to distance the United States and the United Nations as much as possible from the negotiation process. This explained why Begin seemed pleased with the Ismailia negotiations though they achieved nothing, because the Israeli prime minister's only interest was in bilateral talks. This explained Begin's displeasure with the Foreign Ministry gang's insistence on the necessity of American participation and the presence of the United Nations.

It seemed to me that Begin's refusal to recognize the Palestinian people and their right to self-determination stemmed from a stubborn refusal to face reality that was not unlike the Arab refusal to face the reality of Israel's existence. As a result, the Israeli delegation avoided treating the Palestinian issue as a political matter and tried to limit discussions to humanitarian and local administration.

Israel, understandably, was trying to deepen the divisions and disagreements within the Arab world. It was particularly focused on planting seeds of distrust between Egypt and the Palestine Liberation Organization. Begin described the organization as nothing but a tool of international communism, attempting to insinuate that it was a danger to moderate Arab governments and to President Sadat's rule. Sadat did not object to this description.

Begin also soon realized that Sadat's style of negotiation provided a chance for Israel to stir disagreement between him and his assistants. So Begin asserted that it was only Sadat who wanted peace, while the Foreign Ministry was still under the influence of the former foreign minister, Ismail Fahmi, who had resigned rather than travel to Jerusalem. Begin said that "the gang" was working to ensure that Sadat's initiative would fail.

Finally, Israel was determined to get agreement on the practical results of a peace agreement—such as trade and tourism and diplomatic ties—before agreeing to withdraw from Sinai. The Israeli negotiators wanted to deprive the Egyptian negotiators of their most important card. We, on the other hand, wanted to discuss Israeli withdrawal as a prerequisite to other issues.

All this went through my mind while I was in the helicopter headed for Almaza airport. Two exhausting days of negotiations had made it clear that negotiations with Israel would be long, hard, and uncertain. The Egyptian negotiating position was weak, and our style of negotiating only increased that weakness. The Israeli negotiating position was strong, and their negotiators moved according to a cohesive and studied plan to achieve clear objectives related to both the long and the short run.

On December 27 I attended the dinner party that President Sadat held in Abdin Palace in honor of Helmut Schmidt, chancellor of the Federal Republic of Germany. The food was bad, unworthy of a head of state or even of a second-class restaurant and we ate to the sound of an orchestra in a neighboring room, alternately playing Arab and Western music.

The next day I met for lunch with Sadat and Schmidt at the table of the German ambassador in his residence overlooking the Nile. I observed once again the absolute abstention of President Sadat from taking any food. He was satisfied with a small cup of tea. He was equally abstemious in his conversation. We did not touch at all on politics or international issues.

On Friday, December 30, Edgar Faure, the former prime minister of France, visited me in my office. He was head of the International Institute for Human Rights in Strasbourg, of which I was a trustee. Faure described the Israeli state as a "*colonie à métropole diffuse*," that is, a colony belonging not to an imperialist state but to an empire spread out and scattered over the entire world. He was referring to the Jewish diaspora. Faure's conversation was filled with criticism of Israel and its policies. But, he said, "No one can accuse me of being an anti-Semite, since I married a Jewish woman."

Frustration in Jerusalem

In the beginning of January 1978 I traveled with Muhammad Ibrahim Kamil to Aswan, where we stayed at the Hotel Oberoi on an island in the Nile between the rosy desert mountains to the west and the city of Aswan on the east bank. I was amazed to learn from the new foreign minister that in his long diplomatic career he had never visited another Arab country and that his knowledge of the Arab world and the Palestinian issue had little relationship to reality. Our talk led me to expect new difficulties within the Egyptian delegation in the coming negotiations.

Early in the morning of Wednesday, January 4, we waited at the Aswan airport for the arrival of President Jimmy Carter, whose aircraft would be on the ground for an hour to refuel. The weather was stinging cold, but President Sadat insisted on performing the full official ceremonies of reception. So there was a twenty-one-gun salute, the national anthems were played, and the honor guard was presented. All this took almost forty-five minutes, time that could have been better devoted to explaining the Egyptian position to the American president.

In the brief remaining time, the two presidents met privately in the VIP lounge. The two delegations sat outside and discussed the idea of a quick visit by President Carter to the High Dam, but the Americans responsible for security rejected that idea completely. Before his airplane took off, the American president issued a declaration that, for the first time, expressed United States recognition of the "legitimate rights of the Palestinian people" and their right to participate in negotiations determining their future.

This was an important declaration. I discussed it with Musa Sabri, editor of *Al-Akhbar*, the daily newspaper with the greatest circulation in Egypt. Musa Sabri's friendship with Sadat went back to their days in prison during the Farouk period. He was a prolific, honest, and courageous journalist—a unique combination in the Arab world. I now knew that Musa Sabri had been one of the two others Sadat had asked to draft a speech for his use in Jerusalem, and that Musa Sabri's text had been the one chosen by the president rather than mine. In a certain way, Musa Sabri would be my pipeline to

Sadat. He and I agreed that we should try to focus press attention on the fact that the United States was calling for Palestinian participation now, rather than allow it to be interpreted as only talk about "their future."

A week later, on Monday, January 9, I was again in Aswan, this time to be among those receiving His Majesty Mohammed Reza Pahlavi, shah-in-shah of Iran. The weather was much better than it had been the day President Carter arrived. The cold had lessened, and the sun was bright and warm. The Iranian airplane landed; the twenty-one guns went off; the band played the imperial anthem and the Egyptian national anthem. The shah inspected the honor guard and went with President Sadat to the Hotel Oberoi.

I sat by the hotel swimming pool and had lunch with Hosni Mubarak, Mamduh Salim, Muhammad Ibrahim Kamil, and Hasan Kamil.

In the evening, President Sadat held an official dinner in honor of the shah. After dinner the two delegations moved into a grand reception hall for a performance by the Aswan Folk Dance troupe. Their Nubian-Arab peasant show was long and tiresome.

Both Sadat and the shah were at the peak of their power. It seemed clear to us all that if they formed an alliance, they would dominate the entire Middle East as the two superpowers of the region. It was an old friendship; in the 1973 war only the shah had kept oil flowing to Egypt. Israel had long followed the old maxim about being on good terms with the neighbor of your neighbor and had formed a strong relationship with the shah's government as a counterweight to Israel's nearby Arab enemies.

The shah had supported Sadat's trip to Jerusalem. He and Sadat also shared an obsession: to fight communism. As evidence of this they were cooperating to support Somalia in its struggle with Marxist-Leninist Ethiopia. Sadat felt that the United States would look upon this Egyptian-Iranian connection with great favor.

Back in Cairo I attended a meeting of the board of the Egyptian Society for International Law. I agreed with Dr. Hafiz Ghanim that I should submit a proposal to the council to nominate Anwar Sadat for the Nobel Peace Prize. The council accepted the proposal in principle, but I felt that some members, like other Egyptian intellectuals, were not enthusiastic about the idea.

The political committee that had been agreed on at Ismailia was to meet in Jerusalem in three days. At a meeting in Muhammad Ibrahim Kamil's office with the group of experts of the Egyptian delegation, I presented the outline of the speech that Muhammad Kamil was to make at the opening session. It was borrowed to a great extent from the outline of the speech that I had prepared for President Sadat to use in Jerusalem, which he did not adopt. That outline had taken much effort and time; why not benefit from it in the second visit to Jerusalem?

I read the suggested text aloud to Muhammad Kamil, Esmat Abdel Meguid, and the rest of those at the meeting. I sensed that they were not comfortable with it. The cultural and literary aspects of my outline were not in step with the political climate or the requirements of the political committee. I was still confusing the diplomatic and the academic. Perhaps I should have realized that "never the twain shall meet."

But faced with my insistence, Muhammad Kamil accepted some of the expressions from my outline, among them the expression *al-Madinah al-Fadilah* (The Virtuous City), with which I described Jerusalem, and by which I meant to refer to the book by the philosopher al-Farabi, and the expression about "the necessity of establishing peace between the House of Israel and the House of Palestine."

On Saturday, January 14, the day before we were to depart for the political committee meeting in Jerusalem, I received the ambassador from the Central African Republic, who informed me that His Majesty Emperor Bokassa had given his support to President Sadat's initiative. While conveying this message, the ambassador recited all the resounding titles that Bokassa had chosen for himself. Emperor Bokassa later became world-famous for the mass slaughter he had ordered and the pyramids of skulls he proudly displayed. Some of his victims, it was said, had been killed to satisfy the emperor's penchant for cannibalism. When Bokassa's empire fell, he found exile in France.

President Sadat provided his presidential aircraft to transport the Egyptian delegation to Tel Aviv, and we arrived at Ben-Gurion Airport at sundown the next day, on Sunday. After our arrival, Muhammad Ibrahim Kamil read a brief speech in English, reaffirming Egypt's fundamental position on the impossibility of achieving peace as long as Arab lands continued to be occupied and the legitimate rights of the Palestinian people were denied.

Then we were driven to Jerusalem. In the car with me was Ephraim Evron, director general of the Israeli Foreign Ministry. Muhammad Kamil rode in Moshe Dayan's car. We arrived at the Hilton Hotel, where I had dinner with Muhammad Ibrahim Kamil and Esmat Abdel Meguid in Muhammad's suite. Although the Egyptian security experts had inspected the suite and assured us that there were no listening or recording devices, we avoided political topics in our conversation.

On Tuesday, January 17, the work of the political committee began, with the participation of Cyrus Vance. In addition to the Egyptian, Israeli, and American delegations, a representative of the United Nations was included. He insisted that his seat be a foot and a half away from the round conference table placed in the basement of the Hilton. This was on instructions from Secretary-General Kurt Waldheim, to ensure that his presence at the conference would be seen as that of an observer, not a full member.

The participation of the United Nations had required intensive effort by the permanent Egyptian delegation in New York with Kurt Waldheim. The Arabs did not want the UN to confer the slightest degree of legitimacy on Sadat's initiative, and their pressure on Waldheim was raising his fears about the extent of UN involvement.

After the inaugural session Ezer Weizman came to my room. The Israeli minister of defense was careful to assure me that he was not a member of the Israeli delegation and was not participating in the work of the political committee. In my talk with him, I told him that I had found in my room a pamphlet virulently attacking the Palestine Liberation Organization as a communist conspiracy. He said that the establishment of a Palestinian state under the leadership of the PLO would represent a grave threat to Israel's security. Weizman read the publication, then said, laughing, "This is for the benefit of American tourists, not Egyptian ministers!"

In the afternoon, I agreed with Muhammad Kamil to visit Prime Minister Begin in the hope that such a courtesy would lighten the atmosphere. We went to Begin's office in the Israeli Knesset building, where he greeted us hospitably. The prime minister took hold of a book of international law by Professor L. F. L. Oppenheim and said, directing his remark at me, "International law distinguishes between defensive wars and aggressive wars. The 1967 war was a defensive war; consequently, Israel has the right to retain a part of the lands that it occupied in that war." Begin thought he might convince the professor of international law in Cairo University more easily than he could convince Egypt's minister of state for foreign affairs!

Begin spoke with great vehemence about the Egyptian media, saying that they had attacked him in an unacceptable way. After much discussion we agreed that both sides should avoid provocative press and public statements and should practice quiet diplomacy. Begin said to me, smiling, "Now that we have come to an agreement, should I call you Peter or Boutros?" I replied that that depended on the degree of firmness of the agreement. He laughed and, to signal that our relationship was good, said, "In that case, I will call you Boutros!"

In the evening, Menachem Begin gave a dinner party at the Hilton Hotel. This seemed an exceptional gesture, as, by protocol, he could have left the duty to his foreign minister, Dayan. After dinner, Begin gave a long speech in which he attacked the Egyptian position and condescendingly addressed Foreign Minister Muhammad Kamil as "my young friend." Begin's speech was not welcoming; his words were unfriendly and hurtful.

The speech angered Muhammad Kamil, who rose immediately to declare that a dinner party is not an appropriate place to carry out political discussions, which should be reserved for the closed meetings of the political committee. Then Muhammad sat down and refused to converse with the people sitting near him. When Begin offered a toast, he refused to participate.

Back in Muhammad Kamil's suite, we had a long discussion about Begin's motives. What made him publicly attack Egyptian policy when, just a few hours before in his office, we had agreed to a truce in the media battle and to avoid precisely such behavior? Later we were told that Sadat, infuriated when he heard of Begin's remarks, had decided to send an Egyptian air force plane that very night to bring our entire delegation back to Cairo. Clearance for the plane was obtained from the Israelis, but then Sadat dropped the idea.

As a result of Begin's speech, the next day's atmosphere was gloomy. Only marginal contacts took place in the rooms and halls of the hotel. Cyrus Vance did what he could to dispel the clouds, but with little success.

I had lunch in my room with Yigal Yadin. Yadin pointed to my plate and said, "You are eating fish from your Lake Bardawil," a salt-water lake near the Mediterranean in the north of Israeli-occupied Sinai. "When the lake returns to its owners," I replied, "I will invite you to eat the same fish in Cairo, prepared according to the Egyptian recipe." I said to Yadin that negotiations need an atmosphere of calm and confidentiality, and that provocative announcements and media battles could lead only to failure. I dreaded a diplomatic incident, I said, that could cause the peace process to collapse completely. If that should happen, when would another leader like Sadat come forward? Sadat has presented a unique opportunity for peace; it must be seized.

Yadin said that he shared my pessimism. He said that despite being the deputy prime minister, he had been removed from the negotiations, just as he had been removed previously from the Israeli delegation that took part in the Ismailia meetings.

After Yadin left, Colonel Ahmad al-Hifnawi, my security officer, came to inform me that instructions had arrived from Cairo to cut off the negotiations and return to Egypt immediately. I soon saw that an air of hysteria had swept through the Egyptian delegation. Luggage was packed; aides gathered up papers; security agents took out the special telephone. Everyone seemed happy to be getting out; the enthusiasm for negotiating with the Israelis had vanished. I immediately went to inform Cyrus Vance that we had been ordered back to Cairo and to apologize to him. Vance, who had been at the center of this meeting, was the last one to be told of its collapse. I did not want him to be embarrassed. "Don't worry, Boutros," Vance said, "the logic of heads of state is different from everyone else's logic."

I told Vance that President Sadat had recalled us because of our reports to him about the way Begin had received us. Vance agreed that Begin had been provocative but added that the Israeli prime minister resorted to the same style with more than one head of state and more than one guest who visited him in Israel. Those engaged in diplomacy, Vance said, had to bear with such assaults.

I returned to my room to pack. Word came that President Carter was trying to contact President Sadat to persuade him to let the Egyptian delegation continue the negotiations in Jerusalem. As I hesitated in packing, Weizman entered. I burst upon him, attacking the Israeli position strongly. Israel carried the responsibility for the failure of the meetings, I said.

Weizman listened calmly and said, "I will try to save what I can," and left dramatically.

We left the hotel at about nine o'clock in the evening on our way to the airport. Once again, Ephraim Evron accompanied me. When we arrived at the airport, we discovered that the car carrying our baggage had not yet left Jerusalem. We had to wait about an hour for it to arrive.

Dayan made a point of sitting next to me during this period. I understood that there was something important he wanted to tell me. He tried to explain that he had a "special relationship" with Prime Minister Begin and differed with him on a number of matters relating to the negotiations with Egypt. His participation in the Likud government despite his long-term membership in the Labor party, Dayan said, stemmed from his conviction that the time had come to conclude a peace treaty with Egypt and that his presence in the government could help that. This was why, he said, he agreed to be Begin's foreign minister.

Dayan said that the long conversation we had during Sadat's visit to Jerusalem had made a profound impression on him and affected his view of the situation. If a solution with regard to the West Bank was too difficult at present, Dayan said, why not concentrate on the Gaza Strip? He noted that Gaza had been for many years, until 1967, administratively subject to Egypt. Dayan said that he hoped that he and I could cooperate to remove obstacles to progress in the service of our countries and the cause of peace. My attitude toward Dayan changed. I began to appreciate the man. He was never a sympathetic character, but he wanted peace. I felt that if it were just the two of us, we could actually accomplish something.

We arrived in Cairo near dawn, tired and embittered by the failure of the mission.

CHAPTER TWO

❖ ❖ ❖

Sparring in the Third World

I wanted world opinion to know the truth of what happened in Jerusalem. I told the Cairo correspondent of *Le Monde* that even now Sadat's historic visit to Jerusalem had not received a serious response from Israel. I explained that the negotiations had not collapsed but had been halted, and that Begin's public statements were the reason.

On Friday, January 20, 1978, I was with President Sadat at his rest house at Al-Qanatir al-Khayriyah when he met with Cyrus Vance and agreed to go to the United States to explain the Egyptian position to President Carter. Sadat asked me to go to Yugoslavia to meet with President Tito. Under the powerful leadership of Tito, Yugoslavia had become a world power in diplomacy. Tito used communist ideology to forge an ultranationalist movement in a country that otherwise would be highly fractious. And Tito had used the concept of nonalignment to create an influential worldwide movement. Yugoslavia was the epicenter of the movement, which had been inaugurated in Brioni in 1956 at a summit that included Prime Minister Nehru of India and President Nasser of Egypt.

I left Cairo on January 28, after midnight, heading for Belgrade on a Yugoslavian plane. The director of my office, Ambassador Ala' Khayrat, and Ahmad al-Hifnawi, the security officer who was like my shadow, accompanied me. The weather in Belgrade was bitterly cold, and ice covered the airport. Deputy Foreign Minister Lazar Mojsov received me and accompanied me to the hotel. Mojsov's diplomatic style was unique, at once sweet and politically acute. He would later become foreign minister and then hold one of Yugoslavia's rotating presidential positions.

The Egyptian chargé d'affaires in Belgrade was a former student of mine, Sa'd Durayd, who, as ambassador ad interim, was excited to receive his former professor as a minister. He showed me a copy of the letter from Tito to Sadat, dated January 24, which had led to my trip. I could scarcely believe that I had been sent to Belgrade without ever having been shown this letter! The Foreign Ministry had not received a copy of the letter from the presidency of the republic.

President Tito's letter was a long explanation of his conviction that Israel was not ready to conclude a comprehensive peace agreement with the Arab states because it would not recognize the Palestinian people and their right to self-determination. President Sadat's initiative, Tito wrote, would produce a situation of the utmost danger—the internal division of the Arab world. This division, in turn, Tito said, would undermine the unified front of the nonaligned movement. Tito called on President Sadat to return to Arab solidarity. Other Arab leaders, too, he declared, desired Egypt to return to its leading role in the common Arab front. Tito invited Egypt to come to Belgrade for a conference of the foreign ministers of the nonaligned nations to assess the Middle East crisis.

I did not imagine that my assignment with President Tito would be easy, but after reading the letter, I understood that the gap between the two presidents was enormous. After resting briefly, I was driven back to the Belgrade airport to fly to the Adriatic coast near Dubrovnik to see Tito. But when we reached the airport, we could not take off because of the weather. It appeared that we would have to travel to Dubrovnik by train, an idea that I welcomed, but the protocol officers discovered that the train schedules would not permit me to arrive in time for my scheduled appointment with President Tito. They decided that I must travel by car to the shore of the Adriatic. Within minutes they changed their minds again and informed me that I would travel by a special military airplane. Shortly before midnight we arrived at a military airport about thirty miles from Belgrade. There a military airplane took off despite the bad weather and the strong winds. After we landed, at about two in the morning. I was deposited at a huge hotel called the Croatia, where I fell instantly asleep.

Tito Condemns

I awoke a few hours later feeling fully restored. The weather had improved, and through the hotel window, I saw the sea as if it were a magnificent painting. I was taken to President Tito's palace, a towering building on a mountaintop. I entered the reception hall, and seconds later two little dogs entered the hall, followed by the president. He was stout, even fat, with a wide face. From a distance he appeared strong, but up close his face was sallow and lined and his hair inexpertly dyed. Although immensely sure of himself, he made me feel at ease. Tito was not the slightest bit patronizing or imperious; he talked to me as a true comrade. No staff or aides were in the room; only a translator. Tito asked that I speak in Arabic. The translator introduced himself as Izaevich. I found that he had been born in Egypt, where his father was the owner of the famous *ful* and *ta'miyah* (bean and falafel) restaurant on Tahrir Square in the center of Cairo, which I had frequented in my youth. President Tito welcomed me with a broad smile and invited me to review developments since President Sadat's trip to Jerusalem.

When I finished my presentation, Tito began to speak slowly, pausing from time to time to take a puff from his long, fine cigar. He spoke of his doubts that Israel would withdraw from the entire Sinai Peninsula. He said Israel would pressure Egypt for more concessions on the rights of the Palestinian people. He feared the matter would end with a unilateral solution, division would spread in the Arab world, and the nonaligned movement would be weakened everywhere. The Yugoslav president then invited me to share a glass of beer with him. I declined. He ordered a glass for himself and continued his conversation as he drank.

He said he was sorry that President Sadat had gone to Jerusalem. Israel depended on its military superiority, he said, and it knew that the United States lacked the will to exert effective pressure on Israel. Tito interrupted his conversation, once more insisting I have any drink I wished. I proposed coffee, which he ordered for two. When he finished the beer, he turned to the coffee and lit another huge cigar.

He regretted that relations between Cairo and Moscow had worsened. He felt that Egypt was leaning toward the United States. The present danger to the nonaligned movement lay, he said, in the great powers' polarizing key countries like Egypt and tying the interests of these countries to their side. Every country had the right to plot the course of its international relations, but siding with one side against the other upset the balance and harmed the nonaligned movement, he said.

While Tito spoke of balance between the superpowers, what struck me most was that his talk was filled with orthodox Marxist terminology. He seemed old and out of touch. I assured the president that I had participated in all stages of contacts with Israel and had been negotiating with her since the trip to Jerusalem. There could be no doubt, I said, of Egypt's integrity regarding the Palestinian issue and the rights of the Palestinian people. Then I asked: as long as President Tito was not happy with the steps Egyptian diplomacy had taken, did he have any alternative suggestions that would open the way toward comprehensive peace?

Tito replied that it was necessary, as a prerequisite, to achieve mutual recognition between Israel and the Palestine Liberation Organization. The Geneva Conference should be reconvened so that both superpowers could fulfill their responsibilities for establishing peace in the Middle East. We talked for two hours; I was unable to persuade him to accept Sadat's position.

I returned to the Croatia Hotel. A question heard in Cairo before my departure came to my mind as I wrote down what had been said during the interview: Was Tito's position precipitated by President Ceauşescu of Romania's role in Sadat's initiative? Ceauşescu had encouraged Sadat's decision, saying, "I know Begin, and you can trust him." Did the traditional rivalry between Tito, who headed the nonaligned movement, and Ceauşescu, who sought a policy independent of Moscow, lead to Tito's opposition to President Sadat's move? This was not an important question, I concluded; the real question was "Is Tito right or wrong?" I was shaken by what Tito had said. His opposition to Egypt's policy raised doubts in my mind about whether we were making a terrible mistake.

In the morning I flew back to Belgrade, which was blanketed by snow. From the airport I proceeded to the party headquarters of the League of Communist Yugoslavs. The secretary of the foreign-relations committee of the party was waiting for me. We spoke about the cooperation between the Egyptian political organization and the Yugoslav league.

He showed some interest in what I proposed and asked about the extent of freedom the new Egyptian political parties had to contact foreign parties. I explained that such contacts must be made through the Arab Socialist Union and under its auspices. I hoped my explanation was convincing. Perhaps I took care to assure him of the benefits of the Egyptian system because I myself was not convinced.

He told me how difficult he had found it to communicate with the Arab Socialist Union. The truth of the matter, which I did not reveal, was that since I had been appointed minister of state for foreign affairs, I had given up the responsibility for foreign relations of the party and no one had been assigned to replace me. It was difficult to tell the Yugoslav official of the extent of the disorganization in the Arab Socialist Union.

I left the meeting realizing that the foreign relations of our party were nothing but an empty slogan with no portfolio, in reality, except trips by parliamentarians, traveling the earth without a clearly defined goal. My talks with the Yugoslavs made me realize that in the eyes of the socialist camp, Egypt had abandoned the movement.

I recalled the opinion of an Algerian friend who had said to me, "I don't understand why you people in Egypt are not concerned with ideology. The ideological weapon is stronger and more effective than a cannon or a bomb. A rifle without ideology is just a piece of solid iron in the hand of the fighter." I myself was deeply affected by the ideology of the Palestinian cause. Sadat, however, was all realpolitik. I could neither understand nor fully accept his realism.

For poor countries that lack economic, technological, or military power, ideology is a substitute for power. Ideology offers an explanation for their underdevelopment, a tool for their international relations, leverage in world politics, and a dream of the future. Without such a dream, the life of the poor would be unbearable.

The next day, February 1, I met with the Yugoslav foreign minister, Milos Minik. He told me he had read the transcript of my meeting with President Tito. Transcripts of meetings of President Sadat would reach the relevant minister only after a week to ten days, if at all. I was angered that the inefficiency of the Egyptian system put me at such a disadvantage.

Minik indicated that he wanted to complete the conversation I began with Marshal Tito. He made it clear that Yugoslavia utterly disapproved of President Sadat's initiative toward Israel. Israel, he said, was unable to rise to the level of responsibility needed to take firm steps toward peace. I told the Yugoslav minister that I was there not to argue whether Israel would be responsive, but to urge that Yugoslavia give President Sadat's initiative a chance. I felt that his judgment was too hasty.

The foreign minister answered, with Marxist arrogance, that the Yugoslavian position was based on an "objective analysis" of the facts: Israel was militarily superior; Egypt was partly occupied; the Arab world was divided; Israel now could deepen that division; and the Israelis knew that President Carter would not and could not put any pressure on them.

I left the office of the foreign minister with a feeling of helplessness. The deputy minister tried as best he could to lighten the tense atmosphere, but he did not succeed. Despite the diplomatic smiles and the courteous expressions, the dry and cold style of my Yugoslav colleague mirrored the fact that he, like me, was acutely aware of the distance between our positions.

Beyond this lay another misunderstanding. Tito imagined that Egypt's withdrawal from the political-committee meeting in Jerusalem in January was a first step toward the retraction of President Sadat's initiative and the end of negotiations with Israel and the return of Egypt to the Arab family of states.

President Sadat, on the other hand, after reading Tito's letter, must have felt that we could convince the Yugoslav president of the importance of continuing the initiative. He had sent me to Belgrade to resume the political dialogue between Cairo and Belgrade and obtain Tito's support.

I left Belgrade in the evening, aware that I was speaking in one valley while the Yugoslavs were in another valley.

I landed at Cairo International Airport just before dawn. After a few hours I was back at the airport to take part in the farewell to President Sadat as he left for the United States. I gave him a quick report on my talk with President Tito. The president made no comment. He seemed distant and indifferent. I felt that my trip to Yugoslavia had been a double failure: I had failed to convince Tito, and I had failed to convince Sadat of the significance of Tito's position.

The Somali Syndrome

While President Sadat was in America, I intended to make a diplomatic tour of nonaligned nations of Asia and Africa in order to counter Tito's interpretation of the Egyptian initiative, but Vice President Mubarak asked me to delay my trip. The military confrontation between Somalia and Ethiopia was mounting, and he wanted my advice on the situation there. Mubarak invited me to his office in Abdin Palace, where I had taken my oath of office. He wanted my views on the deteriorating situations in Somalia and in Chad, where a civil war encouraged by Libya's Qaddafi was worsening. I was happy to find the vice president concerned about African issues, aware of the latest developments on the continent, and understanding the importance of Egypt's role in the black continent. I brought him a book I had written on African affairs. "Do you want me to read eight hundred pages?" he asked. "No, Excellency," I replied, "just those on Somalia." Mubarak grunted and told me to speak with General Abd al-Ghani al-Gamasi, minister of defense, about the military situation in Africa.

Egyptian policy favored Somalia, a Muslim country whose ports had been taken by Egypt during the "Egyptian empire" of the Mehmet Ali dynasty, a part of the Ottoman Empire. Strong ties to Somalia existed in the minds of many in the Egyptian military. To Sadat, Somalia above all was anticommunist. He saw his support for Somalia as a way of containing Soviet influence in Ethiopia and of improving his relations with the United States.

I found al-Gamasi at his headquarters in the barracks at Heliopolis. He was a thin man of average height with a straight carriage. Very sure of himself, he was direct in his speech, avoiding the circumlocutions of the diplomat. He had intellectual curiosity and a reputation for great integrity in all matters. He was not much interested in Africa. I explained to him my opposition to Egypt's complete public alignment with Somalia against Ethiopia. We should avoid, I said, making an enemy of Ethiopia. Egypt needed to preserve a sort of neutrality in order to play a mediating role in the conflict. He seemed to believe that I was favoring Ethiopia because it is a Christian state. "Do you want to defend the Coptic Church in Ethiopia?" he asked.

"It is Marxism that prevails in Ethiopia today," I replied. "The Coptic church in Ethiopia is suppressed and powerless under Mengistu. In any event, more than half of Ethiopia's population is Muslim." But I did not convince General al-Gamasi. He thought my views were colored by religious considerations and personal leanings. In fact my position was based on the reality that more than 85 percent of the water of the Nile has its source in Ethiopia. Any project requiring more water in Egypt—and almost every project did—would require the approval of the government of Ethiopia.

An urgent request had come from the government of Chad for military assistance to confront Libya's aggression against Chad. There was a similar and no less urgent plea from Somalia for Egyptian help against Ethiopia. On Thursday, February 9, 1978, Vice President Mubarak held a meeting at Abdin Palace on the crisis in Chad and the Horn of Africa. I attended, along with Mamduh Salim; Lieutenant General Abd al-Ghani al-Gamasi; Nabawi Isma'il, minister of the interior; a portly officer in the police with a reputation for successfully organizing covert operations; and General Kamel Hasan Ali, head of general intelligence, whom I met for the first time.

We reached no conclusion after almost three hours of discussion. I was directed to get further information from the ambassadors of Ethiopia and Somalia. After listening to each ambassador defend the viewpoint of his government and accuse the other government of aggression, I remained hesitant, unable to advise whether or how Egypt should respond to the requests for military assistance.

The shah's ambassador in Cairo, Bahram Bahrami, who had been chamberlain at the court of the shah, came to see me. We continued the talk we had begun in Aswan when the shah stopped there. This time Bahrami spoke more specifically. Iran, he said, had decided to offer arms to Somalia and, in addition, intended to extend aid to

Sudan through Egypt. This meant that the Iran-Egypt alliance that I had envisioned at Aswan was beginning to take shape. Iran was, in fact, financing Egypt's assistance to key African countries.

I was learning of important decisions taken by the shah and President Sadat, not from my own government but from the Iranian ambassador. As I gained experience in my new role I learned that the most effective way for me to inform myself was from nongovernmental sources. Sadat would not keep his advisers informed; my colleagues considered information a source of power and hoarded it accordingly.

On Wednesday, February 15, came news that Kenyan authorities had impounded an Egyptian airplane, a Boeing 707 headed for Somalia with a cargo of arms. Kenya had asked the aircraft's pilot to turn back to Cairo. This he declined to do because of lack of fuel. The Kenyans asked him to land at Nairobi to refuel. But when the Egyptian airplane landed, Kenyan forces surrounded, stormed, and searched it. The Kenyans confiscated the weapons and ammunition and refused to permit the crew to leave the aircraft.

Mamduh Salim, the prime minister, asked me to initiate urgent contact with the Kenyan government to get the airplane released immediately. I resorted without hesitation to Willie Morris, the British ambassador and an old friend. Although Kenya had long been independent from Britain, Her Majesty's officials still had contacts in Nairobi. I asked of Morris that the British government exert its good offices to end the matter before it escalated. I made a parallel approach to the American chargé d'affaires—the ambassador was in Washington in connection with President Sadat's visit—and stressed to him the importance of speed in ending the situation before it became a public crisis.

A call came from Mamduh Salim. Egyptian authorities had retaliated. We had forced down a Kenyan passenger plane and placed it under guard at Cairo International Airport. I lost my temper. This was nothing but piracy and would severely damage Egypt's international reputation, I told Mamduh Salim. He rebuked me pleasantly and calmly, saying, "Dr. Boutros, forget that you were a professor; international problems are not handled by international law."

A second phone call came, this one from General al-Gamasi. A second Kenyan plane was being held on the ground at Cairo airport after it, too, had been forced to land. It had come from Europe, destined for Nairobi. Both planes would be kept until the Egyptian airplane impounded in Nairobi was released, al-Gamasi said.

A third phone call, this from Vice President Mubarak: he urged me to reclaim Egypt's cargo of arms from Kenya. Our position was hardening. Before, I was to demand the return of the airplane and the release of its crew; now I was also to demand the return of the weapons. Those who had seized the Kenyan airplane no doubt were aware that the two airplanes impounded at Cairo International Airport represented half of the Kenya airline's entire fleet.

"Can't we forget the subject of the arms?" I asked Mubarak. "Then this dispute could be settled quickly, before it reaches proportions that would not be in our interest." Mubarak strongly rejected this view, saying, "You want us to forget a cargo of arms worth several million pounds?" I had not imagined that the value of one planeload could reach such tremendous sums! In the course of an hour I received two additional telephone calls from the prime minister and three more from General al-Gamasi, pressing me to produce results.

At about six o'clock Willie Morris called to ask, "What guarantee is there, if the Egyptian airplane and its cargo are released, that Egypt will release the two Kenyan airplanes?" I hesitated, then said, "The guarantee is the word of honor of your obedient servant, the Egyptian minister who is responsible for resolving this crisis."

Morris was silent, so I added, "Mr. Ambassador, the go-between has to guarantee each side vis-à-vis the other side. With your diplomatic skill you should not find this to be a difficult enterprise."

Next I received the ambassador of Kenya—for the fourth time since the beginning of the crisis. The ambassador, shy and softspoken, informed me that Kenya agreed to return the "equipment" it had confiscated. He did not use the word "arms." I was careful to follow the same style in my speech.

The ambassador confirmed that the Egyptian plane would take off from Nairobi that evening, carrying its full cargo and its complete crew. I then passed word that the aircraft in Cairo must be released at the same time our plane, cargo, and crew were permitted to leave Nairobi.

After long hours in my office, I went to a dinner given by the ambassador of Iran at his residence in Misr al-Gadidah. Willie Morris was among the guests. The British ambassador smiled mischievously and whispered that he had good news but would not give it to me until after dinner, as a treat to accompany dessert.

As soon as the guests had finished eating and drinking, Morris returned to me. Looking at his watch, he said, "The Egyptian airplane took off from Nairobi airport a few minutes ago, with its cargo. Its expected time of arrival at Cairo airport is early dawn." I gave Morris my profuse thanks for his efforts and for the role his government had played in ending the crisis. Willie Morris gave me a very serious look and said, "I hope that the two Kenyan airplanes will have in fact left Cairo airport at the same time." I replied that there was no need to worry; I had given him my word of honor.

Then I remembered that the next day would be Friday. The weekend break might have led to a delay in executing the agreement to release the airplanes. I headed for my office in Midan al-Tahrir in Cairo. It was 1:00 A.M. I called Cairo airport. One Kenyan airplane, I was told, had taken off, but the other was still on the ground!

I was upset. The situation reflected on me personally. I was sure that the Egyptian authorities had resorted to this delay to ensure that all the arms that Kenya had seized were returned. I asked to speak to the officer in charge at the airport. I burst out, exclaiming, "Who permitted you to detain a Kenyan airplane? How can you not obey an instruction given by a minister and jeopardize an agreement between the Egyptian government and the Kenyan government that the two airplanes will leave at the same time?"

"Mr. Minister, please let me explain," he said. "I don't want an explanation," I shouted. "I want the airplane to leave immediately!"

"I must tell you what happened," he said. Technical reasons had prevented the airplane from taking off. "What technical reasons?" I asked. He hesitated a bit, and then explained, with some embarrassment, that the Kenyan airplane crew had overindulged in liquor and were in no condition to pilot the airplane. Because of that, he had delayed their departure until the early morning so that the effects of the liquor could wear off.

I asked whether the government of Kenya had been informed of the reason for the delay. The man said quietly, "I can't telegraph Nairobi airport that the crew are drunk."

I told him to send an urgent telegram confirming that technical causes had prevented the airplane from taking off, but that it would take off at eight the next morning, and that the Egyptian authorities were not responsible for the delay. I apologized to the officer for thinking ill of him and losing my temper and thanked him for his patience. It was three in the morning when I returned home.

The next day the Kenyan ambassador and I exchanged congratulations on resolving the crisis. The ambassador said that he was instructed to request a formal assurance from the Egyptian government that Kenya's airplanes would be allowed to pass through Egyptian airspace unimpeded. I tried unsuccessfully to reach the defense ministry or Cairo International Airport. Then I remembered that it was Friday and government offices were closed.

The Kenyan ambassador called again. Taking a risk, I promised him that Kenyan airplanes could pass through Egyptian airspace without any danger of interception. But I feared that some weakness in the Egyptian bureaucracy could prove my promise false.

Palestinian Terrorism in Cyprus

On Saturday, February 18, I received a phone call from Nicosia. It was the foreign minister of Cyprus, Christophides, offering me his condolences. Yusuf al-Siba'i had been assassinated in Nicosia by Palestinian terrorists. Yusuf al-Siba'i and I had been colleagues for years, ever since he took over as editor of the Al-Ahram publishing house. He was warm, charming, and deliberate in his speech. I held his friendship dear and valued his manliness and morality. He was a former officer of the Egyptian army, a prolific writer of light novels, which were made into films or television dramas. He was a close friend of President Sadat, which may have been the reason he was assassinated.

I was deeply saddened by his death. That he was killed at the hands of Palestinians added to my sadness, for I knew the extent of his conviction in regard to the rights of the Palestinian people and the effort and sacrifice he made to help them. President Sadat reacted with intense emotion to news of his friend's death. He was determined to catch and punish the Palestinians who had killed Yusuf al-Siba'i.

I contacted Mamduh Salim, the prime minister, who asked me to come immediately to his office. We discussed the political repercussions of this crime. Mamduh Salim felt that al-Siba'i's assassination could be part of a terrorist campaign against Egyptian officials who accompanied President Sadat on his trip to Jerusalem. This may be the beginning of a confrontation between Egypt and extremist Palestinian groups, he said. He asked me to take special precautions for my own safety. Abd al-Mun'im al-Sawi, minister of information, was sent to Nicosia on a special plane to bring home the body of al-Siba'i.

I took part in the blessed Yusuf al-Siba'i's funeral, and I was deeply moved by this sad occasion. The funeral cortege began at the Umar Makram mosque near Midan al-Tahrir and continued past the Ministry of Waqfs and the old Al-Ahram Publishers building. Hundreds of protesters began to chant, "No Palestine after today, no Palestine after today." They were fed up with the Palestinians. This act of Palestinian terrorism had set back the Palestinian cause. I walked beside Dr. Mustafa Khalil, who whispered that we had better distance ourselves from the crowd because he feared there would be violence.

We left the main road and used several side streets to reach Kikhya mosque, where cars awaited us. Dr. Mustafa Khalil said to me, "If these assassinations and terroristic operations are repeated, the Palestinian issue will be lost completely." As I thought about it I put it somewhat differently: if there had been any uncertainty in Sadat's mind, this assassination would end it; Sadat would put Egypt's interest first and relegate Palestinian interests to the bottom of the list.

I returned to my office in the Foreign Ministry. Mamduh Salim called to ask me to hurry to the Prime Ministry. Matters had become more complicated. The Palestinians who assassinated Yusuf al-Siba'i had hijacked an airplane and taken twelve hostages, both Egyptian and non-Egyptian. They had ordered the pilot to fly to Benghazi in Libya, but the Libyan authorities had denied them permission to land. The airplane then headed for Djibouti, where it landed on Sunday afternoon, February 19. Plans were begun to send a team of Egyptian Sa'iqah (commandos) to Djibouti to seize the plane, but after the plane had refueled, the terrorists decided to return to Cyprus. The Sa'iqah team was then ordered to proceed to Cyprus.

"Has the government of Cyprus approved of the Egyptian Sa'iqah carrying out this operation?" I asked. The prime minister answered, "I have contacted the Cypriot authorities and explained everything."

I asked him once more, "Did they agree?" According to international law, I said, our undertaking such an operation without the approval of the government of Cyprus would be . . .

But Mamduh Salim interrupted me, "Doctor, I told you before that international law does not have the slightest thing to do with international relations." Then he asked me to study the repercussions of cutting diplomatic relations with Cyprus.

I had dinner at home. At about ten o'clock the phone rang; it was an urgent summons from Mamduh Salim. I was not able to reach my driver, so I drove my own car to ministerial council headquarters and at 10:30 P.M. entered Mamduh Salim's office in Princess Chevikiar's old palace in Qasr al-Dubarah.

"There has been a catastrophe," said the prime minister. "A large number of the Egyptian Sa'iqah team have been killed and others injured by the Cypriot forces. You must go to Cyprus immediately. Larnaca airport has been closed because of the carnage and the only available airport is the British Royal Air Force base at Akrotiri. You should contact your friend the British ambassador so he can secure a clearance for you to land there."

I called Willie Morris at his residence, and he agreed to help. Then I called our permanent representative at the UN and asked him to call Kurt Waldheim. We asked him to urge the Cypriot government to avoid escalating the crisis.

Willie Morris called to say he was having difficulty reaching London. Egypt's telephone system was almost useless. Mamduh Salim immediately contacted the international telephone administration and gave instructions that the British ambassador's call to London was to be given top priority.

It was two o'clock in the morning. Mamduh Salim was showing signs of fatigue as we awaited the British response. I suggested to him that he go home to rest. As soon as the British clearance arrived, I said, I would take off for Cyprus. There was no need for him to wait with me any longer. Salim agreed and left.

I found myself alone in the office of the prime minister. It was a large room, one of those used as a reception chamber by Princess

Chevekiar. The furniture was government-issued, without style. Many telephones covered the desk. The shelves of the armoire were filled with unread books. I noticed a large photograph of President Sadat. I sat and waited. Every half hour a servant entered with small cups of tea and coffee, some with sugar and some without. Silently he pointed to indicate which was which. At four in the morning I received the awaited call from Morris. The British military authorities had agreed to give my aircraft clearance to land at Akrotiri airbase.

I hurried home to change my clothes and tell Leia that I was going to Cyprus and that I did not expect to be gone more than one day. She was vehemently opposed to my going and warned me that I would meet my destiny in Cyprus.

I went to the military airport west of Cairo. A group of officers there invited me to have tea with them while final preparations were made for the plane's takeoff. I was impressed with these men, who had just lost dear friends yet kept their composure.

At approximately six in the morning one of the officers informed me that contact had been made with Akrotiri; the British military base had not received clearance from London for an Egyptian aircraft to land. I tried calling Willie Morris to inform him that his government's approval had not yet reached Akrotiri, but to no avail. The phone lines in the Egyptian military base were out of order! I had to return to my office in Midan al-Tahrir one hour away and call the British ambassador from there. He confirmed that they had received approval for me to land. I started back to Cairo airport. I found there the Cypriot ambassador to Egypt, and I saw Hamdy Fouad, a journalist who covered the Foreign Ministry. He insisted on coming with me, and I agreed. "This will be the scoop of my career!" Fouad exclaimed. He later followed my career step by step and telephoned me weekly when he was *Al-Ahram*'s Washington correspondent and I was in New York as secretary-general of the United Nations. When Fouad died in 1995 in Washington, Egypt lost a great reporter and I a valued friend.

I boarded the aircraft, a Hercules C-130, a plane that can transport cars and heavy equipment and a large number of troops. Inside the plane I was astonished to find a group of officers and armed men. Could they be planning a second assault under cover of my mission? I demanded that the captain tell me their purpose. "Maybe they are here to protect you," he said. I told the captain that these men and their weapons might suggest to the Cypriot authorities that we were coming to execute another armed attack. We should leave them behind, I said. "I have my orders," the officer replied. "I cannot question them."

In about two hours we landed at Akrotiri, where I was received by a British officer, who saluted and told me that a three-seat helicopter was ready to take me to Larnaca. The Egyptian officers and troops did not leave the Egyptian C-130. The helicopter transported us to the Cypriot presidential headquarters. It was about 2:30 in the afternoon when I met with Cypriot president Spyros Kyprianou, his foreign minister, his interior minister, and a number of dignitaries.

Before we discussed anything, President Kyprianou politely asked me to instruct Ambassador Hasan Shash, Egypt's ambassador to Nicosia, to leave the room. He said that the ambassador was a liar and he could not trust him anymore. The atmosphere was tense and Kyprianou seemed shaken. I asked Ambassador Hasan Shash to wait for me outside, swallowing this open insult for the sake of my mission, something all diplomats must learn to do.

I sat down before a group of Cypriot officials. At this moment fatigue and exhaustion set in, as I realized that I had not slept or eaten in the past twenty-four hours. The purpose of my mission was clear: to get the Cypriot authorities to release the Egyptian officers and troops of the Sa'iqah and to ensure that the assassins of Yusuf al-Siba'i were arrested. But the means of achieving these objectives were not at all clear.

I looked at the president of Cyprus. He exhibited the same signs of fatigue and exhaustion that I was feeling. His eyes were bloodshot and his hands were trembling. He, too, had not slept for many hours and was surviving on his wits. In that sense, the Egyptian negotiator and the Cypriot negotiator were on equal footing.

I asked for tea. I said that I would like my chief of staff, Ambassador Ala' Khayrat, to join us if the Cypriots were unwilling to have Ambassador Hasan Shash join me. They agreed to my request.

We started the negotiations at approximately three o'clock in the afternoon and continued until sunset at about 6:30. President Kyprianou began by recounting events from his point of view: at 5:30 on the morning of Sunday, February 19, he said, the Palestinian terrorists' airplane landed at Larnaca airport and parked about one hundred yards from the airport's main building. Fifteen minutes later an Egyptian airplane landed.

Kyprianou said that Egyptian prime minister Mamduh Salim had informed him that Egypt's minister of information would arrive in Nicosia aboard a private Egyptian plane to continue the negotiations with the terrorists. Mamduh Salim had said nothing of the presence of a group of Egyptian Sa'iqah aboard the same plane.

When Cypriot officials found a group of Egyptian commandos with weapons, equipment, and vehicles on the aircraft instead of the minister of information, they immediately contacted the Egyptian ambassador and made it clear to him that the Egyptian commandos would not be permitted to leave the plane or to carry out any operation on Cypriot soil. He said that if the Egyptian commandos attempted to approach the Palestinian terrorists' plane, Cypriot forces would open fire on them.

The Egyptian ambassador, Hasan Shash, assured the foreign minister that Egypt would not undertake any military action. He remained in constant communication with Cairo. The Egyptians knew full well that negotiations between the Cypriots and the Palestinians were going on. During those negotiations neither the Egyptian ambassador nor the military attaché tried to suggest how to solve the crisis. Kyprianou repeated that both the Egyptian ambassador and the military attaché had assured him that the Egyptian commandos had no intention of trying to arrest the terrorists.

But at 8:30 the doors of the Egyptian airplane opened, a jeep sped toward the terrorists' airplane, and an Egyptian commando attack began. Cypriot forces opened fire, killing fifteen members of the Sa'iqah and wounding sixteen. Six members of the Cypriot national guard and police were injured. When the fight was over, the Palestinian terrorists surrendered to Cypriot authorities and the twelve hostages were released.

"This is exactly what happened," Kyprianou said. "I am prepared to swear on the Bible that what I have said is the truth."

I responded immediately that I was prepared to swear on the same Bible that what I was about to say was the truth. Then I made the following points:

First: Mamduh Salim had informed Kyprianou's secretary that a group of Egyptian commandos would arrive in Cyprus, and the Cypriot government had agreed to this.

Second: when the Egyptian military plane appeared in Cypriot airspace, the Cypriot authorities gave it permission to land at Larnaca. It was obvious that the Egyptian information minister alone would not need a huge military aircraft to fly to Cyprus. The Cypriot authorities realized this perfectly well.

Third: the Cypriot authorities could have ordered the Egyptian plane to take off immediately when they "discovered" that it contained a group of commandos. The Egyptian plane arrived at a quarter to six. The Egyptian Sa'iqah's attempt to free the hostages did not begin until about three hours later. During all this time the Cypriot authorities made no objection to the continued presence of the Sa'iqah team.

Fourth: it would have been easy for the Cypriots to prevent the Sa'iqah from reaching the terrorist plane by blocking the rear-door ramp of the aircraft so that it could not be let down to permit the jeeps and the troops to leave the plane.

Fifth: the violence that Cyprus showed in confronting the Egyptian commandos did not match its laxity at the time of the assassination of Yusuf al-Siba'i, the taking of the hostages, the hijacking of the plane, and its departure and return to Larnaca.

I said that I would like to be frank with the Cypriot president. My government's view of these regrettable events was that we were faced with a Cypriot conspiracy aimed at embarrassing the Egyptian armed forces, forces that came to assist the Cypriot government with its permission. What took place would not have been possible without prior intent and arrangement.

A hubbub rose from the Cypriot group. President Kyprianou seemed startled, and Foreign Minister Christophides shook with rage. The atmosphere had become electric. I continued, deliberately showing flexibility and good spirit. No matter how dangerous the events we were discussing, and no matter how we differed about who was to blame, we should agree, I said, on the necessity of solving the crisis peacefully and without delay. I said that my mission was not so much to gain the release of members of the Egyptian force as it was to maintain good Egyptian-Cypriot relations. The Egyptian government had sent its minister of state, not its minister of war. Choosing me, a diplomat, instead of a military leader, was evidence that Egypt wished to maintain good relations with Cyprus. I moved on to the two Egyptian demands: first—the Palestinian terrorists must be turned over to us to try them in Egypt for the murder of Yusuf al-Siba'i; second—the Egyptian Sa'iqah group must be returned immediately with their weapons and military equipment.

The Cypriot minister of interior spoke up: "Doctor, you are a man renowned for wide experience in the law. You must realize that the Palestinians cannot be turned over to Egyptian authorities. The crime was committed on Cypriot territory; therefore, Cypriot courts must try them."

I said that I had no objection to his legal explanation, but what I was suggesting in the name of the Egyptian government was a special agreement between Egypt and Cyprus on this particular matter, so that the terrorists could be tried by us in Cairo.

Then President Kyprianou spoke at length about his government's position. As I listened to him I remembered a recent conversation with Mamduh Salim in which I had told him that the Egyptian demand that the culprits be turned over to be tried in Egyptian courts was impossible from a legal standpoint. The Egyptian prime minister's response had been to rebuke me: "You and your international law."

Kyprianou said that he was willing to explore the possibility of reaching a special agreement with Egypt but that it would take time and would require the approval of the Cypriot Parliament. And it was very possible that Parliament would refuse to sanction such an arrangement because it was unconstitutional.

Then let us, I said, temporarily put aside the issue of the terrorists and discuss the return of the Sa'iqah with all military equipment to Egypt.

Kyprianou spoke excitedly about the "Egyptian aggression" against Cypriot sovereignty. The attempt to take military action on the soil of a foreign state without its permission was unacceptable. He said he had no objection to the Egyptian troops returning but that they would have to leave their weapons in Cyprus.

I knew the difference between a military man retreating with his arms and retreating with weapons left behind, which would connote surrender and humiliation.

I asked President Kyprianou to let me contact members of the Egyptian Sa'iqah. He directed me to an adjoining room where I was able to talk to an officer from the Sa'iqah by phone. I assured him that I was delegated by the Egyptian government to gain their return to the homeland without delay, that the Cypriots had suggested that the Sa'iqah men return to Egypt without their weapons, and that I would like to know his opinion on this matter.

The officer did not hesitate. The Sa'iqah men would return to their country only with their weapons and holding their heads high.

I returned to the meeting room. "The Egyptian colonel refused the Cypriot suggestion absolutely and has confided in me that he will not leave Cyprus without his weapons."

I said that I agreed completely with his point of view. If we wished to find a peaceful solution to this crisis and maintain diplomatic relations between our two countries, then we would have to take the position of the Egyptian officers and troops into consideration and respect their traditions of military honor. Otherwise I would return to Cairo immediately to inform my superiors that I had failed to fulfill my mission.

The Cypriots then presented a number of arguments and military, legal, and historical precedents. I refused to back down. Faced with my insistence, they agreed in principle to the Sa'iqah team's return with all its weapons. As a compromise we agreed to arrangements whereby the weapons would be placed in sealed boxes and transported in the same vehicles that would transport the men from Nicosia to the British airbase at Akrotiri. Here a new obstacle arose. After I secured the Cypriots' agreement to this compromise, one of them pointed out that no arms were allowed on the British military base and foreign forces were not allowed to enter it with weapons and equipment.

I left the operations room to telephone the British commander. He confirmed that there was a strict moratorium on weapons entering the base. I explained the situation to him and said, "We are requesting permission for the Egyptian Sa'iqah team to enter the base, with their weapons, en route to Cairo." I asked him to give me the telephone number of the British minister of defense in London so that I could call him directly.

The British officer said that he would relay my request to London and try to secure a positive response; if he was unsuccessful, I could contact the British minister directly. I thanked him and said that all that was needed was half an hour's exception for our men to reach the aircraft and for it to take off to return to Egypt.

On my way back to the meeting room, it occurred to me that no doubt hundreds of press and photographers were awaiting the outcome of the negotiations. Photographs of the Egyptian officers and troops as they proceeded to Akrotiri without their weapons could ruin all my efforts. I decided that the transfer of the Sa'iqah would take place after nightfall at an unannounced time to avoid photographers. Then we discussed the vehicles in which the Sa'iqah members would ride to Akrotiri. After much give-and-take we agreed that the vehicles would be driven by Cypriot drivers with Egyptian officers seated next to them.

A Cypriot civil servant entered the room. The British base commander would like to speak to me, he said. The British officer informed me of his superiors' approval of my request on condition that the boxes containing the weapons not be opened until loaded aboard the Egyptian aircraft and that British drivers take the wheels of the vehicles upon entering the base's territory. I agreed and contacted the Egyptian Sa'iqah officer to explain what had been agreed on. He welcomed the arrangements and felt that they preserved his men's honor. I then returned to the room to begin discussions on the custody of the Palestinian terrorists. The Cypriots held to their position, so I made no progress.

To tell the truth, I feared that a decision to cut diplomatic relations with Cyprus might already have been taken in Cairo. I felt the delicacy of my situation, as my discussions with the Cypriots were based on the necessity of preserving friendly relations between the two countries.

President Kyprianou wanted to inform the press of what we had agreed on. I told him I preferred not to make any press statements, because I felt that I had not fully succeeded in my mission. The meeting with the press, therefore, was limited to Kyprianou's brief announcement of the agreement to release the Egyptian Sa'iqah personnel. It also had been agreed, he said, that the current crisis would not affect relations between the two countries. I remained silent.

I shook hands with President Kyprianou, thanked him, and proceeded by helicopter to the British base. The British command had prepared dinner for me, which I welcomed, as I had not eaten for a very long time.

From Akrotiri, I contacted Mamduh Salim to inform him that the caravan of vehicles transporting Sa'iqah personnel and the dead and wounded was on its way to Akrotiri. Mamduh Salim welcomed the news and said, "The Egyptian cabinet will adjourn in its entirety to Cairo airport to give the Egyptian forces a hero's welcome home." I was very surprised at this but did not wish to question Mamduh Salim about it. Hamdy Fouad filed his report to news agencies around the world; he had his great "scoop."

The caravan transporting the Egyptian force arrived. I preferred not to leave the room so that I would not have to see the condition of the injured and the bodies of the dead for fear that I would lose my composure. Soon I was informed that all personnel had boarded the plane. The equipment, vehicles, and weapons had also been loaded and the plane was ready for takeoff. I boarded the plane and sat in the cockpit. With me was the Cypriot ambassador to Egypt, who had accompanied me since the beginning of the trip from Cairo.

The plane took off, and one of the pilots gave me a cup of tea, saying to me kindly, "We apologize, Doctor, for troubling you." I felt all the meanings the man intended with this simple phrase. If the Cypriot ambassador had not been present, I would have cried. I felt as though I had been one of the commandos taking part in the assault.

We arrived at Cairo International Airport at 1:30 in the morning and found Mamduh Salim and the entire cabinet there to receive us. The Sa'iqah members shouted their motto, "Sacrifice, Devotion, Victory!" General al-Gamasi gave a speech, but amid the crowd and noise I could not hear what he said. Everyone cheered "Long live Egypt! Long live Egypt!" Then I entered the VIP lounge. Before Mamduh Salim asked me about the details of my mission, he chided me, saying, "Why are you so late? We have been waiting for you for hours!"

I learned that the cabinet had decided, in an emergency meeting that lasted until midnight, to recall its Egyptian diplomatic mission to Cyprus and to ask the Cypriot government to recall its diplomatic mission in Cairo.

The news hit me like a stroke of lightning. I almost exploded. Could not the cabinet have held out a while longer until the minister assigned the official task of trying to resolve the crisis with Cyprus had returned? Did my fellow ministers think what the consequences might have been had the president of Cyprus known of this decision before the Sa'iqah men left Cypriot territory? The Cypriot authorities could have refused to turn them over. They could have arrested them, in fact, and tried them! I took hold of myself, trying to put up with the mistakes and contradictions of my government patiently and calmly.

Many questions still needed answers. How was the decision to undertake the Sa'iqah operation taken? How did the person in charge of the operation think that it could be carried out without the approval of the Cypriot government? It was obvious that such an operation could not succeed without the approval and assistance of the local authorities. Otherwise, those assigned to the operation would have had to face two fronts, the terrorists on one side and the local authorities on the other. Was the command of the Sa'iqah group in contact with Cairo via the Egyptian ambassador or the military attaché? Did Cairo approve of the action that was taken? Did not the command of the Sa'iqah realize what the Cypriot forces were indicating by surrounding the airport? Did it imagine that the Cypriots were only threatening verbally and that they would not attack the Egyptian force? If the intention of the Sa'iqah command was to attack, why wait for two hours on the tarmac and lose the element of surprise?

I was told that Brigadier General Nabil Shukri, commander of the operation, simply carried out orders he received from Cairo. Why did not Cairo alter those orders and instructions according to changing circumstances and new developments?

I also had questions about the Cypriot role in all this. I was told that certain Cypriot politicians had embraced the rejectionist Arab position and sought to punish Sadat by inflicting humiliation on Egypt after they had killed Sadat's friend al-Siba'i. What was the role of the Palestine Liberation Organization representatives who hurried to Cyprus and were in the Larnaca airport building during the attack on the terrorists' plane? What was the role of a certain Arab military attaché, who spent many years in his post in Cyprus and was at Larnaca airport during the battle? What about another Arab ambassador to Nicosia, whose activities were suspicious? Had this catastrophe been arranged by Cypriot elements allied with Arab rejectionists? Was the attack on the Sa'iqah forces a continuation of the attack that killed Yusuf al-Siba'i? Or was this all the result of errors by Egypt and the Cypriots?

At first, I concluded that this had been not a planned conspiracy but the result of stupidity and thoughtless improvisation. As time went by I was not so sure. Sadat's enemies hoped to create unrest within the Egyptian army by humiliating it. The international press was comparing the failure of the Egyptian commandos with the success of the Israeli operation to rescue their hijacked passengers at Entebbe.

On Wednesday, February 22, I took part in the state funeral for the Sa'iqah personnel who had been killed in Cyprus. Sadat was present with all his cabinet. Amid the grief an air of hostility toward Cyprus prevailed. President Sadat announced that Egypt had withdrawn its recognition of Cyprus and of President Kyprianou as Cyprus's president. I tried to convince Mamduh Salim that such a declaration had no precedent in diplomacy and international life. "Then do something," he said, "that is what the Foreign Ministry is for!"

After the funeral the ambassador from Greece came to my office. I asked him to convey to the Greek government our hope that it would use its good offices to calm things down and halt the deterioration of relations between Egypt and Cyprus.

On February 27, I took part in the session of the People's Assembly dedicated to discussing the fiasco in Cyprus. The debate and recriminations went on for seven hours. I was left utterly drained and discouraged. Today, years later, the mystery still has not been resolved. President Vassiliou of Cyprus, with whom I have negotiated on the Greek and Turkish Cyprus problem as secretary-general of the UN, could provide no clue as to what had been behind the 1978 catastrophe. Whatever the cause or reason, it was an act of stupidity, because terrorism is always stupid.

Chapter Three

❖ ❖ ❖

Friends on the Road

As opposition to President Sadat's initiative increasingly isolated Egypt in the world, I set out on a long series of travels to South Asia and Africa. My purpose was to try to strengthen understanding for Egypt's position among the nonaligned and African countries. Tito's message was there to remind me that Egypt would be confronted by the rejectionists within those two groups of states. Their goal was either to force Egypt to change its policy toward Israel or to isolate Egypt in the event that Sadat would not back down.

South Asia and Astrology

I began my trip to India accompanied by a large number of security men. After Yusuf al-Siba'i's death, security arrangements increased noticeably. I do not claim courage, but I do believe in destiny and so put aside any concern about an attack on my life. Leia did not share that conviction. What I regard as equanimity and trust that the flow of events cannot be changed she regards as giving up. Therefore, when I embarked on the trip, the tension heightened at home as my wife attempted to convince me of the importance of adhering strictly to the security men's instructions.

It was almost dawn when I arrived in New Delhi on Saturday, March 18, 1978. India's foreign minister was waiting for me at the airport despite the early hour. I rode with him in an armored car from the airport to the visitors' palace. I was told it was the only armored car in the Indian capital.

In New Delhi I was escorted to the former palace of the Nizam of Hyderabad. This huge building reminded me of my uncle Wasif's palace, which used to be next to the French embassy on the banks of the Nile at Giza. The size of the building and its style, the French furniture made after World War I in the Majorelle style—all this reminded me of my childhood and the happy days I spent in my uncle's palace. I was so spoiled that whenever I asked, my parents would send me to my uncle Wasif's residence. And whenever one of the three children fell ill, my parents would send the other two to the residence to avoid contagion.

The foreign minister held a dinner in my honor. In my speech I pointed out the connections between Egypt and India since the days of the Egyptian monarchy when Gandhi and Saad Zaghlul were in contact as opponents of British imperial rule. These ties continued during the time of the Egyptian Revolution with the meetings between Nasser and Nehru. I said that my task was to assure the continuation of friendship between Cairo and New Delhi.

After meetings with Indian prime minister Moraji Desai and other officials, I proceeded to Bombay surrounded by security men. The assassination of Yusuf al-Siba'i had transformed the security situation around the world.

In Colombo, the capital of Sri Lanka, I was met by Foreign Minister Hamid, who compared my position as a Christian in a Muslim state with his as a Muslim in a Buddhist and Tamil state. I tried to convince him that I represented not the Coptic minority but Egypt as a whole. But the Sri Lankan minister was not convinced, and continued to talk about the subject of minorities, clearly a sensitive subject for him.

I met with the prime minister and then with the president of Sri Lanka at his residence. At the end of a long day of talking, I felt that my journey had contributed to Egypt's position in the nonaligned movement.

At Egypt's embassy in Colombo, our ambassador, Mustafa Ratib, a demanding and difficult man, insisted that I consult an astrologer. My "special situation" necessitated this, he said. I was hesitant, but Mustafa Ratib insisted, stressing that the Sri Lankan astrologers were world-famous.

I met with the astrologer in a closed room in the embassy. After he studied my palm and summarized my life story, he told me of a bright future. I would become very famous, he said, and rise and remain in ascendancy, reaching one of the highest positions in the world and then would be assassinated at the age of seventy-five. I was flattered, pleased, and reassured by his prediction. Seventy-five was a long way off. Perhaps, I thought, there is something to astrology after all.

Then the astrologer paused. Besides his work as an astrologer, he said, he was a journalist. Now that he had concluded his work with me as an astrologer, he would like to practice his trade as a journalist, and he asked me if he could interview me. I was furious and embarrassed. This was no seer, but a reporter. "I advise you to attend my next press conference," I said and stormed out of the room.

When I left South Asia on Swissair, I felt as though I had actually arrived in Switzerland. There was cleanliness, order, calm, and serenity in the Swiss style. If poverty exists in Swiss society, it is hidden. In fact, Europe as a whole has not succeeded in overcoming poverty, but it has succeeded in hiding it. On the plane I enjoyed the music of Rimski-Korsakov and Borodin. I realized that while I firmly belong to the Eastern and Arab world, I am inextricably tied to European culture.

Back to Africa

In March the Israeli army invaded southern Lebanon to try to root out Palestinian guerrilla camps there. This operation was a sharp blow to Egypt's position. It was the occasion for vicious attacks in the Arab world press on Egypt's "betrayal" of the Palestinian and Arab causes. I was a favorite target for denunciation as the "academic engineer of Arab defeatism," a traitor from a family of traitors who deserved to be "liquidated" as my grandfather had been. My photograph appeared in a magazine calling for my death. The entire Arab world was convinced, with good cause, that Israel would never have dared cross the border into Lebanon unless it felt that its southern border with Egypt was secure. President Sadat's negotiations with the Israelis had given them the freedom to attack other Arabs. Egypt was placed in a most difficult position as a result. The majority of Arabs remain convinced that the war in Lebanon was due to Egypt's betrayal of Arab solidarity.

On Thursday, April 13, the Committee on Foreign Affairs in the People's Assembly met under the chairmanship of Dr. Gamal al-Oteify. I responded to requests for a briefing about Israel's aggression into southern Lebanon and its use of various types of banned weapons, including cluster bombs. I told the committee that Egypt would gladly welcome an Arab summit conference on the current crisis; that Egypt had been the first to move diplomatically to halt and condemn the Israeli aggression; that we were in close communication with the Palestine Liberation Organization. And I outlined the efforts I was taking to advance Egypt's standing in the nonaligned movement, and, most immediately, among Asian and African states.

On April 24, I met in my office with Joshua Nkomo, leader of the National Liberation Front of Zimbabwe. Nkomo weighed some 270 pounds. The chair that he was sitting on collapsed under his weight, and Nkomo would have fallen to the floor if I had not caught him. The African leader apologized for the damage. Egyptian bureaucracy was such that it took six months to get the chair repaired.

A good-humored man with a sharp intellect, Nkomo firmly believed that his country would triumph over Rhodesia and that the struggle against the white minority would end in victory. He asked for financial and military assistance from Egypt. I charged Ambassador Ahmad Sidqi, the brilliant and energetic director of the African Directorate in the Foreign Ministry, to take care of the African leader and arrange meetings and a program of visits for him in Cairo. I also asked him to arrange a press conference for Nkomo so that he could convey his point of view to the world from Cairo.

On Thursday, May 25, we commemorated Africa Day and the establishment of the Organization of African Unity (OAU). In press conferences I sought to convince Egyptian public opinion of the importance of the African continent in relation to Egypt and began to prepare for my own travels through Africa.

On June 2 I went to the Armed Forces Hospital on Meadi Road to visit the vice president of the republic of Uganda, who had been injured in a car accident and evacuated to Cairo for surgery. It was said that the accident was arranged by his boss, Idi Amin, to teach his deputy a lesson. The wife of the official was at his side when I entered his room.

I tried to begin a conversation, but quickly realized that neither the vice president nor his wife understood English well. So I made do with sign language and tried to express my hopes for his recovery. I was able to make him understand that I planned to visit Kampala soon. Was there any message that he wanted me to convey to his president, Idi Amin? I understood that his health was improving, thanks to the Egyptian physicians, and that he did not want me to convey anything to the president of his country except his complete obedience and allegiance and readiness to return when called.

The next day, Saturday, June 3, I began my trip to African capitals. We left Cairo in the morning on the Mystère jet, heading for Khartoum. With me were Ambassador Ahmad Sidqi, director of the African Directorate; Ambassador Ala' Khayrat; First Secretary Hasan Fahmi; Colonel Ahmad al-Hifnawi; and two other security people. Just before we arrived at Khartoum airport, a strong sandstorm almost dashed the small airplane to the ground several times before landing. Thank God a disaster did not happen. But we were all terrified, especially Ala' Khayrat, who begged me to leave the private airplane in Khartoum and travel via a commercial airline.

I had long been interested in advancing the federation of Egypt and the Sudan. During the British era, the economic and geographical unity of Egypt and Sudan had been recognized, and all territory from the Nile delta to the frontier of Uganda was nominally under a single authority. I was convinced that integration was a key to prosperity for both states. Several meetings of the joint Egyptian-Sudanese ministerial committee had been held on the subject, but they accomplished nothing. The talks had no relation to the realities of the issue, yet after each session ended, the representatives of the two sides would congratulate each other with an air of gaiety and achievement, as if major obstacles had been overcome and agreement reached to proceed with vast joint projects of land reform, industrialization, and the construction of dams.

I asked Hafiz Ghanim, the deputy prime minister dealing with Sudan, to justify these pointless meetings for me. He laughed and said, "They are a Muawiyah's strand." This old Arab saying conveys the importance of keeping two parties in touch with each other no matter how slender the thread that links them. We had to continue with these meetings without losing our enthusiasm. One day, integration would be based upon the understanding achieved by these persistent, if tenuous, connections. Since the fall of Sudan's President Nimieri in 1989, Muawiyah's strand has been broken, as a fundamentalist regime has prevailed in Khartoum. This regime represents a real danger to the stability of many Arab and African countries.

My Sudanese counterpart took the opportunity of my presence in Khartoum to ask me, as I proceeded to my next stops in Africa, to work out various scheduling problems for forthcoming African summit meetings. I promised to convey the Sudanese messages down the line. My hosts jokingly declared, "You have become a messenger extraordinary for the Sudan, in addition to your original role as the special representative of President Sadat in Africa!"

I left Khartoum on June 4 in the early morning in the Mystère, heading for N'Djamena, the capital of Chad. When the Mystère landed at N'Djamena airport, no Chadian officials were there to meet my delegation. It was explained that our airplane had arrived earlier than expected. I passed the time by agreeing to be interviewed by a Chad radio broadcaster. Eventually the foreign minister of Chad, Colonel Abdel Kader Kamougue, arrived. A tall man from the Christian South, he welcomed me but said it was not certain that President Félix Malloum would be able to receive me. I told the foreign minister that I was carrying a message from President Anwar Sadat. I expressed my great desire to meet with the Chadian president.

The foreign minister returned after half an hour. President Malloum had listened over Chadian broadcasting to the statements I made upon arrival at N'Djamena airport. The interview had been a kind of test by the Chadian government. Now that the Chadians heard what I said about Egypt's support for Chad, President Malloum had agreed to receive me.

I was invited into a large salon in the presidential residence. In its center stood the president, a tall man, slim, with signs of sadness and exhaustion on his face. He carried a long stick in his hand. The room was elegant, and in it were three large radio sets. The president invited me to sit. I began by saying that I brought the greetings of President Anwar Sadat, but Malloum interrupted, asking, "Where did you learn French?" I responded that I had studied the language in school in Cairo. The president commented that the Egyptians he had met before did not speak French and was delighted to discover an exception. I said, "Every rule, Mr. President, has its important exceptions."

The president's sad and tired expression disappeared in a friendly smile. President Malloum expressed his gratitude for Egypt's support of Chad and condemned Libya's aggression against Chad. The Soviet Union and Cuba are behind Qaddafi, he said, and described what his country was enduring as a result of Libyan intervention. What was going on in Chad, he said, was not an internal struggle; it was an international communist plot. The Chadian president expressed his hope that Egypt would provide quick financial and military assistance. He also asked Egypt to do what it could to persuade Saudi Arabia and Nigeria to assist Chad. Later I attempted this but got no positive responses.

A two-hour flight then brought me to Niamey, capital of Niger. The tire of our aircraft blew out on landing, deepening the fears of my already fearful delegation. President Seyni Kountchi received me in his small office in the middle of a military camp. A huge map of Central Africa hung on the wall behind him. An active and quick-witted military man, the president had a strong personality and a strong will, which were reflected in his features. He was small, thin, and nervous, with rapidly darting eyes, completely different, in form and substance, from President Malloum of Chad. We discussed in detail the war going on in Chad. I felt that President Kountchi did not trust his Chadian counterpart and was not comfortable with him. The president of Niger saw the matter as hinging on an internal problem. The Islamic North, he said, wanted to be represented in the Chadian government, which was composed mainly of leaders from the South.

Since then, I have visited N'Djamena, the capital of Chad, the poorest capital in Africa. As director of the African Fund, I sent technicians, doctors, teachers, etc., to Chad, but to little avail, as the endless civil war has devastated the country.

President Kountchi possessed an elaborate and sophisticated view of world and African affairs. He worried about the Soviet and Cuban presence in the Horn of Africa. He recognized that if Chad had better relations with Moscow, this could help in dealing with Libya. The state of Chadian-Soviet relations when seen in juxtaposition with Chadian-Libyan relations presented both contradictions and possibilities for Chad, as he saw it. He discussed strategy in great detail. I listened patiently.

I then went to the Egyptian embassy in Niamey to telephone Paris to request a replacement tire for our airplane. We had no spare of our own. The pilots had also discovered that the oil filter was faulty. All this, of course, increased the worries of Ala' Khayrat. Again he pleaded with me to complete our journey via scheduled commercial airlines.

On Monday, June 5, President Kountchi opened the new session of the Afro-Arab ministerial conference with a speech that emphasized the importance of cooperation between the Arab and African states in confronting economic backwardness. This organ of Afro-Arab cooperation had been created by the Afro-Arab summit in Cairo in March 1977.

As I was leaving the conference building I was accosted by Ali al-Turayki, foreign minister of Libya. "How could you, after years of writing about Arab nationalism, now seek to destroy it? The government of Libya," he said, "is prepared to cooperate with Egypt if Egypt abandons its practice of direct negotiations with Israel." He spoke with undisguised arrogance, and I found his manner most unpleasant.

I replied that Egypt did not need Libya's advice. Egypt's place in the world at large, and in the Arab world, was in no need of clarification for those who wished to understand. I turned my back on al-Turayki and left him standing at the door of the building of the conference hall. For years after, we often faced each other in acrimonious confrontation at international conferences, but in the 1990s we met at the United Nations in New York and had a reconciliation, recalling with good humor the long war between us in the past.

That afternoon I asked the secretary-general of the Organization of African Unity, the garrulous William Eteki, the former minister of foreign affairs of Cameroon, to see me. I told him I had received information that the OAU general secretariat had accepted a Libyan request to add "the Sadat initiative" to the conference's agenda. Procedures would not permit this, I said. The subject was to be discussed in the secretary-general's report. Eteki apologized. He wanted to be reelected as secretary-general and he needed Egypt's vote. His staff was sabotaging the OAU's work and amending the agenda without his knowledge. He promised to delete the agenda item.

Next I met with the foreign minister of Morocco and leader of the al-Dustour party, Muhammad Boucetta. A white-haired, elegant elder statesman, he was a figure of the ancien régime, a classic aristocratic diplomat exemplified for me by Egypt's ambassadors of the pasha class in the days of King Farouk. An important figure, Boucetta seemed like someone more at ease in a Paris salon than in a multilateral conference in Niamey. He graciously received diplomatic approaches but rarely sought to press his views on others. His outspoken defense of his country's interests were addressed to the world at large. Boucetta did not say a word about President Sadat's initiative or the Jerusalem visit. His sole concern was the Western Sahara, a Spanish colony with a tiny population seeking integration into Morocco and another population living in exile in Algeria seeking independence. I discussed with my Moroccan colleague the preparations for the upcoming nonalignment conference in Belgrade. The following year, 1979, the conference was to be held in Havana. Boucetta attacked Cuba violently. His government, he said, felt that Cuba should be expelled from the nonaligned movement. I pointed out to him the difficulty of doing such a thing and the disastrous effects on the movement that could result from such an attempt. If we want to be realistic, I said, we could try to postpone the Havana conference and use the time to work together to limit the effect of radical countries like Cuba within the movement.

I received another telephone call to assure me, again, that the parts needed for the airplane would arrive early in the morning and that we would be able to leave Niamey airport as soon as the tire and filter had been installed. Once again Ala' Khayrat tried to convince me how unwise it was to use the Mystère. His brother had been a commander of the air force, he said, and knew how dangerous such small planes were. He continued his attempt until the last minute, but, faced with my lack of response, he surrendered to his fate and boarded the Mystère jet.

After about two hours we landed uneventfully at Lagos airport. In the airport I found a group of Nigerian journalists who directed provocative and aggressive questions, American style, at me. They wanted me to admit that Egypt was isolated in the Arab world after Sadat's visit to Jerusalem.

Because the head of state, General Obasanjo, was on a state visit to Poland, I met with Brigadier Shehu Yar'Adua, the vice president of Nigeria and the commander in chief of the armed forces. The vice president was youthful, shy, and spoke little. He appeared to find reassurance in his army uniform. When I tried to encourage Nigeria's support for Chad, the vice president replied that Nigeria would not take action unless asked to do so openly and directly by Chad. My attempt to be an intermediary was unsuccessful.

In the afternoon I asked to visit the Lagos museum, a house of treasures where precious African statues and rare works of art were displayed. Visiting this museum assures one that African civilization is noble and ancient and has firm roots in history.

On our way to the airport to leave Nigeria, our driver lost his way. When, after many attempts, we found our way to the terminal, I gave thanks that we were traveling on a private plane; a commercial airliner would have taken off long before we arrived.

Yaoundé, the capital of Cameroon, is set amid a beautiful landscape, and the city is surrounded by a green mountain chain. I was received at the airport by the chief of protocol of the presidential palace. He conducted himself with excruciating ceremony, moving and speaking very slowly, conveying with his every gesture the grandeur of his role. As he escorted me in the official limousine, he took care to reveal to me that he owned a château in the French countryside. President Ahidjo, he said, would receive me that afternoon at 4:30 sharp.

A quarter of an hour before my appointment with the president, the chief of protocol arrived to accompany me to the president's office. An official motorcade, waiting at the hotel door, was headed by a group of motorcycle riders. A guard of honor stood before the motorcade to salute the Egyptian minister. Then the official motorcade moved very slowly to the presidential palace. The streets, were lined with people waiting to see the foreign guest.

At the presidential palace I found another guard of honor awaiting me in uniforms matching those of the French presidential guard that stands outside the Elysée Palace in Paris. I entered the palace with my delegation. Hasan Fahmi, the first secretary, was carrying the gift I intended to give the president. When the chief of protocol saw the gift, he reprimanded Hasan Fahmi severely. This was a huge ceremonial gaffe, he said. According to Cameroonian protocol, the gift should be presented an adequate time before, and not during, the audience. I asked him to handle the situation with tact and said we hoped to use his wide experience to save the situation.

The chief of protocol then asked me, "What exactly is the title you carry?" I said, "I am a minister, a minister of state for foreign affairs, and President Sadat's special envoy." He said in a decisive tone, "We will employ the second title as it is more important than the first." Then the chief of protocol threw open the door to the president's chamber and shouted in a ringing voice, "Special envoy of President Anwar al-Sadat, the president of the Arab Republic of Egypt."

I entered into the presence of El Hadj Ahmadou Ahidjo, who was standing in the center of the room. The Cameroonian president was, by contrast with his functionary, pleasant and unassuming. He welcomed me warmly and pointed out to each member of my delegation where his seat was. The furniture and the damask that covered the chairs were in the French Empire style. In contrast, Ahidjo wore Cameroonian dress and sandals.

After the meeting, in which the president spoke with extreme clarity about the disputes prevailing in the African continent, I emerged from the presidential palace to find the honor guard lined up again to salute me. I followed the same ceremonies I had gone through upon entering the palace.

In the evening the minister of state for presidential affairs, Beb Adon, invited me to dinner at his home. I had met him years before when he joined the Academy of International Law in The Hague. I met him again in 1968, when he was ambassador to Paris. He invited a large number of prominent Cameroonian dignitaries and scholars of the university to the dinner he gave in my honor.

There is no doubt that a French education and the shared memories of studying in Paris are the common denominator of any conversation with French-speaking African leaders. Any diplomat who does not speak French and does not know French culture cannot succeed in Francophone Africa. Egyptian diplomacy is handicapped in that there are few French speakers in the Foreign Ministry.

As I made my departure from Yaoundé airport, I met a Somali delegation awaiting the commercial airliner to Douala. I could see that traveling on commercial airlines entailed hours of waiting and the uncertainty of irregular flights in this part of the world. With all the extra risk, I preferred my private plane, which would take off when I chose.

An hour after my arrival in Libreville, Gabon, I was received by El Hadj Omar Bongo at his opulent palace on the shore of the Atlantic. I was escorted to a large and luxurious reception room lined in Italian marble. Again the furnishings were in the style of the Napoleonic empire; again the president wore starkly contrasting African dress. At the center of the far corner was a special chair placed on a platform like a throne. Sitting there was President Bongo, wrapped in a black cape, which I imagined had as much to do with the bitter-cold air-conditioning pouring into the room as it did with the requirements of ceremony.

After the audience, President Bongo asked me to speak to the media. I agreed and discovered that the television studio was located within the presidential palace compound. Later in the day I met the Gabonian press and television representatives in one of the chain of visitors' houses erected in the African leaders' village for the African summit held in Libreville in 1977.

Following the interview I toured the abandoned village and visited the grand conference hall. Outside the hall were a number of luxury cars in poor condition, apparently left there without maintenance since the African summit a year before. Too often these African conferences have been an excuse for mad and horrifying waste. It was time to put an end to holding the African summits in different capitals, which led each government to compete for the honor of holding the conference and displaying its ability to host the delegations with greater opulence than the others. Hosting an African summit was no different, in African logic, from hosting the wedding party of a son or daughter. In neither case would one hesitate to spend in excess of several years' income to celebrate and borrow more than could be paid back to do so. Since the organization's headquarters are in Addis Ababa, the answer may lie in holding such conferences there, though Ethiopia has been marked by political instability and has changed regimes three times since the Organization of African Unity was founded.

On Monday, June 12, we left the Gabonian capital in the morning and arrived in Kinshasa, the capital of Zaire. Upon arrival I was told that President Mobutu had left the capital and gone into seclusion in his village, Gbadolite, in the Equatorial Province at a distance of two hours by plane, and that he had refused, mysteriously, to receive guests between June 10 and June 17.

In the evening, however, I was informed that President Mobutu had agreed to receive me early the following morning and had ordered a private airplane to transport me and my delegation to Gbadolite directly, because the airport there could not accommodate my Egyptian Mystère.

When I arrived at the military airport, I found the aircraft that President Mobutu had put at my disposal, a huge C-130 Hercules. The plane was ready for takeoff, but we could not locate its crew. After we had spent two hours searching, the head of the Zairean air force appeared in person, accompanied by the rest of the crew. They had been drinking beer in the airport bar.

We took off without further delay and arrived at Gbadolite after about two hours. President Mobutu received me in his remote private palace, situated among lush gardens and a breathtaking landscape. I thanked him for his gracious agreement to see me despite his desire for seclusion. I pointed out the importance of coordinating Egypt's and Zaire's positions in preparation for the Khartoum summit and the Belgrade nonaligned conference and that we should cooperate to put an end to Cuba's interference in Africa and the forces behind it.

President Mobutu agreed with me in this and in the other points I put forth. Our friendly conversation continued at the lunch table at a gathering held in the president's garden. A large number of Zairois were serving under the supervision of a European head-waiter dressed in a heavy tuxedo despite the midsummer heat. He personally served the finest French wines to us. Each time he poured the wine he would put a mark on the bottle with a red pencil so that no one could pour wine for himself without being detected. I was not tempted to try. I avoided the wine because of the great heat and humidity.

After lunch President Mobutu took me to a small garden that had beds of the most beautiful flowers of various colors. Mobutu said to me sadly that his wife, who had passed away a few months earlier, used to tend this garden.

Suddenly, without warning, heavy rains began to fall, as though all the doors of heaven had opened. We hurried inside the palace and then to the waiting cars and drove quickly to the airport. President Mobutu said that should the rain continue, the runway would turn to mud and it would be impossible for the airplane to take off. We might find ourselves stuck in the village for several days until the airport became operational. Terror must have appeared on my face when the president informed me of this, for he laughed and said, "Do you not wish to remain with us in this pretty country house? Hurry to the plane or you will have to stay here whether you want to or not."

We arrived at the airport and took off in the worsening storm. I sat in the cockpit next to an American who introduced himself to me as Maurice Tempelsman, an attorney who indicated that he was the adviser for President Mobutu's affairs in the United States. He held, he said, the title of honorary consul of Zaire in New York. Tempelsman told me that as a Jew he was greatly interested in Sadat's decision to go to Jerusalem. While the plane was violently thrown around by the storm we conversed about Israeli-Egyptian relations.

Back in Kinshasha I held a press conference at the Egyptian embassy. I had been asked for security reasons to avoid any mention of the time and place of my meeting with President Mobutu. I respected this, naturally, although I did not understand the need for it. That night after dinner I returned to the guesthouse in the village erected for the 1977 OAU summit, intending to go to sleep immediately, but the insects flying and crawling around my room kept me awake until dawn.

On Wednesday, June 14, I made a short stop in Bujumbura. The Burundian capital is a small and beautiful city overlooking a lake. After luncheon I visited the foreign minister in his office. I had hoped to meet the president too, but the foreign minister instructed me, tactfully, that mine was just a passing visit, just a technical stop in my African tour, and that the president was away from the capital. The minister made it clear that if I made a long official visit to Burundi, lasting, say, more than twenty-four hours, the president, no doubt, would be pleased to receive me. I was learning that all over the world concern for protocol is in inverse proportion to the power of a country.

Idi Amin on Paradise Island

We arrived in Uganda after an hour's flight. Entebbe International Airport was run by a group of Egyptian experts, who were doing excellent work; they received us heartily and celebrated the arrival of the Egyptian delegation and crew.

Kampala is about an hour's drive by car from Entebbe. There we went to the hotel, where a special suite was reserved for us on the top floor. It became clear to me afterward that it was the only usable floor. The rest of the floors lay in ruins from lack of care. It was strange to be alone in this vast structure. I was reminded of American horror movies.

On the morning of Thursday, June 15, I was received by President Marshal Idi Amin at a special house overlooking Lake Victoria. I found myself before a terrifying giant standing six feet tall and weighing some 270 pounds. He spoke graciously, and on behalf of President Sadat I presented him with a gift, which he admired very much and studied for a long time. He then summoned the official photographer to take several pictures of our meeting.

Idi Amin then invited me to go from the house to a ship moored on the lake. He asked me to sit with him on a platform in the bow of the ship while the other passengers stayed inside the cabin or belowdecks. The ship then sailed for nearly an hour to an island in the lake that the Ugandan president called Paradise Island. Once the island had been full of snakes, he said, but he had cleared them away. He then had a private house built there for himself and a small number of other houses for important guests. A light drizzle began to fall, and we took refuge in a private presidential salon. He preferred that our conversation be private, he said and that no member of either delegation take part.

When we reached Paradise Island, President Amin walked with me to his modest presidential house, with four very small rooms. He asked that we continue our conversation in private in his bedroom. He began by pointing out the unique advantage of the room we were meeting in. It had three doors, which allowed him a better chance of escape should he be attacked. He saw everyone as a potential killer.

Idi Amin then asked me to set an agenda for our talks. I suggested that the agenda be flexible. President Sadat's instructions to me were clear: I should meet with President Amin and discuss with him any matter he brought up without a prescribed agenda.

But what I said did not appeal to the Ugandan president. "If this is the case and you have not prepared an agenda," he said, "then we must do that now, together. The agenda must include ten items," he said. He began to praise the friendly, brotherly relations between Egypt and Uganda, as well as the work of the Egyptian ambassador to Kampala, and he said that this would be the first item of our agenda.

He then said that duty compelled him to express his appreciation and praise for the efforts and work of the Egyptian experts working in all fields in Uganda, and this would be the second item on the agenda. But no, he then said, this subject really belonged in Item 1. He was annoyed that this reduced the number of the items.

He asked about my visit to President Mobutu and said, "Write the next agenda item: Uganda's assent to participate in a token force taking up a position in Shaba Province of Zaire." If Mobutu requested this, Idi Amin said, he would respond, though the Mobutu regime was corrupt. He added, "No doubt you visited Mobutu's palaces and saw the obscene opulence he lives in. You can compare that to the modest and simple house we are sitting in now on Paradise Island."

He then began to shout in a very loud voice: "There is no corruption in my country! There is no corruption in my country!" I asked him if this phrase would do as an item for our talks. He laughed for a long time and answered that it was a good idea, but it need not be on the agenda. He asked me, "Have you recorded this as the third item?" When he was sure of this, he moved on to the issue of his disagreements with Tanzania and his strained relations with Zambia. "I want Anwar Sadat to mediate between me and Julius Nyerere and Kenneth Kaunda," he said. He added with a wide smile that this could now be inscribed as the next item.

Without pausing, he moved on to talk about the United States of America. "Egypt's relations with the United States are excellent since Sadat's visit to Jerusalem. I hope that you use your good offices with Washington so that it will take a friendly position toward Uganda and the president of Uganda." He grew suddenly angry, "Why have the Americans become more stringent with me? Why are they criticizing me? How can members of the Congress turn down my invitation to visit Uganda?" He said that he would like President Sadat to mediate between him and the United States to alter its positions toward Uganda. Amin said that this issue would be the next item.

Next he said that Egypt should support the selection of Kampala as the headquarters of the African news agency; this was the eighth item. He stopped talking for several minutes to think.

Then he said that we needed two additional items in order to end our important negotiations. I asked if the Organization of African Unity and the upcoming Khartoum conference could be included. "No," he said, "these issues will not do as items in our agenda of talks." I did not have the courage to question this ruling, and we were silent for several minutes.

We continued when the Ugandan president declared that he had found the ninth item. He explained to me that it was a personal matter but would be adequate as a ninth item. The matter, he said, had to do with one of his sons, Ali Idi Amin. The son had refused to carry out his father's orders, so Idi Amin was obliged to arrest and imprison him for over a year. But he had forgiven him, released him, and sent him to study at the American University in Cairo. "I have found out that you were a professor at the university before becoming a cabinet minister; therefore, I want you personally to oversee my son's studies." I promised Idi Amin heartily that I would undertake this task. I told him that as I did not have any children, I would consider Ali Idi Amin my son.

"And why have you not had any children?" Idi Amin asked me. I hesitated. "If you stay two weeks with your wife on this island, for rest and recreation," he said, "you will have many children! You are invited. You will be my guest. You can choose any rest house!"

We were still conducting our talks in his bedroom, beside a huge bed. The rest of the delegation was outside. I could hear the music of an African guitarist. Idi Amin lay down on the bed and told me to lie down on the bed with him to rest. I said that I could not do this. He said that I must rest on the bed with him. To try to satisfy him, I pulled my chair closer to the bed and raised my shoes so that the heels were just hanging on the edge of the bed. I continued to sit in the chair as Idi Amin reclined on the bed.

When he arose, I told him that I had visited his vice president, who was in a hospital in Cairo after his automobile accident in Uganda. Did President Amin have any message for me to take to his vice president when I returned to Cairo, I asked. "Tell him," he said with a fearsome scowl on his face, "that my chief of staff had exactly the same accident but that I sent him to a hospital in Libya." It seemed that President Amin made a practice of ordering accidents to happen to his colleagues. Amin indicated to me that he had sent his vice president to an Egyptian hospital for treatment and his chief of staff to a Libyan hospital for treatment as a way of maintaining balance between those two countries. The vice president should consider himself fortunate to have been chosen to serve Ugandan-Egyptian relations. Treatment in Libya was less than ideal, he implied. He added, smiling wickedly, that this would be the final item on our agenda for negotiation. "Then," he said, "we can say that these momentous talks between Uganda and Egypt have ended in huge success!"

Of course, I agreed and offered my congratulations to the Ugandan president on what he had done to make our talks successful. I then asked him if he would agree to the rest of the delegation joining us in order to have extended talks. Amin replied that he saw no reason for this, as we had agreed on everything and the talks had succeeded. "Furthermore, it is after three in the afternoon and time for lunch!"

We left the president's house to go elsewhere on the island. Ambassador Hazim Mahmud whispered to me that we were headed for the basketball court and that the president often asked ambassadors and ministers to play basketball with him. But this was not what Idi Amin had in mind. Instead, we ate lunch while girls danced before us. Idi Amin ate with his hands and, showing me much courtesy and honor, offered to feed me by hand.

When the dancing ended, the girls came up to be photographed with us. The girls knelt beside Idi Amin and me. "Put your hand on her head!" Idi Amin commanded me. I asked no questions and put my hand on the woman's head. Idi Amin did the same with the girl who knelt at his side. "It is the symbol of power!" Idi Amin declared.

Idi Amin asked me what was scheduled for the evening. I answered that as far as I knew there was nothing. He became angry and summoned one of his ministers and demanded: "What is the meaning of not preparing a large dinner party tonight in honor of my friend and brother Boutros-Ghali?" I interrupted to say that I hoped that he would allow me to apologize for not being able to attend such a function. His anger increased. Why, he asked in astonishment, would I refuse his invitation to spend the night with him on Paradise Island?

Frantically searching for a reason, I hesitated. Should I point out the fatigue I feel, or my desire to watch my health, or my departure tomorrow at an early hour? Before I could answer him, Idi Amin shouted: "I know why you have declined. You want to see yourself tonight on television!" To do this, I would have to return to the city, for there was no television reception on the island. I noticed that his anger was subsiding and so hurried to agree with his explanation of my apology. Displaying admiration that he had grasped the real reason why I was turning down his offer, I asked, "Mr. President, how did you know this?" He laughed and said, "There is much that I know; in fact, I can foretell the future! Ask my ministers!" Three ministers were in attendance. "Yes!" they cried, almost in unison, "Yes! The president can read the future!"

Since our arrival on the island, Ugandan television cameras had recorded our every step except for the private session. Cameramen had filmed the talks that took place at the lunch table and the dancers. I told the president that indeed I did want to watch myself on television and relive the events of the busy day that I had spent with the president of Uganda. So Idi Amin agreed to cancel the dinner party. I left him after thanking him for his extreme generosity and the attention he had given me. After renewing his invitation to me, in tones of command, to return to Paradise Island to produce children, President Amin remained, and I departed by boat, waving farewell to him. When I returned to the Kampala hotel, I sat in front of the television to watch the events of the day I had spent with President Idi Amin on Paradise Island. I wanted to make sure that the Ugandan security agents with me reported to Amin that I had in fact returned to watch myself on television.

What I had seen that day was nothing new in the history of nations. There was Emperor Caligula, who appointed his horse to the Senate. And Nero, who set fire to Rome and then read poetry and played music to the flames. Our African continent suffers from economic backwardness, but it is infected with something more dangerous, and that is the power-mad delusions of some of its rulers. We cannot achieve development in Africa unless we succeed in building the African individual. And we cannot begin to build the African individual until power-mad despots like Idi Amin and the emperor Bokassa disappear from the scene.

I felt great relief to see my Mystère aircraft waiting for us at Entebbe airport. I felt even more relief when the plane's wheels left the ground ruled by Idi Amin. After refueling in Khartoum, we flew home to Cairo. I had crossed thousands and thousands of miles under difficult conditions and weather. Despite my fatigue, I was exhilarated to have reinforced Egypt's bond to Africa. On the airplane I recited to my colleagues the poetic (and controversial) view of Egypt's bond to Africa expressed by the African-American writer whose pan-African vision had a deep impact on me, W.E.B. DuBois: "In Ethiopia the sunrise of human culture took place, spreading down into the Nile Valley. . . . Beyond Ethiopia, in Central and South Africa, lay the gold of Ophir and the rich trade of Punt on which the prosperity of Egypt largely depended. Egypt brought slaves from Black Africa. . . . But she also brought citizens and leaders from Black Africa. When Egypt conquered Asia, she used black soldiers to a wide extent. When Asia overwhelmed Egypt, Egypt sought refuge in Ethiopia as a child returns to its mother, and Ethiopia then for centuries dominated Egypt. . . ."

As soon as I returned, I prepared a detailed report for President Sadat. The African leaders appreciated his initiative, I said, but wanted to keep the Arab dispute over the peace initiative out of the forthcoming Khartoum summit of the Organization of African Unity, which would be stormy enough with the battle over who would be the next secretary-general of the OAU. The Africans were also concerned, I reported, about the nonaligned conference that would be hosted by Fidel Castro in Havana following the Khartoum meeting. The presence of Cuban troops in various African countries presented them with a dilemma. Should the Cuban military presence be resisted as an example of communist intervention? Or should it be used to counter South Africa and neocolonialism? The Africans were divided. I concluded by urging Sadat to demonstrate a personal interest in African affairs.

On Wednesday, June 21, I attended the cabinet meeting, where three reports were presented. General al-Gamasi reported on his mission to Washington and Paris. Dr. Hamid al-Sayih, the finance minister, described economic sessions in Paris. And I reported on my African tour. The first two reports received much attention from my fellow ministers, but my report did not. Egypt's ministers continued to look to the European north more than to the African south.

I spent the next day in the corridors of Ras al-Tin, the rococo summer palace once used by King Farouk and set on a peninsula in Alexandria harbor. I was searching for President Ahmed Sékou Touré's foreign minister and cousin, Abdulai, to seek his agreement on the text of the joint declaration following the visit of the Guinean leader. Meanwhile, President Sadat was in a meeting with President Sékou Touré and President Siad Barre of Somalia in one of the palace halls. I found Abdulai, and we agreed on the joint communiqué. I then headed to the beach at Al-Muntazah, the second summer palace of King Farouk, built at the other extreme of Alexandria. There I found time to bathe in the sea and recuperate in the late-afternoon sunshine.

I awoke in my hotel at four the next morning and left Al-Muntazah, at the extreme east of Alexandria, for Ras al-Tin, at the extreme west. The car followed the eighteen-mile-long corniche. Nightclubs I had visited in my youth were winding down at the end of a long night. I saw waiters leaving the clubs and orchestra members and dancers looking for taxis, and recalled my agitated youth and how it differed from my life now.

I arrived at Ras al-Tin Palace to give my regards to President Ahmed Sékou Touré. The Guinean president, a tall and commanding orator, was fluent in Marxist formulas. He was totally convinced that in Guinea he was mixing a socialist medicine that, if taken by other African states, would cure all their ills. He sought to demonstrate that Marx and Islam could be compatible. He said he wanted to reach Conakry before Friday-noon prayers. President Sadat had put his private aircraft at his guest's disposal for this purpose. Before dawn, Mamduh Atiyah, minister of justice, escorted Sékou Touré in a helicopter to Ganaklis airport, a military air base in the desert, where the president's aircraft took off in time to arrive six hours later so that the president could attend noon prayers in the mosque at Conakry.

The next day, the sixth round of meetings of the supreme ministerial committee on integration between Egypt and Sudan met in the Alexandria office of the prime minister in the Bulkley quarter of the city. The Egyptian delegation, headed by Prime Minister Mamduh Salim, consisted of fifteen ministers, along with six members of the People's Assembly, and Sa'd al-Fatatri, ambassador of Egypt in Khartoum. The Sudanese delegation, headed by Rashid al-Tahir, vice president, included ten ministers and a group of other political leaders.

Mamduh Salim gave a speech welcoming the Sudanese delegation; then Rashid al-Tahir gave a speech. The meeting concluded with a series of dinner parties at the Yacht Club in the fishermen's harbor and the Automobile Club at Sidi Bishr beach, which had been one of the most fashionable clubs of the elite in the time of King Farouk. The Sudanese delegation distributed a selection of gifts to the Egyptian delegation—fine shirtings and leather goods. The colors were in such bad taste that I gave my share of the gifts to the guards accompanying me. Because of this practice of giving away what I received, the guards were always more keen on my participation in these meetings than I was. But the meetings were a waste of time. Nothing of significance toward Egypt-Sudan integration would ever be achieved in this way.

Despite my tour of Africa, despite the visits of Sékou Touré and Siad Barre, despite regular ministerial meetings between Egypt and the Sudan, Egypt was not taking Africa seriously, and Africa regarded Egypt as unresponsive to its needs. I was obsessed with this matter. The dream of Khedive Ismail, viceroy of Egypt at the time the Suez Canal was dug, that Egypt would become a part of Europe was still the dream of the Egyptian intelligentsia, even if it was a nightmare to the fundamentalist Muslim Brotherhood, for whom Egypt's salvation lay in rejection of the West and adherence to pure fundamentalist Islam.

Chapter Four

❖ ❖ ❖

Khartoum–Belgrade–Rome

In my scholarly career I wrote extensively on African and nonaligned organization but only as a theoretician. Suddenly I was called upon to attend three gatherings, each with its own special character. At Khartoum an attempt by Arab-African rejectionists was brewing to isolate Egypt from its ancient and precious African context. At Belgrade an effort would be made to deprive Egypt of its political leadership in the third world. And at Rome I would represent Egypt at a world gathering to mark the passing of a pope. After Sadat's Jerusalem trip, only three Arab countries still maintained diplomatic relations with Egypt: Sudan, Somalia, and Oman. If the Khartoum summit condemned Sadat, an Arab-African-nonaligned coalition would be formed to oppose Egypt, which could be devastating to us. Egypt would lose its leadership in the Arab world, its status in the third world, and its independent position between the superpowers; and Sadat's initiative itself could collapse under the weight of such opposition.

The OAU conference at Khartoum in July 1978 would be a crucial test. But Sadat was not interested. He considered such opposition irrelevant. He was obsessed by his negotiations with Israel; the potential isolation of Egypt seemed to bother him not at all. If he had taken the conference seriously, he would not have left the conference to me, a newcomer. Instead, he gave me a free hand. I took up the task enthusiastically. This would be my first international conference; it would take place at the highest official levels; and I was to be in charge of Egypt's affairs there. I was excited by the prospect of putting theory into practice. The first book on the Organization of African Unity had been written by me, and I had published and lectured for years on nearly every aspect of the pan-African organization, its institutions, activities, decisions, and the political trends that influence its work.

In pharaonic times Egypt paid more attention to Africa than to Asia. During the Middle Kingdom the frontier lay at the second cataract of the Nile, but Egyptian interests extended much farther south. Egypt maintained a colony and a fortified trading post at Kerma, a town south of the third cataract, under the command of a high Egyptian official, who enjoyed a status similar to that of Clive or Hastings during England's increasing expansion into India in the late eighteenth century.

When the Hyksos invaded Egypt about 1650 B.C. the Sudan and Ethiopia became a refuge, both physically and culturally, for the Egyptians. Noble Egyptian families migrated farther south into Africa and intermarried; one such family formed the Eighteenth Dynasty, which freed Egypt from foreign rule. From that time, larger parts of the Sudan and Ethiopia were incorporated into Egypt, and one could properly speak of an Egyptian African empire.

The Hyksos, while driving Egyptians southward, also compelled them to look to the east as a source of danger. Now, because of Israel, Egypt's gaze was constantly fixed on the east at the expense of the African south.

Khartoum

As head of my country's delegation, I would have almost total freedom to maneuver, negotiate, and decide on the major issues before this African meeting. I was optimistic about what Egyptian diplomacy could achieve, because our delegation included a superb selection of Foreign Ministry men who had worked many years in Africa. Among them was Fu'ad al-Budaywi, our ambassador in Kinshasa, whom the Foreign Ministry had decided to nominate as assistant secretary-general of the Organization of African Unity. He was supported by a long list of distinguished Egyptian ambassadors stationed in Africa.

My optimism that I could counter the rejectionists was not widely shared. Khartoum had been the site of the 1967 Arab League conference that declared the "three noes" toward Israel: no recognition, no negotiations, and no peace. Here at Khartoum, little more than a decade later, everyone knew that Sadat had placed Egypt on a road that could lead to "three yesses."

The Khartoum conference was the bid of President Jaafar Nimeiri of Sudan for international stature. African leaders took these summit meetings extremely seriously; indeed, the host of an OAU summit became a person of considerable influence, empowered to speak for all the African countries for a full year, to mediate disputes within the continent, and to carry moral and representational weight for all Africa to the outside world. Nimeiri opened the Khartoum meetings on Saturday, July 8, 1978, with a long speech in which he praised the proposed economic integration of Egypt and Sudan as a goal leading to a better life for both peoples.

His words had a special meaning for me. I had been interested in the Sudan since, as a small boy, I had been told that my grandfather Boutros Ghali Pasha as foreign minister had delivered the Sudan into the hands of the British by signing in 1899 the convention that established the Anglo-Egyptian condominium over Sudan, which Egyptians regarded as their own sovereign territory. This was one reason invoked by those who assassinated my grandfather in a Cairo street. The killer, a man named Wardani, was tried, found guilty, and executed, but he became a national hero, and in the streets the students chanted: *Wardani! Wardani! Illi átal al-Nusrani* (Wardani, Wardani, who killed the Nazarene).

Since my youth I had wanted to understand Egyptian-Sudanese relations more profoundly. I read much on the subject, traveled to the Sudan, and had many Sudanese friends. After taking on my new role as minister of state for foreign affairs, I had managed to involve the Foreign Ministry in the Sudan portfolio, which had long been held by the Presidency as a special and delicate problem. The process of integration was going nowhere, but Nimeiri's speech was helpful because he portrayed Egypt as being more interested in Africa than in the Egyptian-Israeli process.

Mamduh Salim had advised me to seek the help of Prime Minister Rashid al-Tahir of Sudan, the president of the ministerial conference. I met with him and said that I had clear instructions to oppose forcefully any initiative to reproach President Sadat's peace initiative or to compromise Egypt's honor. President Sadat's visit to Jerusalem was a purely Arab matter, I said, and there was no reason to discuss it in an African context. Having that clearly understood would pave the way for Egypt to emerge from the conference relatively unscathed.

Rashid al-Tahir agreed that Sudan, which held the chair in the conference, would try to avoid confrontation on the subject of Sadat. His first responsibility, he said, was to make the conference a success. But at the end of our talk I was not reassured. The two major anti-Sadat countries at the conference, Algeria and Libya, were trying hard to move Sudan from a pro-Egypt to an anti-Egypt position. Sudan both loved and hated Egypt. For the Sudanese, Egypt was like fire: too close and it burns; too far and you are cold. Sudan often tried to play Libya and Egypt off against each other. I believed that Rashid al-Tahir, despite the political attachment he showed toward Egypt, was emotionally inclined toward Libya, and emotion predominates in the Arab world. I felt that I could not rely on him.

The next three days, July 9–11, 1978, were filled with concentrated diplomatic activity as I contacted delegation after delegation. Harold Walter, foreign minister of Mauritius, was enthusiastic about President Sadat's visit to Jerusalem. A former officer in the British army in World War II, Walter was a brilliant and cultivated orator widely read in both French and English literature: He liked to discuss and debate the works of Shakespeare, Camus, and Sartre. Walter quoted a verse from the Gospels: "Oh the walls of Jerusalem sway with pleasure, for the messenger of peace has come." Sadat was pleased with this gesture of support, but it was a personal pleasure, unrelated to the need to win diplomatic support.

The Liberian foreign minister, Cecil Dennis, tall, handsome, and elegant in his white suit, looked like a movie star. A polite speaker, with extraordinary powers of persuasion, he was one of the best-liked personalities in diplomatic circles. Because of Liberia's historic ties to the United States, from which its founders had come as freed slaves in 1840, and the awareness of the new Egyptian-American relationship, a kind of informal Liberian-Egyptian alliance had begun to emerge at this conference.

Alioune Blondin Beye, foreign minister of Mali, was a clever lawyer rather than a diplomat. He would brilliantly alter the tone of his voice and infuse his words with an African enthusiasm that would please the masses. He was vehemently critical of Sadat's initiative, arguing that Egypt had no right to try to speak in the name of the Palestinians. He had been an instructor in one of the French universities when I was a visiting professor at the University of Paris, and he had read my writings published in French about African issues. Even in attacking my position he conducted himself in the manner of the younger scholar addressing his professor. After becoming secretary-general, I appointed Alioune Blondin Beye as my special representative in Angola. He was successful in achieving the Lusaka Protocol of 1994, which ended the conflict between UNITA and the MPLA government.

Such was not the case with Hamdi Ould Mouknass, foreign minister of Mauritania, who had been my student at the University of Paris. Unable to overcome the psychological relation of the student to the professor, he seemed uneasy in my presence and unable to regard me as a colleague, despite my efforts to encourage him in this direction.

On Thursday, July 13, came the news that a military coup d'état had overthrown the government of President Moktar Ould Daddah in Mauritania. Hamdi Ould Mouknass, the minister of foreign affairs, came to my hotel room to ask for my advice. His despair overcame his earlier unease in my presence. The relationship between university professor Boutros-Ghali and student Hamdi Ould Mouknass resumed. "Should I return to Mauritania?" he asked. I said to him that I would suffer more in exile abroad than I would in prison in my own country. He agreed. He returned to Nouakchott and was thrown in prison. Many years later he visited me in Cairo as a successful businessman who had totally given up politics.

The summit conference, which began on Tuesday, July 18, required my delegation to vacate its rooms in the hotel in favor of those accompanying the heads of state. Many of those obliged to leave the Hilton and remove to other hotels in the center of town were angry and dismayed, objecting to the priority being given to "the entourage" over Egypt's ambassadors. I intervened to calm the situation. These are the facts of diplomatic life, I said, which must be accepted along with its benefits.

After long and difficult debate it was clear that the majority of African countries backed Egypt and President Sadat's initiative. The most radical bloc—among the most vocal were Algeria, Angola, and Libya—were unable to turn the tide against Egypt. There were several reasons for their failure:

First, the fact that the conference took place in Khartoum enabled Sudan's pro-Egypt government to make itself felt.

Second, an African conference was not an appropriate setting for the discussion of an Arab dispute. The Khartoum majority accepted the argument that Sadat's policy toward Israel was not a problem for Africans.

Third, a number of friendly nations were particularly effective in defending the Egyptian position. Mauritius and Senegal played this role with great conviction.

And fourth, the Egyptian attack on Cuba for its intervention in Africa seemed to diminish the influence of the pro-Cuba rejectionists. I put forward a resolution stating that acceptance of Cuban forces on African territory meant rejection of nonalignment. My resolution failed, but it drained strength from the radicals. The threat to Egypt had been turned back. Sadat could come to the summit without fear of embarrassment.

President Sadat arrived at eleven o'clock. With him on his airplane were Hasan Kamil (head chamberlain) General Hasan al-Tuhami, Fawzi Abd al-Hafiz (Sadat's private secretary), Dr. Muhammad Atiyyah (Sadat's physician and mine as well), a large unspecified "entourage," and a huge security contingent.

The summit conference began with a closed session restricted to heads of state. Each was to be accompanied by one delegation member. President Sadat asked me to accompany him. I rode beside him to the conference palace in a huge limousine escorted in a stately motorcade by motorcycle riders.

Fawzi Abd al-Hafiz, the personal assistant to President Sadat, whispered that he wished to give me an important message: "You must not forget to take with you the tobacco the president needs for his pipe when the session is over and he leaves the session hall." I listened politely and realized that for this person the tobacco pouch and the pipe were far more important than the conference's resolutions.

President Omar Bongo of Gabon, as the current head of the Organization of African Unity, presided over the session, which elected President Jaafar al-Nimeiri to the presidency of the conference itself. Leaders from several countries were nominated to occupy the positions of deputy heads of the conference. President Senghor of Senegal suggested that one of these posts be assigned to President Sadat, a suggestion seconded by President Mobutu. No one objected.

I watched President Sadat's expressions with interest. He seemed uninterested in the session, as though he were deep in thought on other issues.

When the speeches were over and the heads of state and the premiers left the hall, I almost forgot the tobacco pouch and the pipe. Fortunately, at the last minute, I remembered the task that had been entrusted to me. But the president's aide quickly snatched the pouch and pipe from me as though he thought I was not up to this responsibility. Perhaps he feared my competition should I perform the matter with skill.

After the closed session we proceeded to the great hall, which provided seating for all delegations. As the leader of the official delegation, which included Hasan al-Tuhami, Hasan Kamil, and Fawzi Abd al-Hafiz, I sat to the right of President Sadat.

President Nimeiri delivered the opening speech. Then the secretary-general of the United Nations, Kurt Waldheim, delivered a speech in which he saluted the premiers, Africa, and the OAU. Otherwise, Waldheim played no role.

When Waldheim finished, Sadat stood up. He said he was leaving the session and asked me to remain and represent him in his absence. As he withdrew from the hall, my colleagues, the remaining members of the presidential delegation, went running after him. I tried to persuade them to remain but to no avail. I pointed out the bad image the vacant seats of the Egyptian delegation would make. But they refused to stay, saying, "You won't let down the side, Boutros." Thus I found myself alone in the section allotted to Egypt. Diplomats from my own delegation, seeing this embarrassing situation, hurried to the floor of the hall to join me.

That evening a large dinner party was held in one of the halls of the conference palace. President Sadat wanted to rest and did not attend, and therefore neither did any other members of the presidential delegation. As the sole member of the Egyptian delegation attending the dinner, I faced a barrage of questions: "Where is President Sadat?" "Why has he not taken part?" "Is he ill?" "Where are the members of the delegation?" "Are there political reasons for the president's absence?" A rumor circulated that Sadat had decided to boycott the conference because he was angered by statements that had been made there. I said it was untrue; Sadat had been called to an urgent meeting. Few believed my lie.

I attended President Sadat's meeting with Kurt Waldheim the following day. The secretary-general's primary concern was that no solution to the Middle East crisis be pursued without the United Nations. Sadat assured Waldheim of Egypt's concern for United Nations leadership in the international community. He told me to keep the secretary-general informed of our discussions with the Americans and Israelis.

Sadat next met with President Mobutu. When the Zairean president began to speak in French, I proceeded to translate his words into Arabic. Sadat interrupted me: "No need, I understand French although I do not speak it." Thereafter I limited myself to translating Sadat's words from Arabic into French. An air of total compatibility seemed to prevail between the two presidents. Their friendship went back to the 1973 war, and they shared a vision of world affairs. Mobutu, like Sadat, was deeply anticommunist and preoccupied by the Cuban presence in Africa. He fully supported Sadat's contacts with Israel and the opening of an Egypt-Israel peace process. Mobutu had a vision of an Egypt-Zaire "axis." As Africa's two most important countries, Egypt and Zaire, along with Nigeria, could dominate the region, he felt. Mobutu was very sure of himself, acting as though he were a traditional tribal chief, which he was not.

As the meeting was ending, Hasan Kamil appeared and said that President Sadat should proceed immediately to the meeting hall to deliver his speech. Quickly we left the hotel, and I accompanied the president in his car to the conference hall. There we discovered that we had been misinformed; President Sékou Touré had just begun to deliver his speech, which continued for over an hour. I learned to my surprise that President Sadat was tense and nervous, in marked contrast to his tranquillity during the trip to Jerusalem but I had learned that Sadat was always impassive except in the few moments just before giving a major speech. That had been the case in Jerusalem, too, but I had not been present behind the Knesset platform to observe it.

The contrast between Sadat and his predecessor, Gamal Abdel Nasser, was instructive. Nasser, like Caesar, preferred to be "first in his village," meaning the villages of the third world. Sadat accepted being "second in Rome," meaning the capitals of the great world powers. Nasser was deeply anticolonialist and anti-Western. Sadat admired Western culture and tradition and was ready to ally with the enemies of communism. Nasser came to power at a time of confrontation with the colonial powers, Sadat at a time of reconciliation with them. Thus they represented two distinctly different periods in the history of Egypt. I had participated actively in the political life of each of these different periods.

When President Touré's speech was over, Sadat proceeded to the podium, where he defended his initiative with great oratorical effect and to resounding applause from the conference delegates. President Sadat had barely returned to his seat when he decided to leave the session. His entourage, which had suddenly reappeared at the time of his speech, once more left the hall with him. Again, I found myself alone in the seats assigned to the Egyptian delegation and annoyed by their cavalier attitude.

Word came that President Sadat wanted me to stand in for him during the continuing session restricted to heads of state. Practically there was no alternative. The radical countries, led by Benin, Libya, Madagascar, and Algeria, dominated the flow of discussions and were quarrelsome and provocative. Late at night I went to President Léopold Senghor of Senegal, and asked him, with a note of respectful reproach, why all the moderate delegations were silent, abandoning the floor to the attacks and provocations of the radical minority. The Senegalese president smiled and said quietly, "Because they are moderate."

I deeply admired President Senghor as a great poet. He was a master of the French language and at the same time expressed the unique African sensibility. The intelligentsia of Paris and the elite of the black Francophone world both appreciated his work, but it was not accessible to ordinary Africans. Senghor told me that he had surmounted the language barrier by translating his own poems into native African languages. Senghor impressed me equally as a statesman. Despite his advanced age and the fact that it was then four o'clock in the morning, he showed no signs of fatigue. At 6:00 A.M. he was still at the conference, pursuing his idea of the need to adopt an African charter of human rights when most lesser officials had long since departed for bed.

"Where is Sadat?" everyone asked me. To avoid an irritating confrontation, he had probably decided simply to leave. His mind was elsewhere, in Sinai and Jerusalem, and African affairs were no longer on his mind.

I was greatly impressed with these African leaders. Their facility with the French or English language gained much goodwill from the outside world in a manner rare among Arab leaders. This is not to say that the African heads of state were all excellent leaders. Unfortunately, after years of being in power, many of them could no longer distinguish between reality and their own propaganda. But all had benefited from exposure to European cultures and they understood how to communicate to the world at large.

When Chad proposed a resolution condemning Libya for its aggression against Chad, Sadat asked me to support it. He wrote a note to me: "Dr. Boutros, all available efforts must be exerted to assist Chad in passing this declaration and supporting its case against Libya with all force." In execution of these instructions, I met with President Felix Malloum of Chad. The draft resolution was, I felt, far too harsh in its language to have any hope of support. I said that no one could be expected to cosponsor it. I asked his permission to amend the text. With this change I got four cosponsors to join Chad, but by the next morning all four had changed their minds and were nowhere to be seen. I went to the Chadian president to apologize. In a very sad way he said to me, "Al-Turayki did it." The Libyan foreign minister had distributed envelopes to "facilitate" opposition to the resolution. I had failed and made enemies in the process.

On the morning of Thursday, July 20, I attended President Sadat's meetings with several African leaders in his private suite. The first visitor was President Eyadema of Togo. The president of Togo asked for the support of the president of Egypt for the election of the Togolese foreign minister as secretary-general of the OAU. Despite what Sadat had told me the day before, he did not really grasp the French language. He could catch the general meaning of the conversation, but not its details; he could reply only in generalities.

Sadat then received President Seyni Kountchi of Niger, who began the meeting by praising me, saying, "The Egyptian foreign minister is like a great priest! He is one of Africa's wise men!" I was uneasy. Sadat simply smiled and shook his head, whether in approval or out of lack of conviction was unclear. This made me more uneasy.

After meeting President Julius Nyerere of Tanzania, Sadat turned to me and said, "This man is like a great priest, and he is without doubt one of Africa's wise men; he is brilliant. In fact, he is among the most intelligent of the African leaders I have met." Nyerere was to his people the *Mwalimu*—the teacher—and an aura of simple greatness and sanctity shone around him. But he was a great manipulator as well, and his love for his people did not result in many changes for the better in their daily lives.

Then came Kenneth Kaunda, president of Zambia, who was, in a way, a competitor of Nyerere for the title of the wise elder of Africa. A former Protestant minister, he was a revered statesman. He carried a white handkerchief always in his sleeve, in the old British manner, and would pull it out to mop the tears, which flowed easily, whenever a moving topic was mentioned.

Then President Jaafar Nimeiri of Sudan arrived to say good-bye to Sadat. Nimeiri was at the height of his powers, open-minded, outgoing, and proud of Sudan's new leadership in Africa. Sadat recognized Nimeiri's seniority as a leader, for he had brought about a coup d'état in Khartoum when relatively young. Sadat was also grateful to Nimeiri because Sudan was the only major Arab country to support him after his trip to Jerusalem.

Nimeiri felt the situations offered him a role as a bridge between the Arab and African worlds. He came from Wadi Halfa in the north of his country but felt himself able to understand the animist and Christian Africans of the south of Sudan. Later his attitude changed. He became a fanatical fundamentalist, committing the worst atrocities until he fell from power in 1989 in a coup conducted by even more fanatical fundamentalists.

As Nimeiri and Sadat were exchanging pleasantries and I sat silently by, an aide entered to say that the Moroccan ambassador, Ahmad al-Iraqi, requested an urgent meeting with the two presidents on a matter of grave importance. The Moroccan delegate came in, looking very troubled. Word had reached him that a delegation from the Polisario—the Western Sahara freedom movement—had arrived in Khartoum and would attempt to attend the conference. Should this happen, al-Iraqi said, the Moroccan delegation would be obliged to leave Khartoum immediately.

President Nimeiri assured the Moroccan that he would go immediately to the conference hall to prevent the entry of the Polisario delegation. Nimeiri left with the Moroccan ambassador. Sadat then criticized the Moroccan ambassador for his lack of self-control: "Ambassadors representing kings are pampered and spoiled and are inadequate for serious work at these international conferences." Sadat then turned to me to say, "I am pleased with you, Boutros, for your ability to face difficult situations in this conference without losing your temper. Bravo, Boutros."

A light rain was falling as we proceeded to the airport for Sadat's departure. During the departure ceremonies Dr. Muhammad Atiyyah whispered to me, "The president is very pleased with everything you did here at Khartoum, and in particular your ability to prevent a diplomatic setback for Egypt." I saw the president to the foot of the airplane's steps. "Stay strong, Boutros," he said as he shook my hand.

Back at the Hilton I learned that William Eteki of Cameroon, the present OAU secretary-general, had received instructions from his president not to renew his candidacy for reelection. Mrs. Eteki came to see me on the verge of tears. She asked me to help her husband to accept the painful decision by flattering him and praising his work.

I went to Eteki and expressed my admiration for the way in which he had carried out his duties as secretary-general. But his thoughts were wandering and he did not listen to what I was saying. Eteki felt that a catastrophe had befallen him.

I went to the conference hall, where the session continued until four in the morning. There I witnessed a fierce confrontation between the Somali and Ethiopian delegations and then a bitter argument between Chad and Libya. At about three o'clock in the morning, I had almost succumbed to fatigue and considered leaving one of the ambassadors to represent Egypt in my place. But when I saw President Senghor, who had passed seventy several years before, still in his seat, I decided to stay until the session ended.

What really bothered me was not the task of listening to speeches until dawn but the air-conditioning. I put newspaper pages under my shirt to insulate myself from the cold air. When the session ended the sun had risen and was shining on the Nile as I made my way to the hotel.

Despite my exhaustion I was soon back at the conference, where I witnessed a terrible confrontation between Ethiopia and Sudan, which continued until three o'clock in the afternoon. I then hurried to the hotel, hoping for some rest, because I knew the evening session would again continue until dawn. I did not eat so that I could sleep, and I was able to rest until six.

I returned to the conference hall and sat awaiting the beginning of the session. Chinese music was played, perhaps to remind us that China had erected the conference hall. The recorded music had probably been supplied when the Chinese turned over the conference-hall keys to the Sudanese. The music seemed to have a soothing effect, for the next sessions were less vicious than those that had taken place before. But the speeches continued until dawn again, and I did not get to bed until five in the morning.

I arrived at the conference hall at ten on the morning of Saturday, July 22. It was half empty. The all-night sessions were taking their toll. I sat there listening to the Chinese music and enduring the air-conditioning until President Nimeiri opened the session at 11:30. The Sudanese president was also showing signs of exhaustion.

In the afternoon I left the hall to meet with Sudan's Sadiq al Mahdi at his request. I had cleared this meeting with President

Sadat. Al-Mahdi was Oxford-educated, widely read, and spoke with an upper-class English accent. He was a dreamer, but not as violent a dreamer as his great-grandfather, the Mahdi, the charismatic leader who had led the uprising against the Egyptian Khedive in the late nineteenth century. A growing political force in the Sudan, al-Mahdi realized that he could use rejectionist denunciations against Sadat as a way to condemn and undermine Nimeiri.

Sadiq al-Mahdi's brother-in-law, the Paris-educated Islamic intellectual, Dr. Hassan al-Turabi, was al-Mahdi's close ally. He too was articulate, intelligent, and hated Nimeiri. He was also the leader of the Muslim Brotherhood in Sudan. At Sadiq al-Mahdi's home, we had a long conversation over dinner in which we discussed President Sadat's initiative and I tried to explain the new Egyptian political agenda. We have chosen, I said, negotiation and dialogue over military confrontation and violence for reasons that should escape no one.

I failed to convince Sadiq al-Mahdi and Hassan al-Turabi. Nimeiri's government was pro-Sadat; they were anti-Sadat. In their view, the Jews had betrayed the Arab family. Between 1945 and 1955, they pointed out, there were only seven members of the Arab League. By 1977 there were twenty-two members. The entire Arab world had been liberated except Palestine. Now, they said, Sadat had betrayed the Arab cause by giving Sinai priority over Palestine. Al-Mahdi spoke quietly, reasonably, articulately. Al-Turabi was vehement and severe. In time the relationship between the two deteriorated. By 1995 Sadiq al-Mahdi had been put in prison or under house arrest, and Hassan al-Turabi became a new spiritual leader of fundamentalists all across the Muslim world. At the Popular Arab and Islamic Conference in Khartoum in March 1995, Turabi told delegates from some eighty Islamic countries that "the international mechanism that is called the UN now functions incorrectly, and has become a weapon against Muslim countries."

I returned to the conference hall for another all-night session. There, in the hall for the heads of state, I met Léopold Senghor again. Between five and six o'clock on Sunday morning we had an enjoyable conversation about African culture. From time to time, we would leave the session for some coffee to keep us awake.

At eight o'clock that morning President Nimeiri suspended the session and requested a closed meeting to elect the secretary-general. Heads of state and their representatives retired to a meeting hall on the second floor of the conference hall, where we were given light refreshments.

Because there was a single candidate for the position of secretary-general, Edem Kodjo, foreign minister of Togo, I believed the session would last only a few minutes. But it was immediately pointed out that the OAU charter required a two-thirds majority to elect a new secretary-general.

A vote was taken, but Kodjo did not receive the required majority. I asked for the floor as Sadat's representative and tried to convince my listeners that as there was only one candidate he must be elected, so there was no room for maneuvers.

After a second, third, fourth, and fifth ballot had been cast without the necessary two-thirds vote, President Nimeiri suspended the session to allow for side discussions. I went to Nimeiri and said, "Mr. President, why do you not name a Sudanese candidate?" The president smiled. "I am keeping that card in reserve," he said. "I have a Negro I might propose at the last minute." He felt that this stalemate was an artificial crisis created by the communists in the organization. Gradations of skin color were important to the political balance in Sudan.

It appeared that Nimeiri was thinking of nominating Francis Deng, his own minister of state for foreign affairs. I suggested to Nimeiri that it might also be useful to ask Liberia to nominate its foreign minister, Cecil Dennis, who had ideal qualifications for the job. Nimeiri agreed, but asked if I could persuade Liberia's President William Tolbert to approve. President Tolbert rejected the suggestion, saying that he needed the foreign minister to prepare for the next African summit conference, which would be held in Monrovia. I returned to my seat, realizing that the battle would go on for hours.

Another vote was taken, but to no avail. New side discussions were held. Premiers traded places with their colleagues to consult in whispers. I was about to request a postponement of the session when Paulo Jorge, foreign minister of Angola, whispered to me, "Let us try again. Perhaps this time we will overcome the difficulties preventing the election of your friend Kodjo." I realized that most of the delegates at Khartoum considered me—quite wrongly—to be the mastermind behind Sadat's initiative toward Israel. By extension, they also considered me—quite wrongly—to be the mastermind behind this episode of OAU politics.

I was not aware that the radicals had decided to end their obstruction. President Nimeiri held another vote, and Edem Kodjo was elected. When Kodjo ended his term as secretary-general, conditions in Togo obliged him to seek exile in France until 1993, when he returned to serve for a time as Togo's prime minister.

What was the meaning of all this? Who benefited from these attempts to hinder the election of Kodjo? Why did we have to vote more than ten times if Kodjo was the only candidate and no one was competing with him for the position?

I soon saw that the radical countries wanted to show that they controlled the organization and, if they chose, could block any declaration incompatible with their policy. Perhaps they also wanted to make it clear to the new secretary-general, who belonged to the moderate group of countries, that the deciding word in his election was theirs, and that he must be attentive to radical and pro-Soviet members of the OAU.

This polarization was my strongest impression of Khartoum. A cohesive radical group, operating quickly, could muster a third of the member votes in the organization. They took part in all meetings, contributed to the discussion of every issue, interfered constantly, and remained in their seats until dawn without appearing tired or bored. Meanwhile the "silent majority" of moderates lacked both unity and commitment. They preferred chatting over a glass of beer. They seldom spoke in sessions, and when they did, their arguments were weak, their proposals incoherent, and their statements unconvincing.

After finishing exhausting procedural work, we left Khartoum on Sunday evening and arrived in Cairo at dawn the next day. Egypt's diplomacy, sustained by its friendship for and ties to Africa, had prevented unfriendly states at the conference from damaging Sadat's policy. We had bought time and gained some prestige, but signs of trouble were in the air. Radicals, rejectionists, and Marxists had united against Egypt. They had succeeded in isolating Egypt in the Arab world. They had failed to isolate Egypt from Africa, but that effort would continue. Now they would try to eliminate Egypt from the nonaligned world movement.

Belgrade

Weak states seek to employ neutrality for their own protection, but powerful states often perceive it as hostile. Conducting an effective policy of neutrality is extremely difficult, as Thucydides made clear in his history of the Peloponnesian War. But it is possible to employ neutrality with great skill and success, as the United States did at various times in its earlier history. I wrote extensively on the origins, problems, and possibilities of neutralism and was regarded by some as an authority on the subject.

The roots of Egyptian neutralism go back to the digging of the Suez Canal in the nineteenth century. To be acceptable in a world shaped by the balance of power, the canal had to be open to all. The 1888 Convention of Constantinople declared that "the Suez Maritime Canal shall always be free and open, in time of war as in time of peace, to every vessel of commerce or of war, without distinction of flag."

To maintain his dynasty, King Farouk actively promoted Egypt's neutrality. During World War II Farouk sought to avoid British hostility while keeping in touch with the Axis powers, who might put an end to British rule in Egypt.

Neutrality for Egypt took deeper hold during the years of the cold war. The Arab defeat in the Palestine war of 1948 brought a loss of confidence in the Soviet Union, which supported the creation of Israel. And American backing for the Jewish state made close ties with either East or West seem out of the question. Egypt's geographic position made it seem natural to take a stance equidistant from both superpowers.

Neutralism in its contemporary form began with the 1954 meeting between Gamal Abdel Nasser and Jawaharlal Nehru in New Delhi, which led to an agreement of friendship between India and Egypt. The following year in Bandung, Indonesia, the first major conference of the leaders of what became known as the third world took place. Contrary to its later reputation, Bandung was *not* a meeting of neutral and nonaligned nations but the site of a confrontational debate between partisans of nonalignment and those convinced that such a status was virtually impossible in the cold war. The new nations of Asia and Africa, which had recently rid themselves of their colonial masters, emerged from Bandung with a new concept providing them with the leverage needed to engage in global politics effectively—the concept of neutrality and nonalignment.

The movement was inaugurated in July 1956, when Nehru, Nasser, and Tito met in Brioni. They represented two countries that had thrown off Western colonialism (India and Egypt) and one that had broken free from Moscow's Eastern colonialism (Yugoslavia). The next step was taken by a preparatory conference in Cairo June 5–12, 1961. There, eighteen countries from Africa and Asia were joined by Yugoslavia from Europe, Cuba from Latin America, and the provisional government of Algeria. The conference adopted the five principles of nonalignment: (1) in the cold war confrontation between East and West, they would be neutral, aligned with neither side; (2) in the confrontation between North and South, that is, between colonialism and decolonization, they would not be neutral but aligned with the South and the fight for liberation; (3) they would not become a member of any alliance of which either superpower was a member; (4) they would not agree to enter into a bilateral alliance with either superpower; (5) they would not permit either superpower to establish a military base on their territory.

Being a charter member of the nonaligned movement provided Egypt with a dimension of international authority and leadership.

Belgrade had been, in September 1961, the location of the first official summit of the nonaligned nations. Egypt was celebrated and glorified there for its nationalization of the Suez Canal and its political defeat of Britain, France, and Israel in their war of intervention in 1956. The second summit was held in Cairo in 1964. Since then Egypt had participated in all activities of the nonaligned-movement summit.

On Wednesday, July 26, 1978, I flew to Belgrade, where the ministerial conference for nonaligned nations was being held. There I confronted the possibility that the movement that Egypt had helped to found and that gave Egypt a leading world role conceivably could condemn and ostracize us. Sadat's trip to Jerusalem, Tito said, had weakened the nonaligned movement by betraying the Arab cause. When I went to Belgrade, Egypt's status in the nonaligned movement was an article of faith for the Egyptian people and that faith was about to be challenged.

A large delegation of Egyptian diplomats had arrived in the Yugoslavian capital before me. I withdrew to my room at the hotel to prepare my speech to the conference, which I had decided to give in French. My colleagues, however, insisted that Egypt's address must be in Arabic. Our opponents intended to use this conference to accuse Egypt of abandoning the nonaligned cause in favor of the West and Israel, an enemy of nonalignment. It would not do, they said, for me to speak in a European language.

All Arab countries were represented at the conference. No doubt I would find al-Turayki of Libya, Khaddam of Syria, Saddun Hammadi of Iraq, Boucetta of Morocco, and Rashid al-Tahir of Sudan, all of whom I had seen at Khartoum. They would not make my task here at Belgrade easy.

I took the offensive, and began my address by noting the cold war's poisonous seepage into the African continent, which had transformed it into an arena for intervention by, and confrontation and stalemate between, the superpowers. "Some nonaligned countries have become an instrument to serve policies of power and attempts at hegemony manufactured by a superpower in Africa," I said. I was clearly referring to Cuba and the Soviet Union. I repeated what more than one African minister had said during the Organization of African Unity conference a few days before in Khartoum: foreign intervention will result in counterintervention; using the MiG will bring recourse to the Jaguar, the Mirage, and the Phantom; and when one side hires mercenaries, the other side also hires them.

I was trying to counter Arab radical pressure by obtaining the support of the Africans within the nonaligned movement and I wanted to show that Egypt's leadership in Africa was not affected by radical Arab attacks on Egypt's leadership in the Arab world.

Africa, I said, because of its recent emergence from colonialism, was more endangered by the cold war than any other continent. Africa's nonalignment required the utmost support from the world nonaligned movement. I urged the Belgrade meeting to condemn any intervention from outside the continent of Africa—meaning, of course, the presence of Cuban troops there.

Turning to the question of Egypt itself, no nonaligned member could be expelled, I declared; it would be inconsistent with the basic principle of the movement and would weaken it.

The issue of importance, I said, was the nonaligned movement's decision to hold the next summit in Havana. That decision should be revoked. Cuba was aligned with a superpower. I did not say so openly, but I feared that a nonaligned summit in a communist capital would produce such strong opposition to Sadat that Egypt could feel compelled to leave the movement, align itself with a superpower, and lose its leadership role in the third world.

I also argued against the idea of creating a secretariat for the nonaligned movement. Such an institution would be seized by radicals and used as a machine to twist the movement toward the communist camp.

While I was fighting to keep Egypt's leadership in the nonaligned movement, I feared that Sadat didn't care if we kept it or not, and if Egypt was condemned he would react instantly by leaving the movement. Sadat seemed to believe that the movement was dying from the disease of radicalism and turning toward a Soviet Union that no longer could be considered the wave of the future. Sadat seemed ready to do with Egypt what Kemal Atatürk had done with Turkey—cut it loose from its most important historical, religious, and cultural roots and become an integral part of the West.

It appeared that my tactics had an effect. The focus of the discussions turned from Egypt to Cuba. Yugoslavia feared that Castro was trying to seize control of the movement in order to turn it toward Moscow. While many at Belgrade shared my views about Cuba, a majority could not be found to either cancel or postpone the agreed date and place for the next conference: Havana.

On Saturday, July 29, a frantic young member of the Egyptian delegation interrupted a meeting to inform me that the Cuban representative had begun to attack Egypt. I excused myself and made my way to the session immediately.

The conference president gave me the floor on the principle of the right of response. Cuba, I declared, had ignored the principles of solidarity among representatives of nonaligned countries. Such behavior, I said, is not uncommon to countries like Cuba, which are merely obedient instruments in the hands of Soviet policy makers.

Cuba itself had agreed to serve Soviet hegemony in Africa. How dare Cuba, I asked, be insolent toward Egypt, one of the creators of nonalignment?

My words seemed to halt the Cuban onslaught. I left the conference under the illusion that I had faced down Cuba and preserved Egypt's position. In important side discussions both Khaddam of Syria and Saddun Hammadi of Iraq opposed further efforts to estrange Egypt from the Arab world. I later realized that it had not been my speeches that saved the day but the decision of Iraq, Syria, and other Arab governments that it was too early to condemn Egypt. The fact that Egypt-Israel negotiations were stalemated gave them hope that Sadat would give up his initiative and return to the Arab fold. I returned to Cairo and informed Sadat that Egyptian diplomacy had been able to contain the rejectionists. In reality, the battle had only been postponed.

Despite my feeling of success at Khartoum and Belgrade, I was disheartened after my return to the Foreign Ministry. On reflection I realized the immense opposition to Sadat's policy, which had been contained only momentarily and now was mounting again. Not only Arab and African and nonaligned radicals but also many Western Europeans were opposed to what Sadat had done. The Americans indicated a readiness to support Sadat's initiative, but we were not sure even of them. Our opponents grew more relentless while those who supported us grew increasingly quiet. But Sadat himself never showed me for a moment that he felt the isolation. He reproached me for worrying: "Don't be afraid, Boutros. Be sure of yourself," he said.

On Sunday, August 6, I presented a detailed report of what took place at the Khartoum and Belgrade conferences to the Council of Ministers. When I finished, Dr. Mustafa Kamil Hilmi, minister for education, took the floor and spoke in a wonderful Arabic literary rhetoric, with his deep voice, as though telling a love story, thanking me, on behalf of the Council of Ministers, for the effort I had made and the results I had achieved. His eloquent speech lifted my spirits. I felt that the long nights in which I had struggled until dawn at the conference sessions were valued by my ministerial colleagues. During this meeting I was assigned to represent Egypt at the state funeral of Pope Paul VI.

The Americans had now decided to break the stalemate in the Egypt-Israel negotiations. Cyrus Vance arrived on Monday, August 7. In the afternoon we began a working session at a suite in the Palestine Hotel in Alexandria. Afterward, we went to the president's rest house in Al-Mamurah, a short distance from the Palestine Hotel, where Vance had met with Sadat. The next evening we held a dinner party at the Palestine Hotel in honor of Cyrus Vance and his delegation. After dinner, we headed once again to the president's rest house for another tête-à-tête between Sadat and Vance. When they emerged, I had the sense that no progress had been made, but Vance declared that Sadat's initiative must be taken advantage of as soon as possible or "the Jerusalem visit would just be a footnote in history." Therefore, he said, President Carter had decided to call for another trilateral summit meeting in Washington. To me this sounded like just another unsatisfactory round such as we had gone through in Jerusalem in January. The Egyptian team would be limited in number, I was told, but I would be among those taking part.

When the meetings with the American delegation were over, I fled the journalists to enjoy the sea, if only for half an hour, before returning to the scorching heat of Cairo.

Rome and a Papal Funeral

The gathering in Rome was unrelated to the campaign against Egypt, but it assembled more influential dignitaries than the Khartoum and Belgrade meetings combined. Ambassador Shafii Abd al-Hamid, Egypt's ambassador to the Vatican, telephoned me. He was very concerned about the official attire I would wear at the funeral of Pope Paul VI. Despite Shafii Abd al-Hamid's repeated instructions, I could not get it straight whether I was to wear a redingote, a bonjour, or a frock coat.

My mother, God rest her soul, had, after the death of my father, given his formal attire away. So I called my aunt Anna, who assured me that she had kept all the formal attire of my uncle Najib for her son, Jeffrey, who had died a few years earlier, and that she had left the clothes as they were. I put on my cousin's redingote and found I could wear it without great difficulty. When Shafii Abd al-Hamid telephoned, I told him this, but he declared that the redingote was entirely inappropriate for protocol reasons; he had rented a frock coat for me in Rome. Now the primary concern of the ambassador was the decorations I would be wearing on my chest. When I apologized, saying that I had never in my life received any medal or decoration, al-Shafii could not believe his ears. He was disappointed in me. My wife, Leia, was beside me, listening to my answers to Shafii Abd al-Hamid. She, too, seemed taken aback because I possessed no decorations. I then remembered my only decoration, the medal from General Pinochet that I had received from the Chilean foreign minister, but kept it to myself. Better to have no decorations than just one! Since then I have received dozens of decorations but have never had an opportunity to wear them.

The plane taking me to Rome left Cairo airport about three o'clock on August 11, 1978. On board the aircraft I found the Coptic Church's delegation, which would join in escorting the Roman pope to his final resting place. Heading this delegation was Bishop Amba Samuel. When I taught at Columbia University in New York in 1954, I had known him as a young priest studying at Princeton. He was now a sophisticated cleric of the Coptic Church, and I had participated in many international meetings with him.

At the Rome airport, I was greeted by our ambassador to Italy, Samir Ahmad, and our ambassador to the Vatican, Shafii Abd al-Hamid. I sensed that, following an old, established diplomatic tradition, a keen rivalry existed between the two ambassadors. Two ambassadors in one capital is one too many. Italian security services decided I should stay at the Grand Hotel and posted at my door two men with machine guns. They asked that I take my meals at the hotel, and security agents followed me everywhere.

On Saturday morning I put on the suit al-Shafii had rented for me. I had brought with me my late cousin's suit as well. When I showed it to the ambassador, he remarked with grand disdain that it was old-fashioned, the kind worn in the days of King Farouk or even King Fuad. The rented suit fit me, but the pants were tight. I would have to take special precautions in sitting. With the ambassador I proceeded to the Vatican, where the funeral ceremonies were to take place in St. Peter's Square. Shafii Abd al-Hamid sported a large number of decorations and medals on his chest. One of the priests assigned to the funeral ceremonies greeted the ambassador as

Egypt's foreign minister. Embarrassed, al-Hamid pointed to me. The venerable priest looked perplexed to find the minister wearing no decorations but decided to accept me as authentic. The ambassador offered to lend me some of his decorations. I could not tell whether he seriously wished to save the face of his minister or was being ironic, so I remained silent and undecorated.

I sat on the main platform between the foreign ministers of France and the Côte d'Ivoire. The ceremonies were attended by 177 delegations representing more than a hundred different countries and international organizations of the world, an unprecedented number for the funeral of a pope. UN secretary-general Waldheim was there. I saw President Kenneth Kaunda of Zambia and Rosalynn Carter, wife of the American president. The French foreign minister pointed to the socialist delegates from Eastern Europe. "Is it not curious that these countries should be represented at such a high level at the late pope's funeral?" he remarked.

The splendor of the heavens seemed to have gathered up St. Peter's Square. The sky was pure blue. Sonorous voices echoed across the plaza. I was transported. Prayers were said in many languages, among them Arabic. The French foreign minister whispered in my ear, "Arabic in the Vatican is a new phenomenon no one would have imagined a few years ago." It was true. The Holy See had good reasons to give heightened attention to the Arab world: Israel's occupation of the Christian holy places in Jerusalem, the political and economic power of Arab oil, and new problems for Christians in Lebanon.

I had been interested in Christian-Islamic dialogue ever since, as a doctoral candidate at the University of Paris in the 1940s, I studied with Louis Massignon, the great Orientalist. Massignon was a superb writer, deeply involved with the politics and intellectual forces of the world. He had worked for French intelligence in the Middle East during World War I and recounted for me how he had entered Damascus in the same automobile with Lawrence of Arabia. He converted to Islam and became a Sufi mystic. His Ph.D. dissertation on the medieval mystic al-Hallaj was his first contribution to Islamic studies and brought him fame in intellectual and political circles. He was in regular contact with Islamic, Arab, and third world leaders.

When I first encountered Massignon, he had become a Catholic priest. I paid him a visit once a week at his apartment on the West Bank of the Seine. He was a member of the Egyptian Academy, a professor at the Collège de France, and gave lectures at the institute of political science that I attended at the university. His room was virtually empty. The only furnishings were an empty table and two plain chairs. On the floor hundreds of books were stacked. My association with him was not only that of student with professor; he was at the time engaged in a platonic love affair with Mary Kahil, my mother's friend and the aunt and godmother of my first wife, Leila Kahil. The experience was like that of visiting a guru. Massignon had an enormous impact on me in two ways. First, he talked about North African Arab affairs. In the 1940s I knew almost nothing about the Maghreb, the Arab west, which was separated from Egypt by an impenetrable desert. Massignon talked of the importance of unity between the Maghreb and the Mashraq, the Arab east. Second, he conveyed the importance of religious mysticism as a common feature of Christian-Muslim dialogue. Massignon was one of the great figures of this century, one who is still not sufficiently known.

All this came to me as I listened to the funeral rites for Pope Paul VI. I was brought back to reality when my turn came to offer condolences to the Sacred College of Cardinals on behalf of President Sadat, expressing his sorrow and pain at the pope's death.

That evening I had dinner at Ambassador Shafii Abd al-Hamid's residence, along with the Lebanese ambassador and his wife and my friend Muhammad Sabra, Arab League representative in Rome, and his wife. Shafii Abd al-Hamid suggested I postpone my return to Cairo for a few days so that I could meet with four cardinals, one of whom, the ambassador assured me, would be chosen as the new pope. He analyzed the politics of the Vatican in detail for me and elaborately justified his predictions. By establishing a relation with the new pope before he ascended the papal throne, he said, Egyptian diplomacy could gain from the Vatican's world-spanning influence and come to serve as a bridge between the Christian and Muslim worlds.

I agreed partly because of my own deep desire to spend extra days in the Italian capital, primarily to visit my old Italian tailor, who for years had provided me with superb apparel.

On Monday morning, August 14, I met with Monsignor Giuseppi Caprio, undersecretary of state, who had taken over all papal authority after Paul VI's death. He assured me that under the new pope he anticipated no change in the Vatican's support for a Palestinian state and for President Sadat's peace initiative. The dialogue between Islam and Christianity, I said, could help resolve the Lebanon conflicts as well as African conflicts that are tribal or economic in nature but also have a religious dimension. I was thinking of the disputes between the north and the south in Chad and in Sudan, as well as the ongoing conflict between Somalia and Ethiopia.

I next met with Monsignor Casaroli, the Vatican's foreign minister, who was considered the mastermind of the Vatican state. Our conversation revolved around the Khartoum and Belgrade conferences. Casaroli was brilliant, knowledgeable, and intensely focused on Jerusalem. He admired Sadat's decision to go there. The United States, we both felt, had undergone a political transformation that made it increasingly possible for external powers to have their positions appreciated there. The base of power and political decision making seemed to have shifted from the White House and the State Department toward the Congress; this allowed foreign groups to pursue their work much more actively and effectively than in the past. Casaroli and I discussed how to recalculate and improve our diplomatic action accordingly. I urged the Holy See to encourage the Catholic Church in the United States to support the cause of the Palestinians in order to balance the extensive Israeli influence in Washington. I described the effort Egyptian diplomacy was making with Jewish and Protestant leaders in the United States to bring out the true dimensions of President Sadat's peace initiative.

In Casaroli's apartments, as in other rooms of the Vatican, I was amazed at the tasteful luxury of the furnishings and the works of art.

In the afternoon I received Rolandis, foreign minister of Cyprus, in my suite at the hotel. Following instructions from President Sadat, I told him that we anticipated that Cyprus would carry out the death sentences against the criminals who had assassinated Yusuf al-Siba'i. This had already been agreed to during the visit of the Cypriot envoy, Michaelidis, to Cairo. President Sadat insisted that Cyprus respect the agreement.

The Cypriot minister referred to the difficulties his government would face by carrying out the death sentence. He said it would be the first time since Cyprus had won independence that capital punishment was implemented on the island, and that he would not rule out the fall of his government as a result. He asked if there was anything Cyprus could do to satisfy Egypt short of carrying out the execution. He offered guarantees that the criminals would remain in prison to serve their full sentences. In that case, I said to Rolandis, sooner or later they would have to release the prisoners because of Palestinian terrorist pressure. I said that I anticipated their release before the end of the current year or next year at the latest.

It was evident from our conversation that President Kyprianou would postpone the death sentence for a month and then postpone it again, and then reduce the sentence to extended imprisonment. And after one or two years the killers of Yusuf al-Siba'i would be released!

On August 16, I met with Cardinal Bertoli, another of the "papabili." The late pope had assigned him to try to mediate between the warring parties in Lebanon to stop the civil war. The Vatican's policy toward Lebanon, the cardinal explained, had three bases: independence, indivisibility, and religious reconciliation. The cardinal rebuked Egypt for its passive stance toward Lebanon, urging Egypt to play a role of conciliation. This was Egypt's traditional role in Lebanon, he said, and one it must resume. With the Vatican hierarchy, as well as the foreign delegates I met in Rome, it was clear that a belief had arisen that Sadat's approach to Israel was entirely centered on Egypt's goals to the neglect of other major Arab problems. Israel would never have launched its recent strikes into southern Lebanon, they believed, unless it felt sure that its border with Egypt was no longer an active front. Sadat's initiative to regain Sinai was costing Egypt its leadership, influence, and independent role in foreign policy, Bertoli said.

On Thursday I met with Cardinal Pignedoli, who is responsible for non-Christian and, in particular, Islamic affairs at the Vatican. Cardinal Pignedoli had visited Cairo in April within the framework of the Islamic-Christian dialogue between the Vatican and Al-Azhar, the thousand-year-old Islamic theological university in Egypt. The cardinal was another of the small group from whom the choice of new pope was expected, according to Ambassador Shafii Abd al-Hamid.

Cardinal Pignedoli praised the religious liberalism prevailing in Egypt. He expressed pleasure at the progress of the Islamic-Christian dialogue and hoped that after the new pope was elected the sheikh of Al-Azhar would consent to visit Rome to continue the dialogue started in Cairo.

On our way out to the car after the meeting, Shafii Abd al-Hamid whispered to me that he believed Cardinal Pignedoli would be the new pope. If not, I said, Egypt would be looking for a new ambassador for the Vatican! You should prepare to be accredited to Ouagadougou!

I returned to my suite at the hotel, where I was visited by Virginio Rognoni, minister of the interior in the Italian government. He came not as a member of the government but as president of the Arab-Italian Friendship Association. We discussed issues relating to the activities of terrorist movements in Italy, and the Italian minister wondered about the possibility of organizing a discreet trip to Cairo to meet with the Egyptian minister of the interior to discuss ways of collaborating to fight the activities of terrorist movements. He said this was needed because proof of relations between the Red Brigade, the German terrorist movements, and members of a terrorist group arrested in Egypt in April had been established. He was worried about the collaboration of Iraqi terrorist networks with other international terrorist groups. I shared his alarm and was committed to fight international terrorism.

The cardinals and other Holy See officials were interested that I was a Copt and displayed an attitude of universal Christian unity. The Coptic Church, however, is an orthodox, national, Egyptian church without ties to Rome. The Coptic Orthodox Church is closer to Armenian or Russian orthodoxy. Historically it has resisted close contact with Rome, fearing attempts at proselytization. Should the Copts become identified with an international church, they would be seen as a foreign body within Egyptian society, as a neocolonialist and alien presence. This had always been the position of my Church, which for centuries had opposed too close contacts with other Christian churches in Europe.

Of course, none of the princes of the Church whom I had called upon in Rome became the next pope. Shafii Abd al-Hamid's prophecies had been wrong. As was said at the Vatican, "He who enters a conclave a pope, leaves it a cardinal." The new pope was Albino Luciani, who had never served in the Vatican bureaucracy. He called himself John Paul I.

Thirty-four days after becoming pope, John Paul I suddenly died from a massive heart attack. I did not return to Rome for his funeral, however, because a new and dramatic chapter was about to open in Egyptian-Israeli negotiations.

CHAPTER FIVE

❖ ❖ ❖

Camp David

Arrival

On Thursday, August 24, 1978, I had a long conversation with Muhammad Ibrahim Kamil about the coming conference at Camp David. We did not know how to prepare for the conference. Many papers, documents, studies, and analyses were available, but the general strategy on which to base our moves was not clear, at least to me. Napoleon Bonaparte, it was said, never laid out a military plan until he was on the battlefield. I hoped that we would be similarly inspired when we reached Camp David, but I saw no signs of Napoleonic genius among us.

On August 28 we met for more than six hours at the Foreign Ministry to prepare for Camp David but accomplished little. Our preparatory discussions then moved to Ismailia, where President Sadat spoke to the Egyptian team at a meeting of Egypt's national security council. Sadat spoke in generalities, saying that Egypt would strive to achieve a comprehensive solution at Camp David and that we would never accept a separate peace agreement with

Israel. Egypt had lost thousands of square miles when Israel occupied Sinai. Throughout history Sinai had been Egypt's buffer, providing security along the Nile. More recently Sinai has come to seem to Egyptians much as California seemed to Americans a century ago—a frontier land of great economic potential. Four wars had left thousands of Egyptian soldiers dead in Sinai; it was sacred soil.

But a separate deal with Israel for Sinai seemed out of the question. Egypt was the leader of the Arab world; we could not abandon Arab unity simply to get our own territory back while other Arab lands remained under Israeli occupation. I was not sure, however, despite his repeated assurances, that Sadat shared this view. To him, Egypt came first, and after he came under Arab condemnation for his initiative, he began to scorn the rest of the Arab world as a backwater. The Foreign Ministry "gang" was worried that Sadat's strategy of regaining Sinai first to acquire the strength to recover the other Arab lands later would not succeed. We feared that step one would not be followed by step two because of fatigue and opposition, and because we had no mandate from the Palestinians to pursue a second stage. Although our group strongly favored the Arab cause, we were not authorized to consult other Arabs during our preparations.

We left Cairo for Paris on the presidential plane, with Sadat and his family in the private section. It was critically important to win French and European understanding and support for what Sadat was doing.

From Orly Airport helicopters transported Sadat and the rest of us to the parade ground of the École Militaire near the UNESCO building. This was the first time I had seen Paris from a helicopter. I discovered its streets and landmarks from a new angle and recognized the places and quarters I had lived in years ago. I revisited cafés where I used to sit, bookstores where I used to browse. I walked through the Luxembourg Gardens and stood outside the Faculty of Law. The delegation then settled into cars that took us to the Crillon Hotel, where my suite overlooked a side street; from its window I could see the American embassy.

At a dinner for us at the Quai d'Orsay Muhammad Ibrahim Kamil spoke in English and in generalities, but the conversation was monopolized by Hasan al-Tuhami, Sadat's astrologer, court jester, holy man, and morale booster. A bold and brilliant army officer in the revolution, al-Tuhami had become something of a religious mystic and believed that in dreams he received special instructions from the Prophet. He regarded himself as a sort of Egyptian Saladin, with a special mission to recover Jerusalem and defend Islam. Sadat was at ease with him and enjoyed his company, but we all thought he was mad. He wore a full beard in the Islamic fundamentalist style, which was against army regulations. No matter how bizarre we considered him, he played an important role for Sadat; al-Tuhami had gone secretly to meet Moshe Dayan in Morocco and described this trip as setting the stage for Sadat's Jerusalem initiative. However, Sadat told me, al-Tuhami's contact with Dayan had no role whatsoever in his decision to go to Jerusalem.

Now, at dinner with the French, al-Tuhami was revealing how, at the last minute, he decided not to carry out his plans to overthrow the Afghan government, and recounted many other adventures. The Frenchmen listened with astonishment. One of the diplomats whispered in my ear, "Is he really a deputy to Egypt's prime minister?" I replied that al-Tuhami was indeed a personal adviser to Sadat, but he carried no specific responsibilities or powers in the Egyptian government and he took no part in cabinet meetings. Unsatisfied with this answer, my questioner inquired whether Hasan al-Tuhami would be heading the Egyptian delegation to Camp David. I assured him that President Sadat would head the delegation. "But al-Tuhami is second in command," insisted my questioner. "Theoretically true," I said, "but the foreign minister will be in charge of the negotiations."

As we left the Quai d'Orsay after dinner, Ambassador Ahmad Mahir whispered to me about al-Tuhami, "Scandalous!" Muhammad Kamil, who heard his exclamation, added, "And this is only the beginning." We were all upset by al-Tuhami's surrealistic presence on the delegation.

Back on the presidential aircraft, Sadat invited us to his private salon, his family having remained in the French capital, and we had lunch with him. The president ate nothing at all but drank a cup of tea. Sadat was convinced that all this would soon be over. He would present his position. Israel would reject it. American public opinion would support Egypt. Carter would see that Egypt's position was good and Israel's was bad. The United States would then pressure Israel into acceptance of what Sadat had offered. It was simple, he said. I thought that it was not so simple; I feared that the Americans would not pressure Israel and that Sadat would then make concessions.

We landed at Andrews Air Force Base, near Washington. Vice President Walter Mondale and Cyrus Vance headed the reception committee. Sadat delivered a short speech. Then helicopters took us to Camp David. From the air I saw small, simple cabins scattered in a forest. After emerging from the helicopter, we proceeded on foot to the cabins assigned to the Egyptian delegation. My cabin was large, with two bedrooms and two bathrooms in addition to a spacious salon. The first room was given to Hasan Kamil and Ashraf Ghorbal, Egypt's ambassador to the United States. I shared the second room with Muhammad Kamil.

A short distance away was President Sadat's cabin, built on a small mound facing President Carter's cabin. As for Hasan al-Tuhami, he was given his own small cabin somewhat at a distance. Another cabin was assigned to the remaining members of the delegation, Osama al-Baz, Nabil al-Arabi, and Abdel Raouf al-Reedy.

As we were passing by President Carter's cabin, the president and Mrs. Carter emerged to say hello to us one by one. When it was my turn, he said, "I have read a report about your life and personality." I did not know exactly how to respond and so smiled uneasily. I had never seen a head of state wearing casual clothes. The scene was strange and unnerving.

Then we headed to the dining hall, which was on two levels. The Israelis were eating at a large round table. Among them I noticed Menachem Begin and his wife, Moshe Dayan, Ezer Weizman, and several others. We sat at the next table after greetings that could not be described as cold but that certainly lacked warmth. Al-Tuhami and Muhammad Kamil wanted us to have no personal contact with the Israeli negotiators. Eventually unofficial contacts did take place between individuals, but whenever we were in official proximity as groups, we kept strictly to ourselves.

When dinner was over, Hasan al-Tuhami told us that he had devised a way to stop his heart from beating for a few seconds and then resume its beating. Al-Tuhami's conversation attracted Begin's Israeli doctor and an American physician to our table. The American inquired whether al-Tuhami used yoga to stop his heartbeat. This infuriated al-Tuhami, who said his method had nothing to do with yoga, but he preferred not to divulge his secret technique.

Al-Tuhami then distributed pieces of ambergris to members of the Egyptian delegation, explaining that we were to dissolve it in our tea and it would give us the stamina to confront the Israelis. This smelly substance from the bowels of sperm whales was not for me, but some members of the Egyptian delegation used them.

We found Camp David a strange place to conduct diplomacy. We were used to negotiating while seated at a table, dressed as officials, in a classic diplomatic way with files and pens in hand. But here we would see each other in pajamas, in sports clothes, and on bicycles along the forest paths. A kind of familiar disorder was the rule. The dispersed cabins made communication difficult, not least among our own delegation. But the physical arrangement was not our main problem. It was Sadat's style that disconcerted us. When he met with Carter or Begin, we would never be told what he had said, yet we observed that the American and Israeli leaders briefed their respective delegations before and after each meeting. I was afraid that to regain Sinai, Sadat would make enormous concessions. His tactic was to convince the United States and Israeli delegations that he was reasonable but his delegation was inflexible. He believed that this would reinforce his bargaining position; the rest of us were not so sure.

As we continued to meet with the Americans and Israelis, we came to know the individual delegates. Cyrus Vance was careful. Zbigniew Brzezinski, the special presidential assistant for national security affairs, was eager. Begin was pompous. Weizman was optimistic. Dayan was surly. Aharon Barak was diligent. Muhammad Kamil was tense. Hasan al-Tuhami was dreamy. Osama al-Baz brimmed with intelligence and energy.

One afternoon Sadat, Muhammad Kamil, and I strolled among the trees of a beautiful little forest. Ezer Weizman, riding a bicycle, spotted us from a distance. He pedaled toward us and hurried to greet the president, warmly kissing him on both cheeks. In a conversation far from politics, Weizman returned to what was now an old joke. He asked Sadat, "Do you call him Boutros or Peter nowadays?"

Such pleasantries could not mask our discomfort. The surroundings were odd and Sadat was unpredictable. Al-Tuhami seemed crazed. As delegates we were asked to work on parts of issues, but could see no whole picture emerging. We did not know how long this would go on, as day followed day.

On September 7 Sadat summoned Hasan Kamil, Muhammad Kamil, Ashraf Ghorbal, and me to his cabin at noon. Sadat reviewed what had occurred at a meeting that morning with Carter and Begin. The Israeli prime minister had excitedly rejected virtually every article in an outline we had put together. Begin was particularly agitated by our demand that Israel pay compensation to Egypt.

Begin had returned once again, Sadat said, to his strange theory that legitimate defensive war allows for the annexation of land but offensive war does not. Some legal scholars had embraced this notion in the nineteenth century, but the United Nations Charter in 1945 ruled out any acquisition of territory by force. I had explained this to Begin in detail during my visits to Jerusalem in November 1977 and in January 1978, but apparently Begin did not realize that this worn-out theory had no basis in international law. He kept citing Oppenheim's outdated international legal textbook. To me, Begin seemed as rigid as a Central European lawyer from the early decades of the century.

Ashraf Ghorbal asked Sadat about Carter's stand in the trilateral meeting, and Sadat said that the president simply recorded in a little book every word uttered by the Egyptian side and the Israeli side.

Throughout the afternoon we held a long discussion among ourselves. Then we proceeded to a working session with the Americans, at which Osama al-Baz, Nabil al-Arabi, and Ashraf Ghorbal each presented the Egyptian position very clearly.

In our cabin after dinner Muhammad Ibrahim Kamil and Hasan Kamil asked me to join them in poker to get our minds off the talks. But I went to bed, exhausted. The atmosphere at Camp David was nerve-racking.

On Saturday, September 9, we held a work session in Sadat's cabin. A sharp argument arose between Sadat and Muhammad Kamil. Sadat distrusted his diplomats. Kamil was right, but he couldn't explain his position effectively. We tried to intervene in Kamil's behalf, but Sadat waved us away. Nervous and confused, Kamil was not successful as a negotiator. It was clear that Sadat wanted the Camp David meetings to end with an international document, no matter what the price. Without such a document, Sadat realized, his Jerusalem trip and the ensuing diplomatic initiative would appear to have failed.

That evening Ezer Weizman and I had a long discussion. I explained to him how crucial it was that the Israeli withdrawal from Sinai be linked to withdrawal from the West Bank and the Gaza Strip. Otherwise there could be no comprehensive solution. I believed, in fact, that simultaneous withdrawal on all fronts could be achieved at Camp David if Sadat insisted upon it. When Weizman accused me of "hanging on to an ideological point of view," I told him that I was defending Palestinian and other Arab rights not only because of my deep belief in those rights, but because there could never be a lasting peace unless Israel returned these territories.

I went back to my cabin, where I found a nervous Muhammad Ibrahim Kamil. "Where have you been?" he demanded. I told him that I had been debating Ezer Weizman for an hour and felt I had been able to put across some important points to him. But Muhammad Kamil rebuked me sharply, saying, "Did we not agree not to speak with those people?" I said that we had to talk to them not only to clarify our positions, but to persuade them to change theirs. "Muhammad," I said, "negotiating is not simply a matter of sitting around the table. It is also a dialogue away from the table."

But Muhammad Kamil felt that he had lost control of his delegation. He was humiliated. I understood his fears. In his opinion, Sadat did not know exactly what he wanted to achieve. He was firm at one point and accommodating at another for no apparent reason. Sometimes Sadat seemed to want us to reach an agreement whatever the cost; at other times he seemed to hope the negotiations would fail so that public opinion would go against Israel and Israeli designs be exposed before the international community.

Most of all, Muhammad Kamil feared that Sadat would link failure at Camp David to failure of his peace initiative as a whole and he could not afford to have his visit to Jerusalem seem to be a mistake. I agreed that it would be a good idea to tell the president that there was a wide difference between his Jerusalem initiative and the success or failure of negotiations at Camp David. His initiative stood on its own, I said. Even if Camp David failed, other ways could be found to negotiate. We talked until late at night and ended when Muhammad Kamil said, "I cannot go on. My nerves are about to explode."

On Sunday, September 10, I awoke unusually early and went to the mess hall for breakfast. On my way I met Sadat doing his daily exercise. He insisted on walking two or three miles, for about an hour, briskly and energetically every day.

He invited me to join him. As we walked he spoke continuously and in a high voice as though he were giving a speech. He spoke about the ongoing negotiations and of Israeli obstinacy. He also talked about King Hussein of Jordan—a sensitive matter. For any agreement to be comprehensive and not seen to be a separate peace, Sadat must insist that it deal with the West Bank and Gaza. But how could he do that if neither the Palestinians nor Jordan was involved in Sadat's initiative? Sadat was sure that King Hussein would not raise problems. "Once he gets Gaza," Sadat said to me, "he will accept." Sadat considered Gaza de facto Egypt's responsibility and that he would give it to Jordan, thereby providing Jordan with a port on the Mediterranean—and a lot of angry Gazans as well. Sadat thought that at Camp David he could get the Israelis to agree to turn Gaza over to Jordan. It would be Sadat's "gift" to King Hussein. The king will be delighted, Sadat said, and will join the negotiations. Sadat later talked to King Hussein on the telephone and I heard them arrange a meeting in Europe. When one of us asked about the king's position and the importance of obtaining his involvement in the process, Sadat avoided a direct answer and brushed us off. It was *his* domain.

As we walked and talked I put to him the idea of forming a multinational Arab force to take charge of the West Bank and Gaza for the transitional period after the Israeli pullout. Sadat listened but said nothing.

Detention

As the days went by, Camp David seemed more and more like a prison camp. To provide a diversion for the delegations, the Americans organized a visit to Gettysburg National Military Park. Carter sat with his driver and insisted that Sadat and Begin ride together in the backseat of the limousine. I was with Ezer Weizman, who was thrilled with the symbolism of visiting this important battleground of the American Civil War. Visiting battlefields, he said, always compels the military leader to realize the vanity of war and the value of peace. With Weizman, such an emotion was compellingly real. His son, fighting in the Israeli army, had been wounded by a bullet to the head, which left him helpless and disabled. Weizman spoke of the personal anguish, which turned him into a "dove."

As we walked over the battlefield I found myself between Dayan and Hasan al-Tuhami. The crazed al-Tuhami asked the Israeli foreign minister, "Are you the anti-Christ?" No answer. Al-Tuhami then declared that he intended to enter Jerusalem riding on a white horse and take the post of governor of the city of Jerusalem. Dayan smiled politely but made no comment, which reinforced al-Tuhami in his delusion.

It was obvious that Menachem Begin had carefully studied the details of the battle of Gettysburg. He was flexing his intellectual muscles as he showed off his command of the details of the cavalry charge that took place one hundred fifteen years before. Carter said he was very impressed with the Israeli prime minister's knowledge of the battle; Sadat remained quiet and dreamy, gazing into the distance.

We returned to Camp David and headed directly to the mess hall for lunch. Hasan al-Tuhami insisted on giving me more ambergris and once again asked me to dissolve it in my coffee. He must have felt that I showed signs of fatigue and wanted to strengthen me in my confrontation with the Israeli negotiators.

When al-Tuhami began to expound on Islamic jurisprudence, I told him that I had studied Islamic law (*shari'a*) for four years at the law school of Cairo University and had researched and written several studies on Islamic political thought. Al-Tuhami did not believe me. He demanded that I name the Muslim scholars I had read. I mentioned a number of them, from the most profound and prestigious to impressively obscure Islamic thinkers. I supplied al-Tuhami with a summary of the intellectual achievement of each one and recited verses of the Koran to him. Al-Tuhami was impressed and insisted that I become a convert to Islam. I must convert, he said, at Camp David; my act would be of immense symbolic value for the future of the Middle East. When other members of the Egyptian delegation heard of this, they encouraged me to keep talking with al-Tuhami to distract him from the negotiations. I agreed, and al-Tuhami and I took long walks in the woods, discussing Islamic doctrine at length. I felt strange about this, but it was important to draw him away from the others. I was the decoy.

Late on Sunday, September 10, word spread that the American side intended to present an American paper to President Sadat. I asked for a copy to study in advance, but I was not successful.

The next morning Sadat called us to his cabin. He handed me a document and asked me to read it aloud to the delegation. It was the American paper. On first reading it seemed impossibly long and complicated. When I finished reading the text, Sadat asked each of us to give our comments and opinions. As we did so, it became obvious that Sadat was paying no attention to what we were saying. Muhammad Kamil suggested that we all withdraw to study the document carefully and then reconvene to give the president our opinions. Sadat agreed, and the delegation moved to another cabin, where we read and discussed the text for about three hours. The American plan had two parts, one dealing with peace between Egypt and Israel and the other with the Palestinian issue and a comprehensive peace. Part one provided a basis for achieving a treaty of peace, but part two was far less certain; it would be easy for Israel to avoid an agreement on the Palestinian issue.

When we returned to Sadat's cabin, he attacked the American plan, not because of its inadequacy regarding the Palestinians, but because of its provision for Sinai to be returned to Egypt in stages only. Regardless of the reason, we were delighted by Sadat's anger. Sadat called Menachem Begin intransigent and impossible to deal with. He declared that he would withdraw from the talks and leave Camp David the next morning. This we did not like. Although we disapproved of the American paper, we felt that Egypt must continue negotiations. The sudden departure of the Egyptian delegation from the political-committee meeting in Jerusalem in January had been badly received by international public opinion. If we repeated such behavior, we would weaken international support for our diplomatic battle. Even worse, if Sadat left Camp David with nothing, his government would be weakened at home and could even fall.

When I urged Sadat to stay at Camp David, he grew angry. "You do not understand anything about politics!" he said and dismissed me by saying he wanted to rest. Sadat was truly shocked by the American draft and really wanted to leave. At the same time I feared that if Sadat changed his mind and remained at Camp David, his bargaining position would weaken and make him more susceptible to offering concessions.

When we returned to our shared rest house, Muhammad Kamil spoke at length about Sadat, the negotiations, and the future of Egypt. His nerves were obviously frayed, and he was deeply pessimistic. I did my best to calm him. I pointed out that our role was secondary; the political decision would be taken whether we agreed to it or not. "We must offer al-Raiss [the leader] our advice," I said, "but the final decision is his."

Muhammad Kamil reacted angrily, "But al-Raiss is possessed!"

The next morning, Tuesday, September 12, Sadat told Vance that his delegation was resigning in its entirety and that he and the entire Egyptian team were leaving Camp David. Vance quickly got Carter together with Sadat in an effort to prevent the collapse of the negotiations. When Sadat emerged, he said that Carter had told him that if the Camp David talks collapsed, Carter would not be reelected president of the United States. But if the Camp David talks succeeded, Carter said to Sadat, then in his second term he would ensure that the agreement fulfilled all Sadat's expectations. By promising Sadat the many things he would do as a second-term president, Carter turned Sadat around. I felt that Sadat wanted to be turned around. But did Carter actually make these promises?

As I reread the American plan, I saw that it was not comprehensive but confused. It was a series of compromises—a feasibility study, a preproject, a set of guidelines, but not a real agreement. The first section of the plan—withdrawal from Egyptian land—would not necessarily be followed by the second—withdrawal from Palestinian land. The parts were not linked, which meant that Egypt could be accused of signing a separate peace with Israel and abandoning the Arabs. Sadat, however, seemed oblivious to Arab reactions. He wanted the Americans to ensure that his initiative succeeded. I feared that the Americans were deceiving themselves and that Sadat, as a result, would deceive the Arabs.

That afternoon Egyptians and Americans met in a work session. Members of the Egyptian delegation spoke forcefully and courageously to Vance, Brzezinski, and William Quandt, a member of the National Security Council staff, defending Arab rights. But my impression, sadly, was that little we said would be taken into consideration.

Hasan al-Tuhami continued to act in his mystical way. In the morning he appeared at breakfast to announce that he had spent all night "in communication." "With whom?" we asked. "Up," he gestured, and declared that he had received a message from the realm of the blessed. Al-Tuhami then went to Sadat to tell him the heavenly message had confirmed that Sadat was walking the right road. Then he came to me to try again to convert me to Islam. "Such a grave decision requires much deliberation," I replied.

On Wednesday, the thirteenth, President Carter called Osama al-Baz and Aharon Barak to meet with him. They worked from eight in the morning to five in the afternoon and then continued in the evening from eight until ten. Osama al-Baz was becoming the hero of our "gang," fighting for a formula to recognize Palestinian rights and strengthen the document's comprehensive character. Sadat paid attention only to what really interested him, the total return of Sinai before anything else.

Before lunch President Sadat received us at his cabin. The atmosphere was tense between Sadat and Muhammad Kamil. To ease the situation I told Sadat how Hasan al-Tuhami was seeking my conversion to Islam. Sadat looked at al-Tuhami with amusement and said, "Do not underestimate Boutros, Hassan. You will convert to Christianity before he converts to Islam!"

This infuriated Al-Tuhami. Sadat's attempt at humor only complicated my relations with al-Tuhami.

By this time the members of the three delegations—Egyptian, American, and Israeli—no longer took part in the negotiations. The work was done by Carter, al-Baz, and Barak, although many later claimed to have been deeply involved.

While they worked Sadat received Moshe Dayan in the presidential cabin. I had tried to bring about the meeting for days, at Weizman's request. Weizman had explained to me how complicated his relations with Dayan were. Dayan's former wife and Weizman's wife were sisters. Dayan had been Weizman's commanding officer in the army. Now that Weizman was minister of defense, in the Israeli hierarchy he ranked above the foreign minister. Weizman said that this made matters between them delicate. Sadat made things worse by being cool to Dayan and cordial, even affectionate, toward Weizman. "Weizman can't be a Jew," Sadat said fondly. "He is my younger brother."

I had urged Sadat to meet with Dayan not simply in response to Weizman's request, but to ease the flow of negotiations. But Sadat refused, and I was obliged to relay this refusal to Weizman. Then President Carter, sensitive to the problem, intervened and made the same request of Sadat. This time Sadat agreed to meet Dayan "for Carter's sake." The phrase became popular among the Egyptian delegates. Any request we considered to be against Arab interests was labeled "for Carter's sake."

So when Sadat met Dayan I considered my conciliatory efforts a humble diplomatic triumph. Afterward Weizman thanked me for what I had done to bring about the meeting. But it did not melt the ice between the two. Sadat left the meeting declaring that Dayan was a pessimist, incapable of comprehending the far-reaching consequences of Sadat's peace initiative. I did not agree with Sadat's evaluation. The man, despite his difficult personality, could see far ahead and constantly offered creative solutions for complicated problems. What caused this animosity was not Sadat's disparagement of Dayan's abilities, nor was it just bad personal chemistry. Sadat, as an Egyptian military man, seemed to feel that Dayan displayed arrogance about Israel's defeat of Egypt in battle.

The Egyptian delegates were shocked by the Sinai provisions in the American document. The Egyptian peninsula would be a demilitarized zone monitored by UN forces and an international peacekeeping agency. The plan placed scores of limitations on Egyptian authority. These conditions were humiliating to Egypt.

I went to the Camp David cinema in hopes of seeing a movie that would help lift my spirits. The film was about an isolated tribe in the center of Afghanistan who worshiped the memory of Alexander the Great. A soldier of the British Empire tried to trick the tribe into believing he was the heir of Alexander. I was preoccupied, however, and, unable to follow the film, I left the screening room before it ended.

I returned to my cabin, where I found Muhammad Kamil as upset as I was. This time I shared his distress. Our conversation did not calm our nerves and neither of us could sleep. I admired Kamil's honesty and patriotism, but his inability to control his emotions worried me.

On Friday, September 15, Sadat summoned us to his cabin. He was furious, and announced that he had again decided to stop the negotiations and leave Camp David. He ordered us all to pack our bags that afternoon.

In their cabin, Hasan Kamil and Ashraf Ghorbal opened their suitcases and began to gather their clothes. I refused to do so. There is no need to pack, I said, because I am sure that Sadat will change his mind again in the next few hours. The decision he announced is only a warning and a way of pressuring the Americans and Israelis.

Muhammad Kamil had followed us to the cabin and asked me to join him for a walk. As we walked in the forest he said to me, "Try to remember this day. For I have made an important decision you will know of later." I suspected that he was indicating his desire to resign or to oppose publicly the Camp David agreement. I urged him to stay on course. "We are only at the beginning of a long road," I said; I believed that I had succeeded in calming him down.

The news of Sadat's decision to stop the negotiations and leave Camp David spread quickly and reached President Carter, who hurried to Sadat's quarters. We watched this action as though it were a dramatic film. When Carter emerged, it was clear that Sadat had agreed to stay. In fact, he had agreed to sign a revised document whose contents none of us yet knew. Sadat then came to our cabin to describe his talks with Carter. In his long and rambling description he said that he had agreed to sign because he was convinced that Begin would surely refuse. Sadat frequently said that if he could only expose the Israeli position before American public opinion, the United States would favor Egypt over Israel. Much later, however, I was told by Bill Quandt that Sadat had secretly conveyed his "fall-back" position to the Americans. He wanted Carter to use pressure, but assured him that he would give in whenever necessary. The result was that Carter repeatedly asked Sadat for concessions.

At lunch, Menachem Begin came over to our table and invited us all to attend a concert of the Israel Philharmonic in Washington the day after next. Our suspicions were now so deep that we pondered the meaning of this invitation. Was Begin telling us that the Camp David negotiation had concluded? Or was he suggesting a respite in Washington before a return to Camp David? Or did he mean to convey that Sunday had been set as the last day at Camp David whether or not an agreement had been reached by then? The American vice president, Walter Mondale, then visited Sadat. None of us knew what was said during the meeting, but the Egyptian delegation was always gloomy when Mondale came on the scene. We had the impression that he sought to sway Carter toward the Israeli position.

Again I took a long hike in the forest with Muhammad Ibrahim Kamil. He was still nervous and moody, and he seemed on the edge of a nervous breakdown. He spoke of the special relation he had had with Sadat since their deep friendship in prison. He assured me that he had never wanted to be foreign minister. He was very disheartened because decisions were being made without his knowledge, decisions for which he would be held responsible. Sadat was unpredictable, he said. "Sadat agrees to something in the morning, and an hour later he rejects what he had previously agreed to, and then in the afternoon he agrees to the same thing again!" I had to persuade Muhammad Kamil that diplomacy sometimes requires one to be fickle, but I could not improve his mood.

Returning from the woods, I encountered Hasan al-Tuhami. He was furious, because the document to be signed included nothing about Jerusalem. He directed his criticism at me. "You are wasting your time criticizing the foot soldiers," I said. "You must go at once to al-Raiss and take your stand." He did so, determined that any text signed by Sadat include a statement that Jerusalem must be returned to the Arab world.

After dinner we sat in front of the television to watch the fight in which Muhammad Ali defended his title as world champion. Muhammad Ali had bragged to reporters, saying, "I am the most famous man in the world, next to Moshe Dayan." It was probably true; Dayan's military exploits and his handsome face, made more romantic by his eye patch, were recognizable everywhere. Ali won the fight and his victory boosted our morale. We saw him as an underdog and a fighter who had stood up to the U.S. government (during the Vietnam war) and who had succeeded.

Escape

The next morning, Saturday, September 16, the atmosphere was cheerful and the conversation dealt with the details of Muhammad Ali's victory.

Walking along the Camp David paths, I met Hermann Eilts and again urged that the American delegation link the Israeli withdrawal from Sinai with withdrawal from the West Bank and Gaza. Eilts was tense. Any such suggestion should come from President Sadat himself, Eilts said. I sensed that the confusion within the American delegation was as bad as ours.

Late in the morning we gathered in Sadat's cabin. He received us cheerfully, and we had a long talk about subjects far removed from the negotiations, as though we were having coffee at the Gazirah Sporting Club in Cairo. It was clear to me that we in the delegation had been left out and would have to wait until the final score was announced.

After dinner I met Weizman and Brzezinski, who implied that they too were out of the final game at this decisive moment. This somehow made me feel better.

A heated debate ensued between me and Weizman as Brzezinski listened. I said to Weizman that the security requirements in the West Bank and Gaza, which the Israeli delegation mentioned at every opportunity, and even without an opportunity, were nothing but a feeble excuse. The state of Israel in its infancy, I said, had been able to survive and grow strong between 1948 and 1967 without any security presence in the West Bank or Gaza.

Weizman tried hard, but could not refute this argument, and admitted that Israel was powerful long before it occupied these territories.

I told Weizman once again of the fundamental tie between Egypt and the Arab world, economically, financially, strategically, politically, and culturally. Thousands and thousands of Egyptians worked in the Arab world. Egypt drew diplomatic and political strength from leading the Arab world. If Egypt could not find a solution for the Palestinian issue within the framework of Camp David, Egypt would be isolated amid its Arab neighbors; then Egypt would weaken and the collapse of the Egyptian regime could not be ruled out. The agreement about to be signed would then be immaterial.

My debate with Weizman continued for nearly two hours while Brzezinski listened in silence. At last, exhausted, we ceased talking. Brzezinski said, "I must tell you that this is the best debate that I have heard at Camp David!"

As I returned to my cabin I wondered what use these discussions were. Why should I try to convince an Israeli minister and an American official when the decision was being taken at the top? Neither Weizman, Brzezinski, nor Boutros-Ghali could alter a word of the document that was about to be signed. But my debate with Weizman seemed to strengthen our friendship and perhaps even altered his views a bit.

When I got to my room, Muhammad Kamil was sitting on my bed. He yelled, "Why did you leave me, Boutros? Where have you been?"

I felt very sympathetic toward my friend and colleague, who was severely agitated. I told him somewhat hesitantly that I had been with Weizman and Brzezinski. "Why do you talk to those dogs?" he said. "Muhammad," I said, "believe me, the discussion with Weizman was useful. I have accomplished something that will help us in the long run. We must prepare for the next diplomatic battle." Muhammad interrupted. "We have lost the battle," he said in despair.

By Sunday, the seventeenth, it had been agreed that the remaining differences would be dealt with through an exchange of letters that would be an inseparable part of the documents of Camp David. According to Osama, the subjects covered in the letters would be Jerusalem, Jewish settlements in the occupied territories, and Egypt's taking the place of Jordan in the negotiations should King Hussein decline to participate. This last issue aroused our fears. Egypt might claim a special responsibility toward Gaza, but Egypt could not easily justify speaking for Palestinians of the West Bank.

In the afternoon, Nabil al-Arabi came to our cabin, pointing to a sentence in the document that he felt could not be accepted. "Don't tell us," we said to him unanimously, "go to the president and tell him." We had lost hope of convincing Sadat.

Nabil al-Arabi went to Sadat's cabin but soon returned, disturbed and defeated. His observations had angered Sadat, who exploded at him.

President Sadat (center front) poses with his new government, October 1977. Having just been sworn in to my first ministerial post, I stand at the upper right, At the upper left is Sheikh Sha' Rawi, the fiery preacher of the Koran.

With Tito (far right) in Yugoslavia, January 1978. At my right is Sa'd Durayd, the Egyptian chargé d'affaires in Belgrade, a former student of mine.

Idi Amin insists we talk on the deck of his yacht so that our conversation remains "confidential."

Arriving on Idi Amin's Paradise Island, Uganda, June 1978.

Ordered to do so by Idi Amin, I put my hand on the dancer's head to gain "sexual power."

Touring the Gettysburg Battlefield with Sadat and Carter, in an excursion from Camp David. At the far left, next to me, is Sadat's "wizard," Hasan al-Tuhami.

I am amused by the thought that Hasan al-Tuhami (at far left) might try to convert Menachem Begin (center) to Islam. On the right, Sadat, Carter,and Elie Rubinstein listen to Ezer Weizman (at far right). At Gettysburg, September 1978.

President Carter meets the Egyptian and Israeli delegations at Blair House, October 1978. *Jack Kightlinger, the White House*

In the Oval Office with President Jimmy Carter before the start of the "Camp Madison" negotiations, October 1978.
Bill Fitz-Patrick, the White House

Five generals and one civilian (myself, third from the right). Meeting the Egyptian military delegation in Gen. Kamel Hassan Ali's suite at the Madison Hotel, October 1978.

Moshe Dayan (in the center) visits Kamel Hasan Ali and me at the Madison Hotel, October 1978.

With Israeli foreign minister Moshe Dayan, entering the chamber of the Council of Europe at Strasbourg, where we would debate, October 1978. *Council of Europe*

Flying back to Cairo in the president's aircraft after the signing of the Egypt-Israel treaty of peace, March 1979. At the right of Sadat (in center) is Prime Minister Mustafa Khalil.

At the San Giovanni restaurant in Alexandria are, left to right, Ariel Sharon, Betty Atherton, myself, and Shmuel Tamir, June 1979.

Between Yosef Burg and Shmuel Tamir at the Alexandria autonomy talk, June 1979.

With President Léopold Senghor of Senegal, poet and prophet of *Négritude*, before the Monrovian summit, July 1979.

Meeting Liberian president William Tolbert, a Protestant minister, before the Organization of African Unity summit in Monrovia, July 1979.

With Fidel Castro at the nonaligned summit in Havana, September 1979.
Prensa Latina

Delivering a message from President Sadat to the King of Nepal, in Katmandu, April 1980.

With Indian foreign minister Narasimha Rao, New Delhi, February 1981. *Ashoka News Photos*

Talking with Prime Minister Indira Gandhi in New Delhi, February 1981. *Ashoka News Photos.*

The Camp David agreements had two main parts. The first was the step-by-step withdrawal of Israeli forces from Sinai along with a negotiation effort aimed at achieving a treaty of peace between Egypt and Israel. The second part focused on the Palestinians and involved negotiations on autonomy for a transitional period to be followed by the achievement of a final-status agreement. We Egyptians were concerned that Israel would try to keep the Israel-Egypt relationship strictly bilateral rather than part of a comprehensive peace on all fronts. And we feared that the Camp David process would never be permitted by the Israelis to produce the self-determination for the Palestinians in the form of a Palestinian state.

Rumors swept Camp David that Begin was refusing to sign because Jerusalem was mentioned. Al-Tuhami insisted that Jerusalem be mentioned in the heart of the agreement. Word then came that the Americans had overcome this obstacle. Sadat wrote a letter to Carter stating Egypt's position toward Jerusalem. Begin wrote a letter to Carter stating Israel's position. Carter wrote a letter simply stating that the U.S. position "remains as stated" by the American ambassadors to the UN in 1967 and 1969. The key point for us was that the United States would not recognize unilateral actions affecting the status of Jerusalem: in other words, that Israel's unilateral declaration of Jerusalem as its capital was unacceptable. This was sufficient for Sadat: the impasse was broken! We were informed that we would be going to Washington that evening for the signing ceremonies.

Suddenly heavy rains began to fall and a strong wind blew over the camp, as though nature was telling us to abandon this place. During breakfast, thunder and lightning spread across the sky. One of our diplomats said, "The heavens are angry at what has taken place at Camp David!"

It was time to go. Cars took us to a small airport, where helicopters were waiting. Muhammad Kamil sat between me and Hermann Eilts on the aircraft. Muhammad dropped his head in his hands and refused to speak. I asked him if he was ill, but he said nothing. Eilts tried to talk to him, but then the noise of the helicopter blades made conversation impossible.

The helicopters set us down in Washington a short distance from the White House. We had spent two and a half weeks at Camp

David. Muhammad Kamil said he was exhausted and would not attend the celebration with us. I feared that he had decided to take some spectacular action and tried to convince him of his duty to take part in the ceremony. I urged him to keep up appearances before the Americans and Israelis. Hermann Eilts rode in the car with Muhammad and urged him to appear at the ceremony, but when the car arrived at the White House and Eilts got out, Muhammad ordered the driver to take him to the hotel.

Inside the White House I met Ashraf Ghorbal and told him about Kamil. He rushed to telephone his wife to ask her to go immediately to the Madison Hotel to try to persuade Muhammad Kamil to return to the White House.

I found the Israeli delegation fully assembled in one of the reception halls. Dayan saw me and said, "Thank God you are with us today. We heard that the entire Egyptian delegation had resigned in protest."

I told Dayan not to be misled by baseless rumors. He asked me directly about Muhammad Kamil. "He is ill and apologizes for not attending the celebration," I said. Dayan replied with a sneer, "Ill or resigned?" "According to my information," I said, "Muhammad Ibrahim Kamil is ill."

Then Weizman asked the same thing. "Look, there is Hasan Kamil to the right," I said, "and Hasan al-Tuhami standing beside the window, and Ashraf Ghorbal is here, although you cannot see him because he is too short."

We were invited to go to the second floor, where chairs were set out in front of a platform on which Sadat, Carter, and Begin were sitting. I noticed Sadat's eyes searching for members of the Egyptian delegation. He, too, had heard the rumors and was looking to see if everyone was there. I wanted to wave at him to show that I was present, but withheld this childish behavior. Sadat spotted al-Tuhami and smiled at him, comforted that at least his close friend was there.

Each of the three leaders gave a speech. Begin singled out Hasan al-Tuhami for mention, apparently as a way of disparaging the Egyptian Foreign Ministry "gang." Al-Tuhami beamed; he was delighted because Jerusalem had been mentioned in the exchange of letters. He was uninterested in the rest of the Camp David agreement. For him, only Jerusalem mattered.

The signing took place. There was great applause. The three leaders left. The Americans were joyful. The Israeli side showed similar feelings. The Egyptian delegates were despondent and their feelings showed on their faces.

When Ashraf Ghorbal and I returned to the Egyptian ambassador's residence, news of Muhammad Ibrahim Kamil's resignation was confirmed. We went to the third floor, where we found Sadat in pajamas, surrounded by Egyptian journalists. He was pointing out the positive points of the Camp David agreement. When asked about Muhammad Kamil's resignation, he said, "I consider Muhammad Kamil a younger brother, like my son. We joined together in a secret struggle and went to prison together. I excuse him because his nerves could not withstand the enormous pressures we faced. Some brats at the Foreign Ministry," he said, "have poisoned the air." In fact, he said, one of them had just that afternoon come to give him advice. "Is it logical that a Foreign Ministry civil servant interfere in matters of international policy?" Sadat asked. He was referring to al-Arabi, a senior diplomat. Sadat then looked at me. "Boutros, the Foreign Ministry, which you will supervise, needs cleaning up!"

That evening, in my room at the Madison Hotel, I reflected on the strange pattern of these negotiations. Sadat had been flexible while his delegation was rigid, and he used this as leverage when confronting the Americans and Israelis. The Israeli side was the reverse; Begin was obstinate, while his accompanying delegation seemed flexible and even indulgent.

As for the American side, they simply wanted the negotiations to succeed and were not ready to take into consideration the price Egypt would have to pay in the long run. Carter found the most effective way to pressure Sadat was to imply that if we were not successful, it would mean the end of his political career, and to pressure the Israeli side to imply that if we failed, Israel could not expect his future political support. Thus Carter played on what he considered each side's main weakness.

As for Muhammad Ibrahim Kamil, his resignation showed great strength of character. In the Western world, one can resign in dissent and life goes on. In the third world, resignation is a betrayal of the leader, a decision that led to what the Romans called *mortis civilus*, "civil death." Muhammad Kamil was a career diplomat; if he did not serve his government in that capacity, there was no other employment in Egypt for the skills he had spent most of a lifetime to acquire. Muhammad Kamil believed that Israel was more powerful, more advanced, more sophisticated, more modern than Egypt and had wider world support. Faced with such an adversary, Egypt had only one fundamental source of strength: to refuse to negotiate as long as Arab strength was unequal to Israel's. To many Arabs, "the refusal" was the cement that bonded Arab unity. Once you began to talk, as Egypt had done, half the battle was lost because dialogue implied equality, while the facts indicated an immense imbalance between the two sides. Tito had urged a similar position upon me, arguing that Egypt should not talk to Israel until it could do so from a position of strength. Sadat's view was that he had to talk to Israel to get the Sinai back, an outcome that would increase Egypt's strength so that further negotiations between true equals might take place in the future. My colleagues and I feared that Sadat would lose interest in the process as soon as he regained Sinai.

I wrote these points down at the desk in my suite at the Madison Hotel. An elegant suite, it contained several Chinese-style art objects and luxurious antiques-reproduction furniture. But in this beautiful setting I could not sleep; I had left my sleeping pills at Camp David. I tried, to no avail, to read. I looked out the window at the traffic passing endlessly in the street. Luxurious American cars stopped at the corner near the hotel, waiting for the light to turn green, and then quickly took off to destinations that I could not imagine.

From my window, Washington after midnight seemed calm and quiet. Suddenly I was at peace with myself. The Camp David agreement had many faults, but we had achieved an important first step on the road to peace, perhaps not only to Jerusalem, but beyond Jerusalem.

Chapter Six

❖ ❖ ❖

Camp Madison

Engagement

In the early morning of Monday, September 18, I went to the ambassador's residence, where President Sadat was holding a succession of meetings with prominent Americans. He was at ease with David Rockefeller, but perspiring and tense as usual when he faced a public appearance—he was about to be interviewed by Barbara Walters. "Come on, Boutros," he said, hurrying me in the corridor, "I am about to meet Bar-bar-ah." While Sadat happily submitted to questions from the beautiful Barbara, I slipped out and headed for a clothing store in central Washington, where I found a suit I needed; in fact, I bought two suits.

I then went to Muhammad Kamil's suite at the Madison Hotel and invited him to have luncheon with me. I found him calm, clear-minded, and relieved by the decision he had taken the preceding day. He had no regrets. We discussed his return to Cairo. Sadat would be stopping in Rabat on his way back to Cairo, and Muhammad Kamil's presence among the delegation, after his resignation, would appear strange. Kamil did not know what he should do. He decided to return to Cairo on a commercial airline.

With Muhammad Kamil's resignation, speculation arose as to who would succeed him as foreign minister. Esmet Abdel Meguid and Ashraf Ghorbal, Egypt's ambassadors to the United Nations and the United States, respectively, both wanted the job. Meguid had not been involved in the Camp David negotiations; Ghorbal had. To give Meguid a chance to talk to Sadat, I asked the president's aide to let him ride with the president in his limousine under the pretext that he would brief him on the UN. As they were being driven to Andrews Air Force Base for the departure ceremony, Sadat told Meguid that I was needed in Cairo, so I would not be attending the General Assembly in New York in the fall. Meguid took this to mean that Sadat intended to name me as foreign minister.

As I was boarding the airplane Esmat Abdel Meguid whispered, "Congratulations, I understand from the president that he has decided to appoint you foreign minister." I did not take this seriously and replied jokingly that if so, my main problem would be who would replace me as minister of state for foreign affairs, "because if it is someone like me, it will make the foreign minister's job impossible!"

We arrived in Rabat at sundown and accompanied the president to the guest palace King Hassan had put at Sadat's disposal. The president's wife, Jehan Sadat, and members of his family, who had preceded us to Rabat, were there to welcome Sadat when he arrived.

Jehan Sadat, elegant, beautiful, and intelligent, came over to me saying, "Congratulations, Dr. Boutros!" I thanked her and expressed my appreciation for the president's confidence. I realized that once again the public impression had been created that I was to be foreign minister. Once again, however, Sadat said nothing to me. I could see no good reason why he would make me his foreign minister.

Sadat had planned his stop in Rabat when it seemed that he could obtain King Hassan's support for the Camp David agreement and to meet King Hussein of Jordan there to discuss his entry into the peace process. Sadat was deeply mistaken on both counts. King Hussein thought it was too early to make a commitment, and he was offended when Jordan was mentioned in the Camp David Accords without his approval. I realized how badly we were handling our search for Arab support, and how opposed the Arab world was to

Sadat. The Camp David Accords were being defended by the Americans before being defended by Egypt; this was unacceptable to the Arab world. Sadat was compounding the problem by behaving angrily at every sign of Arab opposition. "Those sons of dogs!" was his reaction. There was a reason for this behavior. He felt that if Arabs supported him, they would demand a say in decision making, and he was fed up with the idea of a collective Arab approach. Opposition only spurred him to show contempt. We of the Foreign Ministry gang, however, were conditioned by a quarter century of Arab solidarity, and we wanted as much Arab involvement and support as possible. We were dismayed to see opposition mount so rapidly against Sadat's initiative.

I had a long and sharp discussion with Muhammad Boucetta, the Moroccan foreign minister, who declared that we had sacrificed Palestinian rights because the agreement did not assert the Palestinians' right to self-determination through the creation of a Palestinian state, nor did it mention the PLO as the sole legitimate representative of the Palestinian people or the Arabs' right to the Holy City of Jerusalem. "You are making a separate peace," Boucetta declared.

But Camp David is only the first step toward justice for the Palestinians, and Jerusalem is mentioned in the exchange of letters, I said. I urged Muhammad Boucetta to talk directly to President Sadat.

Sadat and King Hassan met at the Sukhayrat rest house, a pleasant group of buildings on the shores of the Atlantic about 25 miles outside Rabat. The president explained to the Moroccan monarch the circumstances and environment that had surrounded the Camp David negotiations and reviewed the main points of the agreements. Sadat and the king then entered a room to meet alone. I took the opportunity to promenade on the ocean shore and enjoy the fresh sea air.

When Sadat emerged, I asked whether I should prepare a joint communiqué regarding his talks with the Moroccan king. Sadat angrily replied, "We are not asking them for anything. If they want a joint declaration, they have to prepare one." I gathered that Sadat's talk with King Hassan had not fulfilled Sadat's hopes—even though Morocco had been the country Sadat believed would most readily support what he had done.

I suggested that the president hold a press conference before leaving Rabat to ensure that the European media covered the events positively. I pointed out that his press conference in Washington had successfully affected American media coverage of Camp David. But while the American media wanted to defend Camp David, my reading of European newspapers made it clear that the European media were not similarly inclined. The French press, I said, would influence how Camp David would be viewed in the Maghreb—Tunisia, Algeria, Morocco, Mauritania, and the French-speaking African nations. King Hassan gave instructions to prepare for the press conference and invite the foreign journalists.

Sadat agreed, and I sat beside him as he faced a large group of journalists. As usual, he was nervous before the media. But he calmly and clearly declared that there was a linkage between Israel's withdrawal from Sinai and its withdrawal from the West Bank and Gaza. Sadat's presentation was excellent, and a group of journalists mentioned that more meetings like this one would be needed to correct the confusion provoked by Camp David.

We left Rabat in the early morning. King Hassan came to see Sadat off, accompanied by a crowd of ministers who came forward to kiss King Hassan's hand, according to the Moroccan tradition. Hasan al-Tuhami did not hesitate to take King Hassan in his arms and kiss him on both cheeks.

During the flight I tried to lighten the mood by joking that al-Tuhami had injured King Hassan with his long beard and that the king had issued a royal decree that al-Tuhami must shave his beard immediately. When this was reported to al-Tuhami, he did not laugh.

We arrived in Cairo at noon, where thousands and thousands of welcomers had gathered at the airport to greet Sadat with cheers and slogans.

My wife surprised me as soon as I arrived at my home in Gizah by asking me to resign my ministerial post. "You have finished with the Camp David stage," she said. "You must now leave the next step for others." I explained to her that the battle had just begun and that I would lead that battle on the diplomatic front. She grew increasingly angry. News had reached her from Washington that I had resigned along with Muhammad Ibrahim Kamil and she had been happy to hear this. Then, to her dismay, a correction had come through. She was deeply concerned for my personal safety.

Despite a warm welcome for Sadat at the airport, which undoubtedly had been staged, Cairo friends and colleagues were negative about Camp David. I explained and defended the agreements but was getting little help from others, who seemed determined to supply misinformation about what had happened at Camp David and what it meant for the future.

At his rest house in Al-Qanatir al-Khayriyah, Sadat met on September 30 with Alfred (Roy) Atherton, President Carter's special envoy, and Hermann Eilts, the U.S. ambassador to Cairo. The president arrived by helicopter; with him was Osama al-Baz. Atherton reported to Sadat on the results of his talks in Amman and Kuwait, as well as his contacts with Begin in Israel and with Palestinians in the West Bank. Atherton had not been successful. The diplomatic isolation of Egypt was under way.

In the afternoon I had another meeting with Atherton at the Foreign Ministry in Midan al-Tahrir. As a result of Atherton's trip, it was agreed that trilateral negotiations on the peace process would start the following week in Washington. I would head the Egyptian delegation and Dayan the Israeli delegation.

Atherton stressed that the Americans would wage a diplomatic campaign in the Arab world, sparing no effort to explain and defend the Camp David agreements. I pointed out to Atherton the importance of United Nations participation in the coming negotiations. The information reaching us, however, indicated that the UN was far from enthusiastic about getting involved. Secretary-General Waldheim, we were told, was highly sensitive to Arab opposition to Camp David.

On Monday, October 2, Sadat addressed an enthusiastic People's Assembly on the results of the Camp David talks. His speech was interrupted by standing ovations. On the following day I sat before a joint meeting of key committees: the Foreign Relations committee, the Arab Affairs committee, and the National Security committee. My job was to answer all questions about Camp David. The chairman of the meeting, Sayyid Mari, president of the People's Assembly, declared that every member, regardless of political leaning, would be permitted to express his opinion and that the meeting would not end until everyone had been heard.

The members put forth a huge number of questions, which I tried to answer clearly and frankly. No secret agreements were made at Camp David, I said. Egypt will regain the Sinai in its entirety, and no American military bases will be allowed there. No "special relationship" will be created between Egypt and Israel. A freeze on Israeli settlements throughout the negotiations was agreed, I said. Beyond that, Arab Jerusalem is an inseparable part of the West Bank, and what applies to the West Bank will apply to it. The Egyptian and the American positions are the same on this point, I said. Finally, the Camp David framework opens the way for Syria to reach a negotiated settlement regarding the Golan similar to the one Egypt reached regarding Sinai. So, I assured the parliamentarians, the Egyptian initiative is aimed at reaching a comprehensive solution to all aspects of the Arab-Israeli conflict.

The session went through the entire day. When Sayyid Mari adjourned it in the evening, he announced that it would resume on the following day. The next day I answered every question until the members of the assembly gave up in exhaustion.

Within a week we were ready to go back to Washington to start the detailed negotiations to turn the Camp David framework into a treaty of peace. Sadat called the delegation together at his rest house near the Pyramids at Gizah. Large maps of the Sinai Peninsula hung on the walls. As Sadat talked he would indicate points on the maps so that the television cameras could record his instructing us before our departure.

After the reporters and cameramen left, Sadat asked me to read out the text of the draft peace agreement that Egypt would put forth in Washington. The twenty-two-article plan had been drafted by Dr. Abdallah el-Erian and a committee of experts under my supervision. Then everyone went outside and gathered around the president to let the photographers take pictures with the Pyramids in the background.

As I was getting in my car, Dr. Abdallah el-Erian hurried over to thank me profusely for giving him the chance, for the first time, to make a presentation to the head of state. It was highly unusual, he said, for a minister to permit anyone else to take a prominent role in the presence of the president.

On our way from Cairo to Washington we stopped, as before, in Paris. At the Élysée Palace, Jean-François Poncet, general secretary of the presidency, lectured me on my duties. "If you are unable to reach an agreement relating to the Palestinians before signing the Egypt-Israel treaty, you can be sure that you will receive nothing thereafter for them from the Israelis." Egypt's only leverage, I was told, was not to sign a treaty before obtaining the right of self-determination for the Palestinians.

The Americans felt about the Europeans the way Sadat felt about the Arabs, that if they were involved in the negotiations, they would make them vastly more complicated. As the Arabs, the Europeans, the Soviets, and the Palestinians all had been excluded from Camp David, none felt obliged to support it. The Arabs felt humiliated, the Europeans were antagonized, and the Soviets, ostracized, saw opportunities for political gain in the Middle East. We had thought the all-powerful United States would easily deliver the support of key regional and world leaders, but every day it grew more clear that this was not happening, and we were becoming more and more isolated.

The trip between Paris and Washington was comfortable and seemed quick, perhaps because of the film that I enjoyed watching about an American painter and his romance with a wonderfully beautiful blonde.

In Washington we had barely located our rooms at the Madison Hotel when we found ourselves on the way to the White House, where President Carter greeted us. With him were Brzezinski and William Quandt. The State Department was represented by Roy Atherton and Harold Saunders, the assistant secretary of state for the Middle East.

Carter said that his administration had prepared a plan for the Egyptian-Israeli peace treaty and that the negotiations should not take more than three months. The first stage of Israeli withdrawal from Sinai could then take place in six months, he said. The time needed for full withdrawal, he hoped, could be cut from three to two years.

I told Carter that shortening the time for withdrawal had been one of the demands of the Egyptian People's Assembly. It was clear from

Carter's comments that he, like us, considered it necessary to link the Egypt-Israeli peace treaty with progress for the Palestinians.

Back at the Madison Hotel, the Egyptian delegation was housed on the ninth floor and the Israeli delegation on the tenth. I met Ezer Weizman in a hotel corridor and found him worried and confused. Sadat had appointed a new prime minister, Mustafa Khalil, and as a key part of the shake-up had removed the defense minister, Lieutenant General Abd al-Ghani al-Gamasi.

Weizman had carefully built a strong relationship with al-Gamasi and knew little about his successor, Kamal Hasan Ali. Weizman was convinced that the good working relationship between himself and al-Gamasi would have helped overcome many obstacles. He was concerned that he would not be able to establish a similar relationship with Kamal Hasan Ali.

If Weizman had been any other Israeli, and I had been a conspiracy-minded Egyptian, I would have suspected that he was insinuating that I could take over al-Gamasi's role with him, thereby straining relations between me and Kamal Hasan Ali, the two leaders of the Egyptian delegation. But I realized Weizman's concern was genuine. Kamal Hasan Ali, I said to Weizman, is a pleasant and cheerful man; there was no reason why Weizman could not develop a relationship with him no less deep than his relationship with al-Gamasi. His uncle, Kamal al-Mohandas, had taught me Sharia, and Kamal Hasan Ali had trust in me. I suggested that we both go immediately to Kamal Hasan Ali's suite. Weizman welcomed this suggestion and we went at once. Kamal Hasan Ali was a hero of the Arab-Israeli wars, in which he had been wounded. The Egyptian establishment was a predominantly military culture, and Kamal Hasan Ali was popular within it. His intelligence, charm, sense of humor, modesty, intellectual honesty, and military style quickly won Weizman over.

On Thursday, October 12, the negotiations were formally opened at a White House ceremony. After Jimmy Carter, Moshe Dayan, and Kamal Hasan Ali had delivered speeches, I asked the American president, "What about the Israeli settlements in the West Bank and Gaza?" Carter drew himself up angrily. "I am the president of the United States!" he said. "And this is my problem!" Kamal Hasan Ali kicked me under the table and whispered in Arabic, "Be quiet. Stop!

You are making him mad!" Carter had cause to be angry. He and Begin had exchanged side letters about Israeli settlements. Carter thought he had Begin's commitment to a freeze for the duration of negotiations, but Begin claimed he had agreed to only a three-month pause in settlement activity. At the end of the session we moved to Blair House, the official guesthouse across Pennsylvania Avenue from the White House.

When the first negotiating session ended, we returned to the Madison Hotel, where I met with Dayan in his suite. I reminded him of our talk in the car between Jerusalem and Tel Aviv almost a year before, when I had stressed how imperative it was to find a solution for the Palestinian issue. Dayan said he was willing to search for a suitable formula for improving conditions for the Palestinians in the West Bank and Gaza. I told him of the need to make some progress in order to contain the Arab rejection campaign. Dayan said that the best way to do that was to speed up the process and reach an agreement before the Arab summit conference was held in Baghdad. Can we reach an agreement and sign a peace treaty before the end of October? I asked. That was less than three weeks away. Dayan's answer was yes, but it would not be easy. The Israeli government had to face internal Israeli opposition to Camp David. Egypt's opposition was external, coming from other Arab states. While I wanted broad Arab support, I realized that such opposition could help us fend off Israeli pressures for further concessions.

After meeting with Secretary of State Cyrus Vance late in the day, I asked Dr. Abdallah el-Erian and Amr Musa of the Egyptian Foreign Ministry to suggest various measures that the Israelis might adopt to build confidence among the Palestinians of the West Bank and Gaza. Many of the suggestions that I asked my colleagues to include came out of the long discussion I had had with Dayan. I intended to give this list of confidence-building measures to Vance the next day. It would have been safer to await Cairo's opinion before initiating such a memorandum, but the need to move quickly led me to act without hesitation.

On Friday, October 13, the three delegations met throughout the day at Blair House. Cyrus Vance introduced the American treaty plan. Dayan objected to the plan's link between the treaty and a comprehensive Middle East settlement. The Israeli delegation, he said, had been empowered by the Knesset only to negotiate a treaty with Egypt. Therefore, it would not be possible to link that agreement with other issues.

According to the Camp David agreement, I responded, the Egypt-Israel treaty was only the first step in a series of other treaties, and all steps were linked. Dayan said he was nevertheless obliged to refuse any link between the Egyptian-Israeli treaty and other agreements, particularly as the other Arab parties rejected even the principle of negotiating with Israel.

Meir Rosenne, the Israeli legal counsel, tried to minimize the importance of the paragraphs in the Camp David Accords calling for a comprehensive peace. Vance disagreed, but let it be known that he would not oppose changing the location of some articles in the American plan. As a result, the paragraph relating to comprehensive peace was moved to the preamble to the draft treaty, where, as specialists in international law understand, language is less binding than language in the body of the text.

The meeting revealed deep differences. The disputes were over words, but the words represented facts. Israel wanted to declare an end to the state of war, but how could we agree to that when Israel forces continued to occupy our Sinai?

We also disagreed about the wording relating to the Egypt-Israel border. It could have been interpreted to mean that the Gaza Strip lies within Israel. Israel already had made such claims about parts of territories it occupied; such language would put restraints on Egypt's freedom to defend the rights of the Palestinian people.

Behind this heated diplomatic battle were fundamental differences between ourselves and Israel: Egypt insisted on a comprehensive peace involving the Palestinians and all the Arab parties; Israel was seeking a separate peace with Egypt.

The key to Arab support for Camp David was Saudi Arabia. The Americans had failed to persuade the Saudis and in general had underestimated the depth of Arab opposition. Sadat had sent al-Tuhami to talk to the Saudis, but without success.

Faced with this rejection, the Americans put at our disposal a private aircraft to fly Kamal Hasan Ali and me to Cleveland, Ohio, where King Khalid was undergoing a delicate heart operation. We went from the airport directly to the hospital. King Khalid received us in his hospital room. We simply greeted him, wished him a speedy recovery, and after five minutes took our leave. We then moved to an adjoining room to meet with the king's adviser and ambassador, Prince Bandar. I did not argue for Saudi support for Camp David; they would not, I knew, give us that. Instead, I urged Saudi support for Egypt's efforts to achieve a comprehensive peace that would result in Israeli withdrawal on all fronts.

When our meeting ended, a Saudi adviser whispered, "Thank you for your clear analysis. Hasan al-Tuhami came to us two weeks ago and we could not understand him. He said there are secret texts on several issues, including Jerusalem." I assured him categorically that there were no secret agreements. I told him that I had made it clear to the Egyptian Parliament that no such secret texts existed.

As I was leaving the hospital, I was pleased to learn that the anesthesiologist attending King Khalid was an Egyptian.

After my return to the hotel in Washington, Hasan Sabri al-Kholi, who had close ties with the Saudi ruling family, called me. I asked him to urge the Saudis to use the occasion of the luncheon President Carter would give at the White House in a few days in honor of King Khalid to press the Americans on the need to link Israeli withdrawal from Sinai to withdrawal from the West Bank and Gaza. Al-Kholi telephoned me again, at one o'clock in the morning, to say that our meeting in the Cleveland hospital was positive.

The next morning I handed the Americans an Egyptian memorandum dated October 13, 1978. It stated Egypt's view on what was needed for the West Bank and Gaza: a freeze on settlements; involvement of the PLO if they accepted Resolution 242; inclusion of East Jerusalem in the voting for Palestinian self-rule; return of land seized by Israel in the territories; allowing Arab banks in the West Bank and Gaza; freedom of assembly, expression, and movement for Palestinians in the territories; release of Palestinian political detainees; return of a number of Palestinian refugees from the 1967 war; international or UN observers for the elections of a Palestinian authority; immediate withdrawal of some Israeli forces from parts of the West Bank and Gaza and redeployment of others.

I mentioned this paper to Dayan, who was displeased; for him, no position was valid unless it was part of the Camp David agreement. Dayan was the Israeli brain. He had intellectual courage, imagination, and Begin's confidence. My work sessions with him were always confined to just the two of us. On Sunday, October 15, 1978, at the Madison Hotel, we reached agreement that in addition to the Egypt-Israel agreement, a second agreement attached to the peace treaty could deal with the Palestinian issue.

The Egyptian negotiating team dined at the Egyptian embassy at Ashraf Ghorbal's table. He had invited a number of Arab ambassadors in Washington. I explained the Egyptian effort to them and the difficulties and obstacles we were facing. They listened with blank expressions, saying nothing. They had no instructions and would take no chances. When Sadat learned of this meeting, he was furious and sent a cable to us in Washington. Don't waste time talking to Arab ambassadors was his message. He did not need Arab support, he claimed. Sadat's mood seemed to change almost daily. One day he was contemptuous of the Arabs. The next day he was morose after reading the Arab press's charging him with treason and yearned for Arab goodwill.

In mid-October we received from the People's Assembly in Cairo detailed guidelines for our conduct of the negotiations. The members of the assembly were worried and wanted to take part in the diplomacy. I welcomed their involvement, for now we could show Israel and the United States the constraints that domestic Egyptian politics and public opinion had placed on us.

After a working session on Monday, October 16, Weizman told us that Dayan was pessimistic and angry but he couldn't understand why. At Weizman's request I telephoned Dayan. "Where will you be dining tonight?" I asked. "I eat nothing in the evening" was the reply. "And what do you do when you receive a dinner invitation?" I said. "I accept it if it is formal," Dayan replied. "Then I am extending you an official invitation to dine with me in the hotel restaurant." Dayan replied, "I am therefore required to accept the invitation and I thank you, but why do we not meet in my room before dinner for a drink?"

Over drinks, Dayan and I spoke again about "Gaza first." A temporary Egyptian presence in Gaza could facilitate the withdrawal of Israeli forces, I said. Dayan said he had no objection, but any form of Egyptian presence would come under Palestinian attack. He added sarcastically that an Egyptian office in Gaza might have to be protected by the Israelis.

Our "Gaza first" talk was entirely personal; neither of us was authorized by our governments to negotiate officially on this notion. I mentioned it only as a step toward a Palestinian state. Egypt did not want authority over Palestinians, and Gazans did not want to be associated with Egypt. Gaza had been occupied by Egypt from 1949 to 1967, and neither side was pleased.

The next day I had lunch with Zbigniew Brzezinski and Osama al-Baz in Brzezinski's office at the White House. We talked about diplomatic relations between Egypt and Israel. The Israelis wanted this as soon as possible; I said relations would have to come gradually. There should first be an announcement of diplomatic relations. Then each country would send a diplomatic mission headed by a chargé d'affaires. Finally, ambassadors would be posted to Cairo and to Tel Aviv. I felt that my words were heard politely but would meet with quiet opposition.

In the afternoon President Carter received us. In the Theodore Roosevelt Room, where we sat together around a table, Carter accused me of complicating the issue of diplomatic relations between Egypt and Israel. I replied that the matter was particularly sensitive to Egyptian and Arab public opinion.

We accomplished nothing that day. Our instructions from Cairo were ambiguous. The Israelis were aiming to hurry us into a separate peace with full diplomatic relations after their withdrawal to the Al-Arish/Ras Muhammad line. They were also demanding commercial ties to guarantee that Egyptian oil would continue to flow from Sinai wells to Israel. What Israel wanted was to neutralize Egypt completely and remove it from the Arab arena. Meanwhile we feared that Sadat would make concessions far beyond our worst fears. Sadat was the boss. He could ignore his advisers, bypass the Assembly, override the wishes of the Egyptian people, and he enjoyed demonstrating his power.

On the Palestinian front the matter was even worse. Israel bluntly refused to forgo military control of the West Bank and Gaza, regardless of the form of Palestinian self-rule. It insisted that Jerusalem remain united under Israeli sovereignty as the capital of Israel. The most Israel would offer Muslims and Christians was a promise that they could visit the holy places. The Israelis justified this position on the grounds of Palestinian rejectionism, which also made it easier for the Americans to minimize the importance of linking the Egyptian-Israeli agreement with the Palestinian issue.

Dayan's retort to me was forceful. "How can Egypt demand such a link while the Palestinians refuse to deal with Israel? In fact," he said, "they refuse to deal with Egypt under the Camp David framework." Dayan was right. But I wanted to create a context that would give the Palestinians and other Arabs the confidence to join the process. Instead, confidence was declining every day.

On the evening of October 18 the Americans gave a dinner in the grand eighth-floor diplomatic rooms of the State Department. An American army band played light music and a choral group sang delightfully. During dinner, Bill Quandt and I discussed the idea of beginning the Israeli withdrawal in Gaza and establishing a temporary Egyptian presence there to provide security as Israel departed.

It was clear from Quandt's comments that the Americans knew that my government in Cairo rejected the idea of an Egyptian presence in Gaza. In fact, the Americans knew of the Egyptian decision before our delegation in Washington did. This was not the first time we discovered that the Americans knew about Cairo's instructions before they reached us, the Egyptian negotiators in Washington.

At Blair House on October 19 Atherton announced that President Carter was inviting only three members from each delegation to a working lunch because of the limited seating at the table. Dayan was infuriated. "This is impossible," he declared. "The Israeli delegation has four members and if four members are not invited, the delegation will not attend!" Atherton withdrew for a few minutes and then returned to inform us that the table had been expanded to allow four members from each delegation to attend.

At lunch the Egyptians were Kamal Hasan Ali, Ashraf Ghorbal, Osama al-Baz, and myself. The Israelis were Dayan, Weizman, Rosenne, and Barak. There were three Americans.

Carter assured us once more that he would play an active and positive role. But Dayan was in a foul mood again, and he announced that he was not fully authorized to negotiate and that the key to the situation was in the hands of Cairo and Jerusalem. I felt that Dayan was trying to push the Americans around. When I spoke again about the importance of linking the withdrawal from Sinai to the Palestinian issue, Carter backed me up. There had been no doubt at Camp David, he said, that there was a strong and tangible link between the Egypt-Israeli peace agreement and a comprehensive settlement in general and the Palestinian issue in particular. It would be useful, he said, for all sides to agree to a date for elections in the West Bank and Gaza so that the Palestinians could sense the seriousness of our intentions. Carter then suggested that Israel take specific steps.

I was certain from Carter's remarks that he had read our memorandum of October 13 and been influenced by its contents. I believed he might support the Egyptian position.

Dayan asked for the floor to announce his refusal to link the Egypt-Israel treaty with the West Bank and Gaza. He repeated that the inhabitants of the West Bank and Gaza Strip would not agree with the Camp David agreements and refuse any of its measures. He also objected to any Egyptian presence in Gaza, contrary to our conversation two days earlier. Nothing in the Camp David framework, he said, mentioned such an Egyptian military role there.

I was about to reply that there also was nothing in the Camp David text to prohibit an Egyptian presence in Gaza, and to remind Dayan of his approval, in our private conversation, of the principle of an Egyptian presence in the Strip, but I refrained. Because "confidence building" is also essential between negotiators, what is stated in private talks must not be revealed in official sessions. Carter broke in to say that after listening to both sides, he would ask his aides to prepare a new plan for the treaty, the sixth plan. The Americans—Carter, Vance, and Atherton—were now in effect the drafters of the treaty. Dayan and Barak worked on the text for Israel, and Osama al-Baz and I did the same for Egypt.

On Saturday, October 21, I arrived, as requested by President Carter, at the White House at 7:00 A.M. I had asked Dr. Abdallah el-Erian, the legal counsel of the Egyptian delegation, to accompany me. The sun had not yet risen. Carter entered the meeting room a few minutes after we did, wearing a blue suit and blue tie. He said he had started at five in the morning to draw up the ideas he would be discussing with us.

I said, jokingly, that personally I had not slept all night for fear of being late. Carter ignored my comment. In a mood of total seriousness he proposed an exchange of letters regarding the West Bank and Gaza that would provide a timetable for a meeting between Egypt and Israel to discuss the transfer of authority from the Israeli military to the Palestinian inhabitants of the territories. The timetable would also set the date for withdrawal of Israeli forces and their redeployment to new and specified locations. After going through other detailed proposals, Carter said to me that he now had to leave Washington for a destination elsewhere in the United States. He said that he would pray that we overcome the obstacles that had frustrated our negotiations.

Throughout this session Carter was stern, serious, and humorless. He relaxed only when Ambassador Abdallah el-Erian, a shameless flatterer, heaped an avalanche of praise upon him. He declared that he had read Carter's book *Why Not the Best?* In fact, he had reread it and was reading it yet again. Indeed, he kept the book on his bedside table. He turned to it, he assured the president, for moral support in difficult times.

When I got back to the hotel, I hurried to breakfast and then to Kamal Hasan Ali's suite to brief him on our White House meeting. Then I went to the eleventh floor, where a trilateral negotiation session was under way, although not at the ministerial level. I was taking over temporarily from Osama al-Baz, who had gone to Paris to meet Mubarak. When Dayan found out I was at the negotiations, he, in turn, came to the eleventh floor and a "ministerial session" took place de facto. We began at nine o'clock and continued until four in the afternoon.

As we discussed the wording of the exchange of letters Carter had proposed, a new obstacle emerged. The Israelis insisted on calling the West Bank "Judea and Samaria." Our letters would not match if they used "Judea and Samaria" and we used "West Bank." We feared the exchange would not be a valid international agreement. The discussions proceeded with increasing antagonism. At one point Dayan and we exchanged stormy words; I whispered to Dr. Abdallah el-Erian, "I can't take any more of this man. I am leaving these talks!" But Dr. Abdallah put both his hands on my knees to hold me down and whispered in my ear slowly, articulating each word, "We must endure, Doctor. For the land of Egypt is occupied." I felt the weakness of our position and our humiliation. I envisioned the Upper Egyptian countryside, my fury dissipated and for the sake of that land I was able to continue debating for hours on end.

In the afternoon I attended a celebration of the founding of the United Nations, and later went on to another late social function. A black singer caught my attention with her striking beauty, her bewitching eyes, and her height. I listened to her sing and then asked her to dance with me. I was the only one to dance with her. I had a wonderful evening and forgot the struggle of the day, which had started at seven in the morning with President Carter.

Stalemate

At Blair House on October 25 I met the Israeli oil minister, Yitzhak Moda'i, who had come to Washington for the negotiations on Israel's return of the Sinai oil wells. The Israelis were demanding that Egypt guarantee a continuing flow of oil from these fields to Israel. Moda'i struck me as a man without the slightest sense of humility. He let me know of his studies at a British university, which apparently led him to conclude that he was a scientist and a great intellect. He seemed to regard everyone around him, even his Israeli colleagues, as pathetically ignorant or stupid. I was not convinced that he knew what he was talking about.

Years ago in 1956 I had heard from a friend, Pérez Guerrero, Venezuela's minister of finance, about the idea of creating an organization of petroleum-exporting countries (which was later to become OPEC). Before the 1973 war with Israel I had published an article in *Al-Ahram* mentioning the potential for using oil as a means of massive retaliation against those who opposed the Arab policy toward Israel. Oil, I felt, could become the Arabs' "nuclear weapon," and by decreasing production gradually we could pursue a strategy of "flexible response." My article was widely read, and when the 1973 war resulted in an Arab oil embargo, I was regarded as the mastermind behind it, although this was not true.

Moda'i's personality so irritated me that I decided to study the oil file, a task I could otherwise have left to another member of our delegation. For hours I studied the file in my room. I sent out for dinner and ate alone in my room among the papers and documents. The file was complicated. Kamal Hasan Ali had overseen this side of the negotiations, and presumably understood its secrets. The legal aspects of the problem were important and fascinating. I divided the issue into five parts:

1. Israel's surrender of the Sinai oil wells to Egypt.
2. Israel's demand that the treaty contain stipulations regarding Sinai oil.
3. Israel's demand that Neptune, a company American in name but in fact Israeli, continue to explore and drill for oil in the area of Alma in South Sinai. Israel's claim was based on its preparation of more than three hundred geological surveys of the area. Should another company take its place, Israel said, oil production would decline, resulting in the loss of millions of dollars to Egypt.
4. Israel's insistence on a written undertaking by Egypt that it would export a specified annual allotment of oil to Israel as part of the new relationship between the two countries.
5. Finally, Israel's implied threat to link withdrawal from the Sinai oil wells to Egypt's agreement to these oil demands.

Experts had told me that if the price of oil fell, as it was likely to do, Egypt would need Israel as a buyer more than Israel now needed Egypt as a supplier. The short distance between Egyptian oil fields and Israeli refineries made it a natural relationship. It made sense for Egypt to want a guaranteed agreement with Israel, the experts said. It would help tie the two societies together in lasting normalization.

I disagreed and argued against some of Israel's demands. Egypt had already awarded oil-exploration rights in that area to Amoco. Any decline in production resulting from Neptune's departure was Egypt's problem and was, in any case, exaggerated by Israel. Egypt itself would consume almost all Egyptian oil, and it was the Egyptian government's duty to sell the rest for the highest price on the international market. We could not guarantee that Israel would get an annual fixed amount. And, finally, the exploitation of Egyptian oil in Sinai was a matter of Egyptian sovereignty over its own natural resources; we could not accept restrictions on this sovereignty, particularly in a treaty of peace.

The American position was unclear, although the United States obviously wanted a negotiated solution and saw no reason why Egypt should not give Israel priority to purchase a quantity of oil at the international price.

This oil issue could become another problem blocking progress on the treaty. There were still others. Contrary to the promise President Carter believed he had received from Begin, Israel announced its decision to build new settlements on the West Bank. Carter, at the last meeting at Camp David on Sunday, September 17, thought that he had Begin's agreement to a settlement freeze until the creation of a Palestinian self-governing authority with which an Israeli-Palestinian agreement on settlements could be negotiated. On Monday a letter from Begin arrived stating that Israel would freeze settlements for three months only. Deeply upset, Carter felt betrayed. The only record of the Sunday meeting was in the notes kept by the Israeli legal adviser, which showed both Begin and Sadat speaking only in generalities. The United States was acutely embarrassed, because the State Department had sent telegrams that Sunday night to the Saudis and other Arab leaders reporting that the United States had extracted a prolonged settlements freeze from the Israelis.

On October 28 another rumor spread in the halls of "Camp Madison," as people were calling our hotel: Israel was planning to move its Foreign Ministry and cabinet headquarters to Arab Jerusalem. Having helped initiate these important negotiations, Begin now seemed determined to gain every possible advantage over Egypt, perhaps assuming that the Americans would urge us to go along rather than jeopardize the effort to sign a treaty. But how could we negotiate under such pressures?

We spent the next day, Sunday, in a country house outside Washington, where an American millionaire, a friend of Ashraf Ghorbal, had invited us. The weather was wonderful and the air was clean. We walked in the fields and enjoyed the wonderful scenery. For the moment I had been set free from Camp Madison and the increasingly gloomy negotiations. But the beautiful day soon ended and we returned to Washington and a three-hour meeting with Dayan and Weizman, to be immersed once again in Israeli manipulation and procrastination.

On Monday morning Abba Eban, Israel's former foreign minister and now on sabbatical from Princeton University, came to see me. Eban said he was convinced that the road Egypt and Israel were following had no return and the negotiations would succeed no matter what obstacles appeared on the way. Eban gave me a copy of his latest book as a gift.

In the evening, after dinner, I attended a work session in Kamal Hasan Ali's suite until after midnight. That night I did not sleep well. Despite Abba Eban's encouraging words I was deeply pessimistic.

On October 31 I learned of the election by the United Nations General Assembly of Dr. Abdallah el-Erian as judge in the International Court of Justice. Members of the Egyptian delegation warmly congratulated Abdallah, and I felt that their enthusiasm was perhaps not unrelated to the fact that Abdallah's departure for The Hague and the World Court would leave open his much coveted ambassadorship to Bern.

In the evenings, whenever possible, I had dinner alone in my room and studied the oil file.

On November 2 Kamal Hasan Ali and I met with Roy Atherton, who had just returned to Washington from New York, where he had met with Menachem Begin. Atherton's report indicated to us that the Israelis had become even more rigid. I agreed with Kamal that we had to prepare a detailed report for the political leadership in Cairo. It was clear, from a quick comparison of the three positions, that the Americans supported the Egyptian positions but within definite limits.

I gave an interview to Sana Yusuf, the *Akhbar al-Yom* correspondent in Washington, a diligent and energetic journalist. I asked her to print a statement attributed to "an official in the Egyptian delegation": "The history of the Arab nation must record these talks. Egypt was and still is the Arab country most adhering to the national issue. Its support for the rights of the Palestinian people, obvious and clear by the wars it fought one after the other with Israel, is ever more clear through Egypt's peaceful negotiations to achieve these rights."

On the morning of November 3 a telegram arrived from Cairo requesting my return to the city, with Osama al-Baz, for further consultations. We arrived in Cairo the next day badly in need of rest. As soon as I arrived I learned that President Sadat had refused to receive the delegation of foreign ministers of the Arab countries that the Baghdad Arab summit had sent to Cairo.

I went to the Pyramids rest house on Sunday to meet with President Sadat. I explained the situation to him honestly and briefly but he gave no sign of concern. I also saw that the Baghdad conference condemned Egypt, accusing it of abandoning the Palestinian cause, and refused in advance to support any agreement that Egypt might reach. The decisions also stipulated economic measures against Egypt and an Arab boycott. Some had called for the expulsion of Egypt from the Arab League, the relocation of League headquarters from Cairo, and the need to break diplomatic relations with Egypt.

I left Cairo for Washington on Wednesday, November 8. Immediately after my arrival at the Madison Hotel I met with Kamal Hasan Ali and Osama al-Baz on the issue of oil.

The following day I met with Dayan in his suite with Weizman and Ashraf Ghorbal. At the end of the four-hour meeting I felt that this was perhaps the most important work session on negotiations so far. I spoke of the importance of the confidence-building measures we were asking the Israeli government to take in order to persuade the Palestinians to join the peace process. I spoke enthusiastically of the hope for tomorrow in the framework of peace for all the peoples of the area. The two Israeli ministers listened with interest to what I was saying and did not try to interrupt. When I finished, Dayan said, "I understand the Egyptian government's position, but I cannot promise you anything. If Ben-Gurion were ruling Israel today, the situation would be different."

But, as we would soon learn, the Baghdad decisions only toughened Israel's position. Israeli policy makers thought that our isolation weakened our negotiating position, and they were right.

To celebrate Id al-Adha, the Islamic feast, the Egyptian military attaché, Abd al-Halim Abu Ghazalah, invited us to his home. It was a pleasant celebration with a familial warmth.

In the afternoon we met with the Israeli side, and I informed them officially of Cairo's opinion on the disputed issues.

1. The peace agreement must be linked to the West Bank and Gaza Strip. Withdrawal from the West Bank and Gaza must be correlated with measures for withdrawal from Sinai.
2. It is important that Israel take, unilaterally, a number of confidence-building measures in the West Bank and Gaza. They should include lifting the ban on political gatherings, releasing political detainees, and allowing some 1967 refugees' families to return.
3. Exchanged letters must set a fixed date for the beginning of Palestinian autonomy negotiations between Egypt and Israel, a fixed date for holding elections in the West Bank and Gaza, and a fixed date for the transfer of power from Israeli military rule to the Palestinians.

Dayan repeated the Israeli position. He then said, "It is important to point out to the Egyptian delegation that the Israeli government's promise to stop building new settlements in the West Bank and Gaza for three months ends soon. Therefore, I hope the Egyptian delegation is not surprised if in the coming period Israel builds new settlements." He said that he was not authorized by his government to inform us of this officially; his remarks were merely a personal evaluation, which he thought useful to convey to us.

I left the meeting feeling that negotiations had failed. Kamal Hasan Ali suggested we take a walk to calm our nerves. We walked for about an hour on the banks of a small creek, but I could not overcome my feeling that the negotiations had collapsed.

On Sunday we met with Americans for six hours. The Americans told us of Israel's new positions.

1. Israel refused to exchange letters regarding the West Bank and Gaza.
2. Israel has altered its position regarding withdrawal from Sinai in stages. It wishes to withdraw all at once.
3. The Israelis do not agree to setting a date for elections to be held in the West Bank and Gaza.

Dayan called to say he had been called back to Israel for consultations. I relayed this to Cairo and suggested I also return to Cairo for consultations. This was approved and I left Washington in the afternoon of Monday, November 13.

Drift

In the early morning I arrived in Paris, where the embassy staff told me that Vice President Hosni Mubarak would arrive in Paris early the next morning on his way to Washington with an important message from Sadat to Carter. So I postponed my departure for Cairo in order to meet with Mubarak.

I went to Orly Airport to welcome him, but at the last minute was told that the special presidential plane would land at Charles de Gaulle Airport. I hurried over there and arrived at the airport only seconds before the airplane touched down. I asked for Mubarak's guidance, but he would say only that his visit had no direct relevance to my assignment and that I should go on to Cairo. In his press conference Mubarak told reporters that his travel to Washington was aimed not at bringing new suggestions but at explaining the Egyptian point of view in a more detailed way. In the afternoon I returned to Cairo. Leia met me at the airport, along with scores of journalists whose questions I could not answer.

I resumed my work at the Foreign Ministry. Many details had piled up in my absence. I was scheduled to see Sadat on Friday evening, November 17, but soon learned that the appointment would have to be postponed. I heard from a radio newscast that Weizman had also left Washington and returned to Tel Aviv. Only Kamal Hasan Ali remained in Washington, and he, too, would return soon, Dayan having arrogantly told Egypt "to take the agreement or leave it."

On Monday I met with the assistant ministers and heads of department in the Foreign Ministry to describe the negotiations. They felt left out of the peace process and their mood was one of indifference and distrust.

On Thursday, the twenty-third, Mubarak called a meeting in Al-Tahirah Palace to discuss what we should do, now that negotiations had apparently ceased. Dr. Khalil and I were joined by Kamal Hasan Ali and Osama al-Baz, who arrived directly from Cairo International Airport after leaving Washington the night before.

The next day *Al-Ahram* published the full text of the draft treaty, as the Israeli press had done two days earlier. Publication made further negotiations almost impossible.

We had moved from negotiating to media attack and counter-attack.

That day I walked in the funeral procession for the late father of Hosni Mubarak. Sadat was there, too. He seemed more distant and preoccupied than usual. I offered my condolences.

There was now a new reality. The Israelis had announced their willingness to sign the treaty "as drafted." The American side announced that it, too, agreed with the text. But the text contained Article 6, which stated that the Egypt-Israel treaty would take precedence over all of Egypt's other international agreements. This, I felt, was disastrous; it would entirely separate Egypt from its obligations to the Arab world. I had the answer to the problem, I explained to anyone who would listen: Article 51 of the United Nations Charter provided every nation with the right of self-defense, individually or collectively, and no one should complain if we mentioned this in the text. Doing so would enable Egypt to give silent preference to the Arab Collective Security Pact, signed in 1950, which was based on the right of collective self-defense provided in the Charter. Some of the Americans whispered to me that they agreed, but that I must not argue this case or try to change Article 6 because that would cause the Israelis to demand amendments of other articles, which could cause the whole effort to collapse. The United States wanted rapid progress; Israel did not want to accept provisions that Egypt considered vital. Then I had no choice but to make a tactical retreat. Egypt, I told Mustafa Khalil and Osama al-Baz, should accept the current text of the treaty in order to concentrate our energy on reaching agreement on the future of Palestine. We could not fight on two fronts and still hope to win.

I failed to convince my colleagues. Whereas they earlier had opposed my view of Article 6, I had persuaded them I was right. Now, when I saw a need to retreat, they would not agree to give up the attempt to amend some articles of the treaty. We all were in stalemate.

On December 10 Cyrus Vance arrived. He was accompanied by a huge delegation, including the group that took part in the Blair

House talks: Harold Saunders, who seldom smiled but was friendly and respected; Herbert Hansell, the legal counsel who played an important part in wording the draft treaty; Michael Sterner, who spoke Arabic with a Syrian accent; and William Quandt, the professor who had joined the National Security Council staff. Helicopters took us to Al-Qanatir al-Khayriyah to meet with Sadat. It was soon clear that the American delegation had no new ideas. Cyrus Vance had nothing to add to what he had put to us two months before in Washington. Mustafa Khalil insisted that the wording of Article 6 was unacceptable and must be amended. The Americans said that even to propose a change would stimulate the Israeli side to amend many articles. The discussion was unpleasant.

Sadat listened to Mustafa Khalil and Cyrus Vance and then addressed me: "What is your opinion, Boutros, of the wording of Article 6?" Article 6 implied restrictions on Egypt, I said, but Article 51 of the United Nations Charter would make it easy for Egypt to retain its full sovereign freedom.

Sadat laughed. "It is you, Boutros, who will have to defend this treaty before Parliament. If you think this article needs no amending, I will not oppose you."

At this point, Hasan al-Tuhami intervened, angrily shouting that if Jerusalem was not mentioned in the peace treaty, there would be no peace in the Middle East. The session dissolved in a sharp exchange between Hasan al-Tuhami and Osama al-Baz.

On the way back to Cairo, Cyrus Vance said to me, "Your friend al-Tuhami was strangely excited today." I did not reply.

In mid-January 1979 the Americans sent a delegation consisting of special envoy Roy Atherton and legal adviser Herbert Hansell to Israel and Cairo to try to resolve the dispute over Article 6. The two were joined in Cairo by Hermann Eilts. Atherton asked: what would Egypt do if a fellow Arab country was attacked by Israel? Go to its aid in accordance with its Arab obligations, or stand aside, in accordance with the Egypt-Israel treaty? The American delegation suggested we try to define aggression so as to determine who was the aggressor and who was the victim. Should there be aggression by Israel against another Arab country, Egypt would have the right to assist the Arab country under attack in accordance with the right to legitimate collective defense. Should there be aggression on the part of an Arab country against Israel, Egypt would not assist the Arab attacker, in accordance with the Egypt-Israel treaty.

I rejected this suggestion without hesitation. Egypt's Arab obligations, I said, superseded any other commitment. Egypt alone, sovereign and independent, would define aggression under the prevailing circumstances and conditions and would be free to decide who was the aggressor. Should we now start to negotiate with Israel on defining aggression, I said, it would open the door to never-ending talks aimed at nullifying Egypt's right to individual or collective self-defense under the United Nations Charter. This was unacceptable.

As I explained my point of view, I felt that Hermann Eilts shared my opinion, although he did not say so. Naturally he could not criticize a suggestion put forth enthusiastically by the head of his own delegation.

That evening I dined at the home of Dr. Zuhayr Farid. Eilts was among the guests and, taking me to a corner of the room, he whispered with apparent relief that Washington now supported my objections to Atherton's suggestion that we define aggression in order to end the disagreement about the wording of Article 6.

The Americans departed, leaving the peace process adrift once again.

CHAPTER SEVEN

❖ ❖ ❖

A Halt on the Road

The year 1978 came to a close, and the intensity of the negotiations faded as the Americans withdrew into their holidays. On the day of the Western Christmas, I accepted an invitation from Colonel Ahmad al-Hafnawi and the police officers who carried out security and guard duty during my trips. At breakfast with them at the Police Club I explained the current negotiations and answered their questions about Egyptian foreign policy.

I went to a dinner party held at Al-Tahrir (Liberation) Club, which had once been the old Muhammad Ali Club, *the* club to be seen in before 1952, in the days of King Fuad and King Farouk. The name was changed after revolutionary authorities confiscated the club and put it at the disposal of the foreign minister. The dinner honored Simone Weil, who had survived the Nazi camps in World War II and was now the French minister of health. As we talked we discovered we had been at the law faculty in Paris at the same time, although we could not remember meeting then. My colleagues teased me about the rising influence of France on Egypt, and on me, "the friend of the French."

In the evening I celebrated the end of 1978 and the new year of 1979 at the home of Amin Fakhri al-Nur. He was married to the daughter of my great-uncle Amin Pasha Ghali. The friends gathered there were far removed from the world of diplomacy. Perhaps this explained their cheerful outlook on life.

The next evening I went to the home of my friend Minister of Justice Mamduh Atiyah. There I met the singer Muhammad Abd al-Wahab and sat with him for a while. He was, in voice and personality, both the Frank Sinatra and the Enrico Caruso of the Arab world. He teased me, saying that he had watched my facial expressions and tone of voice during television interviews and had concluded that I should become an actor in the cinema when I left office.

The Shah

On Saturday, January 6, 1979, I held a press conference to mark the beginning of the new year. Beside me on the platform sat Safwat al-Sharif, head of the bureau of information, Ahmad Tawfiq Khalil, permanent secretary of the Foreign Ministry, and my new chief of staff, Ahmad Mahir al-Sayyid.

The first question came from the *New York Times* correspondent: "Why has there not been one word from Cairo about the crisis in Iran?" Israel depended on Iranian oil. Could the suspension of oil supplies to Israel affect the peace process? I said that Egypt was following events in Iran closely and with increasing concern, but we were preoccupied with our own problems. We knew that nothing could possibly endanger the shah. Like students preparing a dissertation, we thought of only one topic: removing Israel from Arab land. I pointed out that the United States had agreed to supply oil to Israel. Egypt, I said, would not provide Israel with any special privileges regarding Egyptian oil, which we would offer on the international market at the prevailing price. Although I did not say so to the reporter, I realized that Israeli demands for Egyptian oil would become more insistent as a result of the upheaval in Iran.

After a visit to Khartoum to promote Egypt-Sudan integration, I returned to Cairo on Monday, January 15, to be handed a message that President Sadat had summoned me to Aswan the following morning to receive the shah of Iran.

So I flew south again. At the Aswan airport the honor guard was standing by to receive the shah. Piloted by the shah himself, the imperial aircraft landed, followed a few seconds later by a second Iranian aircraft. A journalist whispered that the other plane was carrying the jewels and priceless artifacts with which the shah had fled his country.

The shah had a long association with Egypt. In 1939 his father had arranged for his marriage to Fawzia, the eldest sister of King Farouk—an old-style dynastic marriage, meant to create something of an alliance between Iran and Egypt, among the oldest civilizations of the world. The marriage failed; Teheran was too provincial for Fawzia, who, even at the age of seventeen, was used to the glittering society of Cairo under the monarchy. Even though the marriage fell apart, Iran (as Persia was renamed) and Egypt remained politically close. The shah had aided Sadat in the 1973 war by providing oil. And Sadat's initiative toward Israel was approved by the shah; his own secret police had long worked with the Mossad, and Iran and Israel had a common interest in keeping the Arab states geographically between them off-balance.

The imperial Iranian anthem and the national republican Egyptian anthem were played as the shah and shahbanu appeared. The shah's face revealed signs of illness and fatigue. "We are witnessing the end of the Iranian empire," Musa Sabri said to me.

The visit of the shah was a warning that fundamentalism had become a menace to the Islamic and Arab worlds. I asked Musa Sabri, "Is there a risk that the Iranian revolution can spread to Egypt?" Sabri, one of the few journalists who dared to criticize the Ikhwan (Muslim Brotherhood) in his popular daily newspaper *Al-Akhbar*, replied, "The Iranian revolution is a sickness that cannot spread to Egypt. This country is Sunni while Iran is Shia; the two countries are geographically and religiously separated by Saudi Arabia, the stronghold of Wahabism, a third force in Islam." Then he added thoughtfully, "The successive governments of Egypt have contributed in no small way to building up the Ikhwan as a political force. Farouk flirted with them in order to limit the influence of the Wafd, the only popular party in Egypt. Prime Minister Abdel Hady had the courage to destroy the Ikhwan, but Gamal Abdel Nasser made the same mistake as Farouk. He abolished all political parties after his military coup in 1952 with the exception of the Ikhwan under the pretext that they were not a political party but a religious movement. He soon discovered his error when they tried to assassinate him. Then he ordered mass arrests of the Ikhwan and again crushed the movement. President Sadat is on the point of making the same mistake in tolerating not only their reappearance but their activism."

I interrupted Musa Sabri and asked, "You see him so often and can talk freely with him. Why don't you talk to him about this very real danger?"

"Yes, this is a subject that I regularly mention to him. Jehan al-Sadat agrees with me and she insists that this danger must be averted. Sadat answers just as regularly that we overestimate their importance and that he would not hesitate to intervene with force should this become necessary."

I asked, "Do you think, now that the shah's regime has fallen, the 'Raiss' will act?"

"I don't think so," said Musa Sabri, shaking his head, "because half of the people present imagine that the shah will return to Teheran victorious, and the other half think that the Ikhwan can never take over Egypt. Sadat himself still thinks that the real danger comes from communism."

Our conversation ended when we were separated by protocol. On the tarmac President Sadat embraced the shah and kissed him. Then they rode in a limousine to the Oberoi Hotel on an island in the Nile. The shah stayed in Aswan for five days and left for Morocco.

On Sunday, February 11, I departed Cairo for Belgium. Accompanying me in the airplane were Ala' Khayrat, my chief of staff; Izz al-Din Isa, executive director for Western Europe; and a group of security officers.

We arrived in Brussels in very cold weather. I had hoped to stay in one of the Belgian capital's wonderful hotels, but Belgian security decreed that we stay in the official guesthouse.

Our ambassador to Belgium was Kamal Khalil, the brother of the prime minister, Mustafa Khalil. The difference between the brothers was like that between night and day. The prime minister was quick-witted and sharply intelligent, his brother Kamal a dandy who took life more easily. His wife was the sister of Shams al-Din al-

Wakil, my friend from the law school of Cairo University. We met again in Paris at the law faculty, where we were preparing our doctoral dissertations.

The guesthouse in Brussels was an elegant villa surrounded by a park, which reminded me of a villa, Le Prieuré, at Saint-Rémy-les-Chevreuses, thirty-seven miles from Paris, where I often stayed with my uncle and his wife. There was the same kind of furniture, French classical style, the same display of oil paintings.

Claude Cheysson, then a member of the European Commission responsible for cooperation and development with developing countries, visited me at the villa. I quickly felt a compatibility and symmetry in thinking between us. I also discovered that we had mutual friends in France and Lebanon and in other Arab countries. Cheysson, a man of broad education, was particularly aware of third-world issues.

Cheysson expressed much admiration for the bold move taken by President Sadat and said that Sadat's visit to Jerusalem was an event unmatched in history. He said he was prepared to give Egypt full assistance within the scope of the European Community's programs and their aid for economic development.

The next morning I met with Roy Jenkins, president of the European Commission, in his office in the towering building the commission occupies. The position held by Jenkins, a shrewd British politician and a tall man of few words, is the equivalent of general secretary of the European Community.

I spoke at length of the role that Europe in general, and the European community in particular, could play to reinforce the peace efforts. I also explained to him Egypt's position in the peace negotiations. But I felt that Jenkins was not very interested in reviewing matters.

After the meeting and a visit to a neighboring city and its magnificent cathedral, we returned to Brussels and headed to Ambassador Kamal Khalil's residence. There I explained to a number of Arab ambassadors the latest developments regarding the peace negotiations and Egypt's principal positions.

After a reception held by Ambassador Kamal Khalil, at which I greeted more than two hundred guests, I returned to the guest palace and went to bed without having dinner. I am convinced my sleep is easier and better when I do not take dinner. Tomorrow would be full and I needed deep sleep and rest to face it.

The King of the Belgians

The next day King Baudouin received me at his palace in a Brussels suburb. I presented him with a pharaonic figurine I had found in the office I inherited from the former foreign minister at the Foreign Ministry. I had been careful to obtain President Sadat's approval for giving that valuable ancient gift to the king of the Belgians. The king expressed his admiration for the gift and asked me to explain its history and the meaning of the hieroglyphic characters etched on it. I apologized and confessed my total ignorance, saying that I knew nothing about the statue. I thought to myself that if I had had a good executive assistant, she would have contacted the experts at the Egypt museum and secured the facts about this small statue, and I would have been able to tell the king of the importance of the gift President Sadat sent him. But work at the Foreign Ministry was often a matter of indifference and improvisation. My severe embarrassment was evident on my face, for I found the king smiling and saying tactfully, "In any case, Mr. Minister, if your information is somewhat lacking I am confident that your information on modern history is perfectly complete."

The king then listened with interest to my explanation of the situation in the Middle East. "You are lucky to work with a great man like Anwar al-Sadat," he said. At the end of the interview, King Baudouin said that he hoped that in my next visit to Brussels I would ask to see him, because he wished to continue our discussion. I thanked the king and smiled because it occurred to me that on my next visit to the Belgian capital I might not be a minister or a government official. As though he read my mind, the king said, "I welcome meeting with you on your next visit whether in your official capacity or on a personal basis."

At one of the palaces affiliated with the government, the foreign minister, Henri Simonet, held a luncheon in my honor. The Belgian minister delivered a speech of welcome. I, in turn, delivered the speech I had been preparing before leaving Cairo. I gave a historical review of relations between Egypt and Belgium. I praised Belgium for the role it played in Egypt over the period of a century. I mentioned a number of Belgian scholars and professors who played a prominent role in Egypt in the field of pharaonic archaeology, at the universities, and even in the Foreign Ministry. I paid tribute to Monsieur Jacquet, who for years until the early fifties worked as adviser to the Egyptian Foreign Ministry. He nurtured the generation of Egyptian diplomats who served in the post–World War II years, ministers like Ismail Fahmi, Muhammad Riyad, and ambassadors like Naguib Qadri and Gamal Naguib. At one time, I said, they were known as "Jacquet's boys."

I praised the contributions to Egypt of a famous Belgian engineer of the nineteenth century. I told them that the Egyptian constitution of 1923 had been copied from the Belgian constitution. When there were disagreements of constitutional interpretation between King Fuad and the Al-Wafd party, they both requested the Belgian jurist Van der Bosch to decide the matter. And it so happened that Van der Bosch's son was present at the luncheon banquet!

When my speech ended, Henri Simonet rose and, on behalf of King Baudouin, presented me with the highest Belgian decoration. Then an elderly man approached me. He said that many years ago he had known my uncles Wasif Ghali Pasha and Najib Ghali Pasha, and he praised my speech as excellent "despite two errors." The name of the Belgian archaeologist was Jacques and not Henri, and the date the Belgian engineer I had mentioned arrived in Egypt was not 1897 but 1899. I thanked the aged Belgian scholar and praised him for his accuracy.

In the afternoon I gave a lecture at the Royal Academy of International Affairs on the peace negotiations since Sadat's visit to Jerusalem. The main hall was crowded with diplomats, university professors, and journalists.

The next day, after visiting Henri Simonet at home and admiring his collection of priceless works of art, I headed to Ambassador Kamal Khalil's residence for a luncheon party to which he had invited Henri Simonet and the high officials at the Belgian Foreign Ministry.

Before departing Brussels I sent a letter to the newspaper *Le Soir* in response to an article by Menachem Begin it had published. I pointed out that the Israeli prime minister had neglected to mention the Palestinians, as if they were nonexistent.

I left Brussels in the afternoon in a fierce snowstorm. When we arrived in Geneva I found the weather was wonderful, completely different from Belgian storms.

The halt in the road had been brief. Soon we were back on the road again and proceeding at breakneck speed.

CHAPTER EIGHT

❖ ❖ ❖

Treaty!

Upon my return to Cairo on February 15, 1979, I found that I would not be going to "Camp David II." Since the Israeli delegation would include only one minister, Dayan, I was told that the prime minister, Mustafa Khalil, would be the only minister representing Egypt. The two delegations would have to be of equal rank.

I returned home and telephoned Dr. Mustafa. I gave him a brief review of my trip to Brussels and asked him, maliciously, if I would be on the delegation to Camp David. With his customary politeness, he said that the delegation had not yet been formed and that he wished to ask the president's opinion as to who should take part.

"I am Egypt's foreign minister, albeit acting, and therefore important talks dealing with the Egypt-Israel treaty cannot be held without my participation," I said. The expertise I had acquired from the Madison Hotel negotiations would be useful to Egypt, I said, and I wanted to remain involved until the treaty was signed.

I pointed out that since September, six months ago, I had been in an unnatural position. President Sadat had often implied, after

Muhammad Ibrahim Kamil's resignation, that he would name me as foreign minister. But six months had passed and officially I was still only acting foreign minister.

Mustafa Khalil said he would contact Sadat immediately, and called back within a quarter of an hour. To placate me the president agreed that I, too, should travel to the second Camp David meeting. He added that the president said he had not promised to appoint me foreign minister. I was about to reply, "Either I am lying or the president is lying," but I remained silent.

I had hoped that the Egyptian leadership would realize that I should become foreign minister and lead Egyptian diplomacy during this delicate period. But my hope was not realistic, because recognition in politics was a matter of internal balances, including religious currents. Realizing this, I blamed myself for having been unrealistic. I knew that Sadat's hesitation was partly a result of the attack on me and my family by Arab media. For me, it made no practical difference whether or not I bore the title of foreign minister. The job was the same. But I was pained by the increasingly intolerant religious current in Egypt, a sign of intellectual regression. Abbas Hilmi Pasha, khedive of Egypt, had not hesitated to appoint my grandfather Boutros Ghali foreign minister and then prime minister nearly a century ago. Half a century ago a series of Christian foreign ministers had served in the first Wafdist cabinet after the 1919 revolution. Saad Zaghlul, with the approval of King Fuad, had not hesitated to appoint my uncle Wasif Boutros-Ghali foreign minister. But today, in the fourth quarter of the twentieth century, Sadat hesitated to appoint a non-Muslim as foreign minister of Egypt.

Not more than twenty-four hours later Dr. Mustafa Khalil called me to say that the president had decided to appoint him as foreign minister in addition to his post as prime minister. He then added politely that this was just a formality with no substantive effect, because I would continue to undertake my present responsibilities and to oversee the Foreign Ministry in all aspects. He said that his mission as prime minister and foreign minister would be limited to overseeing the peace negotiations until the peace treaty was reached.

Sadat's decision hurt me deeply, though I understood the reason for it. I managed to overcome my feelings and said that I welcomed working and cooperating with Dr. Mustafa Khalil to achieve the peace treaty. There was genuine warmth and admiration between us, although we had disagreed during the negotiations over the past weeks.

I had dinner that night at the home of Dr. Magdi Wahba, a childhood friend, and a wise man who shunned power and its trappings. We discussed Dr. Khalil's appointment as foreign minister. "After the peace treaty is signed," Magdi said, "you must return to the university. There are plenty of politicians, but few good scholars."

On Monday, February 19, we left Cairo in the morning. Four of us were seated in the president's salon on the plane: Mustafa Khalil, Mustafa Kamil Murad and his wife, and myself. Mustafa Kamil Murad, with Sadat's approval, was "getting a lift" to New York. He had been my student at the Institute of Political Science, then served in the army, and later formed a right-wing, pro-free-market political party, something new in Egypt. His party was welcomed by Sadat, who wanted to move Egypt toward a multiparty system and a market economy. Mustafa Kamil Murad's presence was a subject for much merriment as we amused ourselves with jokes about his party's clout, for its membership could be counted on the fingers of two hands.

Mustafa Khalil talked candidly about my not being appointed foreign minister. Several "big names" had wanted the post, he said, and he had to take over the position to protect it from unqualified candidates. He assured me once again that I alone would be in charge of the Foreign Ministry and diplomatic affairs. He said that he would issue a ministerial decree giving me all jurisdiction and stating that he would merely oversee the treaty negotiations.

We reached London in the afternoon. At the prime minister's residence on Downing Street, James Callaghan received us and invited us to tea in the British style. The conversation revolved around extremist religious currents and the danger they posed to peace in the Middle East. I recalled my talk with Musa Sabri when the shah fled Iran. But most of my colleagues assumed that Egypt was immune to religious upheaval just as we had once believed that the shah was invulnerable.

Unlike them, I was concerned about the dangers Callaghan raised. In the time of King Farouk, I told him, religious extremists assassinated Prime Minister Ahmed Maher. Then they killed the prime minister who succeeded him, Mahmud Fahmi Nuqrashi. Farouk's government then decided to smash the Ikhwan—the Muslim Brotherhood, whose Supreme Guide, Hassan al-Banna, was murdered in February 1949. Farouk, as mentioned before, had tried to use the Ikhwan to balance the power of the Wafd, the nationalist party that Saad Zaghlul had led, but the Muslim Brotherhood became a monster. Nasser banned all political parties except the Ikhwan, hoping that the Brotherhood would support him. But then they tried to kill him. When he repressed the Brotherhood harshly, the Ikhwan went underground. Sadat made the same mistake. He opened the cell doors in the hope that the Ikhwan could serve as a counterforce to the communists. On the surface the Ikhwan sought power by constitutional means; beneath the surface the extremists used fear and violence to advance their cause and infiltrated professional groups such as pharmacists, lawyers, engineers, and doctors.

Compromise

On the flight to Washington, Mustafa Khalil and I analyzed the negotiations. I was not optimistic. Failure was more likely than success because, I said, Dayan was not really authorized to negotiate. Begin held the power. On our side too the necessary compromises exceeded the scope of Mustafa Khalil's authorization; only Sadat himself could make the important decisions. The difference was that Sadat would compromise and Begin would not.

Helicopters transported us immediately from Andrews Air Force Base to Camp David. Snow covered the fields. Camp David in the winter was so different from what it had been in September. Ashraf Ghorbal and I were assigned the small cabin that Hasan al-Tuhami had occupied last fall. I told Ashraf that al-Tuhami's ghost would haunt us in that place day and night.

At the dining cabin we found the Israelis—Moshe Dayan, Elie Rubinstein, Eliahu Ben Elissar, and Meir Rosenne. Dayan told me that he too was pessimistic, and I wondered if he meant for me to convey his message to Mustafa Khalil or to the Americans. Or was he truly exhausted and losing faith after long rounds of fruitless talks? Or was he simply a colleague expressing his feelings to another with whom he had shared hours of collaborative work? I supposed his mood had to do with the decline in his relations with his prime minister, Menachem Begin.

The complexity of the debates over words grew ever deeper. At first Mustafa Khalil tried to negotiate alone, but soon realized that this was impossible and sought out Ashraf, Osama, and me to help form a cohesive position.

In the afternoon Nabil al-Arabi, Muhammad Shakir, and Husayn Hassunah arrived from New York and Washington to visit us, all of whom later became prominent Egyptian ambassadors. They relayed to us the rumors they had heard that negotiations had not advanced at all despite Cyrus Vance's huge efforts. This was true. Jimmy Carter had planned to spend the weekend with us at Camp David, but changed his mind in light of the poor progress at the table and the worsening personal relationships among the negotiators.

At a working session on Saturday, February 24, Osama al-Baz directed stinging sarcasm and derision at Bill Quandt, accusing him of being weak and afraid of the Jewish lobby. Quandt exploded. I tried to calm them, and lessen the effect of Osama's words, but a wound had been opened between them. Later I reproached Osama. "It is not good to be so aggressive," I said. Osama fired back: "*You tell me* not to be aggressive! Look at your own aggressiveness!"

It had been raining heavily nonstop since morning. We were all depressed and sullen. To show that Egypt was not pursuing a separate peace at the expense of the Palestinians, I once more approached Dayan with the idea of "Gaza first," but Dayan was dispirited. The impasse had led Vance to consider inviting Begin to Camp David to negotiate with Mustafa Khalil, but Begin would never talk to a lesser figure than Sadat. By early Sunday morning it was clear to all that the negotiations had failed completely. Dayan claimed that he did not have authorization from Begin to negotiate anything. Mustafa Khalil wanted to negotiate with Begin, but Begin would not accept Mustafa Khalil as his counterpart, although both were prime ministers. In Israel, however, the prime minister had real power; in Egypt the power is vested in the president. Khalil was humiliated by Begin's scorn and could never forgive him. But Begin's logic was correct; Anwar Sadat was the decision maker, not Mustafa Khalil. The Egyptian delegation was ordered to return immediately to Cairo.

From Camp David the next morning we were transported directly to the White House, where Jimmy Carter received Khalil and Dayan. I returned to the Madison Hotel. The next morning I went to Bethesda Naval Hospital, where I was tested and examined for over three hours. The doctor discovered a black spot on a lung and did not conceal his belief that it was the beginning of a cancerous tumor. He advised me to have another examination in two or three months at the most.

Ambassador Ashraf Ghorbal sensed my anguish. "In America," he said, "fear of cancer is a more prevalent disease than cancer itself. American doctors see cancer in everything." But his words did not help.

That evening at dinner at the home of Herbert Hansell, the legal adviser of the State Department, news came that the Israeli cabinet had refused to send Begin to Washington to negotiate if his Egyptian counterpart was merely Mustafa Khalil. Everyone present agreed that the peace process had now halted and that swift intervention was required to save it.

The next day, to take my mind off my Bethesda diagnosis, I decided to visit the National Gallery to see works by Matisse and Van Gogh, but the pleasure of the visit was ruined by my preoccupation with my health, with the intrusive presence of my security detachments, and with the failure of the negotiations.

In the evening Ashraf Ghorbal gave a dinner in my honor and invited Cyrus Vance and his wife and members of the American delegation. In a long conversation with Vance I suggested that we might get the talks moving by turning to "Gaza first." Vance listened with interest and asked me to meet with President Carter early the next morning to repeat what I had just said. I returned to the hotel and prepared my notes for the meeting, which I felt could be decisive.

I spent the morning on February 28 waiting for a telephone call from the White House, but none came, so I decided to return to Cairo. I left the hotel at noon for the airport. I was heading for New York to take a plane to Paris. In New York I spent some two hours in a locked, secure room surrounded by American security men until it was time to leave for Paris. When I arrived there, tired and disappointed, I went to the Crillon Hotel, where an old friend, Boula al-Alayli, and the French journalist Danielle Eyquiem dined with me. I ordered champagne and we drank a toast to peace, the unachieved dream.

Ashraf Ghorbal telephoned from Washington to say that he had received a message from Cairo assigning me to head the Egyptian delegation to the Arab League emergency meeting in Kuwait the following Sunday to discuss the aggression of the government of Aden against North Yemen. A second call informed me that the Kuwaiti authorities would do all in their power to ensure my safety.

Leia met me at the Cairo airport and immediately declared that I must decline the Kuwait mission, which she had heard would be hugely dangerous. Extremist Palestinian groups would try to deliver a blow to Egypt and the peace process by assassinating me. I told her not to pay attention to rumors; the Kuwaiti authorities would take all security precautions.

When I saw Prime Minister Mustafa Khalil in his office, he repeated what my wife had said, and urged me not go to Kuwait. He said that security authorities had reports of Palestinian groups planning to assassinate me as they had killed Yusuf al-Siba'i in Cyprus. I told Mustafa Khalil that Egypt could not succumb to threats or we would be ruled by rumors and terrorists and excluded from international conferences by our own fears. I convinced Mustafa Khalil that I should go, but he ordered that my security detachment be strengthened.

I arrived in Kuwait after midnight on March 3, 1979. Kuwaiti authorities had prepared an armored car, which transported me from the airport to the Hilton amid tight security.

When Sheikh Jaber al-Ahmed, the intelligent and powerful Kuwaiti foreign minister arrived at the hotel I told him that I had been instructed to respond strongly to attacks on Egypt or on President Sadat and that this could disrupt the conference, which had been called to deal with the crisis in Yemen, not with the Palestinian issue. The sheikh wanted to avoid this and suggested diplomatically that I might refrain from denouncing the Arab countries if they criticized the Camp David agreements so long as their attacks were directed toward Camp David itself and not at Egypt or President Sadat. I replied that to attack Camp David was to attack Egypt and Sadat.

I dined at a restaurant in one of Kuwait's high towers. Among the Arab leaders attending the dinner were: Mahmoud Riad, secretary-general of the League of Arab States; Saddun Hammadi, Iraq's foreign minister; Abd al-Halim Khaddam, Syria's foreign minister; Ali al-Turayki, Libya's foreign minister; and Fu'ad Boutros, Lebanon's foreign minister. A friendly and pleasant air prevailed during the dinner, and the conversations were far removed from the political confrontations within the Arab world.

The next morning when the conference began, I said to the Libyan foreign minister, teasingly and in a loud voice within earshot of all, "I fear for your political future because you are sitting between two Boutroses, Fu'ad Boutros and Boutros Ghali—a lonely Libyan between two Christians!" Everyone laughed, so al-Turayki had to laugh too, but his laughter was uneasy.

At the official luncheon party held at the princely palace I was seated between Qays al-Zawawi, the Omani minister of state for foreign affairs, and Kuwait's Prince Sheikh al-Sabah. The PLO foreign minister sat with us. Sheikh al-Sabah spoke nonstop about the food he ate and the medicines he took.

At six that evening the conference resumed, and at about nine news spread through the hall that President Carter would visit Cairo in the next few days. This news was electrifying. The delegates fiercely attacked the Camp David agreements and the American role, and continued deep into the night. I did not reply. Shortly after I returned to my hotel at about 3:30 A.M., Prince Saud al-Faisal, the Saudi foreign minister, appeared at the door to my suite. I had asked Ambassador Tahsin Bashir, Egypt's permanent representative to the League of Arab States, to be there with me.

The Saudi minister, a son of King Faisal, told me that his government would sever diplomatic relations with Egypt if Egypt signed the peace treaty with Israel. I defended Egypt's policy at length, stressing that we shared the same goal and disagreed only over how to get there. The Saudi prince listened and said nothing. The Egypt–Saudi Arabia relationship was a foundation of Middle East politics, standing against the Hashemite alliance of Jordan and Iraq both before the creation of the Arab League and during its early years. At around four in the morning I saw my Saudi visitor to the elevator door and thanked him for his visit. Tahsin Bashir and I discussed the flow of events. The timing of the announcement of Carter's visit was unfortunate. The American giant would pressure us to sign the peace treaty without delay. I had not slept more than two hours when the sun invaded every corner of my bedroom.

On March 6, on the airplane carrying me to Cairo, I found myself sitting beside Mahmoud Riad, secretary-general of the Arab League, who talked to me incessantly of the dispute between Egypt and the Arabs; it was detrimental to the Arab League and to Arab solidarity, he repeated again and again. I tried to follow his conversation but my urge to sleep was too strong.

We arrived in Cairo in a bad sandstorm. The *khamsin* winds were blowing across the airport, and we were barely able to breathe even in the VIP lounge because of the sand in the air.

When President Carter arrived at the Cairo airport a few days later I stood in the receiving line to greet him. Carter paused in front of me for a moment and said, smiling, "Back to old times again." Sadat smiled as though this gesture was a welcome sign.

We left for Alexandria on board a special train, which had belonged to King Fuad. It was designed in a kind of railroad rococo style. Every year at the start of the summer season the king had taken this train from Cairo to Alexandria, accompanied by all his cabinet members, making Alexandria for three months the second capital of Egypt. Then in September they would return by the same train, with the same ceremony, to Cairo. For generations, every member of the Egyptian oligarchy had to own a second residence in Alexandria. As a boy, I was obsessed by such social niceties and was humiliated because my family did not own a second residence in Alexandria but only rented a villa there. Every time I asked my father to buy a villa he would ask me whether I would prefer our second residence to be in Alexandria or in Europe. I would always reply, "Europe!" "Then, do you see why we have no Alexandria villa?" my father would ask. On the rococo train proceeding to Alexandria, "first class" was for the two presidents and "second class" for the ministers, experts, and aides. Crowds lined the route cheering Sadat and Carter. As the train driver slowed down at each station, the cheers would grow louder.

The talks in Alexandria seemed to go nowhere, but the prevailing opinion among the Egyptian delegation was that Sadat was prepared to compromise for the sake of a peace treaty. Would these compromises be as dangerous as I feared or as trivial as Sadat assured us they were? The peace treaty, Sadat declared, was far more important than the details we kept raising with him. Sadat followed his vision.

On March 10 Carter departed for Israel. Presidential shuttle diplomacy had begun. A few days later Carter returned, and he and Sadat met privately for an hour in the airport VIP room. A rumor spread that all differences had been resolved and that the shuttle diplomacy had succeeded. I was overwhelmed with worry and said to Ambassador Eilts, "You are pressuring the president to reach a peace treaty at the expense of Egypt's Arab obligations. The price of responding to your pressure will be paid by Egypt and President Sadat."

Explanations

Finally, on March 14, the text of the treaty was ready. We decided to publish it in the Egyptian papers and arranged for Egypt's representative missions abroad to be given an explanation of the major articles and points of the treaty via an urgent cable. Many articles were difficult to explain; side notes had to be considered an integral part of the treaty. My next days were spent in complicated explanations of the text to parliamentarians, the press, foreign ambassadors, and our own government officials.

On Thursday, March 22, I met with members of the Foreign Affairs, Arab Affairs, and National Security committees of the People's Assembly. I told them that what would be signed the following Monday was, in truth, two treaties, not one. The first treaty called for Israeli withdrawal from Sinai; the second treaty called for autonomy for Palestinians in Gaza and on the West Bank. The two treaties were linked in that the signatories were the same; the legal bases, which were the Camp David agreements and UN Security Council Resolution 242, were the same; and the guarantor in both treaties was the United States, which would be a full partner in the execution of both treaties.

Under the provisions of the second treaty, dealing with the West Bank and Gaza, Jordan and the Palestinians were to take part in the negotiations. If they did not, Egypt would negotiate in their behalf. The Palestinians could approve or refuse what Egypt's negotiators might achieve. Egypt would act like a disinterested party negotiating in the name of others without their power of attorney; whatever was agreed to would have no standing without the approval of the principal concerned.

Dr. Abdallah el-Erian, the former legal adviser who was now Egypt's judge at the International Court of Justice, declared that the contractual obligations resulting from the Egypt-Israel peace treaty were in conformity with international law. I had asked him to help me allay the deputies' suspicions of the treaty. We spent long hours answering dozens of questions touching on many aspects of the agreement.

On Saturday, March 24, the presidential aircraft took off in the morning for Washington. The date for signing the treaty had been announced and was only forty-eight hours away. During the trip I sat with Dr. Mustafa Khalil and Hasan al-Tuhami. The president sat in another suite with his wife and children, and we did not see him again during the trip except when the aircraft stopped to refuel in the Azores.

At Andrews Air Force Base a large fleet of cars awaited to transport us from the airport to the Madison Hotel. My suite was the one occupied by Moshe Dayan during the last round of negotiations.

Sunday morning I watched three different American television channels on which Begin, Dayan, and Kissinger talked, one after another, about the treaty. There were no Egyptian or Arab voices to be heard.

I had lunch with Ashraf Ghorbal and Esmat Abdel Meguid, who had come from New York to take part in the signing ceremonies and then returned with them to my suite for a long discussion, which lasted until after midnight. The treaty to be signed the next afternoon in the White House appeared to be a triumph for Egyptian diplomacy, but I felt that it would hurt us, for there was no doubt that the victory had been achieved by marginalizing the Palestinians and decreasing Egypt's leverage on the future of the West Bank and Gaza. Egypt would have peace, but the Palestinians would not have their rights.

At two that afternoon Ambassador Eilts gave us a copy of an agreement between Cyrus Vance and Moshe Dayan that included additional guarantees by the American government for Israel in case Egypt violated the peace treaty. This Israeli-American agreement stated that if the United States found there was a violation of the treaty, or even a threat of a violation, it would take steps to end or prevent such a violation. The language made it appear that only Egypt might violate the treaty, in which case the United States would give "urgent" aid to Israel.

Early in the morning of March 26 Amr Musa ran in to tell me that Dr. Mustafa Khalil had prepared a memorandum objecting to this Israel–United States agreement. Young, ambitious, and dynamic, Amr Musa went on to become foreign minister of Egypt in the 1990s. I went to see Mustafa Khalil and found him in a rage. He was determined to go to Sadat, who was at the Egyptian embassy, and tell him of the hazards of this agreement, which we had discovered only a few hours before the treaty was to be signed. The United States, he said, had given itself the role of referee in deciding when and if the peace treaty was violated, contrary to the text of the treaty, which set procedures to be followed to resolve any difference that might arise regarding implementation of the treaty. I tried to calm Dr. Mustafa Khalil. This agreement, I said, in truth is only a continuation of earlier U.S. assurances to Israel dating back to the 1973 war. I suggested we demand that the American side give us in exchange guarantees that the Palestinian phase of the treaty be carried out according to the timetable.

Cyrus Vance came to the hotel and tried to assuage Mustafa Khalil's concern by arguing that the United States was ready to give Egypt the same guarantee should Israel violate the peace treaty, and added that careful reading of the agreement with Israel, would indicate that it did not include any real commitment to Israel on America's part. Its phrases were broad and elastic; any American aid to Israel was contingent upon the approval of the Congress. In other words, it was not automatic but would require a specific American decision.

I responded by saying that Egypt could not accept such guarantees from the United States, for as a nonaligned country Egypt was barred from any security agreement with a superpower. Dr. Mustafa Khalil agreed with me. After Vance had left, Dr. Mustafa Khalil sent a memorandum to Vance stating that Egypt was deeply disappointed to discover that the United States had entered into an agreement with Israel that we considered to be directed against Egypt, one in effect that could be construed as a future alliance between the United States and Israel against Egypt, and that would have a negative effect in Egypt and provide other Arab countries additional reasons not to participate in the peace process.

When Dr. Mustafa Khalil informed President Sadat of the U.S. commitment to Israel, Sadat, as I had predicted, displayed no interest. For Sadat nothing could diminish the glamour of the ceremony that would take place in the next few hours.

We had lunch at Blair House with the leadership of the three countries and then walked across Pennsylvania Avenue to the White House. The weather was pleasant but chilly. At the signing ceremonies I sat next to Henry Kissinger, who was acting as though he were the groom at a wedding. Many years later Hermann Eilts told me that on that day Kissinger had asked him why Sadat signed this treaty. "I could have gotten him much more," Kissinger said.

When the American military band played Israel's national anthem, the Israelis sang with enthusiasm. When the American anthem was played, the Americans sang. But we were unable to sing when the music played our anthem because it was not an Egyptian tradition to do so. I was dismayed to realize, as I had when Begin, Dayan, and Kissinger appeared on television, that we Egyptians did not belong to the club; we were on the outside looking in.

The shouted slogans of Palestinians denouncing the treaty reached us from outside the White House grounds, and I was reminded again that the treaty ignored the Palestinian people, contributing a sense of bitterness that spoiled the joy of the occasion.

When I returned to the hotel, the American novelist Saul Bellow, who had requested an interview, was waiting for me. I asked him whether he had taken part in the celebration at the White House. He said that he had. I said to him, "And did you hear the shouts of Palestinians gathered in front of the White House? Those voices, I told him, dominated my thoughts throughout the ceremony. "If we have failed to resolve the Palestinian issue," I said, "the treaty signed today will have no future."

"As a Jew," Bellow replied, "I cannot agree, but as a human being, I must admit it is true."

Bellow wrote about our meeting in *Newsday*. "From Lafayette Park," he wrote, "came the amplified screams of demonstrating Palestinians and their sympathizers, kept at a distance by hundreds of riot police." As for me, Bellow wrote: "He is a diplomat whose smooth Egyptian-French surfaces easily deflected unwelcome questions. There were no unmannerly rejections, only an easy, practiced turning aside of things he didn't care to discuss. For these things he substituted certain rhetorical preparations of his own. I have done much the same on some occasions, with less style, and not in a setting of Oriental rugs and cut flowers." Bellow also summarized my long disquisition on Palestinian rights, but he was more interested in how I felt about Israelis.

He said that my view was that "Dayan is Begin's vizier, that between them there is the oriental connection of caliph and courtier-statesman. Ghali sees Weizman as the crown prince and heir-apparent who has the traditional mistrust of the vizier and invariably fires him." As for the relationship between Egypt and Israel, "Ghali," Bellow wrote, "puts cultural relations in first place. . . . The Israelis should learn Arabic, he says. He emphasizes that he does not mean the lower-class Arabic many Jews learned from their neighbors in the old days—the sort of Arabic Dayan speaks."

In my talk with Bellow I tried to express for him the depth of my anguish over Palestinian rights and my commitment to Egypt's policy, but when Bellow wrote a later article about our meeting, he said almost nothing about the substance of our talk and reported only anecdotes about me:

> Ghali speaks often of France and the French, of French intellectuals. He recommends an article by Jean-Paul Sartre on Sadat's visit to Jerusalem. His friends call him Pierre. Sadat, he tells us, calls him Pierre when he is pleased with him and, when he is displeased, addresses him as Boutros.
>
> When we leave his suite we see through the open door of an adjoining room, the Egyptian musclemen, the hulking guards, coatless, taking it easy, their leather holsters creaking as they move about. They are formidably armed.

Later, Bellow writes, he meets me again, at the grand White House party to celebrate the treaty. "I met Mr. Ghali again; he bowed with polite charm; in his black-rimmed spectacles he looked extremely Parisian, something like the late actor Sacha Guitry." How odd to read a Nobel laureate's description of oneself as a poetic, somewhat decadent figure!

At the large dinner party at the White House that night I was seated among a group of Jewish-American leaders, who were extremely happy with the peace treaty and said so at every opportunity, in sharp contrast with my own drained emotions. I left the celebration directly after dinner. My alert American security detachment hurried toward me as soon as I stood up to go and accompanied me to the armored car that the Americans insisted I use. I returned to the Madison Hotel.

On March 27 I accompanied President Sadat to the Congress for a celebration in his honor. I sat next to Ashraf Ghorbal, who told me that President Carter had sent a letter to Dr. Mustafa Khalil regarding the measures to be taken by Israel in the occupied territories in order to build Palestinian confidence in the peace process. Carter's letter was very general and included the statement that Begin had assured Carter that he would try to secure the approval of the Israeli cabinet to transfer the headquarters of Israeli military government outside the city of Gaza. But he made no mention of the West Bank, which again created suspicions in my mind.

I woke up very early the next morning to go to Bethesda Naval Hospital to have a checkup on the black spot on my lung. When the doctors assured me that the spot did not pose any danger of becoming a cancerous tumor, I returned to the Madison Hotel feeling like a new man, prepared to fight anew for the Palestinians against their Israeli opponent.

That afternoon, in a working session with the Americans, a terrible disagreement erupted between Mustafa Khalil and Cyrus Vance. Khalil had decided to publicize the two Egyptian letters objecting to the Israeli-American agreement. For the first time in my presence Vance lost his temper. His face darkened and his voice rose. He said, "Those letters are confidential documents not to be published!" Dr. Mustafa Khalil responded that as Israel had published its agreement with the Americans, surely Egypt had the right to publish its opinion of the agreement. He then left the room. Vance was furious, and as we walked to the elevator, he treated me coldly, which was most unusual for him.

On the flight back to Cairo we stopped in Germany and were received by Omar Sirri, our ambassador in Bonn. Omar whispered in my ear, "Your desperate need for rest is very obvious from your face." As soon as I arrived at the hotel, I went to my room and threw myself on the bed without even removing my clothes.

After hours of sleep I awakened in somewhat better shape. In the afternoon presidential cars took us to the guesthouse where Sadat and his family were staying, about thirty-seven miles from Cologne. There, at a negotiating session with Chancellor Helmut Schmidt, Sadat incomprehensibly attacked Turkey, saying he did not trust the Turks. The German delegation listened in wonderment, respectfully but uncomprehendingly. Sadat's views originated in Egypt's having been a vassal state of the Ottoman Empire. Egyptians had not been allowed to serve as officers in the Ottoman army. The word "Ottoman" had come to mean "non-Egyptian." Consequently, most Egyptians remained ambivalent toward the Turks, unlike Egypt's higher social classes, whose members often intermarried with Ottoman families and were pro-Turkish.

The next day I visited Cologne Cathedral, which I had first seen about a quarter of a century ago. Back at my hotel, I found security guards carrying machine guns standing at my door.

Shortly before we landed in Cairo, the president summoned me to his private suite, where photographers took pictures of our group, including Hamed al-Sayih, Ali Lutfi, and Mustafa Khalil. Sadat was cheerful and said to me teasingly, "You must get ready to meet your friend Menachem Begin next Monday in Cairo, Boutros. You will be his official escort. A minister will escort the prime minister." I was not pleased to hear this.

Autonomy

On April 1, 1979, the presidential office informed me that I was indeed to head the escort of honor for the Israeli prime minister's visit to the Pyramids and the Sphinx. I objected, arguing that my name was at the head of the extremist Palestinian black list; there was no need to antagonize them more. My real objection was that my relationship with Begin was not enthusiastic. I also did not wish to force my wife to accompany Begin's wife on the visit and to be depicted on Egyptian television as the wife of the "architect" of the peace with Israel.

The next day Begin arrived at noon. As the presidential guard band played the Israeli and Egyptian anthems, it occurred to me that the uniform of the Egyptian honor guard resembled that of German soldiers of the Nazi period. Standing next to me was the minister of tourism, Mahmud Abd al-Hafiz, who commented that the Israeli national anthem—*Hatikva*—was melancholic and deep. Everyone noticed the absence of Dr. Mustafa Khalil, who said he was ill, but in reality was still stung by Begin's refusal to negotiate with him at Camp David II. It was clear from the faces of Hosni Mubarak and Mrs. Mubarak that they too were uncomfortable to have been asked to welcome this guest. I was not the only one to feel that Israel was the winner and Egypt the loser in this treaty.

Begin stopped in front of me for a quick second and asked, "And what mood is my friend Boutros in? I shall not call him Peter anymore!"

After the welcoming ceremonies ended I returned to my office. There I found a telegram from a friend and colleague of many years, George Tu'mah, the former Syrian representative at the United Nations: "Your heading today of the escort of honour accompanying the war criminal Begin is a slap in the face of every Arab. And to assure you that Begin is a war criminal I ask you, as a man of law, to refer to the crimes and the killing of hundreds to which he himself confessed in his book *The Revolt*, English edition of 1951." The text then went on to describe Begin's role as a terrorist responsible for the bombing of the King David Hotel in 1946 that killed almost a hundred people, the April 9, 1948, massacre in the Arab village of Deir Yassin near Jerusalem, and the murder of the United Nations mediator in Palestine, Count Folke Bernadotte, in 1948.

The telegram declared that these were all war crimes and crimes against humanity, as set by the Nuremberg rules and trials, to which the perpetrator had confessed and the statute of limitations had not passed. "It makes the heart bleed and renders one embarrassed that you, Boutros-Ghali, a first-class professor and man of the law, ignore the principles of your discipline, and its morals, and your mission. Instead of being among those calling for the prosecution of

Begin as a war criminal, today you receive him as a premier. Every Arab believing in his Arabism, and particularly every Christian Arab whose grandfathers were hanged from the gallows for the great Arab revolution and who continue to provide victims in defence of the holiness of Arab rights to Palestine, whose brows have grown damp with embarrassment that you place political advantage above the eternal principles of law, that you stoop to heading the escort to receive war criminals. Neither the noble Arab people nor humanity will excuse what you have done and the reasons of your boss, Sadat. . . . I will have other encounters with you."

Had I received this telegram earlier, I would have asked without hesitation and with pride to head the escort of honor that received Menachem Begin.

That evening my wife and I attended a large party at the Qubbah Palace in honor of Begin's visit. The weather was warm and pleasant, and the palace garden looked wonderful under the spotlights artistically placed behind the flowers and trees. Amid these trees an orchestra played light music.

At the soiree the Israeli group sat to one side and the Egyptian group on the other side, as though separated by an invisible fence. I recalled Sartre's words, "*L'enfer c'est les autres.*" Mrs. Faydah Kamil, a member of Parliament and a well-known singer, saved the situation by saying in a loud voice that these were our guests and we must speak to and welcome them. Theatrically she crossed the invisible line dividing the two groups, which then began to mingle and soon neither group was "the others" any longer.

President Sadat and Menachem Begin arrived with their wives and shook hands with the guests one by one. When it was my turn, the Israeli prime minister repeated his stale joke, asking me whether he should call me Peter or Boutros that evening. This was tiresome, but it never failed to please Sadat. I was the bad boy, and my behavior provided a ready topic of conversation for the prime minister of Israel and the president of Egypt.

The two presidents and their wives sat at a long table, with Hosni Mubarak and his wife amid many small tables at which ministers and other VIPs were seated. I was seated at a table with Dr. Mahmud Dawud, minister of agriculture, and Nissim Ga'on, an Israeli multimillionaire of Sudanese origin. At the time of the Blessed Socialist

Revolution, he left Khartoum for exile in Europe, where he doubled his millions several times over. During dinner Madame Ga'on, a simple, kindly lady, spoke of her memories of Khartoum while her husband spoke about agricultural projects that he could help to carry out in Egypt. I noted that the delegation accompanying Menachem Begin was made up not of Israeli ministers but of the prime minister's friends, who appeared to have made huge financial contributions to Likud.

After dinner the Reda, Egypt's national folkloric troupe, clothed in peasant dress, danced and sang traditional songs. The Israelis applauded enthusiastically and good cheer prevailed, which I took to be a good omen. Were we seeing the beginning of the fruits of the long-sought peace? But our relations with the Arabs did not seem promising. That same day I had issued a statement through the Foreign Ministry that the decision taken in Baghdad to move the Arab League headquarters out of Cairo violated the League's Charter, was null and void, and could not be used to confront Egypt. I also announced Egypt's decision to take custody of the documents and freeze the Arab League's bank accounts in Cairo.

The next day, because of heavy early-morning traffic, I arrived late at the Qubbah Palace. As he left the salon where he had spent an hour alone with Sadat, Menachem Begin welcomed me in a loud voice and within earshot of the reporters: "Here is my friend Boutros, who is coming to Jerusalem next week to take part in the ceremonies to exchange the instruments of ratification with his colleague Moshe Dayan."

I was surprised by this news and my heart sank. From an office at the Qubbah Palace I telephoned Dr. Mustafa Khalil and said, "It seems the president has agreed in principle to completing the exchange of the instruments of ratification in Jerusalem. Should this happen, it would mean recognition by Egypt that Jerusalem is the capital of Israel. This conflicts with the stance of the entire international community. Even the United States had not recognized Jerusalem as the capital of Israel."

Mustafa Khalil immediately called Sadat and then called me to say me that he had convinced the president of our opinion. Sadat agreed to our suggestion that the exchange of documents take place either in Washington or on the Sinai Peninsula.

Begin left on Wednesday looking pleased with the welcome he had received, the parties given in his honor, and his talks with President Sadat. Once again he spoke to me as he was shaking hands with those seeing him off. He had been told that I was the one who objected to exchanging the instruments of ratification in Jerusalem. He smiled and said, "Despite your objection, I invite you to make an official visit to Israel and to the city of Jerusalem. As for where to exchange the instruments of ratification, you can decide about that with Dayan." Our option was to exchange documents on the line separating the Egyptian and Israeli forces in Sinai at the early-warning station run by American experts.

On April 9, a great debate on the peace treaty took place in the People's Assembly. Khalid Muhiy al-Din, who had been one of the "free officers"—the Junta—in Nasser's revolution of 1952, and now the leader of the Egyptian "opposition," declared emotionally that he would reject this treaty "for the sake of Egypt," a historic phrase that resonated strongly. It had been used to justify the treaty of 1936 under which Britain granted Egypt independence but only under terms that derogated Egypt's sovereignty. Then in 1951 the Wafd used the same phrase, "for the sake of Egypt," when they denounced the 1936 treaty. Khalid Muhiy al-Din said the treaty offered Egypt only a conditional withdrawal from the Sinai that would compromise Egypt's sovereignty over its lands, and that the treaty violated Egypt's Arab obligations and weakened its leading role in the Arab world. He said that the establishment of full normal relations with Israel was a huge price that Egypt would pay before Israeli withdrawal was complete, and that it would leave the Egyptian negotiator no leverage in negotiations for self-rule on the West Bank and the Gaza Strip. Further, he charged that Egypt was achieving not a comprehensive but a separate peace. He said also that the treaty would isolate Egypt in the Arab world, the Muslim world, and the nonaligned world, and it would leave the door wide open for American hegemony over Egypt and the entire region.

I replied that this was not the first time that Egypt had negotiated in behalf of fellow Arab peoples. In 1953–54, a period Mr. Khalid Muhiy al-Din knew well, Egypt negotiated for the Sudanese people and secured self-rule for Sudan, which led to the independence of Sudan as a nation with full sovereignty.

Mr. Khalid Muhiy al-Din rose to rebut me, and when he finished, I was about to refute him once more when a colleague tugged at my coat and whispered that I had said enough.

Then Ahmad Nasar, another leading member of parliament, proclaimed that the treaty signed by Egypt violated the requirements of the Arab League; Resolution 292 stipulated that no member country in the League can negotiate a separate peace or make any peace with Israel. Any country undertaking such a step would be expelled from the Arab League.

While Ahmad Nasar was speaking I recalled my lectures to students at Cairo University in which I confirmed what Ahmad Nasar said about Resolution 292. But I also recalled having taught my students the theory of *rebus sic stantibus*, that is, that continuing validity of a treaty requires that "things remain as they are." So, in international law, when circumstances change, you can rightfully ask for revision of the requirements of the earlier agreement. As I sat in the People's Assembly, I pondered this recollection for some time, and only with difficulty did I turn my full attention to the present, to the members of the People's Assembly, and to the current discussion of the peace treaty between Egypt and Israel.

The members of the People's Assembly continued to point out the many dangers of the treaty: endangering Egyptian expatriates working in the Arab countries; exposing the Egyptian economy to ruin; increasing the possibilities of armed clashes between Egypt and neighboring countries; halting Arab economic aid to Egypt; withholding Arab oil from Egypt; moving the headquarters of the Arab League from Egypt; imposing a boycott on Egypt like that imposed on Israel. Eventually the session was suspended until the next morning at eleven o'clock. When I stepped outside and looked up at the deep blue of the starry Egyptian night, I relaxed for the first time that day.

As I was driven home I thought to myself that Egypt had sacrificed enough lives and money for the Arabs and the Palestinians. The time has come for Egypt to think of itself. Sadat's commitment to "Egypt first" is justified, I thought. I was fully convinced that rejectionists, Egyptian and non-Egyptian, would sooner or later realize that Egypt was right, that the only logical path to follow was the path of dialogue and negotiation with the Israelis.

When the People's Assembly resumed its debate on the treaty on Tuesday, practically the entire Egyptian government was present. Hafiz Badawi, one of Sadat's close associates and former Speaker of the Chamber, gave an enthusiastic speech, which included all forms of rhetoric from rhymed prose to double-entendre and from poetry to metonymy. He closed by saying, "Peace is not from a position of weakness and servitude. Not from a position of humiliation and surrender. But from a position of strength and honor. If not, let us renew the cry and repeat the prayer to the entire Arab nation. Egypt is the eldest sister and shall remain the eldest sister."

The Assembly cheered. Others speaking in defense of the treaty said that the treaty contained no secret clauses, or envisioned a time "when we pray together, God willing, in Arab Jerusalem under Arab sovereignty and when we exchange ambassadors with the Arab state of Palestine, God willing." Mustafa Murad, the liberal party leader who had been with us in Washington, urged that we explain our point of view to the Soviets in the hope that they would ask the UN Security Council to approve the treaty and establish a peacekeeping force for the Sinai—something that could not be achieved without Soviet support.

Mahmud Abu Wafiyah, Sadat's brother-in-law and a provincial lawyer, suggested that we send the minutes of this People's Assembly debate to all the Arab countries. I passed a note to my neighbor: "The honorable member ignores the fact that our Arab brethren will not read!"—just as those who attacked the Camp David framework had not read that document.

Then Muhammad Hilmi Murad, another champion of the opposition who was known for his opportunism, spoke. He presented a detailed ten-point attack on the treaty designed to prove that the treaty was far from the best that Egypt could have achieved, an attack, in other words, on the competence of the Egyptian negotiators. I felt hurt, for myself and for my colleagues.

I asked for the floor to reply to Muhammad Hilmi Murad and refuted his points, one by one, for what seemed like the hundredth time.

Then Albert Barsum Salamah, a former cabinet minister, spoke in support of the treaty. He closed his speech by quoting "Egypt Talks About Itself," by Hafiz Ibrahim, one of Egypt's great poets:

"I am the jewel in the crown at the crossroads of the East
And its fragments are but curiosities in my necklace.
Should God ordain my death
The East will not raise its head after I've gone."

The session went on far into the night, dealing with such issues as the provision prohibiting anti-Israel propaganda in the Egyptian media. Was this meant to ban the verses of the Koran, such as Surah IV.46, that refer to Jews?

After endless speeches the chairman suggested closing the discussion, whereupon a huge furor erupted as members of the opposition demanded the chance to speak. But the chairman interrupted and asked the clerk to read the following: "We approve the peace treaty, signed in Washington on March 26, 1979, between the Arab Republic of Egypt and the State of Israel and its annexes and the agreement regarding the establishment of full self-rule on the West Bank of the Jordan River and in the Gaza Strip with full reservation pending ratification."

Voting on the bill was by name. There were 329 votes approving the treaty, 15 votes opposing it, and one abstention. When Dr. Mustafa Khalil thanked the Assembly, a kind of mass hysteria set in. Mrs. Faydah Kamil, the singer-parliamentarian, stood on one of the seats and began to shout, "Long live Sadat! Long live Egypt!" Assemblymen shouted after her. Then she began to sing, "My country, my country, my country, you have my love and my heart," a very patriotic song, which we all learned in school and which had become the unofficial national anthem. Assemblymen joined the singer-representative in an atmosphere charged with feeling. President Sadat soon decided that this song, to which we all knew the words, would become Egypt's real national anthem.

The next day it was decided to postpone the exchange of the instruments of ratification. Sadat felt that the approval of the treaty by the People's Assembly was not enough. He wanted a popular referendum as well to reassure Israel of Egypt's commitment to the peace treaty. It would also show the Egyptian opposition that the people favored the treaty.

I agreed with Dr. Mustafa Khalil to form a committee for the Palestinian autonomy negotiations limited to the prime minister, the minister of defense, and me. The Israeli side intended to form a committee of five or six ministers. This would be to Egypt's advantage, I felt, because a small committee can be more cohesive and effective. In addition, because of Mustafa Khalil's duties as prime minister and Kamel Hasan Ali's preoccupation with the Defense Ministry, the principal burden of conducting the negotiations would fall upon me, with the help of Osama al-Baz, with whom I had collaborated during the Madison Hotel negotiations.

On April 19, surrounded by a crowd of voters, I cast my ballot in the Gizah precinct on the treaty referendum. I mingled with the crowd and asked why they were so happy. Some said that they had lost a son in battle and now there would be no more war. Others said that now the Americans would build factories in Egypt and everyone would be able to work. And others said simply that Egypt had done enough fighting in behalf of other Arabs, who did nothing. I was happy to hear these statements. They were genuine.

But throughout April our diplomatic isolation deepened. Though we debated at length, we failed to agree on how to present Egypt's case to the Organization of the Islamic Conference, which was seeking to expel Egypt. This diplomatic isolation from brother countries of the Arab and Islamic world was bitter. Nation-states, like human beings, want to live in society and hate exclusion. For the first time I understood the loneliness felt by Israelis because of their exclusion by neighboring Arab countries.

On Saturday, April 21, at the Tahrir Club I gave a dinner for François Blanchard, an able and knowledgeable Frenchman and the director general of the International Labor Organization. I had known him ever since I was appointed to the ILO Commission of Experts years ago, when I was so young that the other members patronized me and the Russian declared that I was no older than his son.

My after-dinner speech at the Tahrir Club strongly criticized the Arab rejectionists. Later Blanchard took me aside and reproached me politely for attacking Arab countries in his presence. As an international civil servant, he said, he had to maintain strict neutrality in disputes among member states in his organization. I had embarrassed him, he said.

Ambassador Saad Afrah, the Foreign Ministry's permanent secretary, would head the Egyptian delegation to take part in the ceremonies to exchange the instruments of ratification in the Sinai. Moshe Dayan had declined to participate in the exchange because, it was said, Begin had not consulted him on the location of the event. Without Dayan, there was no need for me to attend.

Leia and I traveled to Ismailia on April 25 to receive President Ceauşescu and his wife. I had asked to head the escort of honor accompanying the Romanian guest because I felt it important to pay attention to the socialist countries in order to show that Egypt had not entirely cast its lot with the West. Ceauşescu was on his way back from Africa, accompanied by a huge delegation, in ill-made suits. He looked like an unsuccessful businessman, giving no sense of power or authority. Because Sadat would let no one deprive him of his daily solitary walk, I had to take care of Ceauşescu, whom I took to one of the rest houses of the Suez Canal Authority. Mrs. Ceauşescu was energetic to the point of nervousness, but strong-willed. Ceauşescu was constantly attentive to his wife and showed real affection for her. "Look how he pays attention to her," Leia said to me in a chiding way. They sat in the garden of the rest house, debating the names of flowers. I was called upon to tell them the Latin names for cacti, but I could not produce the answer.

Later I took Ceauşescu to the president's residence, where Sadat held a luncheon in his honor. As usual, Sadat had only tea. After lunch we talked. Ceauşescu suggested, as he had been advocating for some time, that an international conference be held to discuss the Palestinian issue. Sadat showed no interest in this. I favored the idea and felt that if it was mentioned in the Romanian-Egyptian joint communiqué, it would strengthen Egypt's bargaining position with Israel and the United States. An international conference might help us avoid international isolation, and any such conference would have to endorse, if only indirectly, the Egypt-Israel treaty of peace. If the peace treaty and the Camp David process failed, an international conference would provide us with a line of retreat. But I did not say this openly to Sadat.

While we were talking in the salon of Sadat's villa I received an urgent call from Ambassador Saad Afrah, from the early-warning station in Sinai. The Israelis were refusing to exchange the instruments of ratification because they included two documents, one relating to the Egyptian-Israeli treaty and the other to the exchange of letters on Palestinian autonomy. The Israelis said that their Parliament had approved only the peace treaty, and not the other agreement. The Israelis were also insisting once again that the expression "Judea and Samaria" be used instead of "West Bank."

I returned to the hall and whispered to Dr. Mustafa Khalil that the Sinai exchange was in difficulty because of Israeli objections. He, in turn, told Sadat, in Arabic. Sadat smiled and said, "The newspapers of the world will fill their pages with this new crisis between Egypt and Israel." Excitedly Mustafa Khalil said that all was going wrong, which seemed to displease Sadat. As though he had not noticed the interruption, Ceauşescu continued talking in Romanian with his staff about, I supposed, an international conference.

I left the room to instruct Saad Afrah not to sign unless the Israelis accepted our position. Saad Afrah called again after a quarter of an hour to say that the Israelis had agreed at the last minute to exchange the instruments. I informed President Sadat, who remained impassive and made no comment as Ceauşescu continued to talk about an international conference.

When I worked on wording the Egyptian-Romanian joint declaration, I found that Sadat was still hesitant about mentioning the international conference Ceauşescu was calling for. I convinced him that my draft simply called for studying the idea without making a commitment to it.

The next morning *Al-Ahram* reported that two terrorists had been arrested at Cairo airport. They said their mission was to blow up my office in the Egyptian Foreign Ministry. I had learned of this plot a week before from Nabawi Ismail, minister of the interior and asked him to keep the news under wraps, because I wanted to avoid familial, and particularly marital, hysteria that could make my life hell. The interior minister agreed but did not keep his promise.

I hid *Al-Ahram*, but Leia on her own discovered it. Meanwhile some friends called to tell her the story, as though to offer their condolences in advance. In a stormy scene my wife insisted that I leave the ministerial position at once. Hermann Eilts, she said, had chosen the treaty signing as an appropriate moment to become a professor at Boston University. "You will soon be sixty," she said, "and it is time to prepare for a new stage in life." I promised her that I would resign as soon as we signed a Palestinian autonomy agreement. She said fiercely, "Your mission has ended with the signing of the peace treaty. What more do you want? A live ass is better than a dead lion." She often used this saying when accusing me of being a "workaholic," but this time her tone was more vehement than usual.

That evening things calmed somewhat. Leia agreed to accompany me to Dr. Mustafa Khalil's dinner for Ezer Weizman. Mrs. Jehan Sadat was among the guests, and the host played records of classical music, which provided a pleasant background to our conversation. Jehan Sadat was cheerful, and the atmosphere was friendly and harmonious. My wife and I were the last to leave, and overheard the prime minister ask that the protocol department send him the catering bill from the Tahrir Club. I commented that this was an official gathering and the Foreign Ministry would carry the expense. But Mustafa Khalil refused. "I want rules for such issues, and my stance must be a lesson for all. Had the function taken place at the Tahrir Club, which belonged to the Foreign Ministry, it would have been official, and the ministry would have covered it. But the function had taken place in a private home, so the host would have to bear the expense whatever the circumstances or positions of the guests. Doing otherwise would open the door for "deviations," meaning corruption. I decided to apply the same rule at the Foreign Ministry.

The next morning, for reasons unknown to me, the guards had disappeared from the entrance to our apartment building. My wife was alarmed, and the atmosphere became tense. When I inquired, I was told it was Friday and they had gone to the mosque to pray. This made no sense. I tried to calm Leia, but she remained extremely angry and refused to accompany me to Kamel Hasan Ali's luncheon for Weizman. My presence at these parties would antagonize extremist Palestinians, she said. I told her how contradictory her positions were. Last night she went to Dr. Mustafa Khalil's dinner, but today she refused to attend Kamel Hasan Ali's luncheon, although both were in honor of Weizman. She responded that the guards were at our door yesterday but were not there today. I could not see the logic of this.

In the afternoon I held a press conference at the Foreign Ministry attended by more than two hundred journalists, who asked about the future of diplomatic relations between Egypt and a number of

Arab countries. Trying to put the situation in the best light, I replied that Egypt's ties with those countries remained strong, and that Egypt's doors were wide open to our Arab brethren. I also pointed to the presence of two million Egyptian experts and workers in Arab countries, and to the transnational lines of communication between Egyptians and other Arabs.

I had asked Egyptian television to play up a meeting on April 23 with the secretary of the Indian Foreign Ministry to show that, despite all efforts to isolate Egypt, representatives of the countries of the world were still coming to Cairo.

That year the May Day celebration was held in Saffagah, a small harbor on the Red Sea. Mustafa Khalil and I had hoped Sadat's speech that day would not antagonize other Arab states, and I had urged Musa Sabri, who was working on the speech, to make sure that this did not happen. We had been negotiating quietly with certain Arab governments on jointly owned defense plants, and we did not want our money in foreign accounts to be seized. The negotiations would go well as long as Sadat refrained from attacking other Arab leaders, which is why Mustafa Khalil and I discussed every word of the speech with Musa Sabri. When we arrived and seated ourselves, Sadat went to the podium with the draft, but he suddenly cast it aside and spoke without notes. Mustafa Khalil looked at me as though the world were coming to an end. I looked back at him in dismay. Sadat began vehemently to denounce the other leaders of the Arab world, their cowardice, betrayal, and their insignificance. As a result, the negotiations on the joint arms factories collapsed and Egypt faced the prospect of litigating for years in foreign courts.

In my office on May 3, 1979, I was surprised by a phone call from an unidentified person who claimed to be Sadat's secretary asking me to prepare a speech for Hasan al-Tuhami to deliver to the Islamic Conference in Morocco. I immediately called Mustafa Khalil to point out that I was not Hasan al-Tuhami's speechwriter. I told the prime minister that sending Hasan al-Tuhami to represent Egypt at the Islamic Conference would be catastrophic. Dr. Suffi Abu Talib, my colleague at Cairo University and the Speaker of the People's Assembly, a man with a strong grounding in Sharia law, would be a far better choice, I said. Mustafa Khalil agreed. I immediately telephoned Dr. Suffi Abu Talib and urged him to accept this special mission, but he wisely declined. I then learned that Hasan al-Tuhami had contacted a number of Foreign Ministry diplomats directly without my knowledge and asked them to become members of his delegation to Morocco. They quickly responded and raced to attend the meetings he convened to prepare for the conference.

Wherever al-Tuhami was involved, confusion reigned. No sooner had he begun to form a delegation than he declared that Egypt should not be represented at Morocco at all. He claimed to have received a promise from "his friend" King Hassan of Morocco that if Egypt refrained from attending, the king would do his best to avoid the suspension of Egypt's membership in the Islamic Conference.

I called the prime minister and told him that the conference certainly would suspend Egypt's membership if we were not represented by a strong delegation, one that knew the procedures of international conferences and could defend our point of view. I won; al-Tuhami did not go to Morocco.

Djibouti, a microstate, politically, economically, and militarily under French influence, had decided to sever relations with Egypt. France could have prevented this, and I angrily remonstrated with the French ambassador in Cairo. I recalled that at Camp David I had told the U.S. national security adviser, Zbigniew Brzezinski, that Arab countries from Djibouti on the Indian Ocean to Mauritania on the Atlantic would sever diplomatic relations with Egypt. Brzezinski had laughed, asking of what value to Egypt was the recognition of the republic of Djibouti. In fact that even Djibouti would sever diplomatic relations with us was a bitter blow to Egyptian pride. The minister of foreign affairs of Djibouti later tried to soothe me by saying that they had not severed but suspended relations. Arab pressure left them no choice, he said.

Then out of nowhere I found myself asked to help solve a family crisis. Third Secretary Kamil Khalil, the son of Ambassador Kamal Khalil, our ambassador in Brussels, had been transferred to Egypt's embassy in Kuala Lumpur in Malaysia. In addition to being the son of our posted ambassador to Belgium, this young man was the nephew of Prime Minister Mustafa Khalil. His wife was the daughter of a friend, Ambassador Samih Zayid, and his uncle on his mother's side was Dr. Shams al-Din al-Wakil, Egypt's permanent representative to UNESCO, and my classmate in Cairo University days. These family ties had made the third secretary incredibly conceited. He considered being transferred to Asia an extreme affront, an insult he could not accept. He said that he was in the process of preparing a doctoral dissertation at the University of Paris and had to remain there. He claimed that the Foreign Ministry was mistreating him because of his family connections, in order to prove that nepotism did not govern its actions, and that he could not object without using his family ties. I did not like the young diplomat's argument and refused to respond to his request. I spoke about the matter with all frankness to his uncle, Dr. Mustafa Khalil, the prime minister, who also refused to interfere in the matter. We finally decided to post Kamil Khalil neither to Paris nor to Kuala Lumpur, but to communist East Berlin.

On Monday, May 7, Egypt's membership in the Organization of the Islamic Congress was suspended, chiefly because Egyptian diplomats were absent, thanks to to Hasan al-Tuhami's interference. Now rejectionist countries would be encouraged to increase their efforts to expel Egypt from the Organization for African Unity and from the nonaligned movement. I simply could not understand why Sadat insisted on assigning Hasan al-Tuhami to delicate tasks. I did not at all doubt the man's patriotism and courage, but I did doubt his mental balance.

On May 10 *Gumhuriyah* printed an interview in which I tried to justify Egypt's position on the coming negotiations for Palestinian self-rule. These would be almost more important than the peace treaty negotiations had been, because they would deal with the future of the Palestinian people and their land in the face of Israel's designs on those lands. The Palestinian authority must take jurisdiction in accordance with international law. According to international law, self-rule is an interim step toward self-determination. And self-determination could result in independence.

It is an unusual irony, I said, that some of the countries that gained independence via self-rule are rejectionist today and claim that self-rule cannot lead to Palestinian independence. As an example, I mentioned Iraq, which was under British mandate, and Syria, which was under French mandate. Both went on to self-rule and then to independence. Algeria passed through a period of self-rule called "temporary administrative authority" before the referendum that led to independence. Egypt sought the same outcome for Palestine after the establishment of self-rule in the West Bank and Gaza.

Egypt did not invent the system of self-rule, I said. It is established in the United Nations Charter in Article 76, paragraph (B), which states that one of the aims of the United Nations is "to promote the political, economic, social and educational advancement of the inhabitants of the trust territories, and their progressive development towards self-government or independence as may be appropriate to the particular circumstances of each territory and its peoples and the freely expressed wishes of the peoples concerned. . . ."

On Monday we learned that Afghanistan had severed diplomatic relations with Egypt. Such news was like a slap in the face. If I made a comment to reporters, the blow would be reported on page one; if I refrained, the story would be on page three. I decided not to comment.

That night I dined at the British embassy in the former palace of the British viceroy. As I entered the old building I recalled the colonial period when the British ambassador represented political power in Egypt and interfered in all aspects of Egyptian life. At the dinner I encountered Muhammad Hasanayn Heikal, who had been the confidant and adviser of Nasser. With his encouragement, I had created a quarterly journal devoted to diplomacy called *Al Siassa al-Dowleya* (International Politics), which is still the major publication on the subject in the Arab world. I had not seen Heikal since taking my ministerial post. He was, as always, nervous, ambitious, intelligent, with vast journalistic cunning. He said to me with great agitation, "Slow down! You must put the brakes on Sadat. There is no need whatsoever to pursue normalization with Israel in such quick steps." Heikal was one of the radical Egyptian thinkers who intellectually could not accept the idea of dialogue with Israel.

On the following afternoon in my office I met a group of Jewish leaders visiting Egypt. I had become a specialist at holding discussions with these Jewish leaders from different parts of the diaspora. They would listen carefully when I spoke of the peace treaty and normalization of relations between Egypt and Israel. But when I spoke of the Palestinian people and their national rights, their faces changed and they heard nothing. Then, usually led by someone who seemed to have been assigned to synchronize the questions, members of the group would question me. Finally the leader would ask members of the group to have their pictures taken with me. Everyone would smile and display goodwill. I often wondered what good these meetings did. These Jewish leaders often seemed more eager to show their support for Israel than the Israelis themselves. Contact with Jewish groups to assure them of our intentions remained a task of Egyptian diplomacy. Sadat was convinced that there were two sources of Israel's political strength: Menachem Begin and the diaspora, especially the Jewish lobby in America. Sadat would deal with Begin; he assigned the diaspora to me.

On Friday we spent a relaxing day at the farm of Magdi Wahba in Dashur near the Pyramids south of Cairo. Returning to the countryside, where I spent most of my childhood and youth, gave me a deeper and stronger sense of belonging to this good earth. Even as my international travels and responsibilities increased, we kept our land in Kafr Ammar, about twenty miles south of Dashur. When the earthquake of 1992 destroyed our old house there, the family rushed to repair it, for it symbolized to us the links between the generations.

On Saturday I dined at Dr. Zuhayr Farid's house on the occasion of Hermann Eilts's departure from Egypt. The guest of honor spoke to me for the first time without regard for his position as the ambassador of the United States. "The Camp David agreements are a catastrophe," he declared.

"A catastrophe for whom?" I asked. "For Egypt or the Palestinians or the United States or Israel?"

Eilts replied evasively. "The answer to your question requires a long academic discussion, one that I suggest take place when we meet in the halls of a university." Eilts was telling me that I too should return to the academic life. He was a true professional diplomat. He revealed his feelings to me personally but would never do anything publicly to undercut what his president had achieved.

The next day a new crisis suddenly arose that affected the withdrawal of Israel from Al-Arish according to the timetable of the treaty. Sadat ordered me to go there at once. On May 23, 1979, I left Almazah airport on board the Mystère. Al-Arish is a city on the Mediterranean coast of Sinai that had been occupied by Israel since

1967. Meir Rosenne, legal counsel of the Israeli Foreign Ministry, was waiting for me. A helicopter took us to the center of the city, which I saw for the first time. We went to a small house, where Moshe Dayan was waiting for me, along with Yossi Ciechanover, director general of the Israeli Foreign Ministry, and Elie Rubinstein, Dayan's chief of staff. Accompanying me were Major General Muhammad Husayn Shawkat, the governor of Northern Sinai, and Ambassador Ala' Khayrat, my chief of staff.

Dayan asked that Egypt allow the residents of the Jewish settlement in the suburbs of Al-Arish to remain there for an additional period so that they could harvest the crops they had planted. According to the treaty, this settlement was to have been turned over to Egypt on Sunday, May 20, but the Israeli settlers refused to leave, which raised the possibility of clashes between them and Israeli military authorities. Dayan made this unusual request politely, saying, "This friendly Israeli request is based on the good relations between the two countries."

I had no instructions from Cairo, but it occurred to me that should I give more time to the settlers, I would establish a precedent the Israelis would use to delay the withdrawal from other points in Sinai. Therefore I promptly said that I was sorry not to be able to grant his request. We then agreed to consider a line passing two kilometers east of Al-Arish to be the dividing line between Israeli and Egyptian forces and not to allow any Israeli presence in the city of Al-Arish after that day, May 25. It was also decided not to allow Israeli fishermen to fish off Egyptian shores.

Weizman joined us. With him was Shmuel Tamir, minister of justice. They had been at the settlement in an unsuccessful attempt to persuade its inhabitants to withdraw calmly—and to try to convince me of the importance of avoiding confrontation.

Over lunch we and the Israelis chatted cheerfully although I had turned down their major request. At the same time I was paving the way for an invitation to Moshe Dayan to visit Cairo in order to maintain balance in our relations with both Dayan and Weizman. I also announced to Israeli journalists that an Egyptian-Israeli committee made up of Foreign Ministry representatives of both countries would be formed to study the issues of normalization of relations. My aim was to establish another political balance in light of the competition I sensed between the Israeli Defense Ministry, which was in charge of normalization issues from a military standpoint, and the Israeli Foreign Ministry, which until then had played no role in the normalization process. The greater probability was that Yosef Burg, the interior minister, rather than Dayan, the foreign minister, would head the Israeli side in autonomy talks. Therefore, forming the new committee was my way of trying to help Dayan.

In the evening I returned to Cairo after a helicopter tour over Al-Arish. The Israelis had done little to improve the small city during the twelve years they had occupied it. It was as though they had always known that they would have to withdraw from it. City government was administered by two Israeli political officers of Egyptian descent who were fluent in Arabic.

I thought that if we want this city to become the capital of Northern Sinai, we should not hesitate to invest millions of pounds to make it a capital worthy of the province we fought for and sacrificed to regain.

On Friday, May 25, 1979, we left Cairo on board the presidential aircraft for the inauguration of the autonomy negotiations at Beersheba in Israel's Negev Desert. Mustafa Khalil refused to preside over the Egyptian delegation because the talks were at the ministerial level and he was the prime minister. He insisted that his counterpart was Begin. So I convinced Kamel Hasan Ali, minister of defense, to take the lead role. He was not keen to participate either, but I pointed out that as one who had fought in Egypt's wars with Israel, his presence as the leader of the delegation and as Egypt's top military figure would have symbolic importance.

In a large building at the university we sat at a table shaped like a horseshoe. Yosef Burg sat at the center with Dayan at his right and Weizman at his left.

The American delegation, headed by Cyrus Vance, included the American ambassador to Israel, Sam Lewis, and Freeman Matthews, the chargé d'affaires at the American embassy in Cairo, who was running the embassy after Eilts's departure.

After each head of delegation delivered a ceremonial speech, a reception was held. Weizman took us to an air force base where, on the runway, we saw dozens of aircraft lined up and ready, and where we met Weizman's daughter and her husband, a fighter pilot working on the base. Again, Weizman put a warm and friendly stamp on our relations with him.

I had told the media, in accordance with the treaty, that normalization between Egypt and Israel would not commence for nine months—not until Israel's withdrawal to the Ras Muhammad/Al-Arish line in the Sinai. Begin, at Ben-Gurion Airport before flying to London, strongly attacked the author of this statement, unmistakably aiming his remarks at me. Begin said that he would ask President Sadat if the agreement made between them on April 2 still stood, as Sadat had already assured him twice before, or did not stand. Begin said that he would ask the Egyptian president: "Has this agreement been voided as Dr. Boutros Ghali affirms in his statements?" He then repeated the "Boutros and Peter" story.

A new step toward normalization between Israel and Egypt took place when Hosni Mubarak, Mustafa Khalil, Cyrus Vance, and I flew from Cairo to Al-Arish. Vance wanted to see the entrance to the Suez Canal, so Mubarak asked the pilot of the Mystère to circle low over Port Said before heading due east.

We landed at Al-Arish, where we met President Sadat and received his guest, Menachem Begin. At lunch in a handsome guesthouse we celebrated the return of Al-Arish to Egypt. The Israelis expressed great surprise at the good condition of the house, as they had seen it only three days earlier in great disrepair. Hasan Kamil said that Egyptian engineers had worked forty hours straight to restore the rooms for this occasion. A meeting was arranged between Egyptian and Israeli war-wounded, some who had lost limbs in the Sinai desert. As the wheelchairs moved toward one another, the horrendous sacrifice of the past impressed upon us the importance of our work for the future. I saw the emotion shown by Sadat, who had lost his younger brother, and by Weizman, whose boy had been left mentally devastated by a horrible war injury.

Airplanes then carried us from Al-Arish to Beersheba for a celebration at the university. Just before the event was to start, I entered one of the side rooms and found Menachem Begin alone, shaving. Hoping to lighten the tension between us, I asked, "Why are you shaving twice in the same day?" He said, "Because this is just about the most important day in my life and I want to look my best. So I decided to shave again." But I would soon learn that my friendly initiative did not transform our relationship.

Sadat rose to announce his decision to open the borders between Egypt and Israel. I felt all eyes upon me. Less than forty-eight hours before, I had said that we would not open the borders between Egypt and Israel for nine months.

Seated on the presidential dais were Cyrus Vance, Hosni Mubarak, President Yizhak Navon of Israel, President Sadat, Prime Minister Begin, and Mustafa Khalil. At the end was Yigal Yadin, Israel's deputy prime minister.

The rest of us faced the dais. An Israeli distributed gaudily colored caps to protect us from the sun. I was hesitant to put on my cap, but when Major General al-Mahi, the chief of the military guard, put his on, I did the same. After a few minutes I looked around and saw everyone with red and green and blue caps on their heads. I took mine off, preferring to suffer the harsh sun rather than wear the cap. We all looked infantile.

A number of the Jewish leaders spoke, among them the millionaire Nissim Ga'on. President Navon stated that Israel had ceded Sinai—as though it had been Israel's to give. Anger appeared on Sadat's face, and he rose to answer Navon. But the tension soon lessened, and the original good feeling returned for the remainder of the celebration. The point of the festival was to convince the Israeli people that Egypt was sincere in its efforts for peace and normal relations with Israel. It was for this reason that Begin considered the occasion so important; he had brought the greatest Arab state to peace with Israel.

The next day I returned to the Foreign Ministry to struggle with the problem of Israeli settlements in the occupied Arab territories. I asked Dr. Hafiz Ghanim, the deputy prime minister in 1977, when I was appointed to the cabinet, and now president of the Egyptian Society of International Law, to meet with the investigative committee of the United Nations. I wanted the UN to know that our concern about Israeli settlements was not limited to the government alone, but was shared in academic and other sectors as well. The Geneva agreement signed in 1949 stipulated the impermissibility of altering the character of occupied lands. Therefore, settlements were illegal under that document. Carter said that at Camp David he had gained a written commitment from Israel to cease settlement expansion during negotiations, but Begin disputed this claim, and the topic has since been enveloped in confusion and bitterness.

After the election of Dr. Abdallah el-Erian as judge of the World Court, his seat on the UN Commission on International Law became vacant. As a scholar of international law, I decided to apply for the seat. But then I learned of a campaign by Arab countries to ensure that I would fail in my bid. This was part of the Arab campaign to isolate Egypt; they wanted to bar any Egyptian role in international organizations. I had discussed with Mustafa Khalil my anxiety that the maneuvers of Arab rejectionists in the corridors of the commission of international law in Geneva might destroy my candidacy. I told the prime minister that if those Arab states succeeded, it would be a blow to Egypt, as I represented the Egyptian government. I said that I was ready to withdraw before the elections if he thought it best. Mustafa Khalil did not agree with me. If I succeeded in gaining membership in the International Law Commission, it would represent an Egyptian diplomatic victory; if I failed in my candidacy, then the media would not make much of it. He urged me not to withdraw.

Mustafa Khalil was right. My election came through at the end of May 1979, just when Egypt was in need of a sign that attempts to isolate it would not succeed.

On May 31 I met with the former undersecretary of the Arab League Muhammad Riyad and with Ambassador Tahsin Bashir to discuss the implications of the Arab League's decision to move its headquarters from Cairo to Tunis. I felt strongly that the Arab League should continue its work in Cairo and that we should try to persuade such states as Sudan, Oman, and Somalia to support us. My idea was that the Arab League should continue in Cairo, with a membership of four states, while the sixteen rejectionist states established their own league in Tunis. Egypt should declare the new league to be a separate and different organization; this policy would enable Egypt to retain Arab League documents and funds in Cairo and would make it easier for the Tunis rejectionists to return to Cairo in the future. I persuaded Muhammad Riyad to take the position of acting secretary-general of the Arab League until matters were clarified. After all, there were once two popes, one in Rome and one in Avignon.

Later that day I gave an interview to the Cairo correspondent of *Le Monde*. Among his questions was one about my cousin Ibrahim Amin Ghali, who had been expelled from the Foreign Ministry by Nasser because of his diplomatic service to the regime of King Farouk. This cousin had consoled himself by becoming a writer on history and politics, and had just published in Paris an anti–peace treaty book, *Israel, ou, la paix rebelle* (The Rebellious Peace). My cousin's objections to the peace agreement were much less serious than those of prominent members of the Egyptian opposition. I explained to the reporter how the opposition within my own family only proved that Egyptians lived in a democratic atmosphere. I shared an excellent friendship with my cousin, as with other friends who believed that I had made a great mistake.

At the airport on Monday, June 4, 1979, I met Moshe Dayan, who arrived with his wife aboard a private airplane. After newsmen took dozens of pictures, a helicopter transported us directly to Ismailia for a meeting with Sadat.

Sadat continued to feel ill at ease with Dayan, whom he found personally unpleasant. I told Sadat that the signing of agreements was not as important as their execution. Dayan wanted a prominent role in normalizing relations, and we should give him the opportunity to do so. Dayan was the most flexible Israeli leader with regard to the Palestinian question. He was utterly free of the religious rigidity that seemed to characterize so many in the leadership of the Likud. Indeed, Dayan did not hide from me his indifference to religion. He said that his office director, Elie Rubinstein, respected religious traditions in every detail, but all that Dayan required of him was that his religious practices not affect his work.

I explained all this to Sadat to try once again to persuade him to work with Dayan. I considered Sadat's agreement that Dayan could come to Ismailia to meet with him to be an immense success for me.

But as soon as he arrived at Cairo airport, Dayan declared to the press that Israeli settlements in the occupied territories were legitimate and Israel would not stop building them. Had Sadat heard this, he would have canceled the meeting with Dayan at once. I replied immediately to Dayan that I totally disagreed with him on the subject of settlements.

As we headed toward Ismailia, I felt that the meeting between Sadat and Dayan might lead to trouble, and regretted my attempt to bring about a rapprochement between the two men. I told Dayan that if he began the meeting by asking Sadat what had inspired him to go to Jerusalem, the chemistry between them might improve. Dayan stared straight ahead as though he had heard nothing, and I feared that I had only made things worse.

Throughout the helicopter ride, Dayan stared down at the desert and the agricultural lands below. As we approached Ismailia, I said to him, "Are you thinking of establishing settlements down there?" He did not reply, and I felt that the atmosphere between us had reached the freezing point. I said to myself that if Weizman were here with me today, he would have received my question in a jovial spirit and would have criticized his government's policy.

At Ismailia a car took us to the president's villa overlooking the Suez Canal. We waited about twenty minutes for Sadat to finish talking to another visitor. I worried that if we sat there any longer, Dayan would feel that Sadat was purposely humiliating him. But then Sadat's private secretary, Fawzi Abd al-Hafiz, came to say that the president was awaiting us. Sadat was with Hosni Mubarak. He greeted Dayan cordially and asked if he knew the Ismailia area. Dayan laughed, saying that he knew it very well, "but from the eastern bank of the canal." I said to myself that if he talked about the war, we were heading for trouble.

Dayan spoke again. "I have a question, Mr. President, that I have been wanting to ask you for a long time. It is a historical question: I want to know when it was exactly that you got the idea for your visit to Jerusalem and your historic initiative."

Sadat smiled broadly and warmly told Dayan that the idea of going to Jerusalem first came to him when he was flying to visit the shah. As his plane was flying over Turkey he was wondering how he could produce "shock waves" to get the peace process moving in a positive way. First he thought about asking the "big five" UN Security Council members—the Americans, Soviets, Chinese, French, and British—to go to Jerusalem. After Tehran, Sadat said, he flew on to Saudi Arabia. Then, on his return flight to Cairo, it suddenly came to him. He would go to Jerusalem himself! Later the Saudis were angry with Sadat for not telling them of his plan, but the idea had not occurred to him until he had left Riyadh for Cairo.

Why did Sadat decide to go? Dayan asked. Sadat said it was because the Israelis had been using as an excuse for their own inertia the fact that the Arabs would not negotiate with them directly; so Sadat decided to call their bluff.

Dayan was crestfallen. The story had been going around that Dayan's secret meetings in Rabat in September 1977, which were arranged by King Hassan, had been the origin of Sadat's trip. Since an Arab-Israeli meeting was publicly impossible, Dayan had gone to Rabat in disguise. "No," Sadat said, "I sent Tuhami there to meet you for another reason, to assure Israel that Egypt would try to prevent the Geneva Conference—which both the United States and the Soviet Union then wanted to reconvene—from failing." Dayan was not pleased to hear Sadat discuss so lightly an event that Dayan preferred to regard as history-making.

Then Dayan, as if to establish that he too was a visionary statesman, said that before 1973 he had been promoting the withdrawal of Israeli forces from the Bar Lev Line in order to allow Egypt to open the Suez Canal to international shipping. But the Israeli cabinet neither understood nor accepted the idea, he said. "This would have been a *chef d'oeuvre*," Sadat replied, looking toward me, as if to be sure I had noticed his French. This amused Dayan. At the end, Sadat was shaking Dayan's hand and bidding him a warm farewell. The meeting did not conclude with an exchange of kisses, but at least a new mood had been created.

On the return to Cairo airport Ahmad al-Hifnawi told me that by now sixty-six security officials were charged with Dayan's safety.

That afternoon I met alone with Dayan at the Foreign Ministry and told him frankly that the number of Israelis visiting Egypt during the first stage must be very limited. The door should not be wide open to travel to Egypt until we were certain of the reaction of the Egyptian people. The more Israelis visiting Egypt, the harder it would be to protect them. If an Egyptian extremist should kill one of them, it would constitute a serious blow to the peace. I admitted that my fears might be more pessimistic than necessary, but the interests of Egypt and Israel demanded the fullest precautions. Dayan and I agreed to limit visits during the initial stage of normalization to journalists, scholars, and writers. We also agreed to limit entry to Cairo International Airport and the port of Alexandria. Arrival overland via Al-Arish or Port Said would not be permitted until normalization of relations between the two states was completed.

After the talks I announced to the press that we had agreed to establish a direct telephone line between the Egyptian and Israeli foreign ministries like the direct line between the two ministries of defense, a step that reflected Dayan's constant rivalry with Weizman, the minister of defense. If the minister of defense had a direct line to Cairo, then why should not the foreign minister have one too? The phone was installed, but it never worked. When it made a strange noise, I picked it up, but no one would answer my greeting. Still, the sight of the telephone pleased me; it symbolized Egypt-Israel relations.

In the evening Leia and I held a dinner party for Dayan and his wife. From the balcony of our home overlooking the Nile, the Israeli visitors enjoyed the reflections of Cairo's lights on the river. Our steward Abudah, who was in charge of the dinner, had been drafted in 1973 and took part in the October War. He mentioned his story to Dayan in a warm and spontaneous way. Dayan responded without warmth—I felt that Dayan was not unfriendly but shy.

Dayan spoke of pharaonic Egypt, of Ramses II, and of the Egypt of the Ptolemies. Mustafa Khalil spoke about economic conditions in Egypt, which seemed to be of great interest to Dayan.

On the next day, Tuesday, June 5, Dayan traveled to Luxor to visit the ruins and monuments. I stayed in Cairo to meet with the American delegation that would take part in the autonomy talks the following Monday in Alexandria. Leading the American delegation was Ambassador James Leonard, a quiet, serious diplomat who spoke slowly and calmly. He had mastered the substance of the negotiations. I felt that he was not pleased with his instructions, but as a good diplomat he never revealed his own opinion. Much later, when he was a member of a committee of experts on disarmament, I met him in Geneva. He commented to me that the American delegation was in no position to exert any real pressure on Israel.

That evening I held another dinner party in honor of Dayan at the Tahrir Club. The Israeli minister had returned from Luxor amazed by what he had seen of the grandeur of the Egyptian empire, and spoke at great length, with emotion and zeal, about ancient Egyptian civilization. When I saw Dayan off at Cairo airport, he seemed to have a profoundly more respectful attitude toward Egypt than before.

On the day that Dayan left Cairo, Yosef Burg, the chief Israeli negotiator, arrived. Burg was a rotund, cerebral, theological politician. He headed the National Religious Party, on which Likud's government depended, and he was a permanent fixture in one Israeli cabinet after another. Of German origin, he was famous for reading the news in Yiddish on Radio Israel. We met for two hours in my office, where Burg held forth on philosophical and conceptual topics, far removed from politics and diplomacy. He told me of his studies at the University of Leipzig, and of how he had propounded the philosophy of Immanuel Kant in his oral examination. During our conversation I said that I had read the Jewish philosopher Martin Buber, who had advocated a binational Palestinian-Israeli state. Burg said that Buber had been his friend and mentor. So I asked the Israeli minister, "Why don't you adopt the ideas of your friend, one of the great philosophers of the twentieth century?" Burg replied with irony, "I became a politician and gave up philosophy years ago."

When Mustafa Khalil and I met with Burg the next morning in the Prime Ministry, Burg suddenly stopped speaking, his face darkened and then turned as yellow as a lemon. He placed his hand on his heart and complained of severe pains. In a faint voice he said that his heartbeat had increased frighteningly. He wanted us to bring him a glass of sparkling water. Khalil looked at me with anxiety and whispered, "It looks like the man is having a heart attack. Get him out of my office. If he were to die here with us, without any witness, they might accuse us of doing him in."

Mustafa Khalil rang the bell with extreme agitation and said to the office boy, "Bring a glass of soda immediately!" The boy returned after some minutes to declare that there was no soda water in the Ministry. Khalil's anger and agitation were evident. The boy grasped the situation and proposed a glass of 7UP. "Bring it immediately!" said the prime minister. Burg was holding his lips, sitting motionless and breathing with difficulty. His eyes were shut, his right hand on his heart; it appeared that he was about to die. Khalil was observing him with heightening anxiety. The office boy returned moments later with a glass of 7UP. Burg took two or three mouthfuls of it. Signs of relief began to appear on his face. It was a magic potion! Mustafa Khalil advised the Israeli minister to return to his hotel room immediately and rest. Burg departed and Khalil relaxed in relief. The prime minister asked me to have a heart specialist go to the hotel at once to check on Burg.

I returned to my office in the Foreign Ministry, where I became so preoccupied with various tasks and problems that I forgot Burg's health problems until the telephone rang. The prime minister was on the line, inquiring about the doctor I was to have sent to Burg. When I confessed to him that I had not called a doctor, he grew angry and demanded that I speedily contact the officials of the Sheraton Hotel, where Burg was staying. After much difficulty I succeeded in reaching the hotel and learned that the Israeli guest had left a half hour earlier. I asked if anyone in the hotel knew where he had gone. I imagined that his condition had worsened and that he had been taken to the hospital. The hotel clerk told me that the Israeli minister had gone to visit the Pyramids and the Sphinx. I telephoned Mustafa Khalil immediately to inform him of this happy news.

I waited until two in the afternoon, then headed for the Sheraton Hotel, where I knocked on the door of Dr. Burg's suite. He opened the door himself, in the best of health, and spoke of his happiness at visiting the Pyramids. I asked him about his seizure in the morning and if he had consulted a doctor. "I don't need a doctor to diagnose me," Burg said. "I ate too much fish for breakfast." I knew that the minister's kosher requirements came to him specially by airplane from Holland on instructions from our Foreign Office. Burg had eaten too much Dutch fish.

Burg said, "In Torah there is the story of the fish that swallowed Jonah. As for me, I swallowed the fish, and could not wait to get rid of it, as the fish of the Torah got rid of Jonah. After I did so, and after the waters returned to their courses, I decided to visit the Pyramids of Gizah."

Although Burg was the leader of the Israeli team negotiating self-rule for the Palestinians of the West Bank and Gaza, it was clear that he knew nothing about the Palestinians. He talked as if they did not exist in the West Bank, Gaza, and Jerusalem, which his government had been occupying for twelve years. Burg, who escaped Nazi persecution and arrived in the Arab world without knowing a thing about the Arabs or the Middle East, continued to know nothing about them after his many years in the region.

With Burg, I raised, for the fourth time, the subject of Deir es Sultan, a small Coptic chapel in the Church of the Holy Sepulchre. I asserted to Burg, as I had asserted previously to Dayan, that the return of Deir es Sultan to the Egyptian Church would help normalization greatly. Burg, as Israeli minister of the interior, had jurisdiction over this matter and promised to investigate ways of finding a quick solution, as had the other ministers with whom I had raised the issue. To this day the problem has not been solved.

When I met with Dayan in Al-Arish, I had told him that the only hotel in Alexandria with facilities for the "autonomy talks" was the Palestine in the Al Montazah suburb. Dayan assured me that this presented no problem and that he was not concerned with hotels and their accommodations. A few days later, however, I received an urgent letter from Burg. It was impossible, he said, to hold negotiations on self-rule in a hotel named Palestine. That would provoke Israeli public opinion. He demanded that we find another place.

I contacted the minister of tourism immediately and asked him to renovate some rooms and salons of the old five-star Hotel San Stefano and to install air-conditioning in the rooms to be used by the Americans and Israelis.

But the Hotel San Stefano did not have a large round table to accommodate the talks. The hotel ordered a carpenter to build a table of the required specifications, he said it would take at least two weeks. One of the junior diplomats working in the protocol office mentioned the table around which we used to eat lunch at the Tahrir Club in Cairo. Then it became simply a problem of transporting this table to the Hotel San Stefano in Alexandria.

Before leaving Cairo, Burg asked if I had found a solution to the Palestine problem—his jocular way of referring to the hotel problem. I informed him that the meeting would be held in the Hotel San Stefano. This inspired Burg to mention the agreement of 1878 between Russia and Turkey in the city of San Stefano, pointing out, as he sought to do ever since we had discussed the philosopher Buber, that Burg had studied history while I was studying philosophy.

On Sunday, June 10, the Israeli leadership arrived, one Israeli minister after another. Yigal Yadin, the deputy prime minister, and I talked for two hours in my office, where I went over my concerns about the talks, particularly that the Israelis face up to the Palestinian dimension of the process. Yadin was a scholar of archaeology, a university professor. At a time when the interpretation of the Dead Sea Scrolls was being kept secret by a monopoly of scholars, Yigal Yadin had located in a shop in Bethlehem the "Temple Scroll," the longest of the finds, and had written a three-volume work on it, which he published only a year before our meeting. He was a first-class academic, but a third-class politician, too subdued to fight for his views or even to defend them. I felt from my first meeting with him, in November 1977, a sense of harmony and mutual understanding between us, but I had concluded there was no use trying to draw political advantage from our relationship. Yadin reminded me of one of Gamal Abdel Nasser's senior ministers, of whom it was said years ago that "like a Swiss watch, he never runs fast and he never runs slow." Yadin could not be moved out of his own special rhythm. He had told me more than once that he opposed the policy of establishing settlements in the West Bank, but he would do nothing to support his conviction.

General Kamal Hasan Ali and I flew from Cairo to Gianaklis airport to meet the final Israeli contingent to arrive, which included Burg, Weizman, Tamir, Dayan, Sharon, and Nissim Ga'on. Then we left by helicopter to Al-Nuzhah airport in Alexandria, where cars were waiting to take us in a long convoy to the Hotel San Stefano. The negotiations began around the round table from the Tahrir Club, which had arrived from Cairo a few hours before.

Dr. Mustafa Khalil, Dr. Burg, and Ambassador James Leonard spoke in turn. The Egyptian complained about Israeli actions. The Israeli spoke only of documents we had signed, and the American said that the time had come to negotiate in earnest behind closed doors.

After this ceremonial session, I went to the Hotel Palestine, where the Egyptian delegation was staying, and had lunch in my room. Back at the San Stefano, the Egyptian and Israeli delegations argued over how to define the presence of the United States of America. Is the United States a party or just an observer? As the argument revolved around their role in the talks, the Americans said nothing. Behind this argument was a deep difference of opinion: Egypt wanted to give the negotiations an international dimension, to reflect an eventual comprehensive outcome. The Israelis wanted them to appear as two-party talks emerging from a separate peace between Egypt and Israel. In the evening the Egyptian delegation held a dinner for the delegates in the yacht club that overlooked Alexandria harbor, and Mustafa Khalil telephoned from the club to Sadat, who was in the United States, to tell him that nothing had been achieved in the talks and that another intervention by Carter was essential.

The third meeting, held on the morning of Tuesday, June 12, produced only a statement for the press and an agreement to meet again. Ambassador Leonard, apparently hoping to please the Egyptian side, told the press that the parties had accepted the United States as a full partner in the negotiations, a statement that transcended exaggeration and approached the realm of diplomatic lie. All that honestly could be said was that the negotiations had been largely wasted in sophisticated discussions of the American role.

A reporter asked me whether the Palestinians would participate in the next round, and about Egypt's contacts with the Palestinians. I said that we had indirect contacts with the Palestinian leadership and that I preferred not to go into further detail. The truth was that we had been unable to preserve a channel of communication to the Palestinian leadership. What contacts we made were limited to non-influential Palestinians in the West Bank and Gaza.

After the press conference I rode to the airport with Yosef Burg, who taunted me, saying, "The conference has succeeded. There is no reason for you to continue to be sharp-tongued. A person can achieve more with calm and leniency than with violence and excitement." From Al-Nuzhah airport, we flew to Gianaklis airport, where the Israeli delegation boarded its flight to Tel Aviv, and the Mystère took us to Cairo. I arrived home in Gizah completely drained.

I felt that these negotiations were leading nowhere. Why, then, were we negotiating? Why were the Israelis negotiating? Had they formed such a formidable delegation consisting of five ministers simply to impress the public and please their American partner, while in fact Israel could enfold, swallow, and digest the West Bank and Gaza?

As for the American position, there were several questions. The American delegation was anemic and without authority. Was the American envoy silent because the head of delegation, Robert Strauss, the personal representative of President Carter, was absent? Or was the deputy following his government's instructions? Was Washington's goal merely to gain time and disguise the weakness of Carter's administration?

Despite these doubts I remained convinced that if the negotiations showed positive results, the Palestinians would agree to participate, and the moderate Arab states would seek a rapprochement with Egypt.

I arrived on the morning of June 13 in Geneva for my first meeting with the International Law Commission of the United Nations. When I first entered the university life, membership in this commission was a dream that I felt scarcely to be attainable. To me it was the summit of intellectual glory for an expert in international law. But after being elected to the commission and sitting through its meeting, I was not as joyous as I had imagined I would be. I spent hours in my hotel room studying the reports of the commission, which consisted of hundreds and hundreds of pages. But I found that I had lost the ability to comprehend scholarly research. Bad money drives out good money, and diplomatic work had driven out the academic and scholarly currency of my life. I took part in the first session of the commission meeting, but the high level of the discussions prevented my sharing in the exchanges. I had lunch with Saad Hamzah, who had presented his credentials as Egyptian ambassador to the president of the Swiss Confederation just two days before. He urged me to undertake an official visit to the Swiss capital, Bern. He whispered that it would be best if I had good relations with the Swiss leadership, because soon I might need to ask them to give me political asylum in Switzerland! "The future of a political figure in our part of the world is highly uncertain," Saad Hamzah said to me. "Between exile and prison, exile in Switzerland is much to be preferred."

On June 17 I traveled from Geneva to Rome, where I stayed in a part of the Grand Hotel that had not yet been renovated. My suite in Rome reminded me of the apartment I had rented in Alexandria in the summer of 1941, when I was involved in a great love affair with a beautiful Cairene. We planned to marry. Henri Matisse had insisted upon drawing her, and in each of his spare yet swiftly curving delineations of her face the same distinctive expression came through, though each work was unique. In 1948 we published our wedding banns in Paris, where she was studying, but our engagement was broken. We were too young to assume the responsibilities that married life entailed. I still cherish Matisse's drawings.

Pope John Paul II received me in his library on Monday, June 18. It was my first meeting with His Holiness, and I was struck by his attractive personality, extreme intelligence, and quick wit. He spoke in French with a Polish accent. We discussed Palestinian self-rule. He said with a smile that he knew well "the mentality of the Jewish leaders that you are negotiating with, because most of the Israeli negotiators have their origins in my homeland," meaning of course that Poland was where Begin, among other Israeli leaders, was from. Then he added, after a moment of silence, "Cooperation with them is not easy, but you must continue to negotiate with them."

I spoke in detail about Jerusalem and referred to the importance of the role of the Vatican in defending the Holy City in the face of Israeli claims. But he did not pursue this suggestion. He just listened without comment.

This was not the case with the "prime minister" of the Vatican, Cardinal Casaroli, and Cardinal Achille Silvestrini, the foreign minister, with whom I discussed the possibility of internationalizing the holy places. Their attitude reminded me of the mystic Orientalist Louis Massignon, who once told me that he could never accept that "the tomb of Christ was protected by Jewish soldiers." These foreign policy leaders of the Holy See were interested in Jerusalem, in the Christians of Lebanon, and in the Palestinians—in that order. I did not mention the Coptic Christians of Egypt, nor did they, perhaps sensitive to my pride in my Egyptian nationality.

In the Rome airport I met some Coptic metropolitans who had come to take part in religious talks with men of the Catholic Church. I asked for their prayers for our safe return to Cairo.

On the airplane taking us back to Egypt, I met the journalist Durriyah 'Awni, who told me, yet again, the allegorical story that was sweeping through the Arab world about the mother with many children who suddenly leaves her home and children and her responsibilities to go off with a *khawagah* (foreigner). The children wail and rebel against their mother and accuse her of treachery and treason.

Although I had heard this story repeatedly, I listened patiently to Durriyah 'Awni tell me about the mother, who represents Egypt, and her children, the Arab states, and the *khawagah*, Israel. For a mother to leave her children to run off with an outsider was a double betrayal. But Sadat ignored this tale. He did not want Egypt to be the mother of the Arabs; he wanted a rapprochement with the West, which he believed would do more to solve Egypt's problems than continued involvement with the Arab world.

On Thursday, June 21, 1979, the ceremonies celebrating the swearing in of Dr. Mustafa Khalil's reconstituted cabinet were held at Abdin Palace.

After the swearing in, President Sadat granted the Order of the Nile to Dr. Mustafa Khalil and the Medal of the Republic, First Class, to Dr. Osama al-Baz and me in appreciation of our efforts in behalf of the peace treaty with Israel. When Mustafa Khalil spoke he could not hide his emotion. He said, "I swear to you, Mr. President, before God and myself, that I am dedicated to my homeland with you and behind you."

What should I say when my turn came? Before I could decide I found myself before the president of the Republic, who was saying to me, "I give you this medal because you have done your work with understanding and effort and in a manner unmatched, may God reward you."

I replied, "Thank you, Mr. President, for this honor. I pray God that a just, lasting, and comprehensive peace will be established in the region on behalf of the attainment of the hopes and rights of the Palestinian people." It was another way for me to argue with Sadat about the Palestinian cause. By now it was well known that I spoke out for the Palestinian cause whenever I could. People thought correctly that I was emotionally committed to them, but as a realist, I took this position for another reason as well: because I knew that if Egypt did not pursue Palestinian interests, we would lose our leadership over the Arab world and the peace with Israel would be jeopardized.

At dinner, Barbara Smith of *The Economist*, the first British journalist to visit Egypt after the 1956 aggression, referred to the book by Arthur Koestler, *The Yogi and the Commissar*. "You used to be a yogi," she said, "but now you have become a commissar." After a period in power, would I thirst to return to being a yogi? I realized that something in my attitude or work habits led people to suspect that I was a driven personality, filled perhaps with some secret, ascetic, mystical passion—a political version of Louis Massignon perhaps. A reporter asked me if it was true that I consulted a spiritual adviser. "No," I replied, "I have no guru." King Baudouin had asked me in Brussels, "What drives you, religion?" I replied with hesitation to a very Catholic monarch, "No, Your Majesty; it is not religion; it is love for Egypt."

On June 23 I met with African ambassadors posted in Cairo to stress to them Egypt's interest in the African summit conference, soon to be held in Monrovia, Liberia. I assured them that President Sadat would take part personally in the conference and made it clear that Egypt knew that some Arab states in league with some extremist African regimes would try to expel Egypt from the Organization of African Unity, as had been done in the Arab League and the Organization of the Islamic Conference. Egypt will oppose this attempt vehemently, I said.

On Monday, June 25, 1979, our negotiating team, headed by Mustafa Khalil traveled to Herzliya Petuach, a suburb of Tel Aviv overlooking the sea. Our hotel, the Dan Accadia, was like a fine European hotel. We expected no progress in this session, because Robert Strauss, the U.S. head of delegation, was again absent, and his deputy, James Leonard, clearly had been given no authority.

In the middle of the session, Yosef Burg turned to me. "Are you circumcised?" he asked. I indicated that the answer to his question was affirmative. "Why do you ask?" I said. "Because," he said, "with your brain and your penis you are one of us at both ends!"

The Dan Accadia talks were like a scene from Pirandello's *Six Characters in Search of an Author*. All were performing roles in a play with no scenario. The purpose of the play was to gain time and disguise the painful truth that there was no intention to solve the

Palestinian problem. Not only was Robert Strauss absent, showing that the session was not an American priority, but two of the heroes of the first act had withdrawn. Moshe Dayan was confined in the hospital after surgery, and Ezer Weizman had left the Israeli delegation for reasons unknown. Later I realized that he did not want to be an actor in this farce.

At one in the afternoon the session ended, and I had lunch with Mustafa Khalil and Yosef Burg at a table in a quiet and secluded corner of the hotel restaurant. I hoped that we could prepare a scenario, but, of course, nothing happened. The food had no taste. Israelis have a world reputation in music, finance, science, and military prowess. But they have failed in the art of cooking.

After lunch, I asked the Israelis to allow me to visit Dayan in the hospital, where a malignant tumor had been removed from his colon. Two security cars accompanied me from Herzliya Petuach to a one-story military hospital in Tel Aviv. I was surprised to find a group of journalists and photographers jostling to cover the story of my arrival at Dayan's hospital room.

Dayan was weak, tired, and voiceless because of the tubes in his throat. Our meeting was friendly and warm. Among the crowd in the room, one of Dayan's security guards shook my hand vigorously and offered me greetings. I recognized him as the guard who had been in charge of my security during Sadat's visit to Jerusalem in November 1977.

I felt a strange affection for the afflicted Dayan. I saw ourselves as two gladiators who had fought each other fiercely and suffered much from the other. Now my opponent was down. If he had fallen by my hand I would have been exultant. But he had been struck down by sickness, and I felt for him the solidarity of one fighter for another.

In the afternoon session at the Dan Accadia Hotel, as the Egyptian delegation raised once more the problem of Israeli settlements in the occupied Palestinian lands and the right of self-determination for the Palestinians, the American delegation, as usual, sat in complete silence.

At the end of the day Burg suggested that we visit Tel Aviv at night. We walked through the city surrounded by Israeli, Egyptian, and American security teams. Tel Aviv reminded me of the cities of the south of France or of Algiers. Burg led the way with the greatest happiness. The applauding crowds were welcoming the Egyptian delegation.

I said to Burg, "Is this tour part of your election campaign?" He said, "I don't need demonstrations like this to strengthen my popularity. My goal is to give you a view of Tel Aviv by night after hearing you complain more than once that you are seeing nothing in Israel but the airport, the hotel, and the meeting hall." Burg and his colleagues were very proud of Israel's wealth, power, and glamour, which they thought would overwhelm me, but they did not. Despite his disclaimer, Burg was manifesting his popularity and high position. He enjoyed the tour and was far more impressed with it than we were.

The final performance of the Herzliya show concluded with nothing of interest or value, although it took many hours and sharp discussions to craft a communique. The sole purpose of the performance was to convince the media that something had happened.

Back in Cairo on the first of July, I received Henry Kissinger in my Cairo office. I was struck by his compelling voice and accent. We sat side by side on the sofa and conversed amicably. Kissinger said to me that his mistake when trying to find a solution to the Middle East crisis was that after achieving disengagement agreements between Syria and Israel and Egypt and Israel, he failed to concentrate on achieving an agreement between Jordan and Israel.

The achievement of even a partial or symbolic Israeli withdrawal from the West Bank at that time would have established an important precedent, Kissinger said, and would have weakened Israel's claims to the West Bank. But Palestinians and other Arabs were to blame for this failure, he said, because they feared Jordanian sovereignty over the West Bank. As Kissinger spoke, I recalled my early years when I had been an Arab federalist, hoping for an Arab federation including Jordan, Palestine, Syria, and Lebanon. Such an entity, I thought, could be a step toward a pan-Arab state. I was thinking of Bismarck's creation of German unity in the late nineteenth century. Federalism was a common dream of Arab students who imbibed its spirit from studying in Europe.

But, as always, my dreams were interrupted by reality. A new problem had emerged. What if the United Nations opposed the

Egypt-Israel treaty and refused to place Blue Helmets in Sinai? This would be a shock, but we had to prepare for it. I met with Dr. Esmat Abdel Meguid, permanent representative of Egypt to the United Nations in New York, to study the situation. If the Soviet Union used its veto, the Security Council could not provide peacekeeping forces for the Sinai.

I issued a press statement saying that if the Security Council did not agree to renew the term of UNEF, the international force in Sinai, then Egypt would seek to create a non-UN multinational force of neutral nations like Austria, Sweden, Switzerland, or African states to take the place of the United Nations forces.

Bob Strauss, the head of the U.S. delegation was a grand seigneur, a jovial, powerful figure. His chemistry was good for us all, but in diplomacy he was inactive. He was a true politician, and as such, he caught the spirit of his boss, Jimmy Carter. Carter was no longer as active as he had been at Camp David. The Israelis had dealt him a serious blow by continuing to build settlements in the occupied territories, and he seemed less eager to engage them. And Iran, now in the throes of revolution, was preoccupying Carter's administration.

When Strauss was replaced by Sol Linowitz, a dynamic lawyer who had successfully negotiated the Panama Canal treaty, the American delegation became more nervous and more active. But Carter had not changed, and the U.S. team still lacked clear direction. Linowitz's activism encouraged the press to believe that progress was under way when, in fact, it was not. He was fond of declaring that the autonomy talks were 80 percent complete. That might have been true, but the last 20 percent was what mattered.

Strauss and Linowitz were both Jews, a fact that Sadat welcomed. He felt that they would be better than non-Jews at getting concessions for the Palestinians while defusing opposition to the peace process from the American-Israeli Public Affairs Committee (AIPAC), the powerful Jewish lobby in Washington. Sadat also felt that, conscious of their tie to Israel, they would "lean over backward" to be fair to Egypt.

But the choice of American Jews as the chief U.S. negotiators only aroused the hatred of the Arab rejectionists, who called us "stooges of Zionist imperialism." It seemed that the Arab world was not so upset by the Egypt-Israel treaty itself, which meant the return of Arab land by Israel; what they feared was that behind the treaty might be a secret alliance between Israel and Egypt, with the backing of the United States. Egypt would be the political leader, Israel the technological leader, and the United States the financial backer, and together this triumvirate could dominate the Middle East. The military power of Egypt and Israel together would be more than any combination of Arab states could contemplate confronting. There was no truth to this claim. It was another example of the Arab tendency to search for a conspiracy to explain events. It would take the Israelis a long time to believe that Egypt really wanted peace. And it would take a long time for Arabs to believe that Egypt did not want to betray them.

CHAPTER NINE

❖ ❖ ❖

Struggles in Monrovia and Havana

Monrovia

On Wednesday, July 4, 1979, I left for the African summit in Monrovia. I expected the worst. Egypt would be under severe radical pressure and could be ousted from the OAU. I was prepared for a diplomatic confrontation.

At Robert Field I found my friend Cecil Dennis, the foreign minister of Liberia, waiting to welcome me and accompany me on the hour-long ride from the airport to the city. Cecil said that he had instructions from the Liberian president, William Tolbert, to support Egypt against Arab rejectionist attempts to revoke Egypt's membership in the Organization of Arab Unity.

I told Cecil that I would preempt a conference battle by asserting that the Arab League should be represented at Monrovia by a Cairo-based delegation rather than by those who had left Cairo to establish the Arab League headquarters in Tunis. Still represented at Cairo were Somalia, Sudan, and Oman; together with Egypt they represented twice the population of all the Arab states that had removed themselves to Tunis. Cecil urged me to drop this idea. He was convinced that Sudan and Somalia would not go along. They could be counted on to refuse to *condemn*, but not to *defend* Egypt.

I listened to Cecil Dennis with respect; despite his youth, he was one of Africa's most experienced and clever foreign ministers. But I did not promise to take his advice. My hope, I said, was that the African summit conference would remain neutral in this dispute between the *de jure* Arab League in Cairo and the *de facto* Arab League in Tunis.

Cecil Dennis replied that when it came to Tunis versus Cairo, Egypt was outnumbered. At Monrovia, he said, there was only one issue: the controversy of Egypt's membership in the Organization of African Unity.

He convinced me. I telegraphed Cairo saying that Muhammad Riyad should not travel to Monrovia as the representative of the Arab League because the possibility of the conference recognizing him as such was minute. But I did not divulge this to Cecil Dennis. I would wait a day or two, so that my change of position would be taken as a concession from the Egyptian delegation for the purpose of making the conference succeed.

Rain was falling heavily. The car made its way slowly and with difficulty to the Intercontinental Hotel, which stood on a hill above the city of Monrovia. A small room rather than a suite had been set aside for me. This did not trouble me personally, but it would be difficult to hold meetings in this room with my delegation or with other ministers.

The heat was intense, the humidity high, and the air-conditioning weak. I could not help comparing the luxury of the Intercontinental in Geneva with the deficiencies of the one in Monrovia; the wealth of the Swiss city and the poverty and backwardness of the Liberian capital. The north-south gap was enormous. It was there to remind me that the east-west conflict would be solved one day, but that the north-south would take generations of hard work, political imagination, and generosity to solve. It is hard for a rich man to give to the poor; it is even harder for a rich state to do so. I thought of the biblical passage that it is easier for a camel to go through the eye of a needle than for a rich man to enter the kingdom of heaven. Those in the wealthy countries of the north did not know camels at first hand as we did. They did not understand the biblical meaning. The difficulty was not only a matter of size but also a matter of attitude.

The rain fell endlessly. I received in my small room Edem Kodjo, secretary-general of the Organization of African Unity. There will be a general attack on Egypt and its policies, he said, led by the Arab states and a group of radical African states. He, too, advised me that the question of Tunis or Cairo as the headquarters of the Arab League had already been answered and Cairo had lost. To try to prevent the recognition of the delegate of the Tunis League as representative of the Arab League at the OAU Conference would be useless.

I had dinner that night at the house of Adil Khayr al-Din, Egypt's ambassador in Monrovia; he had been one of my students in Cairo University thirty years earlier. He hoped that our personal relationship would lead to a post for him in Europe. In a sophisticated and subtle way he used every occasion to demonstrate to me how difficult life was in Liberia; if he was not transferred, he said, he could well spend the rest of his life in this forlorn place. Despite his incessant complaints, the atmosphere at the dinner was pleasant, helped by several rounds of drinks. Life in Liberia without a little alcohol was unbearable.

In accordance with a request of Liberian protocol, I was at the palace of the presidency of the republic before nine in the morning of July 6. For three hours I waited for President Tolbert to see me, and our meeting lasted no more than five minutes. This was often the practice of third-world leaders, meant to impress visitors with their importance. Tolbert, a Protestant minister, retained the style of a man of the cloth. When receiving visitors, he resembled a preacher giving a blessing.

The OAU conference took place in a new hall. President Tolbert opened the general session with a speech calling on Africa to fortify and encourage the constructive trends that had appeared in the Middle East. This was a positive step for Egypt. Tolbert was advising the hesitant and warning the truculent. He meant that Egypt should be supported, not condemned—a good beginning for us.

The foreign minister of Nigeria adopted with me the attitude of the older brother who is defending his younger brother and offers him advice and guidance: "Boutros, don't be afraid. It is not possible to eject Egypt from the Organization of African Unity. I will defend your position." I laughingly replied, "As long as my brother stands with me and supports me, I won't be afraid of a thing." The Nigerian laughed and ordered more beer for us. But it was a serious fear; Egypt had already been ejected from two major international organizations, and I was afraid that even the United Nations itself might turn against us.

In the evening I attended the dinner party for African foreign ministers. After dinner, a musical group played dance music and the dance floor was soon full. I asked Olga, the undersecretary of the Angolan Foreign Ministry and a beautiful communist, to dance with me and found myself among a group of diplomats who were dancing earnestly and happily. Dancing is a major requirement of diplomatic work.

The next day, Adil Khayr al-Din informed me that he had received an urgent message from the American chargé d'affaires in Monrovia asking to meet with me on an important matter. At Khayr al-Din's residence the American brought to me a message from Cyrus Vance: there was a strong possibility that there would be no UN peacekeeping force for Sinai. The United Nations would not endorse the peace treaty.

I returned to my hotel and asked the hotel clerk not to disturb me with telephone calls. I took a sleeping pill. But after only a few minutes I was awakened by the ringing of the telephone. It was the foreign minister of Chad, claiming that he was being confined to his guesthouse and asking me to help him get out. Liberia did not recognize the government of Chad and did not want it to participate in the conference. Contrary to the rules of diplomacy, they had put the Chadian under house arrest. I tried to calm him and promised that I would raise the matter in the morning with Cecil Dennis, who, as foreign minister of the host country, was also president of the ministerial council of this OAU meeting.

I had scarcely returned to sleep when the telephone rang again. On the line was an Egyptian lady journalist whom I knew well. She was speaking to me from the Monrovia airport, where she had landed an hour before and found no one to meet her. Years before, in a similar situation she had appealed to me, saying, "The ministry won't take care of me because I am so ugly." I had kissed her and told her she was beautiful and arranged for the ministry to help her.

Later, when I declined to be interviewed by her, she had cried, wailing that I would not talk to her because she was so unattractive. I had relented and agreed to be interviewed. Now in the middle of the night, she again asked me to help. I told her to take a taxi from the airport to the hotel.

I contacted the telephone operator and complained in undiplomatic terms about the telephone calls. The operator who had taken my instructions had ended his shift and had not conveyed my request to his replacement. Trusting that I would now find the rest I needed, I went back to sleep once more.

On Monday, July 9, I headed from the hotel to the headquarters of the conference. The trip took about forty minutes despite the motorcycle escort and the efforts of traffic authorities to wave through the motorcades of the heads of the delegations.

Seated behind us in the hall was the delegation of the Palestine Liberation Organization. The Palestinians refused to exchange greetings or even to speak to me.

Egyptian Ambassador Abu Bakr Abd al-Ghaffar had tried to arrange a secret meeting between me and the head of the PLO delegation, but the Palestinian delegate refused, saying, "I cannot shake the hand that shook the hand of Moshe Dayan; I cannot enter into discussions with anyone who went to Jerusalem with Sadat!"

Wednesday, July 11, 1979, was a day I will not forget as long as I live. For ten hours I was subjected to fierce attacks, insults, and reproaches from the rejectionist Arab states and the radical African states. Their attack revolved around three points: Egypt had made a separate peace with Israel; Egypt was negotiating in the name of the Palestinian people without PLO authorization; and an imperialist alliance had been established between Pretoria, Tel Aviv, and Cairo.

Nevertheless I was determined that Egypt would not be expelled from its historic position in the ranks of African nations, with whom we had close and ancient ties. I decided to concentrate on one state only, Algeria, for differing reasons. First, the Algerian delegate, Dr. al-Bedjawi, was one of the most eloquent and forceful French speakers and would later become president of the International Court of Justice. Second, Algeria was among the most active and influential nations in the Arab, African, and third world. Third, confining the duel to Egypt and Algeria could lead the African states to realize that this was an Arab dispute, one that should not be decided in an African conference.

I decided not to speak in Arabic, because the translators had been assigned by rejectionist states. In French I said, "I have listened to the representative of Algeria mourn Egypt, console it, and weep over it," I began, "but I would like to say to him that Egypt has not died. Rather, it is alive and strong in its people, its principles, and its courage and will continue on the path of peace despite the rejectionists and their cries of malicious joy."

Algeria wants to fight Israel to the last Egyptian soldier, I said. "The zeal of the Algerian brothers toward the Palestinian question is in proportion to the distance that separates Algeria from Israel." The farther away, I noted, the greater the zeal. I said other stinging things, which made a number of the African delegates smile, even laugh, at the expense of my Arab colleague.

I urged the conference not to judge in haste. We were just starting on the path to peace. Egypt, I said, agreed with the Palestinians regarding the sought-after goal; the difference was that Palestinians were using armed struggle, while Egypt was using diplomatic struggle. The two ways were complementary.

Egypt had not betrayed the Arab cause, I insisted. The ones who have betrayed the cause are those who are isolating Egypt when solidarity is required to strengthen our negotiating position.

As the duel of words went on between me and al-Bedjawi, I noticed that he referred to President Sadat as "Sadat." I raised a point of order and asked the conference president for permission to intervene. I said, "There are African customs that must be followed in this organization. A foreign minister is not permitted to speak of the president of a state in this manner. We must all of us respect the person of each and every president of a state whatever our differences."

This was unfair. Al-Bedjawi's words were not really improper; I had seized on them as a pretext. But when I challenged him, he lost control. In a shrill voice he cried, "I was not attacking the person of the Egyptian president! Saying 'Sadat' was not meant as an insult!" But the president of the conference, who had been talking to someone else and did not hear al-Bedjawi, angrily declared that he agreed completely with me and demanded the adherence of all members to the rules and principles of the OAU.

My friend al-Bedjawi was furious. He renewed his denunciation of Egyptian policy, but his emotionalism weakened his attack. My tactic had left this powerful Arab voice sputtering, but it did not deter the combined attack on Egypt by Tunisia, Libya, and the PLO—and, among the Africans, Angola, Mozambique, and the Congo.

Even more troubling, not one voice was raised to defend Egypt. Each attack encouraged others, so that some states completely removed from the problem, like Mali and Benin, intervened, and their foreign ministers tried to teach me how to behave and how Egypt must support the Palestinians.

With Algeria's al-Bedjawi off-balance, the Palestine Liberation Organization now took the lead in condemning Egypt, but the presentation was feeble. The PLO delegate spoke in Arabic, and much of what he said was lost in translation. Had the Palestinian condemnation been more articulate, more African states might have denounced Egypt.

My Egyptian security officers were following the battle with alarmed excitement, as if it were a football match. They were stunned by the extent of the attack and the undiplomatic language they were hearing. They were hurt that not a single state rose to defend Egypt or President Sadat, or the peace treaty.

I returned to the hotel after midnight, exhausted but proud of having stood alone against twenty states for ten hours without losing my composure once, or at least not more than once, despite the ferocity of the attacks and the wounding expressions. Indeed, I can't say for sure that on the one occasion when I lost my temper, my personal outburst was genuine or a weapon of debate.

In the morning I did not go to the conference hall but asked Ambassador Ahmad Tawfiq Khalil to take the chairmanship of the delegation in my absence.

Instead I visited various foreign ministers in their suites but soon concluded that they were not ready to offer Egypt any assistance in the diplomatic battle.

Finally, I went to Rashid al-Tahir, foreign minister of Sudan, and said, "Where was the delegation of fraternal Sudan yesterday, when Egypt was faced with an attack, fabrications, and false accusations! How could the Sudanese foreign minister not leap to defend Egypt before the accusations of twenty-some African and Arab states against us? How could al-Rashid al-Tahir accept this attack and remain silent? I am ashamed of your delegation's failure to do anything to support us. Egyptian security men and young Egyptian diplomats want to know the reason for this silence. Is Egyptian-Sudanese solidarity a one-way street?" Al-Rashid al-Tahir was unresponsive, as though he had not heard me. I departed.

After the diplomatic battle came the battle of the rooms, which happened each time President Sadat attended a conference. The president's delegation included scores of aides, and aides of aides, and security men, protocol officials, and others. While the number of rooms in the hotel was limited, the number of members of the delegation was not. So delegates already in Monrovia were required to move to other hotels or to share their rooms to accommodate the advance presidential delegation. Even worse, some were exiled to cabins in an old ship anchored in the harbor to serve as a dormitory. A ferocious conflict had occurred last year at the Khartoum Hilton. To avoid a repetition, I charged Ambassador Ahmad Tawfiq Khalil to oversee the assignment of rooms and to settle the crises that were bound to erupt between the Egyptian Foreign Ministry and the Egyptian presidency.

My search for support among the delegation heads gained nothing, so I decided to speak on every item listed on the agenda of the conference in order to show that Egypt's presence was not limited to its own interests, but that Egypt was a leader among nations, strong enough to be concerned at this moment not only with the Middle East crisis but also with African questions. I pointed out again and again that Egypt was every bit as much an African state as it was an Arab state.

In the morning session I spoke about Egyptian-Sudanese economic integration. I expected that the foreign minister of Sudan would speak in turn and support what I said. But he kept silent. Egypt-Sudan integration was, I had to admit, an illusion that each found occasionally useful, and for which there was no political will in either country.

In the afternoon I held a press conference in the hotel for journalists from all over the world. One of them asked me if the ambassador of Egypt in Turkey, Kamal Olama, was a friend of mine.

I found the question strange, until I heard that Palestinian terrorists had seized our embassy in Ankara and taken the ambassador hostage. I sent a hurried telegram to Cairo to find out about the situation.

In the evening I took part in a dinner given by Siméon Aké, foreign minister of Côte d'Ivoire. Also present were Mohammed Ben Yahia, foreign minister of Algeria; Muhammad Boucetta, foreign minister of Morocco; Paulo Jorge, foreign minister of Angola; and al-Rashid al-Tahir, foreign minister of Sudan. The atmosphere was cordial; the conference was one thing and the dinner party something else.

The session of Saturday, July 14, went on all day and into the night until after midnight. As I was returning to the hotel, the rain was so heavy that my driver was forced to drive extremely slowly and the trip was excruciatingly long. When I reached my room, there was a telegram from Mustafa Khalil: intelligence reports led him to be concerned for Sadat's safety in Monrovia. Did I consider the president's presence necessary? The message was drafted so as to encourage me to reply that Sadat's attendance at the OAU summit be canceled. Instead, I sent a telegram saying, "Without the presence of Sadat, we may lose everything here in Monrovia and Egypt may be expelled from the OAU." Sadat said, "I knew Boutros would do that!" and kept to his schedule. Four planeloads of Egyptian paratroopers were sent into Liberia in advance of Sadat's arrival. There were rumors that a Palestinian guerrilla team was in Monrovia to kill Sadat. The rumor was so widespread that his wife and their daughter insisted on traveling to Monrovia with the president.

On Sunday the president's advance party arrived. There was no room in the Intercontinental Hotel for the numerous security men and administrators. The Liberians were shocked by Egypt's decision to dispatch to Monrovia a well-equipped team of commandos, who were to stay in the Egyptian embassy building. Ambassador Adil Khayr al-Din had rows and rows of cots set up in the embassy residence.

On Monday afternoon eighty commandos landed at Robert Field, and shortly thereafter Sadat's aircraft arrived. In addition to his wife and daughter, Sadat was accompanied by his wizard, Hasan al-Tuhami, who sincerely believed that his presence would protect

Sadat from danger. Did Sadat believe it? Perhaps, perhaps not, but why not take the precaution of having al-Tuhami in attendance? Several others who normally would have accompanied Sadat were nowhere to be seen.

As soon as the ceremonies of the official reception, the playing of the republican anthem, and the review of the honor guard were completed, a heated dispute erupted among the entourage over whether the president should go to his rest house by the helicopter that had been transported especially from Cairo for this purpose or by the armored car that also came from Egypt. I intervened, suggesting to the president that he use the car because darkness had already begun to cover the city, and the Egyptian pilots perhaps were unfamiliar with the area where the helicopter was to land. Happily, my view prevailed.

Early Tuesday morning at the City of the Presidents of the States, which had been built near the beach especially for this conference, I met with Hasan Kamil to discuss the list I had prepared of African presidents that Sadat must meet with. Hasan Kamil said haughtily, "The president naturally will not make visits. Anyone who wants to meet with him can submit a request and come to the house where the president is staying." I replied angrily, "The situation is completely different from what it was last year at Khartoum. We need the presidents of the African states more than they need us. The president must visit them in their own quarters." Hasan Kamil said, "You will have to convince the president personally."

When Sadat received me, I pointed out the effort under way to expel Egypt from the organization. Sadat said calmly, "And what is required of me?" I told him, and he immediately agreed to visit the other heads of state. I handed him the list that I had prepared, which included Augustine Neto of Angola, a major African thinker and political figure. Sadat exploded: "Boutros, I will not meet a communist!" With this outburst behind us, Sadat and I walked to the rest houses of the other heads of state on my list. We began with President Omar Bongo of Gabon, who asked to be presented with a gift of armaments. Sadat agreed. Bongo asked if he could send his generals to Cairo to arrange it. "Yes," Sadat said. "Air force, army, marines?" asked Bongo. "Yes," Sadat said; "I will take them in my own plane on my return to Cairo," which seemed to satisfy Bongo.

Then we visited President Julius Nyerere of Tanzania, known as Mwalimu (the teacher), a revered leader of the third world as a combination of sage, ideologue, and simple schoolteacher. He was known to be anti–Camp David. Nyerere, white-haired and spare, listened serenely and said little. We then proceeded to President Jean-Baptiste Bagaza of Burundi, a young officer who seemed vastly impressed by the very presence of Sadat and listened respectfully. Then came Ahmadou Ahidjo of Cameroon, in national dress. He listened to Sadat cordially but gave the impression of strict neutrality. I translated from Arabic to French, elaborating here and there on Sadat's words—with the tacit approval of the president, who nodded his assent at each point when he noticed my contributions to his words.

President Léopold Senghor of Senegal, the great poet and prophet of *Négritude*, did not wait for Sadat to speak but lectured to us on the races of Africa, and how they had mixed with non-Africans. *Métissage*, he declared, would empower Africa and would overcome the problem of separation between black and white. President Sadat listened respectfully, and we moved on.

At the cottage of the president of Guinea, Sékou Touré, whom Sadat knew well and regarded as a Muslim Marxist but not a communist, Touré launched an immediate attack. "You, the big brother, are the one responsible for the difficulties that have erupted among the Arab states. For when a dispute occurs among brothers, the big brother is the one who bears the duty to resolve it. You should have exerted efforts to explain your policy to your brother Arab states, but you have not done so." Sadat listened without comment, but it was obvious that Sadat was highly irritated. Sékou Touré had been patronizing, but as we walked along, Sadat only praised his eloquence and called him a debater of the first rank. Then he paused and added, "Boutros! Beware of the dialectic of irascible Marxists!"

In his rest house, the president of Nigeria, General Obasanjo, began at once to criticize Sadat. Information had reached him "from a great Arab personality" that the 1973 October War had not been a real war. It had been a show. Sadat had agreed on its details in advance with Israel and the United States. Sadat had agreed that Egypt's army would take the Bar-Lev Line and then the anti-Arab Camp David agreements would follow. Sadat said nothing, but the corners of his mouth twitched. I could sense him asking himself, "Why am I here? Why has Boutros brought me to these people who dare to insult and accuse and denounce what I have done?" I felt guilty and embarrassed and even fearful of what was taking place; it was the opposite of what I had aimed for—a civil dialogue between heads of state in which Sadat could explain his policy. Instead, I had led my boss into prosecutorial accusations of conspiratorial treachery.

The deep anger on Sadat's features aggravated my discomfort. After less than a minute of silence, which seemed like a full year, Sadat calmly began to speak. His voice rose gradually as if he were delivering a speech to the masses. "In Egypt we have entrenched family traditions that resemble to a great extent African family traditions. The elder brother is considered responsible for the younger brothers and the elder considers himself in the position of their father if the father has died. I had a younger brother named Atef. Atef was an officer in the Egyptian air force. He was killed in the first hours of the October War. Do you believe that if the glorious October War was just a performance that we were putting on, I would allow my brother and my son Atef to be killed while he was fighting it? Do you imagine that I would distribute the roles in a mere show in which hundreds of martyrs would die?"

General Obasanjo of Nigeria was silent, as were the other Nigerian officials who were listening to Sadat. President Sadat then rose to leave and said farewell without cordiality. We returned to Sadat's quarters. As we walked along, Sadat saw my woeful expression and said with a smile, "Those meetings were useful."

Just before Sadat was to address the full assembly, I went to his cottage to see if I could help him prepare. His smile had encouraged me to tell him the unpleasant truth. I told him about the prevailing hostile atmosphere and explained in detail the criticisms directed at the Camp David agreements. But I seemed only to make him irritable and nervous again.

As we entered the big hall, despite his attempts not to show it, Sadat seemed unsettled. Hasan Kamil, al-Tuhami, and Fawzi behaved as if they were at a tea party. The president took his seat. I approached him and offered him a new memorandum on what had happened in the conference to date. My note was blunt, without diplomatic niceties. As Sadat read it he became more angry.

"Why have you, Boutros, not responded to these stupid accusations?" I told him that I had answered every accusation and returned every attack. But Sadat did not listen to my response. He tossed my memorandum aside and looked dreamily into the distance, as though he were nowhere near this wretched conference.

At the invitation of the president of Liberia, President Sadat went to the podium and began to read the text of the speech that Osama al-Baz had prepared for him based on what my team and I had sent from Monrovia. But after a few minutes Sadat put the written text aside and announced that he would not give the speech that had been intended to be delivered before the conference. He had been surprised this morning, he said, by a brother African president who told him that he had been assured by a great Arab personage that the 1973 October War was not a real war but a concoction and a conspiracy. Sadat then told the assembly what he had told General Obasanjo about the martyrdom of his younger brother Atef al-Sadat. The president told this story with powerful dramatic effect.

Then Sadat renewed his invitation to all sides of the Arab-Israeli struggle to take part in an international conference to be held in Al-Arish at which the United States and the Soviet Union would also be present. He gave his assurance, in the name of the Egyptian people, who said yes to peace, that he was ready to sit down with any party with whom we had any dispute in order to find a solution.

The hall was electrified by Sadat's words. When he concluded, the delegates rose with thunderous applause, which went on for some minutes. Sadat descended from the podium, sweat pouring from his face. I said to him in congratulation, "Mr. President, with your permission, now I am able to order the airplane for your return to Cairo without delay; there is no need for you to attend the remainder of the meetings because you are victorious! You have turned the conference in favor of Egypt."

Sadat smiled broadly, then asked Fawzi Abd al-Hafiz to tell Sadat's daughter, who was in the balcony reserved for guests, to prepare to leave with him immediately.

"You can hold the fort, Boutros," he said. He left, followed by his entourage, and returned to his rest house. That afternoon he met Kurt Waldheim to discuss the Security Council vote on the United

Nations Emergency Force in Sinai that would take place in the next few days.

Many African leaders called on Sadat in his quarters to convey their admiration. When these visits ended, Sadat invited me to have a cup of tea with him. Jehan Sadat joined us. "Bravo, Boutros," Sadat said. "You have exerted enormous efforts and you must rest, for exhaustion is clear upon you." Then, without warning, Sadat suddenly rose and declared that he would leave Monrovia that evening so as to be in Cairo in the early morning. I asked his permission not to accompany him to the airport, which would take more than an hour's ride from Monrovia, so that I could continue working at the conference. All of Sadat's persuasive oratory would be of no value if we were not present when the operative outcome of the conference was being debated.

Sadat immediately excused me from the ceremonial farewell, but the members of the entourage—particularly Hasan Kamil and al-Tuhami—considered my behavior unforgivable. Sadat's aircraft was in the air by 9.00 P.M. without any notice to the attendees at the conference. In his haste to depart Sadat had forgotten his promise to Bongo to transport three Gabonese generals to Cairo, which left me with a problem that lasted for years. Every time Bongo and I met he reproached me about Sadat's unfulfilled pledge. I would apologize each time, citing financial problems as the excuse for our failure to do as we had promised.

The conference focus now turned elsewhere, a good sign for Egypt. With relief I entered the debate over the demand of Algeria and other radical states to include the Sahraoui Republic (Western Sahara) in the membership of the Organization of African Unity. Morocco and a group of moderate states opposed this demand. A feeling of smug relaxation overcame me. Enemies, who had united against Egypt, had now begun to fight among themselves.

The maneuvers and intrigues were remarkable. Whenever another vote was required or a reconvened session led to a new round of speeches, bargaining behind the scenes was intensified, a process that induced the representatives to carry on the debate to the limit of human endurance. The diplomatic battle of the Western Sahara went on until two in the morning of Saturday, July 21, 1979.

I left Monrovia the next day and headed for Geneva. Paulo Jorge, foreign minister of Angola, one of the leaders of the rejectionist camp, was also aboard. He looked at me with rage and spoke about the summit conference of nonaligned states that would soon be held in Cuba: "The next battle, in Havana, will be much more difficult for Egypt. You will be faced by twenty Arab states and twenty progressive states that demonstrate how your policy of Camp David has betrayed the third world."

I held a press conference in Geneva with the hope of building upon Egypt's stand at Monrovia. But the focus was on a new crisis. The Security Council in New York had begun discussions, and journalists had concluded that the United Nations would not monitor the withdrawal of Israeli forces from Sinai and would not provide peacekeepers as contemplated by the Egypt-Israel peace treaty.

Back in Cairo I found a great crowd from the Foreign Ministry and the media awaiting me at the airport. Despite the disturbing news from the United Nations, I was given the closest thing to a conqueror's reception that a Foreign Ministry bureaucracy could provide.

Back to the Autonomy Talks

The next session of talks on Palestinian self-rule was in Haifa. We arrived by Israeli helicopter, and stayed at a hotel on Mount Carmel overlooking the sea. The city of Haifa, rising high above the Mediterranean, was splendid, with many trees and gardens. We held a working session in the afternoon, then had lunch in the hotel. I noted that my colleagues were careful not to have any spirituous drinks and recalled that the month of Ramadan had begun.

In the morning a bitter confrontation occurred between Mustafa Khalil and Shmuel Tamir, the Israeli minister of justice, on the question of Jerusalem. Khalil said that Arab Jerusalem was an inseparable part of the West Bank and that what applied to the West Bank must apply as well to Arab Jerusalem. Shmuel Tamir asserted that the unification of the city of Jerusalem had been completed, and could not be included in a discussion of the West Bank. Neither side could so much as imagine the position of the other.

In the evening, an armored limousine, preceded by a car filled with security guards and followed by a similar guard car, transported us from Haifa to Tel Aviv. We had dinner in the garden of Moshe Dayan's house, which had been constructed to house his private museum of ancient artifacts. The dinner guests included Abba Eban and his wife and Professor Yadin, the deputy prime minister.

I gave to Dayan a gift of gold cuff links with the name "Moshe Dayan" inscribed in hieroglyphics. Dayan's wife happily displayed the gift to all present and especially to Yadin, the archaeological scholar. Yadin read the inscription aloud and commented that there was a "spelling" mistake in the hieroglyphs for "Dayan." He claimed that the last letter should have been written in a different way and began to write on a piece of paper to explain this to us. But Yadin's editing did not dampen the pleasure of the gift.

After dinner Dayan showed us his antiquities. We talked about pharaonic civilization and the African summit conference in Monrovia. None of us referred at all to the current negotiations in Haifa; it was as if they did not exist. When we left Dayan's house, journalists met us in the street; I told them the visit was private and that no reference had been made to the autonomy negotiations.

At the end of our stay in Haifa, as we were heading for the helicopter pad we discovered that one of the members of the Egyptian delegation was absent and we were forced to delay the takeoff. Anxiety began to spread about the fate of Sayyid al-Masri, a diplomat in my office who years before had been one of my brightest students. After a short time he was found; he had been sleeping in his room, had not taken part in the closing session, and did not know that the Egyptian delegation had left the hotel.

The lost diplomat arrived and the helicopter took off. Sayyid al-Masri resumed his sleep immediately on takeoff, which caused Mustafa Khalil to rebuke me for having chosen him as a delegate. I explained to the prime minister that Sayyid al-Masri was very religious and that when in Israel he felt it necessary to pray far into the hours of the night, which forced him to sleep through the day.

The Haifa meetings confirmed that we were at an impasse. The negotiations were more public relations than diplomacy. The Israeli people could see the prime minister of Egypt and a group of Arab officials every two weeks strolling in the streets of Israel's cities. But

I perceived that the Israeli people still did not trust Egypt's intentions. I wanted the talks to reassure them about Egypt's sincere desire for peace and to reassure the Arab world that Egypt was successfully negotiating in behalf of the Palestinians, so that the other Arabs would join the peace process. Neither of my two goals was realized.

To Havana

At a press conference on August 12 reporters asked me if the Havana conference would oust Egypt from the nonaligned movement. I responded that the Arab states had already adopted a resolution at the Baghdad conference calling for Egypt's suspension from the nonaligned movement. I do not, I said, imagine that the nonaligned states want the Arab rejectionists to make this decision for them.

The delegation chosen to accompany me to Havana was similar to that at Monrovia: Ahmad Tawfiq Khalil, Ahmad Sidqi, Ahmad Mahir al-Sayyid, Wafiq Husni, Ala' Khayrat, Amr Musa. Our permanent representative in New York, Esmat Abdel Meguid, was added. It was an active, excellent group able to hold together during continuous work night and day.

To prepare for Havana, I had flown to India to seek support for Egypt's position. Although I was warmly welcomed, it was clear that I should not expect much from that country. India was in transition. The Congress party, which had helped to create the nonaligned movement, was no longer in power, for the first time since India's independence.

At a press conference before leaving for Havana I referred to the attempts of Cuba and other radical states to pull the nonaligned movement toward the communist bloc, thereby violating the movement's fundamental commitment. I denounced Cuban and Soviet activities in Africa. Cuba's role in serving Soviet goals in the African continent conflicted with the principle of nonalignment.

As my departure for Cuba approached, the security service informed me that a group of six Palestinians was ready to travel to Havana to assassinate me. The Interior Ministry had decided to strengthen the guard accompanying me. I told the prime minister that I did not want a crowd of security officers around me; it might interfere with our diplomatic work. Besides, these security people had never been in Havana and none spoke Spanish. Mustafa Khalil angrily told me never to question the Interior Ministry on security matters.

On the eve of my departure, President Sadat wished me success: "You must take the initiative as you did in Monrovia, for there is never any use in keeping to a defensive position—never—never."

I left Cairo on the morning of August 22 with officers and members of the Egyptian delegation. At my stopover in Geneva I noticed that the Swiss authorities had doubled their security arrangements for my protection. Agents sped me quickly to the hotel.

For a year we had been trying to persuade a majority of nonaligned states to shun the Havana conference in order to assure its failure from the start. When it became evident that we were not succeeding, we tried to persuade states that their presence at Havana was vital in order to preserve the nonaligned movement from being captured by Marxists and radicals.

I called on Félix Houphouët-Boigny, the president of Côte d'Ivoire, who was staying at a villa in Geneva. Illness had kept him from the Monrovia meeting. Swiss policemen guided me to the house of the Ivoirien president, who received me with a huge smile at the door. He seemed to be in good health, but I knew that he was sick. I conveyed to him the warm greetings of President Sadat and described to him the fierce attack on Egypt that had taken place in Monrovia. Many African presidents, Houphouët-Boigny said, had not been in power more than a few months or a few years, and were not yet able to understand the significance of Sadat's initiative. The longer these leaders had been in power, the more they understood Egypt's position; those who were new to high office were more likely to be driven by emotion and pressure. Houphouët-Boigny declared that the majority of states participating in the Havana conference were in fact aligned. The truly nonaligned states, like Egypt, India, and Yugoslavia, would form the exception there. For this reason, he said he was convinced that there was no point in Côte d'Ivoire participating in the Havana conference. What he said gave me a shock, because I had hoped that he would attend the conference and that his prestige would help Egypt.

Before I could comment, he added, "Despite that, I have decided to respond to Anwar Sadat's request by sending my foreign minister,

Siméon Aké, to Havana. I am giving him directions to cooperate completely with the Egyptian delegation and to oppose any attempt to disparage Egypt." I thanked Houphouët-Boigny in the name of President Sadat, but I was certain that Siméon Aké, like any foreign minister in the absence of his president would avoid confrontation. I could not imagine that Aké would defend Egypt with the same ardor as he would if his president was present. I left Geneva as pessimistic as I had been after visiting New Delhi.

I was met in New York on August 24 by Dr. Esmat Abdel Meguid, and I asked him to help me at once on suggesting a revision of United Nations Security Council Resolution 242 so that the Palestinians were not referred to solely as refugees, but as a people with the right to self-determination. I had already discussed this initiative at length with Roy Atherton and other U.S. officials, who seemed to favor my idea. But when the Israelis learned of it, they were vehemently opposed. Sadat himself feared that modifying Resolution 242 would weaken the Camp David agreements, for they were based on the text of the resolution as issued in November 1967. If Camp David was weakened, then the peace treaty would be weakened and consequently the negotiations on self-rule could be halted, which might result in postponement of the Israeli withdrawal from Sinai. Sadat told Bob Strauss of these apprehensions and as a result, Strauss actively tried to kill our initiative.

Nonetheless, I asked Ambassador Esmat Abdel Meguid to speak before the Security Council on behalf of the proposal. Dr. Mustafa Khalil telephoned me from Cairo to say that Sadat's opposition to changing 242 was clear, and I must abide by it. I argued that it was a mistake for Egypt to take the same position on 242 as Israel did. Besides, I said, Esmat Abdel Meguid had already registered an official request to address the Security Council. It would be humiliating to retract this request, and if he did speak, it was unimaginable that he would not favor a proposal to depict the Palestinians as a people with the right of self-determination, not as refugees. It was now a matter of principle and of Egypt's honor and credibility, I argued.

Mustafa Khalil was silent. I told him that I would try to find a way to bridge the gap between Sadat's opposition to changing 242 and Egypt's obligation to seek to amend the resolution.

Soon after, I learned that Mustafa Khalil, having no confidence in my approach, had instructed Esmat Abdel Meguid not to participate in the meeting of the Security Council. Esmat, however, persuaded the prime minister that since he had entered his name on the list of speakers in the Security Council, he must not withdraw.

Ambassador Andrew Young, the permanent representative of the United States to the United Nations, knew of my initiative and supported it, but informed us that his government was deeply opposed. Meguid was the first speaker to address the Council, and he made it clear that Egypt favored a change in 242. The proposal for a new resolution was offered by Senegal. But none of the members of the Security Council supported the proposal, and there was no vote on it. Sadat, Carter, and Begin had all opposed any effort to change 242. I had tried to bring about an amendment and had failed, but at least I had succeeded in formally stating at the UN that Egypt would not oppose any effort to give greater recognition to Palestinian rights.

From my suite at the Waldorf-Astoria I watched the live television coverage of Young's farewell speech. He had been forced to give up his position when it was discovered that he had met with a member of the PLO, contrary to U.S. policy. It was an excellent speech, in which Young criticized his government for not recognizing the Palestine Liberation Organization.

After his speech, Young left the Security Council and came to my suite to keep a previous engagement. I received him with warmth and praised his defense of Palestinian rights. Young said to me that he had been inspired by Sadat's courage in confronting the Middle East crisis and told me that he would now be Carter's unofficial emissary to the African states. President Carter, he said, and a number of enlightened American Jews, were pleased with the growing support of black Americans for the Palestinians; it represented the beginning of a change in American public opinion that could balance the Zionist influence.

Young said that his job in Africa would be to help President Carter restore diplomatic relations between Israel and some of the African states, which would strengthen Carter's position vis-à-vis the pro-Israel lobby in Washington. I was struck by the paradox that Young, a hero to the Palestinians for having met with the PLO, was now planning a mission that would weaken the Palestinian cause by trying to help Israel emerge from its diplomatic isolation.

Havana

I left New York on Sunday, August 26, 1979, for Havana, surrounded by a strong security detachment. I feared that Egypt's expulsion from the nonaligned movement was at hand. Of all my worries, this was the greatest, for the nonaligned movement permitted Egypt to play a truly international role. If Egypt was thrown out, we would have nowhere to go but into the American camp, become part of the cold war, and lose our global radiance. Sadat, once again, disagreed with me. He was convinced that the communist camp was falling apart, and was ready to cast his lot with the West.

When I landed in Havana, the Cuban foreign minister, Isidoro Malmierca, approached me stiffly and greeted me with cold *politesse*. I asked to meet with him soon. He escorted me to the thirteenth-floor suite of a hotel on the corniche where I found a selection of wines and spirits and a quantity of excellent cigars awaiting me.

Malmierca responded to my request quickly and we met in the Hotel Havana Libre, which everyone still called the Hilton. I told him that, as President Sadat's circumstances did not permit him to attend the summit, he had charged me to inform the Cuban leadership as soon as I arrived that Egypt wished the conference to succeed in preserving the unity of the nonaligned movement. Egypt was confident that Cuba, in its chairmanship, would avoid exposing the movement to the dangers of division, separatism, and polarization. The political differences between Egypt and Cuba, I said, mainly dealing with Africa, should not cause a confrontation between our two states.

Cuba fundamentally disagreed with Egypt about the nonalignment, Malmierca said. Cuba rejected the idea of placing the movement in a middle position between imperialism and socialism. The nonaligned movement, he said, had stood since its founding against imperialism and colonialism and its plots and threats. The Cuban government had noted Egypt's dissatisfaction with the proposed closing statement of the Havana conference that would reflect this view. He would like to make it clear, he said, that the statement was the result of numerous contacts and consultations that Cuba had undertaken; it had wide support.

When I informed the Egyptian delegation of this meeting, the general feeling was that we were in danger, but that President Sadat did not care. Nonalignment did not interest him. He intended to achieve Israeli withdrawal from Sinai no matter what the diplomatic price for Egypt.

While the ministerial session was taking place I stayed in my room to write my speech to the forthcoming summit conference. Over the opposition of the younger members of my delegation, who insisted that I use Arabic, I decided to speak in French. Again, I did not trust the Arabic translators working at the conference, most of whom came from Arab rejectionist states. I was told that no Egyptian had been invited to serve on the secretariat of the conference and none had been allowed to work as a translator.

Late that evening, Ambassador Mahmud Abu al-Nasr, the Egyptian seconded to the sultanate of Oman, who was working as permanent representative of the sultanate at the United Nations, knocked on my door and told me that Syria had asked the Arab group to condemn and reject the Camp David agreements and that Iraq proposed suspending Egypt's membership in the nonaligned movement. Only Morocco, which asked for time to study the matter, opposed these initiatives. Mahmud Abu al-Nasr asked me to keep our meeting secret. He did not want to be accused of having spied on the Arab group.

By Wednesday, August 29, the direction of the conference was clear. The candidates for the committee of coordination for Western Asia were Iraq, Syria, South Yemen, and the Palestine Liberation Organization—all rejectionists. I asked our delegates to campaign for the sultanate of Oman and cabled our embassy in Muscat to urge the Oman government to instruct the Omani delegation in Havana to proceed seriously with this candidacy. I telephoned the Egyptian embassy in Washington and found the line clear, no doubt a remnant of the old contacts that linked the American and Cuban capitals in the days before Castro. Ambassador Ashraf Ghorbal reported to me on developments in the outside world, because the flow of information to the island of Cuba was severely restricted.

I then visited my friend Cecil Dennis, foreign minister of Liberia and head of the African group. If he could get the African group to stick to the resolutions of the Monrovia conference, which had refused to condemn Egypt, we might fend off the rejectionist assault. Logically the African states should not now nullify the decisions made a few weeks earlier in Monrovia. The expulsion of Egypt, I told Dennis, would be an insult to the African group.

The sessions of the Havana summit began at nine in the morning and ended at nine at night without a break except lunchtime at the residence of Ambassador Nabil Hamdi, who lived in an elegant house that had been confiscated by the Cubans from a rich businessman. The residence sat in a large garden with a swimming pool that was unusable because the apparatus for purifying the water was not functioning.

During the first afternoon session Cuban protocol informed me that the Cuban vice president Carlos Rafael Rodríguez, in response to my request, would meet with me in one of the offices adjoining the hall. Rodríguez, a white-bearded man of years with a charming smile and a reputation as the chief political thinker in the Cuban hierarchy, spoke of the economic cooperation between Cuba and Egypt—we bought Cuban sugar—and the historical connection between our revolutions. I was surprised, I said, to hear the Cuban foreign minister, in his opening speech, refer to Egypt in so unbecoming and unacceptable a manner. He had, for example, claimed that a military pact existed between Egypt and the United States. But Egypt, I declared, had adhered to the principles of nonalignment more than any other country. If political conditions required us to seek American help in establishing a comprehensive, just, and lasting solution to the Middle East dispute, that absolutely did not mean that Egypt had abandoned nonalignment. In March, I pointed out, Egypt had rejected a mutual-defense agreement with the United States modeled on one that Israel had signed with the United States. "But instead of congratulating Egypt for this, and for regaining its territory, you condemn us," I said.

Rodríguez said, with false humility, that Cuba was a small country with limited military and economic power, but it adhered to its principles and expressed its opinions without hesitation. For that reason Cuba did not hide its opposition to the Egyptian position. For any one Arab country to try to achieve peace would weaken Arab ranks as well as itself. He mentioned the Cuban troops that had been sent to fight with Syria against Israel in 1973 by way of emphasizing Cuba's right to pronounce on such issues. The effort must be collective, he said, and the outcome comprehensive. He must have noticed from my expression that I was not persuaded. So he continued slowly and calmly. Cuba, Rodríguez said, was leading the campaign against American imperialism and against Chinese deviationism, but it was not leading a campaign against Egypt.

I tried to reply with similar politeness, for a skilled debater gives the opponent an opportunity to display his own skill and to pursue the dialogue at the same refined level.

But Rodríguez interrupted me. "Cuba supports peace. Cuba believes in dialogue and negotiation. For example," he said, "the confrontation between Cuba and the United States cannot be solved in a military way. If the U.S. wants a solution, it must engage in dialogue."

I was surprised, I said, that Cuba, which considered peace an inseparable part of its political philosophy, would oppose Egypt's peaceful efforts. Raising my voice somewhat, I said, "To this very moment, Egypt continues to be, in its principles, its soldiers, its works, its experts, its teachers, the basic prop of the Arab states in society, culture, civilization, economy, science, and politics. Egypt plays an indispensable role in behalf of the welfare of the Arab peoples. Even the Arab states that are leading the ignoble campaign of attacks against Egypt cannot do without the Egyptians who work in them!"

Taken aback by my vehemence, Rodriguez tried to soothe me: Egypt was the heart of the Arab world. His friend, Houari Boumedienne, had mentioned to him more than once that, despite any differences, one must never forget that Egypt was the most important state in the Arab world.

As our meeting ended, Rodríguez mentioned the reports that extremist Palestinians would try to assassinate the head of the Egyptian delegation. The Cuban government considered itself responsible for my safety, he said, and had adopted all measures for the protection of both me and my delegation.

I thanked him but said that I believed that the date of a man's death is written; consequently I could not change my fate. I left the meeting even more convinced that a clash between Cuba and Egypt was unavoidable.

The next day a Cuban minister called on me to ask why, unlike the other heads of state and delegations, I refused to move from my hotel to the quarters set aside for me as the head of the Egyptian delegation. Did my position stem from any discomfort with Cuban hospitality? I assured him that this was not the case but that I remained in the hotel suite to be near my Egyptian colleagues.

I sought support from African ministers against the attempt of the radical states, led by Cuba, to take over the nonaligned movement. In the midst of this effort, an Egyptian delegate, greatly agitated, came to my room. He had just read Cuba's proposed new closing statement, which was much worse than the first. Not only did it condemn the Camp David agreements and the Egyptian-Israeli treaty, but it called them a plot against the Palestinian people. Egypt, it stated, had abandoned the principles of nonalignment.

I called the Egyptian delegation to my room. Their morale was high and we agreed to resist Marxist hegemony over the nonaligned movement. I directed them in drafting several alternatives to the Cuban text.

Heads of states and governments, including Saddam Hussein, were now arriving in Havana, which led me to expect that the pressures against Egypt would increase.

In the evening I sent a coded telegram to Mustafa Khalil warning him that the rejectionists were doing their best to suspend Egypt's membership while many countries that we counted remained hesitant. Even Liberia was backing away from us in the face of increasing threats.

Instead of having dinner. I took a tranquilizer and went to bed, but the telephone rang. It was Cecil Dennis, almost hysterical. He wanted to see me immediately. I replied that I was in bed, my car had gone off, and the security personnel had departed, all of which made it difficult for me to get to the Hotel Havana Libre, where he was staying. Let us meet each other tomorrow morning, I said.

"No," he said, the matter was urgent and could not wait until morning. I thought of asking him to come to my hotel, but immediately amended this, realizing that my Liberian colleague was the head of the African group and that I must attend to protocol. So I got dressed, and contacted Major al-Hafnawi, asking him to arrange a car to take me to the Havana Libre. I arrived at Cecil's suite at midnight. He said, almost screaming, "Boutros, my brother, my friend, how can I defend Egypt and its policies at a time when President Sadat is inciting world public opinion against Egypt?" Sadat, he said, had just gone to Israel on an official visit, in full hearing and view of the world—at a time when he should have been taking part in the Havana conference!

"The sight of Sadat on the television, standing side by side with Menachem Begin on an Israeli naval ship in Haifa harbor, is a provocation to all heads of state present in Havana. But more than that," Cecil declared, "Sadat, in a statement carried by all news agencies, says that Egypt will send troops to Morocco to help King Hassan in the Western Sahara war."

He cried, "My brother Boutros, you know that the nonaligned majority does not agree with Morocco's policy! Yet the president of Egypt has chosen to support it! How can Egypt's friends help it under these conditions?"

I acted quickly to calm Cecil, even if this required a diplomatic subterfuge, whatever that might cost me. I said without hesitation that the statement attributed to Sadat was out of context. I said that the coming days would witness many plots and charges by the rejectionist states to deepen the division between Egypt and its African friends. It is incumbent on us all, I said, to be watchful and to oppose these lies and not to join in spreading them.

The foreign minister of Liberia interrupted me to ask, "Are you ready to clarify Egypt's position before the conference?" I responded immediately that I would tell the summit conference that Egypt had not offered soldiers or weapons to Morocco. Egypt was only studying the matter. I also told Cecil that I was ready to call a press conference to assure everyone that the statements attributed to President Sadat were inaccurate. I directed an urgent telegram to Prime Minister Mustafa Khalil, reporting this episode. I wanted Sadat to know why I had to disavow his statements, hoping that he would not be angry.

Bit by bit I was able to pacify Cecil Dennis, who eventually said calmly, "Boutros, defending Egypt's position in this conference has not been an easy matter." I feared that he was about to give up. "But you, Cecil," I said, "feel completely convinced of the correctness of Egypt's position. Indeed, President Tolbert promised President

Sadat in Monrovia that the African group, under your leadership, would stand with determination against any attempt to suspend Egypt's membership."

"The hour is late," Dennis said, "and you are as exhausted as I am. Things will look clearer tomorrow. Then we can agree on a strategy to gather the greatest possible number of African states to stand behind Egypt."

Eight months later a coup d'état led by Master Sergeant Samuel K. Doe took over the government of Liberia. President William Tolbert was slain and the cabinet arrested. I asked Sadat for permission to plead in his name and Egypt's that my friend Cecil Dennis and the others in the cabinet be spared. Sadat said yes, but my colleagues urged me not to contact the Liberian rebels, claiming that I would only provoke them to kill Cecil Dennis. All through the night I hesitated. Should I act or not? In the morning of April 22, 1980, I learned from Reuters that Cecil Dennis and the other dignitaries had been stripped naked, taken to the beach at Monrovia, and murdered. In the course of diplomatic protocol I was later compelled to receive Master Sergeant Doe and shake hands with my friend's killer. Samuel Doe himself was to be murdered later in horrible circumstances.

On Monday, September 3, 1979, I had breakfast with the foreign minister of Indonesia in his suite. He gestured strangely to indicate that there were listening and recording devices around us in the room. The rejectionists were pressing Indonesia and other Muslim states in the name of Islamic solidarity. Every time I tried to refute their position, the Indonesian minister placed his hand over his mouth and waved rapidly toward the wall, urging me to be silent.

From this meeting I went to the conference hall to take part in the ceremonial opening of the summit. Present were the leaders of the third world: Fidel Castro, Josip Broz Tito, Julius Nyerere, Kenneth Kaunda, Saddam Hussein, Hafez al-Assad, Yasir Arafat, and King Hussein of Jordan.

Fidel Castro violently attacked imperialism and emphasized the special friendship that linked Cuba and the Soviet Union. As to the Palestinian question, Castro said, "By way of treachery, and the spreading of division, and the encouragement of fragmentation, imperialism tried to impose a faulty peace by its own methods. But it is an odious armed peace, a peace imperfect and unjust and stained with blood. Peace like this cannot be lasting peace." He called the Camp David agreements a betrayal of the Arab world, the Palestinian people, the people of Lebanon, the people of Syria, and the people of Jordan, indeed, a betrayal of everyone, including the Egyptians themselves.

"For these reasons," Castro declared, "the nonaligned movement most thoroughly condemns the Camp David agreements in a strong and clear manner that leaves no room for doubt."

I was enraged. I said to Esmat Abdel Meguid that I must respond to this man's insolence immediately. Esmat agreed with hesitation but insisted that my response be calm, measured, and brief.

As I wrote my refutation my nerves were on edge. President Kenneth Kaunda was speaking in behalf of Africa, and someone else spoke for Asia, and another for Latin America. As the public session ended, I called for a point of order. The president of Sri Lanka, who was presiding, gave me the floor: "I have listened to the attack directed at my country by President Castro. I have the right to reply to the lack of propriety and lack of respect for diplomatic usage in this speech, to the infringement on Egypt's dignity that it contained, and to the directing of false accusations and allegations against Egypt. I demand this right of reply now."

The president of the session seemed confused. He hesitated, then said that he registered my right to respond, but that time did not permit it during the opening session. I replied angrily that I would accept the position of the president but only on condition that I be promised the opportunity to respond within a short time and in open session.

The matter ended thus. While Castro denounced many states in his speech, Egypt was the only one that did not hesitate to respond publicly to his attack. As the delegates were leaving the hall a number of them implied their appreciation for what I had done. They were not happy with the leftist terrorism that they felt was being imposed upon them at the conference.

I repaired to my room to prepare my speech in reply to Castro and finished a text of no more than two pages. That afternoon Castro was in the chair. He opened the session and said with a broad smile, "In my capacity as president of the conference I give the floor to the representative of Egypt so that he can exercise his right of reply." I began to deliver my speech calmly. But I had read no more than a few words when Ali al-Turayki, foreign minister of Libya, interrupted, waving his hands and shouting, "Point of order, point of order."

I stopped speaking. President Castro gave the floor to the Libyan, who declared that it was not customary to respond to the speech of the president of the host state and that the representative of Egypt could express himself during the discussion of the Middle East question. Castro replied to al-Turayki that, despite his appreciation for what the Libyan representative had said, he still desired to provide an opportunity for the representative of Egypt to speak now.

I resumed amid complete silence. As I read my speech I could hear nothing except Esmat Abdel Meguid whispering in my ear in French: "Keep it slow . . . keep it slow." I told the delegates that I was shocked by Cuba's attack against Egypt. "President Sadat is an authentic revolutionary," I said. "He faced the enemy in his own house in November 1977. Egypt went to Jerusalem to liberate Palestine from Israeli imperialism and went to Jerusalem to liberate the Arab lands from military occupation."

As I spoke, my words came faster while Esmat continued to whisper, "Slow down, slow down." I tried to follow his advice. But the more slowly I spoke, the louder my voice became. "I say to you with the utmost objectivity that the only Arab state that is truly struggling in behalf of the Palestinians is Egypt!"

"Stop shouting," Esmat whispered. His whisper sounded as loud as a shout itself. My heart was thumping so loudly that I did not know which I feared more, a heart attack or that the delegates would hear the pounding in my chest.

I went on, "In the name of President Sadat, I announce that Egypt is ready to support any decision issued by the nonaligned or the United Nations or any other organization that can help the Palestinian people get back their homeland!"

There was complete silence in the great hall. How dare this deviant lecture Fidel Castro, the president of Cuba, the president of the summit, the Marxist and the nonaligned Almighty, in this way?

Castro made no comment on what I had said and calmly continued to administer the session. He gave the floor to a representative of Cuba, followed by a representative of Madagascar, then Yasir

Arafat of the PLO, then Mengistu of Ethiopia, then representatives of Iran, Angola, Vietnam, and the Congo. Each of them insulted Sadat, calling him a traitor, a betrayer of his country to imperialism and Zionism, and a back-stabber of the Palestinian people. Paulo Jorge, foreign minister of Angola, reserved his best insults for me. How could this contemptible person attack the giant of the Cuban revolution, Fidel Castro? He could do so only under instructions from his imperialist masters! Then he spoke about revolution and progress in confrontation with reaction and colonialism as if he were Lenin himself.

Unsettled as my nerves were while giving my speech, I was completely calm while listening to the flow of insults from these "progressive and revolutionary" states (most of whom were Soviet dependencies).

Then President Mathieu Kérékou of the republic of Benin asked for the floor. He stood, waving his hands theatrically, and demanded that my speech be stricken from the minutes of the session. The hall burst into applause. I felt that Egypt was about to be expelled not only from the conference but from the nonaligned movement as well at that very instant! I swore to myself that if a decision was issued to expel Egypt, I would remain in my seat even if it meant that force would be used to remove me from the hall.

While this possibility flashed through my mind I was surprised to see the president of Tanzania, Julius Nyerere, rise and say, "If the conference decides to strike the comments of the representative of Egypt from the minutes of the conference, what happens to the comments and speeches that were delivered following his speech and in response to it? The matter will become incomprehensible."

Nyerere's words brought another strange silence in the hall. No one supported Nyerere, and the atmosphere of intellectual terror grew even stronger in the hall.

Castro then announced that the conference had agreed to strike the text of the speech of the representative of Egypt from the minutes of the session, and the room echoed with thunderous applause. Cries of triumph spread among the rejectionist and leftist states. Those who chose not to applaud had withdrawn into themselves, hoping that the storm would pass without harming them.

The session continued, with wave after wave of insults and obscenities directed against Egypt, Sadat, and the junior minister Boutros-Ghali.

That evening Castro held a party for the heads of delegations and stood at the entrance to receive his guests. As I shook his hand he said, "I had heard before your arrival that you were a dangerous adversary and the truth of that became clear to me today." Smiling, he added that he wished me a pleasant stay in Havana. His cordiality only augmented my agitation, for it conveyed Castro's confidence that Egypt's cause was lost.

A few at the reception greeted me with pleasure as the knight who had tilted at a giant windmill, but most spurned me for my impudence toward the Cuban leader. As Egypt's representative, I had been ejected from the Arab League and from the Islamic Conference, and would soon be ejected from the nonaligned movement.

But when I found myself face-to-face with Yasir Arafat he opened his arms, embraced me, and kissed me before I was able to say a word. He had not recognized me in the crowd and acted reflexively. After the kisses and hugs, I said, "Do you know whom you are kissing and greeting so warmly?" Arafat hesitated and looked at me with astonishment. I said, "I am the head of the Egyptian delegation." Arafat pulled away quickly, crying, "Oh, Boutros! Oh, Boutros!"

Tuesday morning the secretary-general of the United Nations, Kurt Waldheim, and Tito, the spiritual father of the nonaligned movement, spoke. Tito, ill and worn-out, spoke in a low voice from his chair. It was evident that his days were numbered; I could not hope to get support from the Yugoslavian delegation for the cause of true nonalignment.

In the afternoon I visited Kurt Waldheim in his rest house. He referred to my speech and said that the time might have come to hold an international conference on the Middle East crisis. Waldheim said that he intended to take advantage of the presence of Hafez al-Assad, King Hussein, and Yasir Arafat in Havana to discuss this with them. Andrei Gromyko, the Russian foreign minister, he said, had made it clear to him that the Soviet Union opposed an international conference because it would mean recognizing, directly or indirectly, the Camp David agreements. Waldheim said that he was convinced, however, that if the Arabs agreed to such a conference, the Soviets would reconsider.

I listened to Waldheim without revealing my opinion that Sadat would not accept an international conference at this stage and would oppose the idea as long as complete withdrawal from Sinai had not been completed. Despite what I had said in my speech, I knew that the idea of an international conference in Gaza or Al-Arish, which Sadat had mentioned in Monrovia a month earlier, was only a diplomatic maneuver to confound the Arab rejectionists. I listened to Waldheim and said nothing.

That evening I returned to my hotel to await the prime minister of Morocco, who had asked to meet me discreetly in my room. The Moroccan arrived at about 10:00 P.M., wearing a long white *shurta* gown and dark glasses, as if he were going to a costume party. He and the Moroccan ambassador to the United Nations, Abdel Latif al-Filali, entered my room after looking left and right for fear that someone might see them.

I invited the Moroccans to partake of the spirits and excellent cigars placed in my room by the generosity of our Cuban hosts and, setting diplomacy aside, spoke candidly. Everyone now knew, I said, that the first contacts between Egypt and Israel had taken place in Rabat with the blessing of King Hassan. Thus the public position of Morocco and His Majesty had come as a great shock for Egypt.

After much discussion, we agreed on three points. First, the states attempting to isolate Egypt differed from those trying to isolate Morocco regarding the Western Sahara dispute. There was no use announcing an Egyptian-Moroccan rapprochement, because that would simply gather the different groups together into a bloc against us both. Second, the Moroccans would make it clear that they were not trying to get the assistance of Egyptian forces in the war in the Western Sahara. But the Moroccans rejected my request that they publicly declare that there was no truth to the story that Egypt would send troops to Morocco in response to a request from Rabat. Third, we would continue to consult through our representatives in New York. I understood from this that the prime minister wanted to keep his foreign minister, Muhammad Boucetta, out of the picture. It was clear to me that this evening's meeting was being held without Boucetta's knowledge.

When the prime minister left my room, he put on his dark glasses once again and hurried away furtively.

The next morning I visited President Moussa Traore of Mali. I was with Ahmad Mahir, who carried with him a large silver tray bearing Sadat's signature. President Traore received his gift with a broad smile.

The air was warm and pleasant. We sat beside a wide window overlooking thick trees that surrounded the villa. Hundreds of birds were singing in those trees. "President Sadat has made a mistake," Traore began. Representatives of the rejectionist states had come several times to Bamako and were now making the rounds in Africa, urging condemnation of Egypt and explaining their reasons for opposing Egypt's policy. But Egypt did not make similar contacts.

I interrupted him, saying, "It appears that His Excellency the president has not followed the explanation that I offered about the goals of Egyptian diplomacy." Traore interrupted me in turn and said with irritation, "If the enemies of Egypt don't understand Egyptian policy and the friends of Egypt don't understand Egyptian policy, do you not agree with me that there is something wrong with Egyptian policy?" Nonetheless he made it clear that he completely rejected the expulsion of Egypt from the nonaligned group.

I left the meeting angry with myself for having lost control of my emotions and interrupted a head of state in a way that was somewhat improper. The Egyptian position continued to deteriorate at the conference and I did not see any way to stop this.

At lunch at the embassy of Nigeria with most of the heads of delegation, there was a consensus that Cuba was running the conference in an authoritarian manner, far removed from the spirit of democracy appropriate to such gatherings. The Indian foreign minister confessed that the coercive atmosphere made him hesitate to express himself frankly on any subject.

The evening session went on until one in the morning. President after president spoke of Egyptian treachery and Egyptian violations of the principles of nonalignment. Then Julius Nyerere spoke and offered a definition for the nonaligned movement:

> We do not form a bloc; our grouping is only a defense of the right of small states to remain free from blocs. Our movement is a progressive movement but is not a grouping of progressive states. Our ranks include socialist countries but our movement is not a movement of socialist countries. If we wanted our movement to turn into a bloc or to include one of the blocs, that would mean the end of its existence and its loss of any influence over the events of the world and of any effectiveness in the work on behalf of peace. . . .

I was delighted to hear this and smiled.

> The nonaligned movement must remain a group of states jealous of their independence, taking pride in their nonalignedness, and adhering to the principle of justice among peoples and nations, and rejecting without hesitation the idea of alliances with any bloc or any of the great states.

Nyerere's speech, in its refinement and substance, stood out sharply from the scores of other speeches that filled the long hours of this conference.

Ambassador Ismat Kittani, of the Iraqi Foreign Ministry, was chairman of a committee charged with reviewing the proposal to denounce Egyptian policy. I met with them all through the night of September 6, 1979, until six-thirty the next morning. The pillars of the Arab rejection took part: Abd al-Halim Khaddam of Syria, Saddun Hammadi of Iraq, Faruq Qaddumi of Palestine, al-Bedjawi of Algeria, not to mention the African radicals.

Khaddam spoke first, and at length, mainly about the wars of the Crusades. Sinai is not Egyptian land, he said, but part of Palestine. His words irritated many of those present, some of whom protested that he was harming the rejectionist cause.

I intervened twice, the first time a little after midnight, and the second just before dawn, as the light of the new day was beginning to show. Algeria, I said, accused Egypt of selling its soul to America at a time when Algeria was selling its oil to the same country. Everyone knows, I said, that Syrian hands are covered with the blood of Palestinians they slew in Tell al-Zaatar. And Jordanian hands remain covered with the blood of thousands of Palestinians killed in "Black September 1970."

Throughout the session, I had left the conference hall frequently to meet African colleagues and urge them to support me. I had met secretly with the representative of Emperor Bokassa of the Central African Republic in the men's room and in this unlikely place got his pledge to defend Egypt. My contacts were fruitful and led a broad group of African delegations to declare their opposition to the initiative of the rejectionist states and their support for Egypt. Zaire, Togo, Liberia, Zambia, Côte d'Ivoire, and Kenya were all supportive, joined by such Asian states as Nepal and Singapore and the Latin states Peru and Argentina. But Sudan, Somalia, Yugoslavia, and India remained silent, which enraged me.

At six o'clock in the morning, the president of the session, Ismat Kittani, speaking in a flat, objective, professional way, indicated that of 49 speakers, 24 opposed the proposal to condemn Egypt and suspend its membership, while 23 states supported it. Noting that decisions of the summit are taken by consensus, Kittani said calmly that the committee had not been able to agree on a unified position. For that reason he decided to put the matter to the summit conference itself. Kittani, whom I appointed sixteen years later as senior political adviser to the secretary-general of the United Nations, told me that Saddam Hussein had sharply reproved him for failing to gain a consensus against Egypt.

Abd al-Halim Khaddam demanded the floor, at which point I said loudly so everyone could hear: "For the Prophet's sake, why don't you go to sleep, and let others sleep as well?" Everybody laughed and I left the hall.

The next morning I learned that while we were meeting until dawn at the ministerial level, a second meeting had been going on that included Yasir Arafat, Fidel Castro, and a number of African leaders. This meeting concluded an agreement to (1) condemn the Camp David agreements; (2) put Egypt on probation under a special committee created to monitor Egypt's actions on the Palestinian question; and (3) call for a report on Egypt's expulsion from the nonaligned movement.

That day I met with Kenneth Kaunda, president of the republic of Zambia, who as he spoke played nervously with a white handkerchief. No one was disputing Sadat's right to restore Egyptian land in the way that he saw fit, Kaunda said, but it would be a disaster if

Sadat lost the friendship of African leaders like Nyerere and himself. What strongly offended him, he said, was Sadat's choosing the time of the Havana conference—a date set for many months—to undertake a visit to Israel and to meet with Begin in Haifa instead of with Castro in Havana. If Sadat had come to Havana, as he had gone to Monrovia, he could have removed any misunderstanding about Egyptian policy. He added, playing with his white handkerchief, that the plight of the Palestinians had a special sensitivity for all Africans because of the similarity between what the Israeli settlers were doing in Palestine and what white settlers had done in South Africa. Indeed, the solid cooperation between the Israeli regime and the racist regime in South Africa was an added cause for offense among Africans, he said.

Referring to Sadat's statement about Egyptian military help for King Hassan in the Western Sahara conflict, Kaunda said, "I wish, I wish, and insist of my brother Sadat, that he not place Egypt in positions opposed to the whole African continent." Kaunda twisted his handkerchief into a knot, and his voice sounded like a sob. In fact, Kaunda was giving me good news: that he had helped draft the proposed Havana decision and that it would have to be based on the decisions already taken by the Monrovia conference.

When the evening session began, the Arab delegations did not walk out of the hall when I spoke. In my speech I repeatedly mentioned Anwar Sadat's name, but my main purpose was to recall for my audience the founding principles of the nonaligned movement. Directing my words to President Castro, I noted that Cuba had participated in producing the five guidelines of nonalignment: pursuit of an independent policy based on peaceful coexistence; support of national-liberation movements; nonparticipation in great-power military alliances; nonparticipation in bilateral military alliances with any of the great powers; and refusal to allow great-power military bases on the territory of a nonaligned state.

By listing these guidelines I emphasized to all present that some governments represented at Havana had not respected these guidelines. Most prominent of these was Cuba, the host of the conference, which had allied itself with the Soviet Union and allowed it to establish military bases on its territory. I said that Egypt had rejected the Soviet Union's pressure for a USSR-Egyptian defense agreement. As Egyptians we were proud of our Egyptian heritage, I said, and as Africans we were proud of our African heritage, and as a nonaligned nation we were proud of our refusal to align with any superpower bloc. I stressed the necessity of the nonaligned movement's adhering to the decision of the Organization of African Unity in everything that related to Africa. That required, I said, that the Havana conference adhere to the decisions issued by the Monrovia conference on the matter of Egypt's policy and Camp David.

Egypt had been able, I said, by virtue of the peace treaty with Israel, to regain its occupied lands and the integrity of its national territory. That should be considered a victory for the Arabs and the Arab nations and a victory for Africa and the sons of Africa, and a victory for the nonaligned states and for the principles of nonalignment.

I paused for a moment, and then directed my words to the president of the Palestine Liberation Organization, Yasir Arafat. "From this podium, on the occasion of the Havana summit, and in the presence of this esteemed gathering of presidents and leaders, I extend my hand with sincerity and honesty to the Palestine Liberation Organization and its leadership. I say officially and without hesitation or reservation that Egypt, the warrior, will continue the fight in behalf of its brothers the Palestinians until the Palestinian state is born. Egypt is ready to extend the hand of cooperation to any Arab state that wants to open a fraternal dialogue toward arriving at a comprehensive and just solution to the struggle in the Middle East."

My speech over, I headed for my seat. As I passed the Zambian delegation, I found President Kaunda sitting there. Dispensing entirely with protocol, I took a seat next to him and said, "Mr. President, you told me a few hours ago that the decision to be issued by the Havana conference would be based on the Monrovia decisions, but now I know that the proposed decision that will be put to the presidents is completely contrary to the Monrovia decisions."

President Kaunda interrupted me angrily and said loudly, "Do you say that I lied to you?" "No, Mr. President," I replied, "Your Excellency is a head of state and I am just a minister. I know my limits. I have all respect for you. I come to you only for your help. President Anwar Sadat told me to resort to you if I found difficulties or obstacles. 'Kenneth Kaunda,' he said, 'is like a brother to me and can guide you toward the right path.' "

I felt the extent of President Kaunda's embarrassment as he simply smiled. Samora Machel, president of the republic of Mozambique, passed in front of us and Kaunda called to him. Machel joined us and said, "Mr. Egyptian Minister, we Africans are fed up with your Arab quarrels. Please give up your seat for me so that I can discuss African issues with my brother Kaunda!" I rose from my place, angry and losing hope. I saw no point in further effort.

On Saturday, September 8, 1979, the decision of the conference condemning Egypt was issued. Fidel Castro rose to pronounce the judgment of condemnation. He made it clear that Cuba, Bangladesh, Congo, Grenada, Guyana, India, Libya, the SWAPO movement, Panama, Korea, Singapore, Uganda, Yugoslavia, Zambia, Iraq, Mozambique, Sri Lanka, and Suriname had all agreed on the proposal. Discussion began at around ten o'clock in the evening and ended at four in the morning with the issuing of the condemnation of the Camp David agreements. Twenty-two states supported the condemnation; only six, including Egypt, were in opposition. The remaining states in attendance, which were the majority, preferred to distance themselves from the battle. The presidency of the conference considered this silence to be consent.

Then the foreign minister of Liberia spoke, in his capacity as head of the African group, and said that the proposed decision contradicted the Monrovia decisions. The foreign minister of Senegal, Mustafa Niasse, rose and attacked the "terrorist" methods employed in the conference and announced his government's rejection of the decision. He scathingly denounced those African states whose positions in Havana were in opposition to their positions in Monrovia.

The vehemence of Mustafa Niasse's speech backfired on us. Kaunda responded that the Senegalese had displayed a lack of respect for the African tradition of respect for heads of state and respect for age. He touched his white head to signify himself as such. When Kenneth Kaunda is speaking, Kaunda said, he speaks in the name of Africa because he is an African leader, but when Mustafa Niasse speaks, he is only a minister who exceeds his competence. If there had been any other official who was thinking of speaking in defense of Egypt, Kaunda's speech silenced him. From what he said, Kaunda clearly supported the rejectionists at the conference.

At four o'clock in the morning Castro announced the end of the conference. I returned to my hotel and took refuge in my bed, but I did not sleep. All the struggles of the session were going around and around in my head, with the images crowding one after another. Although I had lost the battle, I took comfort in the belief that I had undertaken my responsibility properly.

The next morning I summarized my thoughts in my report about the session:

Among those present at Havana there was an almost complete consensus in opposition to the Camp David agreements. The reasoning was that the nonaligned movement had recognized the Palestine Liberation Organization as the sole legal representative of the Palestinian people; that the PLO had condemned these agreements; and therefore that the conference must condemn them also.

The members of the conference were convinced that Egypt had no right to negotiate Palestinian issues in the absence of the PLO.

The general conviction was that the Egyptian-Israeli peace treaty was nothing but a separate peace. Even if some states expressed the view that Egypt had the right to sign whatever agreement with Israel it deemed appropriate to get back its land, not a single state defended the peace treaty.

Likewise there was a conviction among many states that Israel had grown more aggressive since the Camp David agreements, as if by virtue of the agreements it had achieved greater freedom to intervene in neighboring Arab lands.

It was assured that the campaign against Egypt will continue. The battle will shift to the United Nations, where Egypt's enemies will seek a decision of the General Assembly condemning Egypt.

But I also recalled some positive points:

Egypt, at Havana, was able to withstand attempts to assert the existence of a natural alliance between the nonaligned states and the socialist states. Despite the great efforts of the rejectionist states, a decision suspending Egypt's membership in the nonaligned movement was not issued. The existence of a strong and deep African current of support for Egypt was established.

Even though the radical states, with Cuba in their forefront, cooperated with the Arab rejectionist states, they refused to follow the

Arabs to the end of the road. There is no doubt that Castro did not want a decision to be taken in Havana to suspend Egypt's membership. Let it happen later and somewhere else, he seemed to feel.

And I was able to explain the peace treaty and the two Camp David agreements to a number of friendly states, erasing doubts and misapprehensions among many.

One thing of which there is no doubt, I cabled to Cairo, is that the negatives exceed the positive in the final accounting. But that should not lessen our resolve. Egypt's victory will be realized when the withdrawal of Israeli forces from Sinai is completed and after elections in the West Bank and Gaza lead to the establishment of full Palestinian autonomy.

That night a strong storm set in, and all airplanes were grounded. I was indebted to this storm for the hours that it allowed me to rest and to prepare a declaration that I would have to deliver to the European Parliament in Strasbourg in a few days. A correspondent for the weekly *Le Nouvel Observateur* came to me. "You were the chief target of criticism in the Havana conference," he said. Did I expect, he asked, that Egypt's separation from the nonaligned movement would be completed during the conference of foreign ministers of nonaligned states in Delhi a year and half from now?

I replied by referring to the story of Goha, the donkey, and the sultan. The sultan had ordered his vizier to find someone who could teach his donkey to read and write, and said he would reward whoever succeeded in this task and punish those who failed. The vizier could find no one to accept this task except Goha, who asked the sultan for ten thousand dinars and a period of five years. When Goha's friends came to him to find out why he accepted a task in which he must necessarily fail and which would lead to his being hanged, he said to them calmly, "Who knows? After five years maybe the sultan will have died. After five years maybe the donkey will have died. Or maybe Goha will have died." In diplomacy, even twenty-four hours can be a long time.

A New Round in Alexandria

On my way home from Havana via Paris, I met the newly appointed French foreign minister Jean-François Poncet. Adjusting his coat

collar and leaning back in his chair, he said, "Moshe Dayan was sitting in this office, where you are sitting, a short time ago. Dayan said to me without evasion that what was concluded between Egypt and Israel was only a separate peace, and that when Israel negotiates about the West Bank and the Gaza Strip, the subject will not be sovereignty over these areas but only administrative rule for the Palestinians, and nothing else." Thus Dayan had confirmed Israel's intention to retain the West Bank, François-Poncet said. And American diplomacy had erred, for whereas Israel's withdrawal from the occupied lands had once been assumed, now it had become a topic for negotiation.

I almost confided to the French minister that perhaps I shared his view, but I controlled myself and zealously defended our diplomacy. Afterward at a press conference in one of the great halls of the Crillon Hotel, I found a hostile press. Why do your statements differ from those of President Sadat? Hasn't Egypt's treaty with Israel created the Lebanon crisis? How did I feel when I extended my hand to Yasir Arafat in Havana and the Palestinian leader rejected it? I answered energetically.

Back in Cairo I had a telephone conversation with President Sadat on September 21. He said angrily, "I do not want you to be afraid of waging any political battle. We shall continue on this line and in our work regardless of Arab rejection or non-Arab rejection." I realized from his conversation that he had read the cables I sent from Havana. Sadat talked at length while I simply listened or murmured approval.

Two days later the president summoned me to meet with him in Ismailia at noon. I arrived a few minutes late and hurried to the president's retreat overlooking the Suez Canal.

Sadat was wearing a blue exercise suit and white shoes, and I thought to myself that the shoes didn't go at all with the clothes. With the president when he received me was the engineer Uthman Ahmad Uthman, who said nothing until, after the meeting had gone on for some hours, he tried to persuade Sadat to take their daily walk together, but to no avail.

I told Sadat of my fears that Egypt was becoming increasingly isolated diplomatically. Sadat listened to my conversation calmly for some time and then interrupted me, saying, "I want you to move

your chair." I did not understand what he meant. My thoughts were far away from my chair. When I asked him, he repeated the same phrase and said, "I want you, Boutros, to move your chair from where it is so that you can see the east bank of the Suez Canal."

I carried out the president's instructions, and from my new position I could see the glorious Sinai desert on the bank opposite us. Before me were green trees and gardens surrounding the president's retreat, and beyond them the water in the canal shining and reflecting the sunshine. In the distance were the yellow sands of the desert.

The president said, uttering his words with deliberate slowness, "I do not wish to underestimate the magnitude of the problems and worries that Egyptian diplomacy is facing. But all these problems and the worries pale in comparison with this land we have regained. They are not worth one square meter of this land, which we have regained without spilling the blood of my children. Boutros, I don't want to belittle the efforts you are making, but I assure you that a square meter of this Egyptian land is far more important than your diplomatic difficulties. I am not afraid of condemnations. I am not afraid of countries' severing diplomatic relations with us. And I am not afraid of the provocation and trivia of the Arab countries." Sadat talked over the next hours as I listened; he gave me no chance to respond to or comment on what he said. He fiercely attacked the "semi-countries in the Gulf and Africa which are but a little band of no political, cultural, or economic value."

Actually, when the meeting was over, I was fully convinced by Sadat's argument: there was no comparison between the two elements of the equation; the political isolation would end after a while, but the regained land would remain forever ours.

The sixth round of negotiations for self-rule started on Wednesday, September 26, 1979, in Alexandria. The Egyptian leaders, from president to prime minister, had been in Alexandria for about a week. Sadat had decided to make a grand show, to indicate that the period of the autonomy negotiations, now ten months old, had made progress. The truth was otherwise.

I flew to Alexandria with Major General Ahmad Badawi on board the Mystère, which took us from Almazah to Al Nuzhah airport in less than twenty minutes. I noticed that General Badawi preceded me without hesitation when we arrived at the aircraft. Although I

usually was not concerned with such matters, his lack of courtesy and failure to invite me to enter the aircraft caught my attention, particularly as I was his guest. But after we arrived at Al-Nuzhah airport, and I made a passing comment to one of the protocol officers, I was told—I was not aware of this before—that the army chief of staff took precedence, in the rules of protocol, over ministers.

The negotiations began at eleven-thirty in the hall of the San Stefano Hotel. In his opening speech, Dr. Mustafa Khalil said that since the fifth round of talks two important events had taken place: the first was President Sadat's visit to Haifa, which established a positive atmosphere in Egyptian-Israel relations. The second event was my attempt to amend Security Council Resolution 242 at the UN in New York or to have a new resolution issued in its place. Dr. Mustafa said that Egypt had rejected these attempts because it wanted to allow enough time for the self-rule negotiations to produce a solution to the problem. This comment by Mustafa Khalil embarrassed me. I had repeatedly advocated that Egypt would welcome the issuance of a new Security Council resolution that to amend 242 by stipulating the right of self-determination for the Palestinian people. I did not regard this as being in conflict with the Camp David agreements or the negotiations for self-rule. In fact, a new resolution would reinforce the Egyptian negotiating position within the Camp David framework.

The Security Council had not taken action; indeed it had refused to discuss the matter. Therefore there was no reason for Mustafa Khalil to state on record, officially and openly, that Egypt objected to amending Resolution 242. By doing so, he was restricting Egyptian diplomatic movement in the future.

Dr. Mustafa Khalil then expressed his outrage at Israel for announcing, on the first anniversary of Camp David, that Israelis would be permitted to purchase land in the West Bank and Gaza. The American ambassador, James Leonard, added that the United States was publicly and officially opposed to this Israeli decision. As Leonard said this the air became tense. The Israeli delegates nervously whispered to one another while Ariel Sharon jumped up and down in his chair and waved his hand to be recognized. The face of the Israeli minister of justice, Shmuel Tamir, was dark. But Yosef Burg intervened politely. As head of the delegation, he spoke calmly in response to Mustafa Khalil and Leonard. He said that Jordanian law had been instituted in the West Bank and discriminated between Arabs and Jews, for it did not allow Jews to purchase land. During the British occupation, Jews came under religious and racial persecution that also prevented them from purchasing land. So the Israeli government had decided to rectify this situation. The timing of the cabinet decision on the first anniversary of Camp David was an unintentional coincidence. Then the minister of justice, Tamir, offered similar explanations for the Israeli ruling.

As I listened to these fairy tales I nearly lost control of myself. First Mustafa Khalil had undermined Egyptian diplomacy; then Burg and Tamir had exposed Israel's duplicity. It was the drop that made water spill from the glass. I asked to be recognized. "Allow me to disagree with what the Israeli minister of interior and the minister of justice have said. The aim of negotiations we are now undertaking is, at the end, to bring about Palestinian participation in these negotiations. Without the participation of the Palestinians I cannot imagine that any result will be achieved. And there is no doubt that the Israeli government's decision to allow Israelis to purchase Arab lands in the West Bank and Gaza will not encourage the Palestinians to join us in negotiating or in the peace process. This Israeli position has created a new crisis of confidence on the anniversary of the signing of the Camp David agreements."

I raised my voice—as though I were still at the Havana conference—and pointed at Shmuel Tamir: "Allow me to ask you, Mr. Minister of Justice, wasn't the decision issued in 1967 prohibiting Israelis from buying Arab lands in the occupied territories an Israeli decision issued by the Israeli government itself? Why has Israel retreated from this position? Why are you now deciding against what you decided in 1967? Can you answer this? Do you honestly believe that this decision helps the peace process? Without Palestinian participation our negotiations will remain a strictly theoretical exercise that has no relation to reality, and your decision will not encourage the Palestinians to participate in our talks!"

While delivering this speech, I noticed Nessim, the Israeli minister of state, who never spoke in session, whispering nervously in Sharon's ear. As soon as I had ended my speech the Israeli minister of defense leaped from his seat and demanded to be given the floor while Shmuel Tamir fidgeted nervously. Only Dr. Yosef Burg was calm. Showing no anger, Burg spoke as if he were a head priest who every day made pronouncements about which he accepted no discussion: "I completely object to what Dr. Ghali has just said. The United Nations Resolutions of which the Egyptian minister speaks prohibit the acquisition of land by force, but to my knowledge this does not prohibit the acquisition of land by purchase." Burg smiled mischievously. He was much amused by his phrase and fully convinced that with it he had toppled all the arguments I had made. Then Burg added, brimming with self-confidence, "Is it logical that Jews should have the right to buy land anywhere in the United States but should not be allowed to buy land in their own country?"

I said with anger in my voice, "I wonder what our motives are, all of us, in these negotiations? Is not our aim to establish a Palestinian authority in the West Bank and Gaza Strip? I should imagine that when this authority is established, it will be responsible for deciding about the sale and purchase of land. It is not logical or acceptable that every week the Israeli government confronts us with a new ruling aimed at putting before us a new fait accompli. If Israel is to continue in this policy, what will be the duties of the Palestinian authority that we are meeting today to agree to form?"

Burg quickly intervened to ask Dr. Mustafa Khalil to end this discussion because we were assembled to discuss self-rule and not the Israeli government's decision to allow Israelis to purchase land.

Mustafa Khalil replied that Israel's decision to allow the purchase of land was issued under a military government controlling the occupied territories, one that has ways of forcing the Arabs to sell their land. We had all heard the complaints of Palestinian mayors that the Israeli military on the West Bank had forced them to sell their land. At this point Mustafa Khalil declared the session suspended so that everyone could calm down.

As we were leaving the hall Yosef Burg stopped to whisper in my ear, "Why did you start this side battle?" I answered him in a loud voice, "Because this issue is at the heart of the matter and because there is no reason for negotiations to continue if you confront us with a new diktat in each new session!"

The evening session was even more ferocious. Sharon, who had been prevented from speaking in the morning, took the floor and delivered a speech in which he paraded his oratorical muscle. With customary arrogance, he declared that Israel had given Sinai to Egypt and presented it with Sinai oil but so far had received nothing in return.

Now Mustafa Khalil became very angry: "Sinai has been Egyptian for ten thousand years and will remain Egyptian. Dr. Sharon, Sinai is ours." Sharon erupted, shouting that he was not to be addressed as Doctor: "I am just a simple farmer and carry no titles or distinguished academic credentials!" Mustafa Khalil asked whether he preferred to be addressed as Mr. Farmer. The Israeli people wonder, Sharon said, what Egypt has given to Israel in exchange for Sinai and Sinai oil. Mustafa Khalil replied simply, "Egypt gave Israel peace."

Dr. Mustafa decided to suspend the evening session. As we gathered our papers before leaving the room he said to me that he did not think he could stand "these people" anymore, so he would not be able to attend the dinner party that night. I told him he must attend, as he was the host and head of the Egyptian delegation. But he refused, saying, "I do not want to see them again today!"

I arrived at the restaurant San Giovanni on the sea at nine o'clock in the evening to receive the guests in place of Mustafa Khalil. At the table, Burg was to my right, Sharon to my left. The confrontations of the day had left their mark on us all.

Ambassador Leonard tried, in his Anglo-Saxon style, to lighten the atmosphere by recounting some diplomatic escapades, but he was unsuccessful. Mustafa Khalil's absence heightened the tension.

Burg and Sharon dealt with the unpleasantness by piling their plates with food. The huge amounts they dished on their plates amazed me. My behavior was completely opposite. I drank but hardly ate at all.

During dinner Ambassador Muhsin al-Diwani, head of protocol, approached to inform me that an artistic presentation had been arranged and would begin in minutes. Sure enough, an Arabic music troupe entered the hall and began to play, and then a graceful belly dancer appeared and rhythmically began to practice her craft. My neighbor at the table, Ariel Sharon, stopped eating and his expression reflected pleasure and happiness. He turned to me and spoke warmly, "Dr. Ghali, if you would send three dancers like this to Israel, you would not need any other weapon or tanks to invade our country." He laughed and I laughed and so did all those present. The dancer now became the topic of conversation and for the moment reconciled the delegates.

As this was taking place I found that Dr. Burg had disappeared. I asked Ambassador Mushin al-Diwani to find him. He soon came back, whispering in my ear, "Burg left the hall in consternation and is now on the ground floor of the restaurant." I immediately went in search of Burg and found him sitting alone in a quiet corner. Seated near him was an Israeli security guard. "Dr. Burg, what happened? Why did you leave the party?" He gave me a horrified look and said, "Don't you know that I am the head of a religious party and the presence of half-naked dancers making sexual gestures violates religious teachings? With journalists and photographers in the hall I cannot risk having them take a picture of me looking at this dancer."

I apologized and said that I did not think the dancer could cause him any embarrassment. "Dr. Ghali," he said, "you are trying to kill my political career." I denied this and asked what could be done. "Nothing," he said quietly and asked me to return to the dinner and send a messenger to tell him when the performance was over. I agreed and thought as I climbed the stairs that this was the only agreement we could reach during the sixth session of negotiations for Palestinian self-rule. When I returned to the head table, the dancer was still shaking different parts of her body with enthusiasm, while Sharon watched and applauded with commensurate excitement.

As soon as the dancer ended her act, I prevailed on Muhsin al-Diwani to issue instructions to present no further performances and to go and invite Burg to return and join us. This he did, and the dinner party continued late into the evening. Reconciliation prevailed, and there was laughter all around.

In the morning the discussion revolved around the text of the joint declaration. We agreed that the best way to conceal the failure of this round would be to announce the dates of coming meetings. We would state that this round dealt with the reports of the subcommittees and decided that these committees would meet from October 15 to 18 in Alexandria, then from October 24 to 26 in Herzliya, then from November 11 to 15 in Alexandria, and from

November 25 to 29 in Herzliya. All this was to hide the lack of progress and assure the public that the will and momentum to continue negotiating remained present on both sides.

I accompanied the Israeli delegation to Al-Nuzhah airport, where they boarded a military aircraft for Tel Aviv. During the car trip to the airport, Yosef Burg confided to me his difficulties with his ministerial colleagues, referring to their party ambitions and personal differences. I was convinced that the Israelis were not at all searching for a solution to the Palestinian issue. They were using the negotiations to gain time while they gained total control over the West Bank and Gaza through the chain of settlements they were building.

Back to New York

I took the Concorde to New York and on October 1 spoke before the United Nations at the opening of the Thirty-fourth General Assembly. I asked the Palestine Liberation Organization and Israel to agree to mutual recognition in order for the dialogue for peace to begin between them. When I returned to my seat, only a few ministers and diplomats came to congratulate me.

At the head of those shaking my hand was the British representative, Sir Anthony Parsons. Proficient in Arabic, he had listened to my delivery without an interpreter. "It was a great speech worthy of Egypt's standing," he said. I was touched by the ambassador's praise, which compensated me somewhat for the ostracism that I felt.

The pope arrived in New York on October 2, 1979. At United Nations headquarters I stood in line at a large function at which resident ministers and ambassadors were introduced to him. He showed signs of deep fatigue as he stood to shake the hands of the dignitaries. Ambassador Ali Teymour, deputy head of protocol at the United Nations, was introducing the diplomats to the pope, who appeared too exhausted to recognize them individually. When my turn came, Ali Teymour said at the top of his voice in French, and in an unusually theatrical tone, "Dr. Boutros Boutros-Ghali, Egypt's foreign minister." Ali Teymour's voice had its effect and awakened the head of the Catholic Church from his reverie. He looked at me and smiled. He said that he had mentioned Egypt in the speech he gave that morning and added, "Egypt has a special place in my heart." I responded with phrases of thanks and greeting. This conversation attracted the attention of the journalists, as the pope did not speak with any other head of delegation. The media representatives asked me about the content of the conversation and the secret behind the pope's interest in the Egyptian minister. Naturally, I refused to comment, which only increased the journalists' interest.

I met with several foreign ministers who were in New York to attend the General Assembly. Arranging a time was not a problem, but in the chambers and halls around the General Assembly hall there were only five or six places where meetings could be held and only a few seats. Many countries sent a delegate at an early hour to occupy seats in one of these rooms until it was time for their minister to meet another. The delegate had to defend the seats against the attempts of diplomats from other delegations to secure chairs for their superiors. The limited seating in the United Nations building was a cause for continuing diplomatic struggle.

In one of the United Nations rooms the foreign ministers of nonaligned countries were meeting. I felt as though I had returned to Havana. The foreign minister of Cuba, Isidoro Malmierca, presided, and Ali al-Turayki, Libya's foreign minister, and other rejectionists took part.

I decided to avoid this gathering, even though it was to vote on an Iraqi resolution condemning Egypt and Camp David. I do not know if the reason for staying away was mental or physical weariness, but I remained in my room, where delegates came to offer me their congratulations after the radical Arab states failed to secure a majority to pass the Iraqi resolution. Formerly silent countries dared to speak, and hesitant countries dared to clarify their positions. The atmosphere of intimidation that had prevailed at the Havana conference had evaporated.

On Tuesday, October 9, at Charles de Gaulle Airport, from which I was to fly to Strasbourg, an attendant informed me that two VIP lounges in the airport were occupied: one by Moshe Dayan and the other by Crown Prince Hassan, Jordan's heir apparent. The Frenchman asked mischievously whether I wished to share the lounge with the Israeli leader or with the Arab leader. I said without hesitation that I wished the attendant to make the decision for me because he was responsible for protocol. Minutes later Moshe Dayan and I were on board the same airplane going to Strasbourg, where there was to be a meeting of the Council of Europe.

Dayan seemed exhausted, but we had a friendly conversation during the short flight. On our arrival, a crowd from the Jewish community of Strasbourg was present to receive Dayan; only French policemen were there to receive me and take me to a secure hotel outside the city. Terrorists had threatened to blow up the hotel where we were to stay in the city and to blow up the Council of Europe's headquarters as well. The security measures were more stringent than ever.

In my hotel suite I found bouquets of flowers and a Bible with a white bookmark. When I opened the Holy Book to the marked page, I found the passage "Blessed are the peacemakers."

We were informed that dinner would be at a restaurant in the city and that formal attire was not necessary. This upset Leia, as she had been told to wear a long gown for the occasion and had searched the shops of Paris to comply. She criticized my entourage for not providing us with the protocol requirements of our visit to Strasbourg.

The dinner given by the general secretary of the Council of Europe and his wife was limited to Dayan and me and our wives. In his welcoming toast he said that we were living a historic moment; this was the first time that the Council of Europe had invited two ministers to set forth their differing views on a major world issue, the question of peace for the Middle East. Dayan seemed pleased. We both felt relaxed and happy, if only for a moment.

CHAPTER TEN

❖ ❖ ❖

Contending with Israelis

Debating Dayan in Strasbourg

Wednesday was an especially important day in my life. The French post office issued a special envelope on the occasion of the Egyptian-Israeli debate in Strasbourg. It had both my portrait, printed below the Egyptian flag, and Dayan's portrait, below the Israeli flag. Between the two portraits was the Council of Europe building; and below the picture the caption "The two declarations of Moshe Dayan and Boutros Ghali—Strasbourg 10/10/1979."

The president of the Parliamentary Assembly of the Council of Europe invited me into his office. There I met Dayan. The president theatrically positioned himself between us and then escorted us to the Assembly hall.

A French journalist noticed that Dayan and I were both wearing gray suits. She said to me, "Your suits are the same color, but the difference in tailoring is enormous." In fact, my suit was made by an expensive Italian tailor, while the Israeli minister's suit, as he told me, was made in a small Israeli shop.

I decided to speak in French because my French was better than my English and I also felt that French would be better received in Strasbourg than Dayan's English.

The preliminary speakers all stressed how important the Arab-Israeli conflict was to world peace and to the twenty-one nations represented in the Parliament to hear this historic debate.

The president of the Parliament said, "I now invite the minister of state for foreign affairs of Egypt, Mr. Boutros Boutros-Ghali, to come to the rostrum to make the first statement."

I took out the text I had spent so many hours preparing in Cairo and Havana and which I had edited scores of times.

As I began to speak I did not need to refer to my text. I had rewritten it so often and thought about it so much that the words flowed of themselves. "President Sadat's historic visit to Jerusalem on November 19, 1977, was not his first peace initiative," I said. "As long ago as February 4, 1971, the president proposed to the Israelis that the Suez Canal blockade should be lifted and a timetable drawn up for negotiating the implementation of Resolution 242. Two years later, on October 16, 1973, while fighting was continuing after the collapse of the Bar-Lev Line, President Sadat proposed that an international conference be held in Geneva to put a stop to military confrontation. Yet other initiatives, not all of them fully appreciated at the time, were unsuccessful in breaking down the wall of distrust, misunderstanding, and I would even say hate, which existed at the time between Cairo and Tel Aviv."

I paused to survey my audience. In silence, everyone gazed back, waiting for me to continue. I felt that I had to lead this assembly through every step of the negotiations. Only then would they realize what Egyptian diplomacy was doing. Throughout these negotiations, I said, the collective approach has characterized our diplomatic activities, whereas the state of Israel insists on direct contacts and wants strictly bilateral negotiations. "Egyptian diplomacy," I said, "attaches particular importance to the presence of the UN both during the negotiations and during the implementation of any agreements and treaties that may come out of them. Egypt's attachment to the United Nations has been one of the constant features of her foreign policy ever since she contributed to the organization's creation at San Francisco in 1945. Rightly or wrongly, Egypt has always regarded the UN as the only guarantor of international legality and the institutional framework par excellence for the settlement of disputes between states. Our insistence on the participation of the United Nations during our various negotiations has always been received with misgivings—with hostility, even—by the Israelis. In this they share the attitude of the rejectionist Arab states, which, for different reasons, want to keep the United Nations out of our negotiations, so as to accentuate their bilateral nature and thus be able to accuse us of having concluded a separate peace." In short, I said, Egypt was seeking a global peace embracing the largest possible number of Arab or non-Arab states as partners, witnesses, or guarantors, a global peace endorsed by the two superpowers and the international organization, whereas the Israelis want a separate peace and a bilateral solution to the conflict.

My delivery of these words was deliberately unemotional and careful. I wanted to overwhelm them with the details of what had taken place. As I moved from my review of what had taken place so far, my voice grew louder and more emotional as I spoke of those who opposed Egypt's search for peace.

"Egyptian action to promote peace thus finds itself hemmed in by two refusals—the Israeli refusal to recognize a Palestinian entity and the Arab refusal to recognize the peace treaty between Egypt and Israel. . . . Our whole policy and all our diplomatic actions are aimed at overcoming this twofold crisis of confidence, which is endangering the entire peace process set in train by the historic visit of President Sadat to Jerusalem." I cited on the one hand the untimely statements by the Israeli prime minister and his colleagues, the establishment of new Israeli settlements on the West Bank, the authorization to acquire Arab land (decided on by the Israeli government on the first anniversary of the Camp David agreements), and Israel's continued acts of aggression against southern Lebanon. On the other hand I listed the untimely declarations of the Arab leaders, the military activities of the PLO in Israeli territory—all the actions and reactions that were reinforcing the objective alliance between the Israeli and Arab rejectionists.

I called upon my hearers for support.

"What can you do to help us? What can Europe's role be in this many-faceted problem?" The Palestinians, I said, must acquire the citizenship of which they were deprived, first by European colonization, then by Zionist colonization. The Israeli people must acquire the security and dignity which they were denied first of all by a certain European tradition and subsequently by the Middle East situation. "The task of Europe and the Council of Europe is to assist men of goodwill to achieve this twofold aim and restore human rights to this thrice-holy land. Peace is at stake on both the southern and the northern shores of the Mediterranean, the sea that unites us as well as our destinies!"

The chairman of the session then asked Moshe Dayan to speak. He launched an attack on European governments that did not make public their support for the peace treaty. He directly challenged his European audience by recalling how Europe had been a theater for the annihilation of the Jewish people. Dayan's words were strong. As for the Palestinian cause, Dayan was dismissive. Palestinian self-determination was being expressed through Jordan, which after 1948 had given citizenship to the Arabs of "Judea and Samaria." The Palestine Liberation Organization was using terrorism and assassination to destroy Israel. Therefore, Dayan said, Israel would not negotiate with the PLO. The problem of Palestinian refugees should be solved by the Arab countries with vast areas of land and a small population, he said.

When the Israeli foreign minister finished, it was noon and we adjourned to a side hall, where Dayan and I held a joint press conference. I answered the journalists' questions at times in French and at times in English, while Dayan's answers were all in English. This gave me a clear advantage, which did not please Dayan at all.

After meeting the press, the Egyptian and Israeli delegations went to the dining hall, where each lunched separately. The Egyptian group was joined by an old friend, Professor Jean Dupuy, a fellow student of mine in the forties at the law faculty of the University of Paris. He had become one of the premier scholars of international law and held the post of general secretary of the Academy of International Law in The Hague. Jean Dupuy's presence at the table helped distance me somewhat from the miserable political atmosphere prevailing that morning. The nobility of our academic dialogue restored me.

I returned to the Assembly's meeting hall, where Dayan and I were to respond to members' questions. Seventy-one questions were asked; thirty-five were addressed to Dayan, twenty to me, and sixteen jointly to both of us.

The first group of questions related to the peace treaty. Dayan's answers had the ring of optimism. I stressed that Egypt was not seeking a partial or separate peace. "What we are seeking," I said, "is not 'peacekeeping' but 'peace-building.' We have to move from partial, fragmenting solutions to a comprehensive solution that will make it possible to lay the foundations for institutionalizing peace."

The second group of questions dealt with withdrawal. Dayan rejected the principle of withdrawal to the borders before June 1967 on all Arab fronts. He refused to consider Israel's complete withdrawal from Sinai as a precedent for withdrawal from the other fronts.

The fact that Resolution 242 calls for withdrawal from "territories" rather than "the territories" was being cited by some Israelis as meaning withdrawal from Sinai was enough, that no more withdrawals were required. I vehemently attacked this interpretation: "I disagree entirely with Mr. Dayan. The principles are not different because there is a desert between Egypt and Israel but not between the West Bank and Israel. In our view, Resolution 242 has been applied according to the French, Spanish, and Russian texts. The fact that there is a slight ambiguity in the English text makes no difference."

My response increased the tension in the Assembly. When the answer was strong and convincing, the applause was long and loud. When the answer was weak, the applause was light and mild. Truth be told, my answers brought much stronger applause than did Dayan's. This was obvious to the Israeli minister. He appeared disheartened and even angry.

The next group of questions dealt with how European countries could contribute to the effort to solve the Middle East crisis. "Very often," I said, "Europe takes refuge behind the fact that it is the United States that acts as a full partner and is expected to solve this problem; Europe merely plays a secondary part. But it is not a secondary part that Europe has to play; it is a vital one."

Dayan, who was visibly agitated, said, "We often hear the idea expressed that Israel will get some kind of international guarantee. We are told, 'What does it matter if you have to go all the way back and have only fifteen kilometers? You will get instead an international guarantee for your security.'

"I would ask this honorable Assembly—can any single one of you in this hall stand up and say that if Israel is at war, attacked by the Arabs, your country will send its troops to fight for Israel? Did you do it in the past? Will you do it in the future? Can you commit yourselves to that? Can you? None of you can!"

I asked for the floor. "Mr. Dayan said he was not interested in international guarantees because he had no faith in any state, because he placed his trust only in Israel's armed forces. He always looks at things from a very Israel-centered angle, but he should occasionally consider how people feel on the other side of the boundaries. . . . What we want when we think about international guarantees is not so much to safeguard Israel's frontiers or secure the state of Israel as to guarantee the state of Palestine which we hope to create. That state of Palestine has far more need of international guarantees than Israel."

The hall erupted with sharp applause to my remarks. Dayan demanded to be recognized to answer me. He recalled that Israel had offered to give up all its occupied territories to President Nasser in return for a peace treaty, but Nasser went to the Arab summit in Khartoum. "In response to our offer to give back all the territory under a peace treaty, we received three 'noes,' no recognition, no peace, no negotiation. We were told only that what was taken by force would be taken back by force."

I felt that Dayan had responded with great skill. The applause for him was strong. This round he had won.

Following this came a new group of questions on the taking of Arab land for Jewish settlements. The chairman asked Dayan to reply. "We are talking about peanuts," Dayan said, "about very exceptional, rare occasions, which were justified before the High Court only when justified by military need in accordance with the Geneva Convention." The Camp David Accords, Dayan said, must end with a peace treaty with the state of Jordan to decide the boundaries between the state of Israel and the state of Jordan. "The Camp David agreements do not include the possibility of a Palestinian state," Dayan declared. "If the Egyptians thought that the Palestinians should have the right to self-determination, they would not have signed that agreement, which does not include the term 'self-determination.' "

In agitation I demanded the opportunity to respond. "Yes, Mr. Dayan is quite right: there is no mention of a Palestinian state in the Camp David agreements. But nothing is said that would prohibit the creation of a Palestinian state. The whole spirit of Camp David requires the creation of a Palestinian state," I said.

I then attacked Israel's settlements policy as contrary to the Geneva Convention, to international law, to United Nations resolutions, and to the understanding reached between Egypt and Israel. At the top of my voice I declared that "the creation of new settlements and the unilateral statements by the Israeli cabinet are major obstacles to the peace process."

The hall exploded with applause. The applause continued for some time until the chairman of the session had to intervene to curb the representatives' enthusiasm. He said, "I have been lenient until now but I remind you that the Parliamentary Assembly's Rules of Procedure state that 'members of the public admitted to the galleries shall remain seated and in silence.' "

With the sweet taste of victory, I looked at Dayan. I saw that the man was vulnerable. But he remained firm and resolute in the face of general condemnation of the policy he was defending.

Dayan replied to the next questions with quiet emotion: "We consider Judea and Samaria—the West Bank—and Jericho and Shiloh, Bethel and Gaza to be our old homeland. We do not mean that we have a real estate right to it and that we can tell the people living there that because two thousand years back it was Israel, the kingdom of David, it is therefore our land and they should get out. Absolutely not; that would be absurd. . . . The real question, which no one can avoid, is how shall we live with the Arabs? The school of thought to which I belong is that we should live together on equal ground, by agreement, side by side, with the Arabs on the West Bank, in the Gaza Strip, and Jerusalem. It is as simple as that. There is no other way."

In other words, Dayan said, "Another Israeli settlement is not an obstacle to peace. It is an ongoing situation within the system that eventually will be the solution for the West Bank and Gaza. The Jews and Arabs will live side by side without driving away a single Arab."

Dayan's emotional yet calm tone had their effect. I noticed the beginnings of sympathy on the part of a number of the European representatives and decided to launch a new attack with the aim of provoking him to abandon his calm approach. I rose shouting: "When Mr. Dayan says he has a right to buy land on the West Bank, I see no reason why he should not, provided it is the Palestinians who accord him that right and that it is not imposed by him. He seems to forget the eleven years of military occupation with all their attendant humiliation and misery for a people without the right to express a political opinion or to have any freedom whatsoever."

I added, raising my voice further: "Here is a people, the Palestinians, who, like the Israelis, have demanded the right to self-determination and, like them, want to achieve it. The state of Israel came into existence. In a similar way the Palestinians too have the right to create their own state. . . . Unless they get it, there will be no real peace in the Middle East!"

When I stopped talking, strong applause resounded once again and continued longer than a full minute, reaching a level I had not heard before. I realized I had won this round.

Although the tide had turned decisively in my favor, the audience was not ready to release either Dayan or myself.

Dayan continued to read from the Camp David agreements, signed, he said, "not only by Prime Minister Begin but by President Sadat, who, I am sure, is in a position to commit Egypt. He would not have signed anything unless he was ready to carry it out." The Camp David text, Dayan said, made it clear that the other party with Israel would be Jordan as regards negotiations for the boundaries and the peace treaty. "If my distinguished colleague had in mind another state, a Palestinian state, or the possibility of a Palestinian state, he should not have signed this document about which we are now negotiating."

I commented sarcastically, "Mr. Dayan has put a great many words into President Sadat's mouth. When Mr. Dayan attributes to President Sadat the view that he is not in favor of a Palestinian state, I beg leave to doubt that. Egypt's position is quite clear and has been expressed in various statements, official and unofficial. The idea of creating a Palestinian state has been a constant factor in Egyptian foreign policy even before the creation of the state of Israel. In March 1945, the Egyptian negotiator fought for a text that gave clear promise of independence for Palestine, although at that time Palestine was still under mandate."

The final group of questions focused on the future of Jerusalem.

"The Egyptian position is quite clear," I said. "In our view and according to the Camp David agreements, Resolution 242 must be applied *in toto*, which means the withdrawal of Israeli troops from all the territories occupied after June 5, 1967. As the Arab part of Jerusalem was occupied after that date, the Israelis must withdraw from the eastern sector. That is our position, a position laid down by President Sadat in an exchange of letters with the United States government, which endorsed this point of view. Once the Arab part of Jerusalem has again become part of the West Bank, of Palestinian territory, it can negotiate with the Israeli part of Jerusalem to find a modus vivendi that will enable a special relationship to be established between the two parts of the capital."

The president of the Parliament gave the last word to Moshe Dayan. Surprisingly, Dayan did not assert the usual Israeli position that Jerusalem would forever be the undivided sovereign capital of Israel. His tone was soft and strangely yielding: "There are two matters to be raised regarding Jerusalem and we should not mix one with the other. One concerns sovereignty and the other the holy places. . . . We all agreed at Camp David that we should not decide about sovereignty now, but should do so at the end of the transitional period of five years. That includes Jerusalem. It may be that Jordan will ask that we withdraw all the way to the west of Jerusalem. But the time for that will be when the questions of sovereignty and the boundary are discussed throughout the country.

"However, Israel's position on the holy places has been stated by Prime Minister Begin: 'We are for every religion, every faith, to be in full control of its holy shrines and holy places'—the Christians of theirs, Muslims of theirs and the Jews of theirs. Each community or faith should administer its own holy places and that should be established under the law."

The president of the European parliament declared that "this has been a historic day" and closed the session. I shook hands with

Dayan and a number of European parliamentarians. As I was leaving, a crowd of journalists gathered around to congratulate me warmly and say that I had won the debate. One of them said, "The battle lasted nine rounds. You won seven of them and lost only two." Journalists who talked to Dayan were probably saying the same things to him.

After this came a reception. I was exhilarated by my triumph. Wine was poured and I acted like a spoiled playboy. Dayan came up to me. "Stop behaving like this," he said. "Fate has pampered you." He spoke not harshly but almost affectionately. "I did not study at great universities," Dayan said. "I had no opportunity to read great books. I had to learn through the harshness of life and war. I learned English in a British Mandate jail." My first impulse was to reply that a self-made man like himself has a better chance of succeeding than one whose path has been made easy. By this I meant to point out that I, too, had had to discipline myself. But I said nothing, for in truth his words made me ashamed. My wife said to me, "You have not behaved like a gentleman!"

When I returned to my hotel, the Turkish ambassador, a friend since the days he was posted to Cairo, was waiting for me. He said, "I feel sorry for Dayan. Throughout the debate he was on the defensive because of your fierce attacks. Your blows were harsh."

Ten days later I attended a party held by the American ambassador at his Cairo residence. At the head of those invited was Ezer Weizman, Israeli minister of defense. At one stage of the party I was alone with the Israeli minister and we had a frank discussion. Weizman, always optimistic, was even more so than usual. He was convinced now, he said, that the negotiations would soon succeed. The next night I had dinner at the residence of General Kamel Hasan Ali in Zeitoun, a villa reserved for the minister of defense. The grand party was in honor of Ezer Weizman again. Umar Khurshid's orchestra was playing light music. Kamel Hasan Ali whispered to me that Khurshid refused to accept payment and that he was donating his music to the peace process.

Among the invitees were some Jewish millionaires, among them Edmond de Rothschild and Nissim Ga'on. During the party there came a telephone call from Dr. Mustafa Khalil, from Vienna. He asked to speak with Weizman and welcomed him to Cairo, then asked to speak with me.

Mustafa Khalil told me that Dayan had resigned as foreign minister. He asked me what reverberations there were in Cairo over this news. I had no comment, but it seemed to me that Weizman's optimism might stem in part from Dayan's departure. The party lasted until two o'clock in the morning. A cheerful atmosphere prevailed throughout.

In less than two years, on October 16, 1981, Dayan was dead of cancer. When I heard of his passing, I recalled the time at Camp David when we had watched the boxer Muhammad Ali win his fight. Ali had declared that he was "the most famous man in the world—except for Moshe Dayan." Dayan, also a fighter, had lost his fight.

A Storm in Begin's Teacup

"The Soviet ambassador requests an urgent meeting to communicate a very important message." It was Friday morning, December 28, 1979; Cairo was in the midst of its weekly holiday. I agreed to see the ambassador that afternoon in my office. As I left home I wondered whether the minister of the interior had been causing trouble again. Had he arrested a Soviet "expert"? Had houses under diplomatic immunity been searched? I was surprised when Ambassador Poliakov told me he had come to explain the reasons for the Soviet military intervention in Afghanistan. The Soviet takeover of Kabul was based, he claimed, on the right of self-defense provided in Article 51 of the UN Charter.

Whether it was because I had been disturbed on a Friday, or because of the far-fetched explanation, I reproached the Soviet ambassador severely: "You are worse than the old colonial powers. What allows you to intervene? Chinese accusations against you are justified." Embarrassed, the Soviet ambassador swiftly left. I issued an official communiqué of the Ministry of Foreign Affairs strongly condemning Soviet aggression against Afghanistan.

Two days later President Sadat asked members of his inner cabinet to meet with him in Aswan. Sadat's villa, overlooking the old

Aswan dam, contained little furniture, no curtains, not a painting or an engraving on the walls. It was an ascetic's cell, bitterly cold. Some little electric radiators tried, in vain, to fight the cold. We sat around a table on which tiny cups of tea had been placed. After discussing Egyptian domestic issues, Sadat turned to me and said, "I liked your communiqué, but I want a plan of action to stop the Soviet aggression in Afghanistan."

Back in Cairo, I telephoned our permanent representative at the United Nations to propose a Security Council resolution condemning the Soviet aggression. When the Soviets vetoed this, as they surely would, the only choice would be to seek a resolution in the General Assembly, which would require mobilizing Arab and other Islamic states.

On the following Sunday I was back in Aswan for a session of the National Democratic party's political bureau, though I was not yet a political bureau member. A controversy broke out between Sadat and his prime minister, Mustafa Khalil over the Arab League's decision to move its headquarters from Cairo to Tunis. Sadat wanted to retaliate by creating a League of Arab Peoples. By this Sadat was referring to Arab opposition parties and movements that could meet in Cairo. Mustafa Khalil was opposed, saying that such a project would be difficult to achieve and dangerous. Irritated by this opposition, Sadat spoke to us as though Mustafa Khalil was not present. He told us that he had known Mustafa Khalil as a young minister under Gamal Abdel Nasser. "I respect him for his integrity, but he is extremely obstinate," the president said. Mustafa Khalil replied that he respected and admired his leader Sadat as a statesman and as a man of vision, but that his duty was to express himself when he disagreed with his leader. Sadat could accept criticism in private, but he could not tolerate public contradiction.

The dispute was halted by the arrival of lunch, served with pleasant simplicity by Jehan Sadat. After lunch, Sadat returned to the issue of Soviet aggression in Afghanistan. He seemed to be more obsessed with international communism than with his status in the Arab world. But the coming visit of the Israeli prime minister, Menachem Begin, compelled his attention.

Sadat believed that only Begin could make peace and "deliver" on it, so Sadat focused all his attention on Begin. If Begin the hardliner made a concession to the Arabs, the Israeli people would abide by it. I was not convinced. True, Begin could deliver, but he was ideologically unable to agree to full Palestinian rights on the West Bank, and as long as those rights were denied, there could not be a true or comprehensive peace in the Middle East. I repeated on every occasion that peace between Egypt and Israel must be linked to progress for Palestinians in Gaza and the West Bank. But such linkage was something that, for different reasons, both Begin and Sadat preferred to let fade away. I was the irritant, and increasingly Begin was getting fed up with me.

Begin arrived at Aswan airport on the morning of Monday, January 7, 1980. The military band played the Israeli national anthem. Begin reviewed the guard of honor, then disappeared with President Sadat. We passed our time in the restaurants and lobbies of the Oberoi Hotel on the island. I was furious at being kept away from the talks. General Kamel Hasan Ali helped me remain patient. He suggested a boat ride with our wives to the botanical gardens on another island, but I preferred talking to the Israeli journalists, with whom I had very candid conversations. That evening at the official dinner in honor of Begin, I was seated next to Begin's daughter, a rather shy and awkward young lady. She signed, left-handed, the menu, which was circulated for signature and which would end up in the archives of the Israeli delegation. After dinner we were entertained by the Aswan folk troupe, an ordeal we had already suffered with the shah of Iran.

The next morning I acquiesced in the boat ride to the botanical gardens with General Ali and our wives, but in the afternoon I returned to my continuing debate with the Israeli journalists. I explained my point of view as I had done since the signature of the Camp David Accords: the normalization of relations between Egypt and Israel must occur in tandem with the normalization between Israel and the Palestinians. The Israelis reacted to my words much as Sadat did, with aloof disdain.

The Sadat-Begin summit, however, appeared to be a success. The press reported that "the personal acerbity that had characterized so much of their relationship between the first meeting in Jerusalem, in November 1977, during the Camp David negotiations in September 1978, and even later, seemed to have vanished without a trace. They were now true friends and even more important, they wanted the whole world to know this. Everything they did seemed geared to putting each other at ease."

On Wednesday I was still languishing in the Oberoi lobby, subject to the aggression of Israeli, French, English, and American journalists. At lunch, there were Sadat's youngest daughter, Nana; General Kamel Hasan Ali and his wife; Hasan Kamil and his wife; and Kadria Sadek, who was Mrs. Sadat's lady-in-waiting. It was a nice group, relaxed about the peace negotiations.

When I returned to the journalists, they asked, "You are considered a traitor by the Arabs and the rejectionist front, and a disrupter of the peace process by the Israelis. How can you remain enthusiastic?" I was about to reply when I was interrupted by a telephone call from Ibrahim Nafei, editor in chief of *Al-Ahram*, who told me that Sadat was very angry at the statement I had given to Radio Monte Carlo condemning the Israelis' negative attitude toward the Palestinians. Monte Carlo had picked up my statement from a tape-recorded interview I had given the *Jerusalem Post.* The peace treaty would be a "hollow shell," I said, unless the Palestinian problem was solved. The autonomy talks, I charged, were being wrecked by endless debates with Dr. Burg that were nothing but *pilpul* (I used the Hebrew word for Talmudic hairsplitting). It reminded me, I told the press, of the Byzantine Christians debating the sex of angels as the Turks lay siege to Constantinople. Israel, I urged, "should capitalize on Sadat," for there would be no comparable Egyptian leader in the decades ahead.

The Israeli journalists requested an urgent meeting with me. Mr. Begin, they told me, has asked Mr. Sadat to get rid of Minister Boutros-Ghali, whose policy of obstruction was a major obstacle to the peace process. Sadat has promised, they said, to pull his minister's ears and keep him away from the peace process. The journalists declared that I would be removed in a cabinet reshuffle that would take place in a few days. At the airport the reporters' statements appeared well founded. Begin did not greet me. Sadat turned away and pretended not to see me. My colleagues and Sadat's courtiers all noticed. In the airport lounge I sat alone, surrounded by silence. Even the waiters seemed to shun me and would not serve me coffee. I was considered unclean, banished in complete isolation. The Israeli journalists' predictions had come true.

Jehan Sadat noticed me sitting by myself. She kindly called me to her side, asking, "Dr. Ghali, why are you so far away from us?" As I was to be removed from office, I thought that I might as well tell Sadat what I had been told by the journalists. I approached the president and quietly said, "Begin has informed the press that you have made new concessions to hasten the process of normalization between Egypt and Israel, that the airlines will start flights between the two countries . . . but that we have not had any progress concerning the Palestinian problem." Sadat interrupted me in a loud, angry voice: "I had to make these concessions to limit the damage of your recent statements to the international press. Begin came to see me this morning. He has not slept all night, he is very upset, very pale. He feels offended by your stupid statements. I was forced to calm him and to make concessions to hasten the normalization process. Stop talking to the press. I want you to stop giving interviews and making statements."

I hurriedly changed the topic and asked the president, "Have you finished reading my long position paper on 'Egypt and the New Arab Situation'?" Sadat's demeanor changed immediately. He smiled; his anger disappeared. "Yes, I have finished the paper. Congratulations, it is excellent. You are a true scholar. I know that you are supposed to depart for Cairo with your colleagues, but they can wait. Come with me, let us examine the position paper together."

For the next two hours, Sadat and I examined my paper page by page. It was a text that my close aides and I had spent three months preparing. In sixty pages it analyzed Egypt's contribution to the Arab world, the crisis as a result of the peace process, and Egypt's stance toward this new situation. Sadat had heavily annotated the paper, even correcting typographical errors and grammatical mistakes. "You have forgotten your grammar, Boutros," he said with delight. The mood was relaxed and friendly. Sadat seemed to have forgotten his reproaches to me and his promise to Begin to keep me away from the peace process. But I knew Sadat only too well. This friendly session did not mean a thing. I knew that when it suited his interests, he would not hesitate to remove me from the cabinet, or at least from the negotiating team.

Back at the airport, my ministerial colleagues asked me about the cause of the long delay. I told them I had stayed behind with the president to discuss the situation in Afghanistan. It was half true; during the discussion Sadat denounced the Soviet intervention more than once.

In Cairo I told the prime minister what had happened to me in Aswan. He tried to reassure me: "You know how much President Sadat appreciates your work. This anger will pass. As for the normalization problem, it depends on the prime minister. We always possess the possibility of delaying the process, even if the kings or heads of state request it, or if the Israelis remain intractable on the Palestinian question." I did not know whether the prime minister was simply trying to cheer me up or whether it really was true that the prime minister's office could wield such power.

The next morning Mustafa Khalil telephoned me; Sadat had ordered that my position paper be adopted as the policy of the National Democratic party and therefore a policy of Egypt. I felt great satisfaction and said so.

On the Israeli air force plane returning from Aswan, Begin told reporters that I had been rebuked by Sadat for stressing the linkage between normalization and autonomy. Once back in Israel, Begin launched a personal attack on me. "Boutros-Ghali wants to be more Muslim than Mohammad!" he said. The *Jerusalem Post* editorialist, however, described my words as having rendered a useful service to Israel no less than to Egypt. My statements, the newspaper noted, were unpleasant for Israelis to hear; they could not abide the reality that the Arab world was more crucial to Egypt's future than was Israel, and "that for ideological and practical reasons, Egypt cannot just let the Palestinians go hang."

Sadat, as a visionary, could afford to take the long view, to be patient with a difficult partner. I, as the press noted, was a professional and a technician. I had to attend to the day-to-day implementation of policy, and in my role I had to be more confrontational than Sadat.

"Thus it was Ghali," the *Jerusalem Post* stated, "who had to beat back the fierce assaults on Egypt's peace policy made at the recent African and third-world conferences in Monrovia and Havana. Those experiences, obviously unsettling, reinforced Ghali's conviction that what he viewed as Israel's procrastination on the autonomy was costing Egypt's policy all its credibility in the eyes of its most natural allies."

It was soon clear that Sadat had not forgotten my statements in Aswan that had provoked Menachem Begin's ire. Sadat saw Leia when she was accompanying Mrs. Sol Linowitz in a call on Mrs. Sadat and said, "Tell Boutros to shut his mouth, and to stop making statements."

With those instructions ringing in my ears, I left on Wednesday, January 30, 1980, for Tel Aviv to start the eighth session of negotiations on Palestinian autonomy. We went back to the same hotel in Herzliya. In the summer it had seemed like a five-star European hotel; in the winter it just seemed badly heated. It was very cold as the wind whipped up the waves on the Mediterranean shore. Our ambassador, Saad Mortada, provided whisky to help fight the chill. As I sipped Scotch, I read the Israeli newspapers, which described me as the bogeyman of the Egyptian delegation.

A plenary session was held in the hotel ballroom in the morning, filled with the usual ritual speeches. When we moved to our rooms to negotiate with Sol Linowitz, Yosef Burg, and Ariel Sharon, we let the youngsters prepare the final communiqué. Except for an agreement to follow an intensified schedule, and an expression of satisfaction with the progress made so far, the communiqué said absolutely nothing.

As I left Israel the journalists' questions implied that the Aswan row had not blown over, and that Begin's revenge would follow me.

With every day that passed, the Israelis presented us with a new development. They destroyed Palestinian houses, confiscated more Palestinian land, imprisoned or expelled Palestinian leaders. A Jewish student was murdered, and in reaction the Israeli cabinet declared that Jews had the right to resettle in Hebron, a dangerous step. The United Nations Security Council in Resolution 465 unanimously censured Israeli settlements, but then Jimmy Carter disavowed the U.S. vote. Our position was increasingly untenable and ridiculous. The Americans hid their passivity by claiming the need to be neutral toward the negotiating parties. Sol Linowitz and his U.S. delegation had no intention of exerting pressure on the Israelis. The PLO regularly condemned the negotiations that we, Egypt, were conducting without their approval and that were against their interest.

Yet despite these frustrations, we had no choice but to keep trying. Palestinian self-rule was the indispensable pillar of an eventual comprehensive solution. Should we fail, it would mean a crisis between Egypt and Israel that would halt Israeli withdrawal from Sinai. It would be a victory for the rejectionists, for they tirelessly repeated that Egypt would fail to produce anything for the Palestinians. How could we resist the temptation of a separate peace toward which both Israelis and Palestinians were pushing us in their obstinacy—calculated and rational for the Israelis, emotional and irrational for the Palestinians?

In March 1980 Yitzhak Shamir was named to replace Moshe Dayan. Shamir, a former member of the Jewish underground and later of the Israeli intelligence service, was thought to be a former terrorist. His appointment clouded the scene.

I understood Yitzhak Shamir. We always spoke in French. He was a good listener, and when he spoke he conveyed a desire to make the autonomy negotiations succeed. Whenever he complained to Sadat about me, he did so in my presence. Shamir's complaint led to Sadat's first defense of me ever: "I listen to many points of view, so I listen to Boutros." Sadat added: "After all, you opposed Camp David, but I still listen to you!"

Terrorism came from the Arab side. Palestinians crossed into Israel from Lebanon to attack a kibbutz and take hostages from a children's dormitory. This led to an Israeli military assault into Lebanon.

The autonomy talks in Herzliya in May 1980 were held in a setting of terrorism, invasion, and recrimination. While they were going on, six Jewish settlers were killed and sixteen wounded in an attack in Hebron. Israel deported Palestinian leaders in retaliation, an act the United States declared to be contrary to the 1949 Geneva Convention.

In Herzliya Dr. Mustafa Khalil came to me in confidence to say that because of a variety of intrigues Sadat had asked him to resign. "Prime Minister," I said, "do you not think it is also time for me to resign? The autonomy talks are at a dead end and the Israelis blame me as the obstacle to progress." Mustafa Khalil said, "In our political system one never resigns; one is asked to offer one's resignation. You represent continuity at the Ministry of Foreign Affairs. You still have the strength to resist the pressures of these talks." Sadat needs you, he said.

This was all very depressing. We had formed a good team: Mustafa Khalil as prime minister, Kamel Hasan Ali at the Ministry of Defense, and myself at Foreign Affairs. If Mustafa Khalil left, I would have to start from scratch, and what would my position be in the reshuffle?

Our May 5 session with Sharon was painful. Sharon could not mask his anger and was terrorizing his colleagues, Burg, Nessim, and Tamir. Earlier they had agreed that the question of security in the territories should be an item for discussion. No, declared Sharon: "The question of the security of Israel [by which Sharon meant the occupied territories as well as Israel itself] is not open for negotiations, as it is part of Israeli sovereignty. It must not be discussed in the autonomy talks."

General Kamel Hasan Ali calmly explained to Sharon that the Camp David Accords provided for the Israeli military administration in the occupied territories to be replaced by a civilian administration, and that Israeli troops would have to be redeployed in certain military bases. It was therefore natural to form a commission to deal with these issues. Sharon was not listening. He was red-faced and seemed on the verge of a stroke.

Burg intervened with the smooth manners of a prelate. Nessim showed no trace of emotion. Shamir masked his feelings as well, and Tamir appeared to be somewhere else. The meeting was adjourned.

The plenary session being postponed until the next morning, I decided to go for a walk on the beach with Herbert Hansell, the legal adviser of the U.S. State Department. I told him that the time had come to suspend the negotiations. Preserving the public credibility of the autonomy talks, even our own credibility, was a more difficult task than the negotiations themselves.

At the closing plenary session we were all exhausted and dispirited. A final communiqué was read out. Despite its optimistic language, nothing had happened. During the return flight to Cairo, Mustafa Khalil's wife, Malak, did her best to lift the spirits of our somber group.

Mustafa Khalil's "resignation" was confirmed. He asked me to prepare for him a new diplomatic passport, giving his function as "former prime minister." He wished to leave for Paris on the morning of the formation of the next cabinet. "If I approve such a passport," I said to him, "the whole ministry will know that you have resigned." He replied, "Dr. Boutros, the whole of Cairo knows that I have resigned."

Two days later, on Saturday, May 10, I was summoned by Vice President Hosni Mubarak. He had been chosen by Sadat to be the next prime minister, in addition to retaining his position as vice president. Mubarak informed me that I would be a part of the new cabinet and that I would retain my current functions. "And who is to be the next minister of foreign affairs?" I asked. "General Kamel Hasan Ali, who is to leave the Ministry of Defense," he replied. Once again I was disappointed, although I knew by heart the list of reasons why I would not be foreign minister.

"Come now, Dr. Boutros," Mubarak said, "don't let these details bother you. You know quite well that you are the person responsible for the whole ministry. Don't be in a hurry, and you will obtain everything you want when the moment comes." When I met General Kamel Hasan Ali, our friendship was strong enough for me to tell him, quite frankly, that I was disappointed. "I am even more so," he replied. "You have lost nothing; you have retained your old position. I have been, to a certain extent, demoted. For the last forty years I have served at all levels of an empire that I eventually came to direct. Now I am given a ministry that has a budget equal to one tenth of the budget I managed at the Ministry of Defense."

That evening, at a dinner held at the British embassy, the mood of dismay wafted away on wine vapors and cigar smoke.

May 15 was the fourth time in three years that Sadat had changed the government and the fourth time that I had taken the oath of office at Abdin Palace. Sadat was in a very bad mood. He criticized all the ministers who had just taken the oath. He turned toward me and said, "And you have not yet reformed the Ministry, which is still staffed by 'daddy's boys.' " On our way out, General Kamel Hasan Ali teased me: "How can you reform the ministry? You're a daddy's boy yourself!" This was quite wrong and unjust. In three years I had carried out many reforms, such as changing the entrance requirements, regulating foreign postings, publishing a series of white papers, and streamlining the departments.

But the mood soon shifted to one of crisis. Weizman resigned. I learned later that he had informed Sadat of his intention to do so some months earlier. Begin announced that the Israeli prime ministry would be moved to Arab East Jerusalem. The Israeli Knesset on July 30 voted formally to annex Jerusalem. In a meeting in one of the halls of Abdin Palace I persuaded Sadat to allow me to announce the suspension of the autonomy talks. I prepared a communiqué, which I read at a press conference at the Foreign Ministry. That evening I had a long telephone conversation with Sadat. We discussed how to conduct our foreign policy in a world without the autonomy talks.

With the departure of Mustafa Khalil, a new chapter of my political saga began. I would no longer be alone at the Ministry of Foreign Affairs. I would no longer have the support and friendship of the two main actors of our foreign policy: the prime minister and the minister of defense. My task would be complicated. The vote at the Knesset rendered our relations with the Jewish state more and more problematic. The year 1980 was becoming a disaster for Egypt.

Opening a Dialogue with Labor

By October the United States had succeeded in getting autonomy talks reconvened, but they were a sham—a cover for Israeli aggression. Begin declared that Israel would never leave the Golan Heights. The Arab League at its summit meeting rejected the entire Egypt-Israel peace process. My experience with Begin had reinforced my conviction that Sadat was right in believing that only Begin's Likud could achieve a peace treaty with Egypt, but he was wrong in failing to see that only the Israeli Labor party could achieve peace with the Palestinians.

Since the Jerusalem visit of 1977, the Israeli Labor Alliance had recognized Sadat's bias toward Begin and had complained with good reason that it was neglected by the Egyptian government.

Professor Steve Cohen, a Canadian professor of political science, regularly transmitted the complaints of the Israeli Laborites to me. Professor Cohen added his own arguments: Egypt should not cut itself off from other influential political sectors in Israel; Labor represented the majority of Israelis and was closer to the Palestinian position than Likud; Labor could well win the next Israeli election, and by dealing only with Likud, Egypt was creating an impression that it was more interested in getting Israeli troops out of Sinai than in full normalization of relations with Israel.

Cohen's views were close to my own. I wanted to help Labor win the next Israeli election. I had often tried to obtain Sadat's support for rapprochement with Labor. In the first week of August 1980 I had the opportunity of a tête-à-tête with the president, and I tried once more: "I should like to issue an official invitation to the Israeli Labor party to visit Cairo."

Sadat looked surprised, then after a moment of silence said, "I do not trust the Israeli Labor party, but I do trust Begin to keep his word regarding the autonomy of the West Bank and Gaza. Before the end of next year it will all have been settled. The Palestinians and the Jordanians will join the peace process, which will triumph. If I hold a meeting with Labor, it will sour my relations with Begin."

I did not insist. I had failed in my attempt to get François Mitterrand invited to Egypt, as Sadat did not want to sour his relations with his friend Giscard. I had made the error of insisting, by trying to explain to Sadat that the rules of French politics allowed meetings with leaders of the opposition. He replied that he followed the rules of Egyptian, not French, politics. Contact with the opposition was out of the question.

I then thought of having an unofficial meeting between the two political parties: the National Democratic party (of which Sadat was president) and the Israeli Labor party. I decided to act through Mustafa Khalil, who was appointed vice president of the party after his resignation and who shared my views, and through Anis Mansour. Mansour and Musa Sabri were the journalists closest to Sadat. I suggested to Anis Mansour that the meeting take place as a symposium organized in his office by *October*, the weekly he edited, which regularly carried exclusive interviews given by Sadat.

Surprisingly, it seemed to work. Sadat agreed to meet the Israeli delegation at the end of the symposium. The Israelis complicated matters by insisting that the meeting be held in the offices of the National Democratic party. But I refused to change the venue, knowing that this would lose Sadat's approval.

The Israeli delegation would be led by Shimon Peres and include Abba Eban, Haim Bar-Lev, and Yossi Beilin; on the Egyptian side would be Mustafa Khalil, Ibrahim Helmi Abdel Rahman (former minister of planning), Anis Mansour, and myself.

On November 4, 1980, Ronald Reagan was elected president of the United States. Sadat was disappointed, as he had hoped for the reelection of his friend Jimmy Carter. A few weeks earlier I had telephoned Sadat to tell him that Carter probably would not be reelected. Sadat was angry: "Ya Boutros! You always listen to rumors and believe they are reality." Now, with Reagan's landslide victory, Sadat telephoned to ask me to prepare two telegrams, one for Reagan and the other for Carter, and said, "You know, Boutros, I knew he would not be reelected." Of course, I did not remind him of my earlier warnings. The text of the telegram for Carter was friendly and sentimental; the telegram for Reagan was formal.

During the Camp David negotiations, and frequently thereafter, Sadat would say to me, "When Carter is reelected, he will obtain concessions from the Israelis and solve all our problems. You must learn how to wait. Ya Boutros." Now, indeed, we had to learn how to wait, wait for the formation of the new American administration, wait for the result of the Israeli elections. I was secretly hoping that the success of Labor at the next elections would "solve all our problems."

On the day after Reagan's election I went to Anis Mansour to receive the Israeli Labor party delegation. Shimon Peres was at the top of his form and full of hope. Abba Eban had put on weight and sounded even more like a university professor. It was my first encounter with the new Labor generation in the person of Yossi Beilin, who seemed improbably youthful.

Friday is a holiday in Egypt. Nevertheless, we were all present at nine o'clock on November 7 at Dar Al Maaref, a nationalized publishing house directed by Anis Mansour where the weekly *October* was edited. On the veranda of the penthouse, with a panoramic view of the Nile and the island of Gezira, the mood was relaxed and cordial. Mustafa Khalil put every one at ease. It was the first time Helmi Abdel Rahman had met Israelis, and he was shy.

Like tentative lovers on the threshold of a long-term romance, each side began by telling about its many past affairs: alliances, betrayals, breakups, dreams shattered and pursued, and the structure of their present life—all, of course, suitably edited for the purpose of building confidence in the newly encountered other party. The Israelis knew that they had a rival for Egyptian affections, the Likud of Menachem Begin. Shimon Peres portrayed the Likud in terms designed to woo us away.

"What is the future of Likud?" Peres asked. "Labor is an organic party. We have an uninterrupted history. The Likud is made of two different parties [the economically driven Liberals and the politically driven Likud]. I would say its future can be predicted as an outcome of marriage between George Bernard Shaw and Marlene Dietrich: their child will have the beauty of Shaw and the brains of Dietrich."

Abba Eban revealed, however, that the last Labor alignment had its own problems because of its statistical dependence upon the parliamentary majority of the National Religious party, the Mafdal. "We made an interim agreement with Egypt in 1974 based upon withdrawal along the Suez Canal. We made an interim agreement with Syria in 1974, based on the withdrawal from Quneitra on the Golan Heights. The natural next step would have been a similar agreement with Jordan based on withdrawal from Jericho."

But, Eban said, Labor's political commitment to the Mafdal required either the religious party's approval "for the surrender of any territory of *Erez Israel* west of the Jordan River" or taking the issue to the polls. "That is why," Eban said, "it is so important for [Labor] not only to win the election, but to win it with a margin that frees it from dependence on parties of different ideologies." I agreed and shared Eban's hope that Labor would win the next Israeli election.

Peres spoke in eloquent, prophetic, indeed rhapsodic, terms about a far future of boundlessly rich and cooperative economic progress that would bind Arabs and Israelis forever in mutual prosperous endeavor. Hospitals, water conservancy, a common market—all would be our shared future. For example, he said, Israel has no automobile industry, so it "may agree that Egypt will be the producer of cars for us," getting preferential treatment to do so.

Then, Abba Eban, apparently believing that his party leader had drifted a bit too far into the future, delivered a monumental disquisition on the past of the Jewish people and the indelible mark it has left on the Israeli present. He sought to bring us back to earth.

"Since we will have elections next year," Eban said, "our thinking on foreign policy is pragmatic. It is not merely conceptual. There is a sharp sense of tragedy that can only be explained by our history—the experiences of the people and of the state; the dominant theme is the fragility of life. It is the sense that physical life has been less secure for our people than for other people, and less secure for our state than for other states. That is why the worst security scenario is going to leap at you whenever you discuss any new proposal with Israelis. Some people say we have an obsession about security. We never objected to that definition. We are a sovereign state and we are entitled to our sovereign obsessions. We do criticize some of our fellow citizens for being too much anchored in history. Some Israeli governments seem to have been too extremely concerned with history. We think in our party that we have to build a bridge between our experiences and our vision, between our past and our future."

Then, having said what Israelis agree upon, Eban spoke about what they did not agree on: "If we agree with the other party, why should we try to replace them? If we don't agree with them, then we ought to make it clear in what we do not agree."

Eban began elaborately to set out what he said were five points of difference between Labor and Likud. First, he said, Labor saw the Palestinians as a true people with a right to their own political destiny. As Eban's words rolled on, Mustafa Khalil listened carefully. Anis Mansour's face revealed his reaction to every Israeli point. Helmi Abdel Rahman looked absently away as though hearing nothing. My head was bent over the table as I tried to note everything down.

Second, Eban said, Labor wanted to share territory and share sovereignty with the Palestinians. Eban was speaking without notes and without any indication that he was addressing a group of listeners. It was as though he were speaking to a television camera. He continued at great length to point three, which was that Labor had a far more limited view of Israeli settlements than Likud. Fourth, Labor regarded Palestinian autonomy as an interim, not a permanent, status.

We all eagerly hoped that Eban would now turn to his fifth and final point of difference between Labor and Likud, but he did not. I looked up at Helmi Abdul Rahman, who was seated in a gallery above. His face was a blank, indicating that his mind was elsewhere.

"So here," Eban said, "we have four matters on which we have an approach distinctive from Likud. I would say that between the two major parties in Israel there is probably a sharper difference than between the American Democrats and Republicans, or between the British Conservatives and Labor."

Finally Eban came to his fifth point. Labor differed with Likud about Jordan. "We don't say any longer that you can solve the problem with Jordan and without the Palestinians, but we think it is irrational to say that you can solve it with the Palestinians, and without Jordan. If you take away Jordan, you are left with a chemical reaction that just doesn't work."

Eban said that even within the Labor party there were "hawks" and "doves." He was categorized as a dove. "In Hebrew literature," Eban said, "we have the story of Noah's ark. The only animal that knew what it wanted was the dove."

It was an ordeal for us, sitting silently for so long as Eban talked on and on. But what he said was welcome and bore out my conviction that the Arab cause could not be satisfied until Labor defeated Likud at the polls. When Eban paused briefly for breath, Mustafa Khalil asked about the meaning of security to the Labor party, and Shimon Peres jumped in to answer by stressing the danger of terror, "which is a speciality of the PLO," the danger of invasion, the danger of falling behind technologically, and the danger of placing the security of Israel in the hands of America, the United Nations, or the Russians. "Israel has to be self-reliant when it comes to defending our country," he said.

Peres was very animated. His images were captivating. "There are two main bodies: one the people of the West Bank and the other the people in the Gaza Strip. They are different, you know. . . . I was once in charge in those areas, and to make the situation less tense and demanding in Gaza, we offered some of the refugees the chance to go to the West Bank and live. It was a total failure. The people on the West Bank did not receive them, did not absorb them, and the people of Gaza felt that they were secondary citizens; they did not like it. I don't want to say that they cannot live under the same framework, under the same umbrella, but they are different people."

Peres, unlike other Israeli leaders such as Sharon and Burg, knew that Palestinians existed. He had thought deeply about them, but we did not like what he was saying, for it argued against the possibility of Palestinian solidarity under PLO leadership. And worse, Peres argued forcefully against a Palestinian state. Whatever Arafat might agree to, Peres said, it would never satisfy the Palestinian radicals. The PLO, he said, was incapable of agreeing in a united manner. "You cannot have a glass of wine in a broken glass," he said. "If there would be a separate Palestine state," Peres said, "the war will go on; it won't stop in spite of all the kisses."

At 1:30 P.M. the talk, which had been almost entirely dominated by Peres and Eban, became ragged and unfocused. It was time for lunch.

At the Meridien Hotel a beautiful hall with an unusual view of the Nile had been reserved for our party. At three-thirty we returned to the discussions. After more talk about the differences and similarities of the two political parties, I was invited to speak about foreign affairs and the peace process.

As Eban and Peres had been the spokesmen for Israel, I now felt that I must match them, and more, with point after point in support of Egypt and the Palestinians. We must maintain the momentum, I said. It is slipping away. "There will be a kind of vacuum from November 1980, the date of the American elections, to November 1981, the date of the Israeli elections. So how can we keep the peace momentum?"

"It is essential," I said, "to build confidence among the Palestinian population in the West Bank and the Gaza Strip—and the Palestinian population of the diaspora, Palestinians in Lebanon and Palestinians in Jordan, Syria. Why? Because as long as the Palestinians in the diaspora remain refugees, they will be subject to the influence of the radicals. But the day they have a passport the whole situation will change. They will be citizens of a federation, or of a state, or of whatever will be the entity, and they will have the protection that exists now in international law. Their situation inside the diaspora would be completely different. There were something like three hundred thousand Syrians and three hundred thousand Palestinians living in Lebanon; both of them in a certain way were the underdogs of Lebanese society. But whenever the Syrians were unhappy, they just took the taxi from Beirut to Damascus and the problem was solved. But the Palestinians were refugees, and their only solution was to become radicalized or to become terrorists. The day they get a Palestinian passport, their status as foreigners will be different, they will be citizens with foreign passports, and not refugees.

"You were talking about the Israeli obsession with security," I said to Abba Eban. "You must know that the other side has a terrible obsession with security. After thirteen years of military occupation, you cannot imagine their complexes, their trauma."

I felt that these Israelis had no sense of the position Egypt was in. Only when they understood this would they realize the damage that Israel's insistence on hard, even maximum, terms would do—and already was doing. "The real price Egypt has paid for the peace treaty is not so much the isolation of Egypt from the third world, but Egypt's inability to play the role it has played during the last ten years. Egypt was the moderator, the source of new ideas, from Bandung to nonalignment to African unity. Now we see Soviet infiltration in the region not because of the failure of the Palestinian negotiation but because of the peace treaty. The consensus of the third world, even of the Arab countries, is that it is our right to conclude a peace treaty. But they attack us for speaking in the name of the Palestinians without a mandate; for having obtained nothing; and for the fact that the situation of the Palestinians is worse after the peace treaty than it was before."

Shimon Peres attempted to refute me: "You keep asking us how much we are giving. Are you ready to give? Do you agree with us on the following points: that there was never an international marked boundary on the West Bank, and that the question of boundaries on the West Bank is an open question? You cannot take a position totally opposite to our own. You cannot insist that because the '67 War ended along a certain line, this line all of a sudden became sacred. It doesn't make sense. So we would like to see if you're showing also a little bit of flexibility, not just us."

At the end of eight hours of discussions, Abba Eban said that he wanted to come back to Dr. Boutros-Ghali's statement about the immediate future, how to live in the next year with some kind of movement. There was little the Labor party could do, he said, to build confidence among the Palestinians. "But I wonder whether you do not exaggerate confidence-building measures. You do not give enough weight to the intimidating effects of the PLO on the

Palestine residents. They threaten with assassination those who otherwise would choose what would seem to be in their interest. The PLO exercises intimidation and nobody stands up to PLO intimidation. I wonder whether the answer wouldn't be a much more obdurate, rigorous attitude towards the PLO in order to encourage the inhabitants in the West Bank and Gaza to go ahead with what is really in their interest, which is to achieve an organization that expresses Palestinian identity."

"I completely differ with you," I said. "Because what was in the Camp David agreements is still in the Camp David agreements. The Palestinians see nothing there—even the moderates among the PLO who have been ready to give the green light to the Palestinians in the West Bank and Gaza Strip to participate in the peace process. If you were a Palestinian, you could see that the situation is worse after the peace treaty than it was before. I don't want to underestimate the activism of the PLO. Nevertheless the action that has been adopted during the last sixteen months by the Israeli military administration is certainly the main reason for this crisis."

Shimon Peres had the last word: "There is no sense, I believe, in talking between us to raise all the points of disagreement. Who agrees one hundred percent? Nobody does. But we believe we have enough common ground. . . . We have to do it like bricklaying, one after another. I don't think that we can have the whole construction overnight, and if we wait, nothing will be built. You disagree. We disagree. We can argue about it. But let's really try and cement the agreed parts and use them as momentum for peace; that is what I really suggest."

Sadat received the Israeli delegation at his residence in Al-Qanatir al-Khayriyah. The talk was friendly. Sadat declared that the autonomy talks would end in agreement, and that Jordan and the Palestinians would join the process in the course of 1981. I accompanied the Israelis back to the airport. They seemed pleased. The expression that Abba Eban used in many interviews that followed was "Peace is irreversible." That expressed the first aim of our symposium. The second aim was more ambitious: we wanted to contribute to the victory of Labor in the coming elections.

When Peres and Eban returned to Israel, word was out among the press that they had told Sadat more about "the Jordanian option" than they had ever shared with the Israeli public. Eban declared that indeed the Jordanian question was one on which Labor had the greatest agreement with Egypt and that "Sadat and his associates do not think it possible to solve the problem without Jordan." Indeed, Eban said, by signing the Camp David Accords, the Likud had "become prisoners of the Jordanian option," for there was no more Jordanian document than the Camp David framework: Jordan appeared in the autonomy talks as the country with which Israel must make a peace treaty, and as one of the parties that would fix the final status of the West Bank and Gaza.

CHAPTER ELEVEN

End of a Saga

Spurned at the Source of the Nile

Sadat's obsession with communism intensified. He had opposed my effort to send the Egyptian ambassador back to Moscow. He had refused to see Neto of Angola in Monrovia when we needed Neto's support. He had shut down the consulates of the Soviet Union and Eastern European countries without warning. What complicated my life now was that his anticommunism extended as well to Mengistu Haile Mariam, who had overthrown Emperor Haile Selassie of Ethiopia. To carry forward my Africa policy, I had to deal with Mengistu, the Ethiopian Marxist-Leninist leader. Sadat's hostility toward Mengistu was matched only by Mengistu's hostility toward Sadat. Egypt was providing financial and military support to Ethiopia's enemy, Somalia, as well as to the Eritrean rebels who sought independence from Ethiopian rule. Neither policy helped Sadat's relations with Mengistu.

I tried repeatedly to convince Sadat of my views and maintained that Egypt's national interest required us to establish relations with

Ethiopia, where 85 percent of the Nile waters originate. To guarantee the flow of the Nile, there is no alternative to cooperation with Ethiopia, particularly in view of the Ethiopian irrigation project at Lake Tana, which could reduce the Nile waters reaching Egypt. As long as relations between Cairo and Addis Ababa were strained or hostile, we risked serious problems. Preserving Nile waters for Egypt was not only an economic and hydrological issue but a question of national survival. As Herodotus declared, "Egypt is the gift of the Nile," and our security depended on the south more than on the east, in spite of Israel's military power.

One evening, after a long telephone conversation, Sadat agreed to write to Mengistu and authorized me to go to Addis Ababa on an official visit to attempt a rapprochement. Mengistu knew me; we had often met. I felt sure that I could engage him in a productive dialogue. The letter to Mengistu that I prepared was friendly and courteous. I did not deal with specific issues, but mentioned the historical, political, and economic importance of Egyptian-Ethiopian relations. To my surprise and pleasure, Sadat signed the letter without modification.

Sadat agreed with my request to take Anis Mansour with me. A writer, journalist, and former lecturer on philosophy at Cairo University, Anis Mansour was very close to Sadat, serving him as intellectual adviser and spokesman. I needed Anis Mansour's support for my plan to establish solidarity among the states of the Nile, incorporating as a first stage Egypt, the Sudan, and Ethiopia, and later the other riparian states—Kenya, Tanzania, Uganda, Burundi, Rwanda, and Zaire—so that together we could create an authority for the Nile that would provide water, energy, and communications for all the peoples on the banks of the Nile. So that Sadat would feel comfortable, I promised him to counterbalance the visit to Addis Ababa with a visit to Somalia. He proposed that I also stop in Nairobi to see Daniel Arap Moi, the president of Kenya, the host of the next OAU summit.

I left for Addis Ababa early in the morning of March 28. At Luxor we stopped to refuel. The airport was empty, and I walked with Anis Mansour along the tarmac in the dry, bracing air, far from the oppression of bugged meeting rooms. I told him in great detail about my plan to associate all the states bordering the Nile in a common supranational authority. It would create a highway from Alexandria to the heart of the continent, an electricity grid taking advantage of all the new dams on the river. We could even export electricity to the European Economic Community, I said. It could be, in its way, a Sadat initiative as dramatic as his trip to Jerusalem. I urged Anis Mansour as one of Sadat's privileged advisers to support my project and persuade Sadat to make it his own. My attempt at a rapprochement with Mengistu, "the red emperor of Ethiopia," I said, constituted the first stage of this project.

Anis Mansour listened with care but said, "Sadat is at the zenith of his glory. He is not ready to become enthusiastic about a new project that might end in failure and thus diminish his glory." Sadat was not interested in the Nile, Anis Mansour said, because those responsible for water and irrigation will never tell him the true extent of the problem. Sadat, to persuade the Israelis to return the West Bank and Gaza, had offered them water from the Nile for their irrigation projects. That had raised an uproar in Egypt, as well as in the states upriver, who were furious that Sadat had offered the waters of the Nile without their approval. This attempt, Anis Mansour said, made acceptance of my project by Sadat quite difficult. "Like all politicians, he is more interested in today's problems than in tomorrow's."

Twenty minutes after takeoff we were over Lake Nasser, the artificial lake formed by the Nile behind the Aswan High Dam. I continued to ponder my grand design. Lake Nasser, with Abu Simbel and its temple, restored by UNESCO, as the capital of this new region, would become a population center with new fields, towns, and tourist projects on its banks. Now it was a barrier between Egypt and the Sudan, but it could become a magnet drawing the region together beyond the megalopolis of Cairo. We would conquer the desert. Anis Mansour listened skeptically but let me continue. Soon Lake Nasser was behind us and we were flying once more over the desert, then over Khartoum. I could see clearly the junction of the Blue Nile and the White Nile, where they united to form the river-god, which gave rise to one of the oldest civilizations of the world.

At last we were over Addis Ababa. To our consternation, the airport refused us clearance to land. I asked the pilots, "Can you land in Djibouti or Nairobi?" Not enough fuel, they said. The airplane circled above Addis Ababa. Anis Mansour was terrified. "Do something or we will all die!" he exclaimed. My delegation was in panic. The atmosphere in the plane was electric. I ordered the pilots, "Tell the airport we are running out of fuel and are going for a forced landing."

We landed safely. What was going on? In the VIP hall we found the Egyptian ambassador, Mahmoud Kassem, and a few Ethiopian officials. The ambassador looked embarrassed, ashamed even. He whispered in Arabic, "This is incomprehensible. Mengistu refuses to see you. First they say he is out of town inspecting his troops, then they say he is chairing a cabinet meeting. The political situation seems serious, but the city is calm."

Furious with the ambassador, I said, "You should have warned me, sir. It was you who led me to believe that relations had improved. You suggested this visit. It was you who suggested a message from President Sadat, which I obtained with great difficulty. And now, because of your lack of judgment, we are headed for even worse relations between Egypt and Ethiopia."

I turned toward one of the Ethiopian officials, who was attending with the unctuous obsequiousness of a court chamberlain, "Does not President Mengistu know that I am carrying a message from President Sadat?"

With exaggerated deference, the Ethiopian suggested that I hand over the message for him to transmit to the minister of foreign affairs, who would then present it to President Mengistu. I turned to my pilots and made sure we had taken on enough fuel to fly us to Nairobi. I then told the official, without hiding my anger, "Please telephone the presidential palace immediately. I have precise instructions from President Sadat to hand over the message to President Mengistu Haile Mariam personally. If this is not possible, I shall leave immediately without transmitting the message."

The official disappeared only to return in a few minutes to inform me that he had been unable to reach the presidency. He repeated his offer to take the message himself. I announced our immediate departure. I refused the cup of coffee I had been offered. I left the VIP hall and its velvet armchairs, and we took off for Nairobi.

Anis Mansour, who had witnessed everything, teased me: "You kept calm when we were refused clearance to land, but lost your composure when we were refused a meeting with Mengistu." I could not find an explanation for this diplomatic incident. How would Sadat take this arrogant behavior? Had the Ethiopians discovered that we had made a new weapons delivery to the Somalis? Were there outside powers opposed to a rapprochement between Cairo and Addis Ababa? How could our ambassador have been so wrong? The strangest ideas were going through my mind. Months and months of hard work had been destroyed, and I did not even know why. "The press must never learn of this incident," I said. Anis Mansour spoke quickly, "I am not here as a journalist, but as a member of the minister's delegation."

At five o'clock in the afternoon we landed in Nairobi, and I was soon back in my old suite in the Intercontinental. The next morning I boarded a small propeller plane for Nakuru, where I met with President Daniel Arap Moi at one of his residences. Tall and gray-haired, Arap Moi spoke smoothly and slowly. He carried a staff of authority in his hand and carried out every gesture with stately deliberation, in the style of the traditional African leader. I informed him that I was on my way to Mogadishu. I would be prepared, I said, to undertake a mission of good offices with President Siad Barre of Somalia. Relations between Nairobi and Mogadishu were difficult, even though Mogadishu had abandoned its territorial claims on northern Kenya, a semiarid region inhabited by Somali tribes. Arap Moi did not reply to my offer of good offices, but expressed the hope that the next OAU summit, in Nairobi, would bring about reconciliation. At Nairobi airport, when we were about to take off for Mogadishu, the Coptic bishop of Nairobi appeared with a dozen priests, who accompanied me to the steps of the plane, praying and chanting for the success of my mission. "With all the benedictions," said Anis Mansour, "I hope we shall fare better in trying to land in Mogadishu than we did in Addis Ababa."

The prayers yielded immediate results. A large crowd was waiting at Mogadishu airport: Egyptian technical experts, Somali ministers, and an excited crowd lined the street from the airport. Why this huge reception? Was it because no high Egyptian official had visited Somalia in years? We were housed in a bungalow in the president's compound. Three quarters of my bedroom was filled by a king-size bed. An enormous rococo armoire, one door of which had disappeared, took up the rest of the space. In the bathroom, French perfume bottles vied for space with toothbrushes and beauty creams, but when I turned the tap there was no water. Anis Mansour said this rest house reminded him of an ancient pharaonic temple, with false windows and doors. The minister of foreign affairs, President Siad Barre's half brother, informed us that the president would meet us the next evening.

The next day I visited a refugee camp forty miles north of Mogadishu. Anis Mansour, terrified of "germs," washed his hands obsessively and wrote about health problems frequently in his newspaper column. The prospect of a refugee camp alarmed him, and he refused to accompany me. I insisted, reminding him that he was a member of the official delegation and that his absence would be misinterpreted. The camp was enormous. Hot, humid, dusty, and swarming with flies, it was made up of hundreds upon hundreds of small round huts, covered with plastic sheeting, resembling igloos. As I entered a school the children started singing a martial song: " 'We are fighting, fighting to regain our lands! We shall exterminate our enemies!' " meaning the Ethiopians. We were invited to lunch by the governor, who talked incessantly of Ethiopian atrocities against Somalians.

Back in Mogadishu, I prepared for my evening meeting with the president. Siad Barre was superficially smooth but actually ruthless and ready to kill his opponents without hesitation. My relations with him had always been rather difficult. He considered me pro-Ethiopian and feared that improvement of Egypt's relations with Ethiopia would be at the expense of Somalia. I tried to explain that I was pro-Egypt, neither pro-Somalia nor pro-Ethiopia, and that Egypt's interests were to have good relations with the country that controls 85 percent of the Nile flow to Egypt. But for Siad Barre one is either for or against; he did not understand neutrality, and strategic reasons carried no weight. Siad Barre was convinced that I, as a Copt, must favor Ethiopia, a country whose religion is largely Coptic. He distrusted me, and I reacted accordingly. In 1991 an urban uprising would overthrow Siad Barre, and a year later, when, as UN secretary-general, I was involved in the crisis of Somalia as a "failed state," I was accused by Somali factions of having been pro–Siad Barre more than a decade earlier.

Despite his suspicion of me and despite pressure by Arab states, Siad Barre had been in favor of Egypt and the Camp David Accords. In return, he expected increasing military and financial help from Egypt. Ethiopia and Kenya were allied against Somalia, and even Djibouti, Somalia's other neighbor, had difficult relations with Mogadishu. The Somalis saw Egypt as a big brother who could support their claim to a greater Somalia, which would include Djibouti, Ethiopian Ogaden, and part of Kenya.

I was received by Siad Barre at eleven o'clock at night. With him was his brother Simantar, the regime's strong man. Our talks, which ended at one o'clock in the morning, were dominated by Somali requests for assistance. "Somalia could be the granary of Egypt. Why don't you send your peasants and your technicians to cultivate our land?" It was late, and I took my leave, promising to transmit his request to President Sadat. I mentioned to Siad Barre the importance of his attending the OAU summit. He would not be in Nairobi, the capital of Kenya, he said, but in Nairobi, the seat of the next OAU summit. I assured him that Sadat would be there. I hoped that this would be the case, but I was far from sure.

Back in Cairo I learned that Mahmoud Kassem, our ambassador in Ethiopia, was not to blame for misinterpreting the internal Ethiopian situation. Mengistu wanted to start a dialogue with Egypt and had been ready to receive me as the special envoy of President Sadat. But on the eve of my departure for Ethiopia, Sadat had issued a statement to the press criticizing Mengistu and his corrupt regime, to the point of threatening him with military intervention if he dared touch the waters of the Nile. The text of this attack reached Mengistu a few hours before my arrival. Mengistu was furious and gave orders to prevent my plane from landing.

Why did Sadat make this declaration? Was it intentional, a way of canceling out the friendly letter? Had Sadat forgotten he had sent me to Addis Ababa to see Mengistu? Mengistu's affront to Sadat's messenger was mentioned neither in the Egyptian nor the Ethiopian press. And Sadat himself never mentioned the incident, although Anis Mansour, with his unequaled talent as a storyteller, did not miss the opportunity of describing what had happened in every detail. Whatever his motives, Sadat had delivered a setback to my grand design.

I am haunted by the myth of Sisyphus. It came to mind whenever I thought of my master plan for the Nile. The flowering of one of the most destitute regions of the planet. The transformation of a barrier into an immense communication link between the Mediterranean and the heart of Africa. The Nile would be the axis of prosperity. I felt that I was pushing a boulder endlessly up a hill whose waters fed the Nile.

Rejected by the United Nations

The treaty of peace between Egypt and Israel signed on March 26, 1979, called upon the parties to request the United Nations to provide forces and observers to supervise the implementation of the return of Sinai to Egyptian sovereignty through a series of phased Israeli withdrawals. The UN peacekeeping operation was to be operational as of January 26, 1980.

But now, over a year later, the strong opposition of the Arab states, the Soviet Union, and others to the Camp David Accords had blocked the creation of a UN force. President Carter wrote to Sadat and Begin to say that the United States would exert its utmost effort to get Security Council approval, but if the UN would not agree, Carter would "take those steps necessary to ensure the establishment and maintenance of an acceptable multinational force."

In the face of opposition to the Camp David Accords, the UN did not renew UNEF's mandate when it expired in July 1979. In response to a written request from Egypt, the president of the Security Council on May 18, 1981, advised Egypt that there was not sufficient support among the members of the Council to provide a UN force. A Soviet veto was certain should the matter come to a vote. It was a disgrace that the Israel-Egypt treaty, the greatest contribution to peace since the end of World War II, had been spurned by the United Nations. The United States and Egypt had no choice but to try to put together something that had never been achieved before: an entirely non–United Nations peacekeeping force.

Moshe Dayan, who always prepared for the worst, had asked me on one of the many days when negotiations were stalled, "In the event that the Soviets use their veto to oppose sending Blue Helmets to Sinai, what do we do?" An American had suggested an ad hoc peacekeeping force, with U.S. involvement but no link to the UN. The Israelis were enthusiastic; they deeply wanted Americans on the ground in Sinai. I was not so pleased and had been convinced that Washington would use its influence to get the treaty and the peacekeepers approved by the Security Council. To my dismay, I was proved wrong.

Roy Atherton had informed us that the United States would send a thousand men to Sinai, and had gotten Fiji to agree to add a few hundred soldiers so that the force would be "multinational." This was ridiculous!

I protested this in the strongest terms to the American ambassador. "Egyptian public opinion would then be justified in saying that the Israeli occupation of the Sinai has been replaced by an American occupation force. We shall be accused of having allowed the establishment of an American military base in the Sinai, flagrantly violating Egypt's nonalignment policy." Prime Minister Mustafa Khalil and General Kamel Hasan Ali strongly supported my position.

Atherton replied, "If you want a different composition to the multinational force, then you will have to assume responsibility for the whole operation; the United States has fulfilled its commitment. But," he added, "obtain Israel's approval of the nationality of the various contingents. Israel will refuse to accept any state that has broken diplomatic relations with Israel over Camp David—and that's a lot of states."

President Sadat was informed of what I had said to Atherton. "As Boutros raised the problem, let him try to resolve it," Sadat said. The problem was not so easy to resolve. Atherton was right. Israel would not accept forces from any country with which it did not have diplomatic relations. The majority of African and Asian states had broken diplomatic relations with Israel and were thereby excluded from the multinational force. The Europeans, who had kept away from the peace process, had made their Venice Declaration, which focused on the PLO, and that disqualified them not only in Israel's eyes but with the Americans as well. My only hope, therefore, was the Latin American states.

Seeking Latin Support

About twelve months before this time I had persuaded Sadat that I should go to Latin America to try to strengthen support for Egypt's policies.

Whenever the Egyptian minister of foreign affairs or a high official in the Foreign Ministry was going to be sacked, or put on early retirement, he was sent on an official mission to Latin America. The distance involved gave the Egyptian authorities the time needed to put an end to the services of the diplomat. The absent diplomat could do nothing to prevent his own dismissal and would return to face a fait accompli. Therefore, when I discussed with my colleagues the possibility of a Latin American tour, they reminded me, at once amused and worried, that this might be seen as my farewell tour. I ignored their fears and submitted the proposal to President Sadat. I explained the importance of diplomatic relations with Latin America and listed the number of official visits we had received from Latin governments. I had long sought to promote Latin American relations with Egypt in every way, including presiding over the erection of a statue of Simón Bolívar in a square in Cairo. I told Sadat how the Latin nations were important in the Group of 77, in the nonaligned movement, and in OPEC. In stressing their importance to Egypt, I avoided speaking of "the isolation of Egypt," which always highly irritated Sadat.

The president, who had listened to me without much attention, interrupted, "You want to travel again?" He then corrected himself: "You are right, we must not neglect Latin America. Have you already been there?" "No, Mr. President, it will be my first time." "I haven't been to Latin American either," he remarked, and the conversation was finished.

My tour started in Buenos Aires and took me to Santiago de Chile, Lima, Quito, La Paz, and then to Mexico City. At the last capital I was received by José López de Portillo in his villa in the middle of a large garden. There also was the minister of foreign affairs, Jorge Castañeda, a brilliant academic and jurist, whom I knew from the time when he was Mexican ambassador in Cairo. During this meeting we prepared a project titled "The Afro-Latin American Seminar" to bring together, for a few days each year, Latin American diplomats, academics, and businessmen with an interest in Africa and the Arab world, with African diplomats and experts with an interest in Latin America. I had thus set the basis for a diplomatic and cultural infrastructure of relations between Egypt and Latin America.

So in early July 1981 I set off a second time with Leia for Latin America with a clear goal: to obtain Latin American contingents for a non-UN multinational force to be deployed along the Egyptian-Israeli border in the Sinai after the withdrawal of Israeli forces. This would be an immensely difficult mission. Sinai must have seemed like terra incognita for Latin Americans. Furthermore, it would be difficult to explain why we wanted to set up a peacekeeping force outside the authority of the United Nations, which had invented the concept. We would have to prove to the Latin Americans that the Security Council would not even examine our request for a UN peacekeeping force. Finally, the very presence of American troops in the multinational force would dissuade many Latin Americans from participating.

I started in Uruguay because of the economic relationship between Cairo and Montevideo. Egypt was the largest importer of Uruguayan beef at that time. I arrived in Montevideo on the afternoon of July 13, 1981. We went directly to the Ministry of Foreign Affairs to sign a cultural accord between our two countries. Speeches, journalists, television—the welcome was enthusiastic; it had been a long time since Uruguay had received an Egyptian minister. That evening at a large reception the generals ruling the country received me with warmth.

The next morning I was received at the presidential palace across the square from the hotel. The president, a smallish gentleman, was seated in the center. To his right, three generals in uniform were seated on identical chairs. I presented President Sadat's message, which the president read slowly and carefully. The first general on his right took the letter impatiently and each read it in his turn. The letter contained a message about the friendship between Egypt and Uruguay, but said nothing about the multinational force or Uruguay's possible participation in it. This delicate subject was left to the messenger.

I explained the reason for my mission and the importance of the multinational force. It would reinforce our political and economic links, I said. The generals were bored. They would study President

Sadat's request with care. The meeting was over. At a ceremony surrounded by Uruguayan troops, I laid a wreath at the tomb of the Uruguayan Unknown Soldier.

That evening I gave a lecture at the University of Montevideo. The mood was solemn: the national anthem was followed by the rector's introductory speech. It was the first time, and probably the last, that the University of Montevideo would host an Egyptian minister of foreign affairs lecturing in French on African and Latin American influence on international law. I spoke of the significance of the doctrine of *uti possidetis*, that is, the decision of African and Latin leaders after decolonization to let the boundaries imposed by the European imperialists not only remain in place but be declared inviolate. This helped the two continents remain relatively free of the kind of border disputes that had devastated Europe.

Back at the hotel, I met the American chargé d'affaires, who had been one of my Fulbright students in Cairo at the end of the 1950s. He had received instructions from Washington to assist me, he said, but relations between Washington and Montevideo were difficult at the moment. He did not expect me to get my military contingent, no matter how much beef Egypt imported from Uruguay.

Later, there were cocktails for "*tout* Montevideo" at the Egyptian embassy. I tried to make my appearance brief, but the ambassador insisted I remain; he hoped to receive the fourth general, the real boss, that night; if I could convince him, Uruguay certainly would join the peacekeeping force. Despite the ambassador's insistence, I was on my way out, when suddenly the whole room went silent. The supreme power had arrived. A charming, smiling man in civilian clothes walked into the drawing room. Everyone smiled and bowed at his passage. This clearly was the one and only ruler of Uruguay. I wasted no time in proposing a private talk, and together we went into a small study. With us was Elias Ibrahim, the small, rotund Egyptian millionaire who was the largest meat exporter in Uruguay. The meat king offered the general an enormous Havana. The general smiled, carefully lighted the cigar and listened. I spoke in two languages, switching from French to Arabic for no obvious reason. I was instinctively searching for the best way to persuade the general. The meat king was an excellent translator from French and Arabic into Spanish.

The general spoke: "First, this is an American, not an Egyptian, problem. If we participate in the multinational force, we are doing a favor to America, not Egypt. Second, why should we be the first?" Looking at the meat king, who was also smoking a Havana, I answered that I started my tour in Montevideo because of the close Egypt-Uruguay economic ties. The general ignored my remarks and asked, "What are the risks to my troops if I send them to the Sinai?"

"Practically none at all, General. Egypt and Israel are at peace. These troops will be military observers for a limited period. When the international situation changes, they will be replaced by Blue Helmets," I replied.

He listened carefully while clearly enjoying a satisfying smoke. "You know the American administration; what can you do to improve Uruguay's relations with the United States?" I immediately answered, "Your participation in the multinational force will favor a rapprochement."

Drawing on his cigar, he asked mischievously, "If you were my political adviser, what advice would you give me?" I did not hesitate. "I would not participate in the multinational force if Uruguay were the only Latin American country to send troops along with the United States. But if another Latin American country were to send troops, then I would advise Uruguayan participation. This will strengthen relations between Egypt and Uruguay. It will also serve to bring Uruguay and the United States closer together."

The general appeared satisfied. "Listen, Mr. Minister. I appreciate your frankness. If other Latin American states participate in the multinational force, I shall be able to convince my colleagues to send a contingent in the Sinai." I thanked the general for his support, and took my leave.

The next morning, as I was preparing to depart for Buenos Aires, I saw the communiqué issued at the end of my visit: "The Minister Boutros-Ghali explained to the Uruguayan Minister in detail the matters regarding the Multinational Force and Observers to be stationed along the Egypt-Israeli frontier. The Minister of State for Foreign Affairs of Egypt submitted an official invitation to the government of Uruguay to participate in the Multinational Force. The Minister of Foreign Affairs of Uruguay stated that his Government would consider with interest the stated invitation."

In Buenos Aires, a beautiful city that reminded me of Madrid, I was received by President Jorge Rafael Videla. The next morning's newspaper cartoon showed two Argentine soldiers in tears with the caption "I do not want to go to Sinai." In the afternoon there was a solemn ceremony attended by the minister of foreign affairs for the signature of a joint communiqué that mentioned the Egyptian request. At a press conference I was asked my reaction to the Israeli bombing of Beirut. I was taken aback, as I had not heard of the bombing, and gave a vague and awkward answer. Argentina's answer to the Multinational Force and Observers (MFO), as the peacekeeping entity was called, was no. I had failed in Buenos Aires.

In Caracas I met the playwright Arthur Miller and his wife, Inge Morath, a photographer whom I knew from an earlier Cairo encounter. They took us to meet American ambassador and Mrs. William Luers for drinks at the ambassador's magnificent residence overlooking the city. Modern paintings borrowed from American museums decorated the walls. I was then taken for dinner to the splendid villa of a Venezuelan millionaire and patron of the arts, where the conversation revolved around painting and music. It was pleasant to return to the kind of intellectual atmosphere I had abandoned for foreign affairs.

On July 20 I was received by President Luis Herrera Campins in a room freezing from air-conditioning. The president was sympathetic to my request but made no commitment. I then went to lay a wreath on Simón Bolívar's tomb, recalling that I had dedicated a monument to the great liberator at the center of one of our main squares in Cairo. The monument had been my idea, and it had not been easy to get the approval of the Cairo municipal authorities, who had no interest whatsoever in Bolívar, if they even knew who he was. At that time I had had to insist on the importance to Egypt's foreign relations of this gesture to Latin America and to go to Sadat himself for approval. On this day I was glad that I had succeeded.

I failed again in Venezuela and so proceeded to Bogotá. There, after leaving a bouquet of flowers at Bolívar's house, I was received by the president of the republic, Julio Turbay Ayala. The president, who was of Syro-Lebanese origin, followed with care the situation in the Middle East. He was a friendly listener and promised to support my request. That evening I was awarded a Colombian decoration. The United States ambassador, whom I had met previously in Ougadougou, came to whisper that the Colombian government's attitude was very positive to my mission, but I received no commitment.

In Panama City, Foreign Minister Jorge Illueca, tall and dark, a brilliant lawyer who was very prominent in the nonaligned movement, fulminated against the American presence in Panama. On Sunday morning I visited the Panama Canal to watch the opening of the locks and the passage of a ship. The manager of the Panama Canal, an American citizen, with a high opinion of himself, was full of contempt for Panamanians. I could feel the source of Illueca's ire. A little airplane took us to spend the day with him at the Pacific Panamanian resort of Contadora, where we swam and, wearing guayaberas, toured the small island. Minister and Mrs. Illueca showed me the villa where the shah of Iran had lived for a few weeks. The tropical humidity was intense. The shahbanu, Farah Diba, told me that she spent the worst months of her life on that island when her husband was dying of cancer.

My official visit to Panama started on Monday, when I presented a wreath at the national monument. The military band played the old Egyptian national anthem that dated back to the days of King Farouk. It was strange to hear, in Panama City, on a scorching day, during an official function, music that had moved me forty years before. When I was a Boy Scout, I had stood at attention when that anthem was played and imagined that, like Michel Strogoff, I had been given dangerous missions to perform for King Farouk and Egypt. My mission now was not dangerous, but it was as difficult as anything faced by Jules Verne's hero. After the ceremony I reproached the Egyptian ambassador, a retired general, for this grave error. The ambassador answered placidly that the government of Panama had only the music for the former national anthem, and rather than not play any anthem, they had preferred to play the music of the former monarch. Then, he added with a smile, "Cairo is far from Panama City. They will not know of the incident, and perhaps it has brought back youthful memories for Your Excellency."

My delegation informed me that the committee in charge of preparing the joint communiqué had a major problem. The Panamanians refused to mention the Egyptian request for participation in the multinational force for Sinai. I went to Illueca. He said that if the Egyptian request was mentioned, the communiqué would also have to state that Panama had refused; to avoid offending me, they would rather be silent. I objected and said, "Why do you not at least express support for the peace process and Egyptian policy? Our countries both belong to the nonaligned movement."

He then said, "It is precisely because we are nonaligned that we reject a request that would, in the final analysis, confirm American military presence on Egyptian soil. To legitimate the establishment of a new American military base in Egypt would be contrary to the principles of nonalignment." I tried to alleviate the worries of my Panamanian friend. It is because we are nonaligned that we want a multinational force—to ensure that there are no foreign national troops on Egypt's soil. Colombia was nonaligned and had not raised this objection, I pointed out. After long negotiations we reached a compromise. The joint communiqué stated: "The two Ministers discussed the issue of the Multinational Force and Observers to be established as a temporary substitute for the United Nations Peacekeeping force." It was a very long and ambitious communiqué, which expressed a program of action very close to third-world ambitions to bring together all "the wretched of the earth," but with no link to reality. My failure in Panama was visible, undeniable, and humiliating.

On July 29 I reached Guatemala City. The minister of foreign affairs, Rafael Eduardo Castillo Valdez, a Mormon, had asked his wife, daughters, and son to come from Salt Lake City to receive me and my wife. The situation was tense in Guatemala because of the civil war. As soon as my visit was over, the minister said, he would send his family back to the safety of Salt Lake City. The next morning, the president of the republic, General Fernando Lucas García, received me in a castle with Art Nouveau furniture, Chinese carpets, and bodyguards at every door. In a large, half-empty drawing room, he asked his minister of foreign affairs to translate President Sadat's message.

As his only reply to Egypt's request, the Guatemalan president said, "Tomorrow, Mr. Minister, I shall take you to the south of the country, where you will witness the distribution of land to the peasants." The next morning at dawn an airplane flew me to a wilderness. A helicopter took me from the airport to a village deep in the jungle where a stage had been prepared on top of a hillock. I nearly slipped climbing the hill, but was caught by Minister Castillo Valdez. "Suppose one of these armed guards should slip and his gun go off," I asked. He smiled. "There would be a mass killing. The other guards, thinking it an attack, would immediately shoot. We live dangerously here, you know."

Hundreds of peasants assembled around the stage. There were long speeches on land reform. During his speech, President Lucas García announced that a guest of honor was in attendance. "It is the minister of foreign affairs"—he hesitated—". . . of Israel."

At lunch I was seated next to the head of the armed forces, for no apparent reason. Next day I was taken to the Petén region in Tikal to see the Mayan temples. A large aircraft was at my disposal. Another plane transported the staff, the food, and a marimba band. The band played while we ate lunch in the shadow of the great Mayan pyramid. This was only the beginning. The next morning the minister took me to Antigua, the old capital. Ancient churches and houses with romantic patios were surrounded by colorful flowers. Never had I seen a place of such antique charm and atmosphere. As if to live up to their surroundings, the people of Antigua seemed always to be dancing, laughing, and embracing. As we walked we heard an explosion. The bodyguards whispered something to the minister, who suggested we continue by car, but I asked to continue on foot. So Castillo Valdez said, "Let us walk, then," and we visited another church under the reproachful eyes of our guards. There was a second explosion. This time the guards insisted that we continue by car. We had lunch and were entertained by folk dancing. Enormous balloons were released to the sky to welcome us to Antigua. I danced with the ballet folklorico dancers. None of this served the purpose of my mission, which was not succeeding.

On the way back, Castillo Valdez asked me what I intended to do in the evening. "My wife understands Spanish and will watch television. I want to sleep," I replied. "In that case," my host said, "your wife may well find out from television the information I have hidden from you. The explosions you heard during our walk were two bombs that were set to explode in our path. We found them and detonated them."

"Was it an attempt on my life or yours?" I asked. "What does it matter?" was the reply. "If the attempt was directed against me," I said, "it proves that Palestinian terrorists have a frighteningly long reach. but if the attempt was directed against you, this is less serious, at least for me." Minister Castillo Valdez, still smiling, reassured me, "The bombs were for me, but they were also aimed at you, the honored visitor, to humiliate my country for being incapable of protecting its VIP guests. Don't worry, they do not even know your name or nationality, they know only that you are a foreign dignitary." Fifteen years later when I returned to Guatemala as secretary-general, another bomb attempt was made on my life. The bomb exploded, killing a woman and injuring the man who was carrying it, near the presidential palace, where we were the guests at a presidential banquet. Again I was told that the bombers did not care who I was; it mattered only that I was a foreign dignitary whose violent death would embarrass the government.

My stay in Guatemala was the best holiday I had experienced in years, but it gained nothing for Egypt. The next day in Tegucigalpa the president of the Honduran republic, General Policarpo Paz García, was not interested in my request but expressed his admiration for President Sadat as one of the century's greatest men of vision. During my stay, the French foreign minister, Claude Cheysson, arrived in the capital. After a dinner at which the Honduran foreign minister, a colonel, recited poems of García Lorca, Claude Cheysson and I met at midnight. I told him of my purpose in Latin America and asked France to participate in the multinational force for the Sinai. Cheysson was genuinely surprised to hear this but made no comment. Nocturnal diplomacy, especially in far-off places like Tegucigalpa, is often more productive than official daytime encounters, but on this occasion I got nothing from Cheysson but a promise to mention my request to President Mitterrand.

On August 5 in Mexico City, I found that my old friend, Foreign Minister Jorge Castañeda, had been closely following events in the Middle East, but Mexico would not be able to participate, even symbolically, in the multinational force. Another failure. But on the morning after my return to Cairo on August 9, I was told that Colombia had agreed to be part of the multinational force. I was immensely happy. A few weeks later Uruguay announced that it, too, was participating in the multinational force. The general had kept his promise. My trip to Latin America was not a diplomatic farewell, as my Egyptian colleagues had joked, but the start of practical steps toward peace between Egypt and Israel.

By September of 1981 Israel was satisfied with a multinational force that would be made up of the United States, Fiji, and the two Latin nations. But the Americans, particularly Secretary of State Alexander M. Haig, wanted, as he put it, "real countries," so the Americans approached the European Community, primarily through the British foreign secretary Lord (Peter) Carrington.

Carrington's first reaction was that Britain should stay out of any such effort so that it could remain politically free to pressure Israel with regard to withdrawal from the West Bank and Gaza. Under continuing American urging, however, four European Community nations—Britain, France, Italy, and the Netherlands—informed Egypt in early November that they were willing to contribute troops to the MFO. The four attached "clarifications" to their agreement, most notably saying that their decision was based on the policy stated in the European Community's Venice Declaration of June 1980. In that document the Europeans had set out their view on the Middle East peace process. It called for Palestinian self-determination and for full participation by the PLO in negotiations.

This, of course, was not acceptable to Israel. It also was not acceptable to Haig. When Carrington informed Haig on November 4, 1981, of the four nations' agreement to join the MFO, the United States replied that the conditions attached were unacceptable, because the Europeans appeared to be trying to place the Venice Declaration in a position superior to the Camp David Accords and to avoid any recognition of the Egypt-Israel peace treaty. Haig felt that the European documents would produce an explosive reaction by Menachem Begin. Haig himself was livid and asked the Europeans to put the effort on hold. He told Carrington that he didn't even want to pass on to the Israelis the European "acceptance" of a role in the MFO. Ashraf Ghorbal, the Egyptian ambassador in Washington, felt that Carrington was bungling the whole affair.

Nonetheless, on November 21, 1981, Carrington sent a letter to Haig stating that the four would join the MFO and included all the conditions that the United States had rejected. On November 23 the four made their position public. The Israelis reacted, they said officially, with "horror" to the European position and pointed out a variety of additional unacceptable points in the European documents, such as the apparent willingness of the four to serve only in order to secure Israel's withdrawal from Sinai and not, by their presence, to guarantee freedom of navigation through the Straits of Tiran. This raised in Israeli minds the 1967 withdrawal from Sinai of the United Nations Emergency Force, an episode cited ever afterward by Israel as evidence of the unreliability of peacekeeping operations.

Just as Begin had previously referred to me as Peter, he now started to refer to Carrington as Boutros as a way of denouncing Britain for seeking to serve the Arab cause. Begin categorically rejected the European proposals as "foolish, insulting, scandalous, and arrogant." It was not only the Israeli right that opposed the European position. Abba Eban remarked that "For the one hundred soldiers (whom the British are prepared to send) there was no warrant for one thousand words. It is carrying pretentiousness altogether too far for a country summoned to perform a limited and modest task." Eban felt that the Europeans should not have been invited in the first place, for, in his view, they had dissociated themselves from the Middle East peace process since 1973. "Insofar as they did put their spoke in, it was to heap obstacles on the USA," he declared.

The Americans rushed in to try to salvage this diplomatic disaster. They quickly worked up a joint U.S.-Israel statement that reaffirmed that the MFO would be based on the Camp David framework: "The basis for participation in the Multinational Force and Observers is the treaty of peace between Egypt and Israel originated in the Camp David agreement and the protocols signed between Egypt and Israel and witnessed by the United States on August 3, 1981, based upon the letter from President Carter to President Sadat and Prime Minister Begin of March 26, 1979."

The Israeli foreign minister Yitzhak Shamir informed Haig that Israel considered this U.S.-Israel joint statement as a means of rendering European involvement possible. Israel proposed that the statement be transmitted to the four Europeans and they be asked to give their "confirmation" to it. This effort was interrupted by Menachem Begin's sudden and completely illegal attempt in late November 1981 to annex, or apply Israeli law to, the parts of the Golan Heights occupied by Israeli troops and settlers. On its face inexplicable and universally denounced as invalid and unacceptable, this action apparently was taken by Begin to appease radicals within his coalition, and it focused all attention on international steps to counter Begin's decision.

The MFO effort did not emerge again until January 4, 1982, when Carrington wrote to Haig and to Begin confirming that the four European nations had "no intention of seeking to put any gloss on the various agreements entered into by Egypt and Israel, still less on the Egypt-Israel peace treaty itself."

But then occurred one of those textual aberrations that have periodically disrupted the smooth course of diplomacy over the centuries. In the letter from Carrington to Haig, no reference was made to the European letter and public announcement of November 21 and 23, 1981, in which the Europeans had grounded their participation in the Venice Declaration, so odious to the Israelis. But in Carrington's letter to Begin, these documents were mentioned, if only by reference to their dates ("our agreement was made public in a statement of 23 November 1981").

This convinced Begin that Carrington was trying to outwit him. He erupted in anger again, and once again the effort teetered on the verge of collapse. The United States rushed into action. Haig sought to get the Europeans to replace the text they had sent to Begin with the text they had sent to him. The Europeans declared that they had no ability to withdraw a text that had already been delivered, but Haig won from them the statement that they would "attach no conditions" to their participation.

Haig flew to Israel to try to convince Begin to agree to the European MFO. He succeeded, and the Israeli cabinet on January 31, 1982, approved European participation. In late March the MFO was deployed. Its members were Australia, Colombia, Fiji, France, Italy, the Netherlands, New Zealand, Uruguay, and the United States. Its military commander in Sinai was Lieutenant General Fredrik Bull-Hansen of Norway; its civilian director-general based in Rome was Leamon (Ray) Hunt of the United States. The MFO was never replaced by the United Nations. In my view it was of more psychological than real value and was needed only for the transitional period. But we could not find a way to bring it to an end. The powerful opposition to this operation and to the entire Camp David process was viciously demonstrated once again, however, when Hunt was murdered by leftist terrorists in Rome. "We must claim the attempt on General Hunt, the guarantor of the Camp David Agreement" was the telephone message from someone claiming to be speaking for the "Fighting Communist Party."

Entering a Time of Trouble

In early 1981 the Israeli election campaign was in full swing. In May I had a long meeting with David Landau of the *Jerusalem Post,* who was convinced that Begin would win because of Sadat's evident conviction that only Begin would make peace for Israel. I was convinced that the opposite was true. Begin had used the end of Israel's confrontation with Egypt to turn more aggressively toward his enemies to the north. A crisis was reached in April, when Syria moved Soviet SAM missiles into position near Zahle. The Arab world felt, understandably, that Israel had duped Egypt into a separate peace in order to free Israel for combat elsewhere. On June 7, 1981, Israeli air force planes destroyed Iraq's nuclear facility at Osirak. A war between Israel and Syria seemed all too possible. Israel's battles with other Arabs were being played down in the Cairo press; we feared the news would undermine Egyptian public support for the peace process. Israel *still* occupied Sinai. Meanwhile I sought to give support to Israel's Labor party. To me, they were the true peacemakers.

On June 30 at midnight I received a telephone call from my friend Israel Gat in Tel Aviv. Labor had won the Israeli election! Begin was out! I could not conceal my joy and congratulated Israel Gat. He read me a message from Shimon Peres, who would now be Israel's new prime minister. Peres was asking me to call Sadat urgently to ask him to issue a declaration in favor of Labor's victory. "But my dear friend, it is after midnight," I protested. "I cannot awaken the president of the republic at this hour." But he urged: "We know Sadat works late at night and you have a hot line to the Presidency—please do it! I'll call back in ten minutes to find out what President Sadat has decided." I accepted his mission and reluctantly telephoned Sadat. I told the duty officer it was very urgent. A moment later Sadat was on the line.

"Ya Boutros, what is so important for you to telephone me in the middle of the night?" It was an important message from Shimon Peres, I said. Labor has won the election and would like a message of support. There was silence. I could hear Sadat express his astonishment by a series of sighs and grunts: ah, ah; hum, hum; uh, uh. Almost a minute passed. "Mr. President, what should I answer? They will call again in ten minutes!"

Sadat stopped hemming and hawing and said with a firm, imperative voice, "Listen, Boutros, you tried to telephone me but could not get through. Inshallah tomorrow you will try again."

I stayed up in vain to await the second call from Israel. The final electoral results had changed the outcome. Begin had won. The next morning I was careful to avoid Sadat's eye. A few days later we discussed the Israeli election results, but he was kind enough not to remind me of the nocturnal telephone call. Much later, during a conversation on another topic, he cocked his head at me and said with a little smile, "Your Israeli friends couldn't get elected, could they?" I noted timidly that the president's position had contributed to their defeat. "Ya Boutros, Egypt's position is one of strict neutrality. We never intervene in the affairs of another state."

In July 1981 Israeli fighter jets struck at will at Palestinian targets in Lebanon. On the seventeenth they bombed Beirut—an Arab capital—in a raid that killed some three hundred people and injured almost three times that many. Despite this, Sadat proceeded to try to make the peace process work. On August 3 in Washington, Egypt and Israel signed the agreement that inaugurated the Multinational Force and Observers for Sinai. In early September a new U.S.-Israel doctrine of "strategic cooperation" including joint military maneuvers was agreed on by Begin and President Reagan in Washington. The Arab opposition to Egypt howled in frustration.

At the end of August, Begin, Sharon, and the whole Likud team received a triumphal reception—staged by the Egyptian president—in Alexandria. Sadat welcomed them warmly and housed them in the former palace of King Farouk's heir, Prince Muhammad Ali, a wondrous piece of late Ottoman architecture on a small hill overlooking the sea. On August 26 they reached agreement with Sadat to restart the autonomy talks.

Sadat was now under sharp and relentless attack by Muslim fundamentalists. Sermons in the mosques denounced him every Friday. Sadat was heedless in his treatment of the internal Egyptian opposition. He ordered arrests of the Muslim Brotherhood. He decided to break relations totally with the Soviet Union. I was alone, at the Council of Ministers on September 15, in criticizing Sadat's decision. The USSR and China, I pointed out, were in the midst of profound ideological and even military confrontation yet maintained diplomatic relations. Why was it necessary for Egypt to throw out the Soviet envoy and lose this channel of communication? My colleagues were shocked at my presumption. No one listened to me.

No group was spared Sadat's wrath. The Coptic patriarch Shenouda retreated to Wadi Natrun, a monastery in the desert. Sadat declared that he must stay there under house arrest and forbade him to run Coptic Church affairs. Sadat named five bishops to take over Church affairs from Shenouda. Having decided to crack down on Islamic fundamentalists, Sadat seemed to conclude that he needed to display the same stiff attitude toward Coptic Christians.

I was afraid that Sadat would depose Shenouda and replace him with a Coptic bishop of his own choosing. House arrest in the desert would project a bad image for Egypt abroad, but the main point was to maintain Shenouda's status as the spiritual leader of the Copts. Faced with this Coptic crisis, from behind the scenes, working through Musa Sabri, I urged Sadat to receive a Coptic delegation, including my cousin Mirrit Boutros-Ghali and Magdi Wahba at Sadat's house in his home village. I had two purposes in mind: to protect Sadat from negative world opinion, and to show him that he must not try to intervene in Coptic Church matters. At the village meeting Sadat had vegetarian food prepared for those who were observing a Coptic fast. They discussed state-Coptic relations and tensions were somewhat relieved, but the patriarch was not freed. Sadat sent me with a message to the pope in the Vatican. The message conveyed the official Egyptian position that Shenouda had gone to the monastery for security reasons and that his retreat did not diminish his spiritual authority as head of the Coptic Church. The Holy

Father received me at Castel Gandolfo and read the message without comment. He was not convinced by Sadat's message or by me.

Dr. Burg Returns

Despite general public indifference or even hostility to the idea of negotiations with Israel, we resumed the autonomy talks on September 22, 1981. I was now so frustrated that the very idea of resuming talks was depressing.

Dr. Burg arrived for the first time not by special Israeli government aircraft but on a scheduled El Al flight to Cairo airport. With him were Nessim and Sharon, and a new deputy minister of foreign affairs of American origin, Yehuda Ben-Meir. Burg had put on weight, and he looked tired and fed up. We immediately began arguing over the agenda and soon were deadlocked. The next day I arrived at Mena House quite early and resumed the previous night's conversation in Burg's room. Same disagreement. I argued that measures to change the quality of life in the occupied territories were an essential basis on which to resume negotiations in a new atmosphere. For Burg this subject was not within the competence of the talks. We all had lunch on the veranda of Mena House. I sat next to Sharon and raised with him Israel's confiscation of Palestinian land. Between mouthfuls of rice and fish, he said, "This is a lie." I showed him the cables of *Agence France-Presse* received that morning giving details. "This is a French brochure," said Sharon as he continued to stuff himself. "The French are all anti-Semitic; you must not believe them." Burg, who was following the conversation, could not stand this kind of language. He intervened with a quotation from Goethe: "*Ich bin der Geist der stets verneint* [I am the spirit that always denies]."

In the afternoon, after painful negotiations, we reached a compromise. Instead of adopting an agenda, we would prepare a joint communiqué in which all themes would be mentioned as a narrative. Thus, we would say that Sharon had described the measures taken to establish a new atmosphere of trust among the Palestinians, and we would say that measures would be taken to encourage the Palestinians to participate in the peace process according to the Camp David agreements.

In the evening, over a drink, I gave an interview to my old friend David Landau. I think he suffered more than I did from the presence of Likud in these negotiations. Another Israeli journalist pounced on me after dinner: "Have you calculated the cost of these negotiations—travel, receptions, dinner, lunch?" To which I replied: "Certainly less than a military parade or the maintenance of a tank."

The next day's session was painful. We squabbled over the text of the final communiqué. Sam Lewis, the American ambassador to Israel, adroitly intervened to save everybody's face. Kamel Hasan Ali whispered compromise solutions in my ear. He imitated Sadat's voice: "Ya Boutros, stop exasperating the Israelis." We decided to postpone the joint communiqué until after a trip on the Nile. The Nile at dusk was infinitely beautiful. The Egyptian countryside, looking like a pharaonic fresco, had the power to calm us as we sailed upriver to Maadi. But back at Mena House we fell to wrangling again, emerging only with a clumsy compromise to paper over the failure. I was bitter and frustrated. I would have preferred to negotiate with Peres, Rabin, and Eban, but that could not be.

Parade's End

Ever since Egyptian forces broke through Israel's Bar-Lev Line on the Sinai front, a great military parade had been held each year on the sixth of October—our most important patriotic day of celebration. I had always been allergic to such displays and managed to be traveling abroad on every such occasion. This year, however, I was in Cairo and under great pressure to attend. It would be highly unusual for a minister not to attend under these circumstances. But I was tired and wanted a weekend in Alexandria. The city was empty at this time of year. The weather was fine and the sea would be beautiful. I had met my wife in Alexandria and the call of nostalgia was overwhelming. We would be staying with our friends the Wahbas.

I told General Kamel Hasan Ali of my decision. He was reproachful in a friendly manner. "I realize you are tired, but if you do not attend the military parade, the Raiss will notice your absence and you run the risk of displeasing him. He imitated the voice of Sadat: "Ya Boutros, Ya Boutros." And we laughed together. Again he urged me: "Try to be at the military parade. The president places great importance on the presence of all ministers and your absence will be misinterpreted. I am a military man," Kamel said, "and I can assure you we are sensitive to civilian attitudes toward us."

I did not take General Kamel's advice. I wanted a few days of rest. Leia and I left for Alexandria by motorcar. She allayed my remorse: "Nobody among the crowd of dignitaries and diplomats busy watching the parade will notice your absence."

We were happy to meet the Wahbas. After dinner we had a fascinating talk, continuing a dialogue I started forty years ago with Magdi Wahba, when we were students at the faculty of law. Magdi expounded: "The regime is losing speed. Sadat has lost his popularity and all his credibility. The arbitrary arrests of fundamentalists, Wafdists, and Muhammad Hasanayn Heikal were made more for Sadat's personal revenge than for reasons of state. You are in power; therefore you are isolated in your ivory tower. You have lost all contact with political reality. Your foreign policy may crumble if you do not take into account what is happening inside the country." Our dialogue went on late into the night despite the intervention of our wives, who insisted that one must not talk politics on holiday.

On our second glorious day at Montazah the beach was empty. An autumn sun gently warmed us, the sea was calm. It was poetic. Magdi Wahba was an admirer of the Alexandrian poet Constantine Cavafy, and I caught some of the poet's mood. The sea seemed to me to hold in its immensity the entire history of Alexandria. I had a feeling of plenitude and well-being. In our bathing suits, lying on deck chairs, we were having lunch, talking quietly as only old friends can talk. A lady, well on in years, stopped in front of our group. "You are Minister Boutros-Ghali, aren't you?" she asked.

"Yes, madam, what may I do for you?" I replied.

"Have you heard Radio Monte Carlo? A serious incident has occurred this morning during the military parade, which has been interrupted," she replied.

"Madam, do not listen to foreign broadcasts; they are biased" was my rejoinder.

The lady left us and we turned again toward the sea and the serenity of the day. Then she reappeared and said, "I am sorry to bother you once again, Mr. Minister, but the BBC has just confirmed that a serious incident has happened during the military parade."

We turned on the Egyptian radio service, which confirmed that the military parade was over, but mentioned nothing out of the ordinary.

The old lady returned for a third time, even more insistent: "This time it is the Voice of America, which confirms what I have just heard."

Suddenly the atmosphere darkened and I was filled with foreboding. Some lines of Cavafy's came into my mind:

> Why this sudden unrest and confusion?
> (How solemn their faces have become.)
> Why are the streets and squares clearing quickly,
> and all return to their homes, so deep in thought?

I decided to return to town, but the driver and bodyguards were absent, as we had intended to spend the day at the beach. I was advised against taking a taxi. We found a friend, who took us back to the Wahbas's residence, where security officers were waiting at the front door. My presence was required in Cairo, they said. It was preferable not to return by motorcar, but to take the six o'clock train, where a compartment had been reserved. "We know exactly what has happened in Cairo, an attempted coup; the situation is serious," they told me.

At the railway station I was surrounded by four bodyguards, who took us to the compartment that had been reserved. News became more precise. There had been an attempt on the life of President Sadat, who had been seriously wounded and taken by helicopter to the military hospital in Maadi. The train stopped at Benha, one hour from Cairo. One of the guards came near and announced Sadat's death in the hospital. Rather than leave me alone, he insisted on staying next to me. It seemed he wanted to know my reaction. I tried to hold back my tears, but I could not overcome my emotions and I wept. I saw again and again, as in an old film being rerun over and over, the elderly lady coming up the beach with the news. Her image fragmented until it seemed that three witches were warning me of future disaster in Egypt. Images, phantasms crowded one another in my mind. I thought of the time we prayed at Al-Aqsa mosque in Jerusalem when I was in fear of an assassination. Now, four years later, it had happened. Sadat was killed by the same kind of fanatic who killed my grandfather in 1910. Like Moses, Sadat would not see the promised land. He would not see the return of the Sinai, the great dream for which he had risked and sacrificed so much.

The whole edifice we had built so painstakingly threatened to fall apart. Would the Israelis retreat from Sinai now that Sadat has disappeared? For the Israelis, Sadat was not Egypt; he was someone apart. I had spent months and months explaining that Sadat *was* Egypt. "And if Sadat disappears, will Egypt continue its search for peace?" they had asked. Now the assurances I had so often made would be put to the test. Would Sadat's succession take place peacefully? Would Israel go through with its withdrawal from Sinai? Sadat had been killed by people who passionately hated the idea of peace with Israel.

Despite these fears, I was worried more by the international than by the internal repercussions of this horrible assassination. I found my motorcar waiting at the railway station in Cairo and went directly to the Ministry of Foreign Affairs, where I found General Kamel Hasan Ali. We embraced in silence. Then he said, "It is an irreplaceable loss; it was a coup of great magnitude."

"Was the army infiltrated by the fundamentalists?" was my first question.

Kamel reacted quickly, "The army will never be contaminated by the fundamentalists nor by the communists. The army is, above all, patriotic." Then he paused and looked at me and quoted the Arabic proverb, " 'Your mother's prayer protects you' " adding, "You are lucky not to have attended the military parade; there have been many dead and wounded at the presidential podium." Then, with a sardonic smile, he said, "It was a plot on a national scale. We have found the list of personalities who were to be assassinated. Do you know who was first on the list? Boutros-Ghali. And who was second? Kamel Hasan Ali." I laughed. "This is discrimination—why you second?" We laughed ruefully at the misfortune of our country.

As I was leaving he embraced me again. "Tomorrow we shall have to start a new battle, more difficult than the ones we have fought together already."

Back home, I contemplated the Nile, which flows indifferent to events, this river-god that my ancestors worshiped and that I look at with love and respect from my window at dawn and sundown each day. A page of the history of Egypt, thousands of years old, had been turned that day with the death of Sadat. The myth of Sisyphus, which has haunted me from my youth, came back to me again. I shall have to roll the rock up the mountain again, this time without Sadat. The road beyond Jerusalem would be steep. But Egypt, as she has done since the dawn of time, would produce a new leader to take up the journey for peace.

Index

ABOUT THE AUTHOR

BOUTROS BOUTROS-GHALI was secretary-general of the United Nations until December 1996. As Egypt's minister of state for foreign affairs, he was a chief participant at the meetings that culminated in the Camp David accords between Egypt and Israel. Dr. Boutros-Ghali received his doctorate from the University of Paris. A distinguished academic, active in many international associations, he has written a number of books on Egyptian and international politics and has contributed to many journals. He has been a member of the Faculty of Political Science at Cairo University and of the Parliament of Egypt.

ABOUT THE TYPE

The text of this book was set in Janson, a misnamed typeface designed in about 1690 by Nicholas Kis, a Hungarian in Amsterdam. In 1919 the matrices became the property of the Stempel Foundry in Frankfurt. It is an old-style book face of excellent clarity and sharpness. Janson serifs are concave and splayed; the contrast between thick and thin strokes is marked.